# FlameMaker

## Lorraine Eljuga

Essential Earth

Lorraine Eljuga's website can be visited at
http://www.lorraineeljuga.com

First published 2020 Essential Earth Pty Ltd
Copyright © Lorraine Eljuga, 2020

*Cover design: Natasha Snow Designs*
*(https://natashasnow.com/)*
*Publisher: Essential Earth Pty Ltd*
*Printed & bound: Ingramspark Australia*
*ISBN 978-064899-61-4 (Paperback)*
*ISBN 978-064899-68-3 (eBook)*

*From the ashes*
*emerged a hero*

# ONE

**WATER** levels rise, eyes filling to its limits, lashes not yet wet. A misty veil is all that separates me from two black, marble headstones.

I try to walk and stumble. I concentrate harder this time, more conscious of slower, deliberate steps, knees shaking, hands trembling, breath unsteady, heart barely keeping me in this world.

This is my first visit to their graveside.

I know I should've come sooner, but I couldn't. I just couldn't.

The dam breaks, spilling onto my cheeks, trying to blind me.

Too much pain, I'd told myself. Too many memories of what I'd had and will never have again. Too many sleepless nights, reliving the worst moment of my short life.

I can say it now. Aloud, and for everyone to hear. I was scared to come.

I'm still scared.

Scared of what my life might look like without them. Scared of remembering them too much *and* forgetting them a bit more. Scared of shattering the flimsy, make-believe world I'm trying to exist in, and realising that no amount of wishing or praying is going to bring them back.

I read their names over and over, struggling to process it's been a whole year since they were killed.

1 drawn-out, devasting year they haven't watched me grow.

12 agonising months without love.

52 weeks of gut-wrenching loneliness.

365 days of no warm hugs or a kiss on the cheek to welcome in the day.

8760 hours wondering how this happened to my life.

525,600 minutes of sleeplessness and nightmares of fire.

31,536,000 seconds since I last saw their faces.

The thought of my parents being so close, and yet so far away, is life's meanest trick. Their coffins are empty – "No remains recovered" they'd said to me afterwards at the hospital. Erased … like they'd never existed.

Glass everywhere … in my eyes, scratching out tears, in my throat, slicing away words I never got to say to them.

I swallow hard.

Air disappears from my lungs.

My legs no longer want to hold me.

I drop. I fall.

The dewy grass that once tickled my feet all those seconds ago seeps through the knees of my jeans.

'WHY!' I scream out. 'Whyyyy? Why didn't you take me with you? Why did you leave me here? WHY!'

Bitterness rises. I want an answer!

I deserve an answer.

Anger empties into my *almost* perfect life. 'It's not fair,' I sob to an urn that's never seen flowers. I didn't think to bring any. Up until fifteen minutes ago, I didn't think I would be here myself.

Silence.

I drop my head, hands covering my face. 'How do I go on?' I want to stay here forever. I want to leave here and never come back. A trickle of sweat follows the line of my hair to my ear. I reach up to sweep it away, only to discover my palms collecting little puddles of their own.

Instinctively, I wipe my hands down my jeans.

It does nothing.

I seem to have sprung a leak. The puddles return, quicker and in greater quantities. I rub harder, the course denim chafing my skin. My palms, now red, hold more heat than is humanly possible. My stomach squirms, registering unnerving panic.

*What's happening?*

I look around.

Glance upwards.

The late August sun isn't even a consideration before 9am, not in England anyway, especially Gloucester, regardless of what Good Morning Britain's latest prognosticator says. But heat is coming from somewhere … and at a fierce rate. I draw my eyes from the tombstones to see if someone nearby is lending their body heat to me.

Apart from a bird, its feathers the colour of soot, watching me from the graveyard gate, I am alone.

Heat begins to gather all around me, wrapping me in a thick, suffocating duvet, with hot water bottles dangling off me and radiators sewn into the lining.

No. Wait!

Wait a minute.

Not *around* me.

*Inside* me.

My temperature skyrockets. The stream of water down my back has nowhere else to go but the waistband of my jeans. The soft polyester sticks to my skin as a cool breeze tugs at my shirt. I fan my face with my hand and blow out a breath, trying to cool myself. *What's happening?*

Heat stroke … not likely. Menopause … definitely not!

6

My body is a sauna, my blood the steam, organs impersonating smouldering hot coals. Something inside me screams out "spontaneous human combustion".

Panic grips me.

The real kind of panic when your heart is beating too fast for its own good and nothing in this world is going to stop it except a logical answer, or unconsciousness.

I look around in search of help. The solitary crow flaps its wings and takes off. *Great! Thanks!* I reach for the coldest thing I can see, the marble headstone. Both hands desperately seize the black wedge, to help steady myself, to cool myself, to hold onto something that's real. Before my eyes, I watch my fingers cut through the marble like a knife through soft cheese.

I withdraw them sharply, heart thumping in my throat.

Two perfectly carved handprints have been chiselled into the smooth stonework.

I check out my palms, turn them over, turn them back, turn them over again, inspecting them for clues. A fine layer of black dust is all that's left.

*What's happening?* I can't believe what I've just seen, what I've done. That's impossible, I tell myself.

Impossible!

Flesh cannot disintegrate marble!

I pinch myself hard. And then harder still until I squeak my discomfort. I am *not* dreaming. I am not *dreaming*. Realty kicks in.

I'm a freak. I'm a walking, talking freak.

Which means I have another secret to keep. No one can know. No-one.

And then nothing.

*Nothing*!

As quickly as the heat starts, it slithers away, returning my temperature to normal, and my hands to their customary dry state with my standard ten icy fingertips that never seem to thaw.

# TWO

$I$ know The Creeper is coming for me before I hear his heavy footsteps on the landing. Call it an aura, if you will. My mother used to say she could feel a migraine coming an hour before it struck. Is this her gift to me, because if so, I don't want it. It's more like a curse.

Floorboards groan. His feet shuffle closer.

I hold my breath and squeeze my eyes tight.

*Please, please, I'll do anything.*

Tears, as useless as rubbish, wet my face, wet my pillow. I brush them away.

I hear a footstep. Then another.

Heavier footsteps drum inside my ears, blood trying to escape. Nowhere to run. Nowhere to hide. Heart racing, bursting, desperate for a rest.

The footsteps stop but the pounding in my head doesn't quite drown out the sound of the door handle turning.

I feel sick.

I'm one breath closer to terror, one squeaky floorboard away from losing my innocence.

'Please, don't let it be him. *Please*! I'll do anything you want ... *anything.*' The words turn to steam in my pillow.

Take a breath.

Take another.

I need to remind my lungs what to do. It seems they have forgotten. No air. No air. No air means death. I don't want to die.

The doorknob clicks.

Then nothing. Feel everything ... and nothing. Numbness where sensitivity should dwell. Death where life should exist.

My fingers twist into the duvet, knot tightly at my neck. No easy entry in. Not even air.

The doorknob rattles.

Each breath in now hurts, each breath out, quivers against my tongue. Copper strands slides across my face, hiding the panic only a camera can capture.

Then voices.

I hear voices.

*I'm saved!*

It's Aaron.

His soft and gentle voice says he's hungry and wants his Frostie Flakes in his special tiger bowl.

My heart soars.

From outside my door, I hear the whispered, guttural growl of The Creeper. 'I said, back to bed, boy, before I slap you this side of Tuesday.'

Aaron's soft footsteps pad back along the landing until they fade to nothing. That dreaded nothing again.

Aaron's door clicks shut, sealing my fate.

Not saved.

*Doomed.*

My door opens. And closes without a sound. The Creeper's presence fills the room. The residual smell of camel cigarettes. The faint aroma of Blue Stratos aftershave.

*I don't want to look at him.*

*I hate looking at him.*

I hold my breath to punish those damn heightened senses for meticulously journaling the entire event. *Why can't they be numb like the rest of me?*

A breath in is the only clue he's closer, stench stronger. My hands grip tighter. My throat burns, teeth clench, jaw fighting to relax. I struggle one measly swallow. Eyes stinging, tears ready for the second round, waiting for the permission that will never come.

*Please*!

He's standing behind me. My time for begging has run out.

'Close your eyes,' he hums into my ear.

They're already closed but I force them tighter, lids aching, eyelashes flickering, squeezing like I never want to open them again.

*Ever.*

He sits too close, the top sheet pulling tightly around my body, becoming my prison.

My bed is a coffin, my body … a corpse.

It all started a few months ago when I woke in the middle of the night to find him standing over me, twirling a strand of my hair. It's got worse since then.

*Please, please, I'm scared. Can't you see that? I don't want you near me.*

I gasp as his fat, moist fingers snake their way across my cheek and through my hair. Every cell, every molecule, every atom in my body tries to crawl into the spaces furthest away from his touch … to the tips of my fingers and the edges of my toes. Desperate to move away. Desperate to escape.

The first touch is always the worst, and he draws back the covers and crawls in behind me.

The bed, barely big enough for one, leaves me balancing on the edge of the mattress. His stubby, round belly, all sweaty and hairy, presses into the small of my back as he wriggles in closer.

10

I bite down hard into my lip.

An old wound opens. Rusty blood seeps into my mouth.

'Ems,' he coos. 'Turn over and face me.'

I do as he says. It makes him angry if I don't.

One stroke of my face and my body goes stiff. I know what's coming next. I swallow the urge to dry reach as he kisses me, his moustache scratching across my lips like razor-wire.

And here is where I check out.

I say check out, because I can't be here to listen to the putrid things he says or to be conscious of the places his hands venture to. So, I shut out everything. Everything becomes stillness and white. Numbness climbs inside my skin and becomes my best friend. It comforts me and fills in all the gaps where pain resides, and emotions leak out.

Life ceases to exist when I check out.


Celeste storms into the kitchen that morning and kicks at the leg of my chair.

'Where did you put my hairbrush, you thieving bitch? I know you have it.'

Celeste is a year older than me and loves to remind me of that crucial fact. According to her, this makes her more beautiful, more intelligent, and more knowledgeable about boys than me. Maybe she does know more about boys. She's certainly dated a heap of them.

I glance up from my breakfast bowl. 'I haven't seen your brush,' I mutter into my spoon. *My* comb is tangled around her not-so-natural, honey-blond hair.

Her eyes bulge. 'You're a frigging liar, Ember Riley. Ever since you came here, you've been nothing but a thief and a dirty little liar. Look at her face, Mum? Are you going to allow this kind of thing in *our* home?'

The net-curtain, hanging over the kitchen window, is hardly anything to be enthralled by, and yet Rose Burberry simply skols the last of her cold tea and continues to stare out of it.

'MUM,' screams Celeste again, her lips now tighter than her school shirt. 'The bitch has got my brush and won't give it back. Make her … NOW.'

Aaron giggles.

Without warning, Celeste cuffs him around the back of the head, sending her g-zillion bangles into a melody of jingles. 'And you, you little snot. I don't care if you're hungry. Get your own breakfast.'

From under my lashes, I send a pleading look in Rose Burberry's direction.

'Leave him be,' Rose murmurs in her usual aloof manner. She lights a cigarette and sits down next to Aaron, exhaling lethargically. Smoke hangs over his head and begins to drift all around him as though he's hitched a ride to heaven on a cloud.

Celeste stomps her foot hard and backhands Aaron's plastic bowl off the table. I risk another glimpse at Rose Burberry, who is now staring vacantly at her son as milk trickles from the corner of his cheeky smile.

Celeste scowls. '*Well* …aren't you going to search her room or something?'

Rose Burberry draws deeply and longingly on her cigarette and says nothing. Her dark brown hair flickers with silver streaks when it's washed. Today, it trails untidily down her back in oily threads.

'God! I can't believe this bullshit,' huffs Celeste. 'You wait till daddy gets up.'

The air suddenly seems lighter, somehow easier to breathe, the second she leaves.

I force down the last of my cereal, rinse my bowl and spoon, and place them on the drainer to dry.

'You'd better get a wriggle on, Aaron.' I say, picking up a wet cloth. The splash of milk and soggy Frosties are still sliding down the cupboard door.

A grateful smile breaks through the emptiness on Rose Burberry's face for a full second, before returning to its normal, expressionless state. I want Aaron to hurry for my own reasons. I want to be out before The Creeper is up.

'I'll pick him up today, if you want?' I add. I catch myself staring at her back, her thin cotton t-shirt tracing the outline of ribs that need more meat.

Rose Burberry turns and nods. Her lips look like they want to smile again, yet the effort seems far beyond her reach.

From under my hair, I glance at the clock and clap my hands softly behind Aaron to get him moving. 'Hurry up, T-Rex, or we're gonna be late.' He's the little brother I didn't have.

Aaron's pointy, freckled nose scrunches as he grins. 'I'm a Triceratops today,' he informs me and lets out a fierce growl. He slips down from the table and disappears around the door.

The Creeper's voice severs the breath from my lungs in mid-inhale. Instinctively, I wedge myself up against the corner of the chipped, laminate cupboards.

'Morning,' he says chirpily. I hate his jovial moods.

I steady my breathing, lace my fingers behind my back, search out the cupboard door handle, and when the round, wooden knob nestles perfectly into my palm, I tighten my grip and squeeze the life out of it. The tremble in my legs eases just a little.

As though he's read my mind, The Creeper leans in closer and inhales deeply, his nose *almost* brushing the collar of my shirt. I slide sideways along the cupboards away from him, snagging my skirt pocket on the handle I'd seized only moments ago. It restrains me, holding me prisoner as though the two of them have a secret pact. The Creeper rests his hand on the fake stone worktop, blocking my only exit. His index finger inches towards me, mimicking a lonely caterpillar, and I draw my hand away and hold it to my chest. Some kind of disgusting snicker

13

comes out of his mouth as he reaches up to pluck a mug from the rack behind me. The quiver moves from my legs to my stomach. I fight back the urge to pee.

Rose Burberry hasn't moved either since he came in and The Creeper backs away slowly and plops himself down into the chair with a groan and a huff.

I unhook my skirt.

'I'm going to be late tonight, cupcake,' The Creeper says, addressing his wife and patting down the wide comb marks running down the length of his thinning hair. He unbuttons the jacket of his pinstripe navy suit, exposing his usual white shirt and dark blue tie and even though I can't see under the table, I know his bulbous stomach is resting heavily on his thighs.

'It's Phil Caruthers' retirement party. You remember me telling you about him, darling, don't you?' He gives his wife no chance to answer and carries on stirring his coffee with avid interest. 'The party's tonight and knowing Phil, and the kind of parties *he's* used to …' he pauses to give me two quick winks, 'anything goes.' His fat head rotates on his equally fat neck to face his wife before pivoting back to me, jowls swaying above his tightly collared shirt.

'Can you leave the key under the milk crate, petal? I'll be back late.' He gives me another wink.

Heart stops.

Beats a few times.

Stops. And then flat out chases my pulse around my body as though it's the last race it will ever run.

*Hurry up, Aaron,* I silently pray as another gallon of crude oil empties into my body, slithers beneath my skin, claws wrapped around my throat, panicking the blood inside my veins. Fear has found another way in.

Aaron returns, boisterously swinging his school bag over his shoulder. 'Can I have some dinner money please, Dad?' His hand stretched out, his fingers wiggling. Aaron's tie is crooked and his shirt untucked. I will see to it before he enters the school gates and ensure he has his jumper.

The Creeper extend his leg and reaches deep into his trouser pocket. 'There … now quit bugging me, boy.' He dumps a handful of silver on to the table, and Aaron sifts through the coins and slides the money into his pocket. No smiles or hugs. No "have a great day at school". Nor are there enough words in the English language to describe how much I hate The Creeper.

I feel him staring at me. 'Ems, do you need some money, love?' I cringe, keeping my eyes on the mosaic-patterned lino. I hate the name Ems.

In seventeen years, nobody has ever called me Ems, except him. I grind my teeth until my jaw aches knowing it's a memory that won't purge.

'No, thank you, Mr Burberry,' I mutter, my fake smile straining against gravity. I raise my head, allowing my eyes to devour the hob that hasn't seen a clean cloth in a month. 'I've already made my lunch.'

He chuckles again, sending his baggy pelican throat into a ripple of jiggles. 'I should think after a year, Ems, you could refer to me as Darryl. Don't you think, dear?'

Nothing in this world will ever make me say his first name. To me, he is … *him* or The Creeper. His leering stares with no blinks, midnight stalking's and the seductive lick of his lips when he thinks no-one is watching have turned my days into a succession of stand-alone anxious moments and bone-chilling nightmares.

This time Rose Burberry does look up and offers a hum of acknowledgement. Dark crescent moons shadow beneath her eyes.

'Well. I think it's time,' he says, running the tip of his middle finger along the length of his moustache. He smiles at me, slow blink by slow blink, removing my clothes, layer by firmly tucked in layer.

Aaron bounds over and threads his fingers into my hand. He pulls me towards the kitchen door. 'C'mon, Ember, we're gonna be late.'

I am thankful, if for nothing else this morning, for the swift exit and the opportunity not to respond.

# THREE

*IN* the heavens above this dodgy little terrace house I now belong to, there's a debate going on. The sky's still deciding whether to be blue or grey, the sun as always, excused from the discussion. It's not that unusual really, for an autumn day in Gloucester. The long, hot days of August are over, not that there were many of them to remember, and the beginning of a new school year means my second Christmas as an orphan is almost here.

I miss them most at Christmas.

I step outside, onto the doormat that has never said welcome in its life, and pull the door closed. The letterbox clatters.

The small front yard, the width of one window and a front door, can't really be classified as a garden. It's mainly concrete, apart from the partially dug flowerbed under the window that bear no plants. A few of Aaron's old Tonka trucks are embedded up to the wheels.

I throw back the hood of my jacket and look to the sky. 'At least, it isn't raining,' I say, trying to stay cheerful as

Aaron tugs at the gate. The row of terrace houses in front of us could do with the water though, the archaic bricks dating back to the war, are grimy with age.

As if out of a deliberate act of defiance, a spot of water lands on my cheek. Water and I have a love-hate relationship. I reckon it leaking out of my skin, confirming how *un-normal* I am, gives me grounds to detest it. It also fails to wash off The Creepers dirty pawprints after he's done, but worst of all, it wasn't there when I needed it twelve months ago, dousing the flames that took my parents life. And yet it's simplicity, shape and feel calms me to the point of unconsciousness. Water and I definitely have issues.

I yank the gate open and swipe a glance back at the Burberrys' house. Number forty-seven Lilac Road sounds innocent enough. But there is the illusion. It should say six six six 'welcome to hell street.'

'I like the rain, Ember,' says Aaron, wriggling his fingers into my hand. 'It always washes the dog poo into the gutters and makes the streets all nice and clean again.'

Despite my melancholy, I find a smile for him.

As we walk, we chat about Aaron's favourite subject – dinosaurs, and which dinosaur he wants to be when he grows up. By the time we arrive at Hudson primary, I can recite the names of the coolest herbivores and carnivores from Aaron's top twenty list.

The playground is littered with kids wearing fawn coloured shirts and blue trousers. I bend down to Aaron's height, tuck in his shirt tail, reposition his tie, and plant a quick kiss on his cheek.

'Not in front of my friends, Emm-ba,' he whispers, dragging his sleeve across his face as he speaks. For a six-year-old, it's still cute.

I stand for a minute, watching him.

It takes me back to when life was simple, and the only dilemma I had, was deciding what colour nail varnish to wear.

'Bye, Emm-ba,' Aaron calls out.

I shake off the hopelessness of a life I will never have again and sling my bag over my back. Every morning, my eyes still open, towel not ready to be thrown in just yet.

The back gate into the high school is where it all happens … according to the cool kids. But, what would I know? All I see are the same faces from last term milling around, checking their phones and prolonging the inevitable. So, as usual, I keep my head down, commit the patterned stitching of my shoes to memory, until I'm sure I've left the seasoned smokers behind with their disapproving stares, and the groups of girls with their standard knee-length skirts eight inches shorter than everyone else's. It doesn't matter it's been a year since I survived the crash; as far as gossip goes, it might as well have happened yesterday. They all wanted to know back then, and still want to know now, how I got out of that car, except, I don't know. The incident hangs around my neck worse than a bad reputation.

'Who's the redhead?'

My feet suction to the concrete, leaving the top half of my body free to spin around to see who'd spoken.

A boy, hands deep in his pockets, is staring intently at me. Not smiling. Not frowning. Not blinking. Just staring.

I find myself staring back, cheeks hot and cherried, my mind cloudy and not my own. Bars spring up in front of me, walls surround me, his eyes holding me prisoner. Eyes that are not simply blue, not cobalt, or azure, or even cerulean. They are a blue that has never been seen before. Colour without a name. Beauty without a reason. So unique, so unbelievably unique, so breathtaking that I want to smile and laugh for no reason at all. His black hair, a little spikey in places, barely registers, as does his angled jawline. And forget about asking what he is wearing or what bag he is carrying. His eyes refuse to allow me the pleasure of looking.

I can't move. No thoughts. No words. No breath.

Out of nowhere, heat begins to build inside me, just like last month at the graveyard. And like a week ago and only two days ago after Celeste 'accidentally' smashed a photo of my parents.

But this is a different … *somehow.*

No lagoons fill my cupped palms. No exaggerated perspiration. No water leaking out of my skin.

Instead, my heart thumps louder, harder, faster than it's ever done trying to cope with this new fiery hotness. My face burns too, like a tidal-wave of heat has tsunami-ed down my neck and across my chest. Most would pass it off as heatstroke without the rash, but I would bet my crystal rocking horse I'm more a cooked lobster now than suffering a mild case of measles. My low wedge school shoes could be stilts for all the good they're doing to steady me.

Time stops.

The world stops.

My heart stops.

And then beats again.

Someone's laughter breaks the spell his eyes have over me. I wish I could stay here forever. The soft whisper of leaves above my head gently brings me around, reminding me of the breaths I've forgotten to take.

I inhale and breathe out.

I take a second breath and then a third.

A dog barking several streets away nudges me further into reality.

The rubbing of shoulders and brushing of backpacks skim across my body as kids manoeuvre around me to avoid walking in the mud.

I blink, dazed, check myself.

I'm standing in the middle of the path; inquisitive faces pass me. The boy with the blue eyes is still there although his attention is now elsewhere.

My legs feel the breath of life again. Blood slows, heart slows, breathing slows.

The furnace has dulled to a simmer, and my cheeks feel more pinched by cold than by embarrassment.

I pause for another second.

It feels so much longer.

I urge my legs to carry me from this weirdness I have no idea how to explain. Slowly, one foot in front of the other, I move until the invisible connection binding me to this blue-eyed god snaps like a bungee cord at full stretch. It propels me forward into a run, and I steady myself hoping nobody saw me. I take one quick glance backward to find him staring at me again, a hole, the diameter of a plate scorching into my back. I pick up my pace, partially blinded by those vivid blue eyes and head for the sanctity of F Block.

I reach the courtyard in one piece and throw my bag onto the table. The flush of warmth lurking in the deeper layers of my skin remains, even after the removal of my jumper.

My thoughts go back to last month and the black marble headstone. I double-check my surroundings, deciding it's a perfect opportunity to put this weird melting *thing* to the test again. It worked the other day when I managed to soften my bread knife enough, I could tie it in a knot.

Blinking and blinking, the flaking green paint scorches away to nothing the second I place the flat of my hand against the table. I almost let out a squeal in total amazement as the wood starts to smoulder. Wood responds so much faster than stone or stainless steel and yet my rational brain insists this isn't possible.

Humans cannot do these things!

But some can.

I can.

The distinct aroma of charcoal and paint fumes tells me this is not my imagination, and the scorched handprint left behind is not an illusion. I can't deny any longer that I possess some weird, freakish power.

I trace the outline of each charred finger, if only to verify its existence. It makes me smile, something I don't do enough of according to my best friend, Rachel.

My thoughts flash back to the boy who triggered this heat, his hands in his pockets and his head cocked to one side.

*Holy shit, here we go again!*

I fan my face with my hand, sensing my core temperature rising a few degrees more. I blow out a hearty breath, trying not to think of myself as a recently boiled kettle. I replace my hand over the print, this time, searing the wood much quicker, leaving a clear indentation, several inches deep.

My lips turn up more until a soft snigger breaks rank.

'What are you laughing about?' Hastily, I throw my bag on top, before swinging around to see Rachel walking towards me. She is as different to me as fire is to ice. 'I'm not saying it's a bad thing,' she continues, dumping her bag next to mine before readjusting the clip in her blond hair. A few strands always manage to escape and dangle around her face, even when she's not trying to look gorgeous. 'I love seeing you laugh. It's just ...' her eyebrows pull unnaturally close together.

'I know, I know, I don't do it often enough,' I add before she has a chance.

The weight of this morning's ordeal must make its way to my eyes because Rachel pounces. 'Are you frigging kidding me? Did he come into your room again?' she growls, lowering her voice. She looks over her shoulder to see if anyone heard her. 'That pervert should be in jail.'

Rachel knows. I told her everything.

Her voice softens. 'You've gotta tell someone, Em.'

I let out a breath. 'Who's going to believe me? *Rose Burberry*? She's stuck in her own little world of daytime soaps and cold cups of tea. She'll never believe it in a million years. Not with his "darling" this and "petal" that.'

I swallow a raggedy breath. My throat wants to close over; to not talk about him, them, my life. I see it in Rachel's eyes she won't let it drop. I must end this … now.

'He's made it clear if I ever told anyone, he'd make life so unbearable, I'd wish I was dead. And he's a lawyer for fuck's sake. What chance do I stand against him?'

Rachel throws her arms around my neck and hugs me tightly. 'Not much at all, the fat bastard,' she says softly. She rubs my shoulder. 'Don't worry, he'll get what's coming to him, even if I have to sneak around in the middle of the night and cut off his favourite appendage. It's only a matter of time, Em … I'm telling you. It's coming for him.'

Her words sound more like a promise to herself than reassurance to me. I raise my eyebrows.

'*What*?'

'Nothing,' I reply.

'All I'm saying is I *could* live with myself if I did something like that. That's all.'

A tiny smile breaks through my lips. Her face is so sincere, so serious, with the customary frown pinched above her nose. One second is all it takes for us both to burst into fits of laughter. It's never quite as serious when she talks about it and, although it may sound disingenuous to most, to me it's her way of lifting me out of my crappy world for a few seconds, to enjoy a little of her uncomplicated life.

'Can I stay at yours Friday night?' I ask, anxious to be off the subject.

Rachel blots her recently applied lip gloss and throws the bottle back into her bag. 'Goes without saying. You always stay over at the weekend.'

'I know,' I mumble. 'I don't like to presume.'

Rachel shakes her head and laughs. 'Being presumptuous isn't in your nature.'

'I know, but …' I stop in mid-sentence. The warm glow from before is escalating at an alarming rate. Someone has

23

let off a flare in my stomach, and heat and fireworks rocket up from my chest to my face. My cheeks feel like a Catherine wheel, spitting out white-hot sparks.

I twist around, hearing my name spoken.

Again.

The new boy, with eyes as blue as the ocean, is standing across the courtyard. His head is angled to one side, looking straight at me, staring, concentrating.

Heart double thumps.

Breath disappears.

Full on body tremors.

He nods once in my direction before going on his way.

'What was that all about?' Rachel's head is flicking back and forth between us in case she misses something.

At first, I can't speak.

'Em?'

'What?'

Rachel grumbles. 'I said, what was all that about?'

'Err, I'm not sure.'

Something inside me does know. Unconsciously, I'd acknowledged his presence in a way that made my whole body come alive with fire.

# FOUR

*LAST* year, I sat next to Lee Nightingale in English.

He's pretty harmless, as far as boys go, however, picking his nose with the end of his pencil and wiping it on the side of the desk, isn't an experience I'm keen to share with him again this year. So, I take the shortcut through the science corridor, down the stairs where most year elevens go for a quick snog at lunchtime, and then bolt across the quadrangle, until I come to the undercover bike racks. On a patch of mud right next to it, stands four free-standing, demountable cabins, the first being my English classroom.

Not surprisingly, I'm the first to arrive. I take a quick peek at my timetable, prise the lid off my lunch box and remove an apple. Sarah Turner and Monique Hudson are the next to arrive, and my lips twitch into half a smile at them. The last bite of my apple, however, has me looking around for a bin.

Without warning, the inferno is back.

So soon.

Three times in one day! Or should I say three times in less than an hour. That has never happened before.

A volcano holds my body captive, setting me alight, heat rushing through my blood, desperate to consume me.

I struggle for control. A sharp gasp escapes my lips.

Monique and Sarah stop talking and spin around to face me. I cover my mouth, trying to pass it off as a yawn, but who am I kidding. I feel like I'm about to explode.

Thankfully, they turn away and I press my palm to my cheek.

My face is super-hot.

*What is wrong with me today?*

I scan my immediate environment.

Holding the lid of the rubbish bin, a short distance away, is the boy with the wondrous blue eyes.

Our eyes lock. My legs lock into place. My heart locks itself away, afraid to be given free will after our last meeting. I have no keys for any of them.

Silent questions float somewhere in the gap between us.

Seconds tick by. Minutes dissolve into each other. All I can think of is ... I can't move. I don't want to move.

Eventually, his eyebrow lifts. 'I'm not standing here all day.'

His gruff tone snaps me to attention.

Apart from the dazzle in his eyes, his face shows no emotion.

Shyness creeps in, and my gaze drops, finding comfort in the last pair of shoes my father brought me. I'm safe, where I'm standing ... back here in the trenches where my legs don't work, and my heart does what its told. Crossing no-man's land, a mere fifteen yards away, to be closer to him, has me all nervy and flustered. But I can't stay put. I'm feeling more and more like an idiot.

I breathe out, wriggle my toes into action, and take my first step. I wobble, like it's the first time I've learnt how to walk. I feel his eyes on me, my body smouldering like

I've been doused in petrol and set on fire. I bridge the distance between us, the tiny hairs on my arms prickling to attention. It's unnerving and yet strangely exhilarating.

I drop the core into the bin and wait for him to speak. Again, he says nothing. I contemplate looking up, except he'll take me again, I know he will, and put me under his spell that doesn't sound as scary, as far as spells go.

He clears his throat and without thinking, my eyes betray me, and I look up. I have become the snake, and he is the charmer.

He replaces the lid, and I partially recover, enough to at least acknowledge him with a nod. Words dormant, out of order, away on holiday at the coast.

A light switch's on inside me, dim at first and then brighter until an image of us together burns against the back of my mind. An image of us, both naked, two black silhouettes tangled in a fiery embrace that would make many blush and then look away.

The moment passes between us and then is gone.

I don't indulge in fantasies.

This isn't a time for fairytales.

He retreats although doesn't venture more than a few feet before stopping. He doesn't turn around.

Heat begins to burn my organs one at a time, transforming my blood to boiling tomato soup. I want to scream. I want to cry out in pain, anything to rid my body of this firestorm.

*I need air.*

*Fresh, cool air.*

Monique and Sarah cock their heads in my direction again, and this time, I opt for a slow steady breath.

It doesn't help.

*What's happening to me?*

The boy's shoulders stoop a little; enough for me to notice, and his head falls forward. He shakes it so slowly as though he's talking to someone.

Turn around, I want to call out. Turn around and explain this strangeness I feel when you're near me.

He doesn't.

He walks away like he can't stand to be near me another minute. The invisible connection between us breaks and I watch him disappear from sight.

A few drops of rain land on my face and I crane my head backwards to question the clearest, bluest sky, waiting for the rest. Thankfully, none comes.

Fire extinguished.

English, with Miss Freebody, starts the same way it does every year – with an oral presentation about yourself and what goals you hope to achieve by the end of the school year.

My body wilts at the prospect.

The narrow classroom, with its twenty-four desks divided equally on either side of the room, blaze a path down the middle for the annoying pacing back and forth Miss Freebody likes to do in her soft Hush Puppy shoes.

Flashing off her new engagement ring, she waltzes into the classroom, hair streaked red and cropped short at the neck, and wearing an outfit more suitable for a woman in her twenties. A dramatic overhaul, I must say. Not a floral print skirt or ponytail in sight. Not that this matters to me. Whichever way I look at it, Miss Freebody's makeover isn't going to change how she runs her class first day back.

And I *hate* talking about myself … in public. What I dread more are the three questions the other students get to ask afterwards.

When the first two rows complete their speeches, I know I'm next. I make my way to the front and stare down each student individually, visualising them as nursery rhyme characters like my father had told me to do on my first day of school.

*I can do this.*

I take a deep breath.

'My name is Ember Riley. I'm seventeen years old. I don't wear jewellery because I don't like it ... and this time next year ...'

I pause.

My words trip over themselves in a rush to get out. Blood stains my cheeks and hitches a ride south to my neck. This time next year, I want to be living somewhere other than with the Burberrys, except I can't say that aloud. It would prompt questions I have no intention of answering.

With my fake smile in place, I say the first thing that comes into my head. 'And this time next year, I would like to be cross-country skier.'

Of course, I haven't the faintest idea about cross-country skiing and, never had the desire to do it. I also know nobody wants to know about it either.

Miss Freebody glares disapprovingly at me, and my two-line autobiography, before addressing the class. Hands shoot up immediately.

'Yes, Eliza,' says Miss Freebody.

Eliza Campbell-Jones lowers her hand and grins at me with all the warmth of a barracuda. Last year's poll had her topping "the bitchiest girl in the year" award, a title she hasn't shut up about since. Fake is her middle name – from her nails, lashes, and hair extensions down to her topped up solarium tan lines. *And who gets a boob job when you've got an extra two servings?*

'EM-BA. You said you don't wear jewellery because you don't like it,' she begins, exaggerating each word slowly, 'my question is ... why don't you like it? Is it because you can't afford it, now that your parents are dead?'

A hush falls over the class. Even the birds outside stop their pleasant chattering.

My parents. My poor, innocent parents.

I feel unsteady and a little bit sick. My hand searches for something to hold on to but find nothing but air.

Desperately, I pinch the side of my skirt. *Something to hold onto, something to hold onto ...*

Malice, that invisible wound that doesn't bleed. That doesn't cut tissue or bruise skin, but tears away at you sharper than any knife, poisoning your whole body with a handful of nouns and a few adjectives. It shakes my world right down to my feet, making my knees, calves, toes, throb. I want to yell "you have no right to even mention them ... you have no idea of the guilt that lurks in the blackness around me, pinching at the ragged edges of my resolve".

A procession of snorting piggy giggles belongs to an unnaturally blond, pouty, pink-lipped girl sitting beside Eliza. Cherie Bennett is Eliza's equally evil twin. Her hair not quite as long or blond, make-up not quite as perfect and fake tan not quite as orange.

'Enough of that,' Miss Freebody scolds, glaring at Eliza. 'You don't have to answer that question, Ember, if you don't want to.'

My stomach is still twisting, still breaking down and digesting the words as quickly as it can to rid the feeling from my body. The glass from ten broken bottles finds its way into my throat. I swallow, pushing the pain down further into the places I can't allow myself to visit.

'It's okay,' I reply timidly. If I don't give Eliza an answer, she will continue to drag this out for months, like she did last year when it was fresh and new, and I didn't know how to handle it.

All eyes fall on me.

*Now I am the nursery rhyme character.*

I can't tell them I've had to stop wearing every piece of jewellery I own since my visit to the cemetery. Since I've been capable of vandalising school property and re-sculpting cutlery. It seems gold and silver either turn my skin black almost instantly, resembling charcoal in colour *and* texture or has a strange habit of turning necklaces, bracelets, rings and earrings into soft squishy lumps of metal.

*Do they need to know I'm a freak?* I think not.

So, I sugar-coat it the only way I know how. I make fun of myself.

'Actually, Eliza, I'm allergic to it.'

The grin on Eliza's face fades fast behind three inches of foundation, and Cherie, whose mouth is gaping like a goldfish, looks as though she's been asked how many sides an isosceles triangle has.

'Yeah,' I add quickly, pleased by their reaction, 'it's disgusting. My skin bubbles up with these tiny little blisters, and then when they pop, this putrid yellow liquid oozes out.'

Some girls groan.

Eliza sits rigidly in her seat. Her lips form a snarl as the flats of her hands press down on her desk. Her elbows shake, her eyes taking me apart one thick mascara blink at a time. 'It does not, you liar. *Miss*, are you going to allow lying in your class? I've never once seen Em-BA with these blisters.' The similarities between Eliza and Celeste are uncanny. I can't help wondering if they were separated at birth.

'If you ask a silly question, Eliza, you're going to get a silly answer.'

I ward off the urge to grin back. If Eliza doesn't believe it, nobody will, and being formally shut down in class, there's less chance she'll bring it up again. Eliza's hand flies into the air again.

'You know the rules. One question only,' Miss Freebody says abruptly, and moves right along to the next person.

Troy Finnegan's hand is up first. 'Yes, Troy. Do you have a *sensible* question?' Miss Freebody's eyes flick back to Eliza, who has now slumped back into her chair with her arms folded awkwardly across her bulging bust.

Troy, who appears to have forgotten to brush his gingery-brown hair this morning, scratches his head nervously.

'Umm, yeah. So, you said you're seventeen. What date is your birthday, then?' His freckles peer out from under a slow developing blush.

Wolf whistles echo around the room and I mask my embarrassment with a weak smile.

'The twenty-third of August,' I answer firmly. I want to add the word 'why?' when I see Troy jotting down my answer on a piece of paper.

'And the last question is from …' Miss Freebody scans the faces. 'Adele.'

Adele Quirk hardly ever speaks, so when she does, everyone spins around in their seats in interest. Scarlet ribbons fasten her plaits to the top and bottom of her hair making her look twelve not nearly old enough to vote.

'Ember, I was wondering where your name came from?'

Troy's head jerks up again, pen at the ready.

I am off-footed by her question, although more confused by Troy's sudden eagerness in my life. Adele doesn't indulge in gossip, and her face is always sincere that making a joke of her question, wouldn't feel right.

'Obviously, it's to do with the hair,' Eliza interrupts, swishing her hair in protest.

I ignore her comment, regardless of Miss Freebody's wide eyes and raised brows which have lunchtime detentions behind them.

'Adele, even before I was born my mum wanted to call me Ember. She said from the moment she found out she was pregnant with me; I was like a little ball of fire in her belly, keeping her warm. Once I was born, my skin was as red as my hair,' I rake my fingers through it, 'and she knew no other name would fit.'

Adele's smile widens, a huge contrast to the trollish sneer on Eliza's face.

The rest of the class falls silent.

Everyone knows I live with foster parents. Tongues will wag, and rumours will flourish. Miss Freebody offers me a sympathetic smile as I take my seat and I observe Troy scribble down one last word and stuff the paper into his pocket.

The rest of the lesson runs as smoothly as an English lesson can run, with quotes from this scholar and that poet and everything else with a quote in between. At last, the bell rings, and I'm more than keen to leave.

So is Troy, I notice.

His books are packed away, and his backpack is on his shoulder, ready. He doesn't see me watching him. He's more interested in who is outside the classroom.

'Okay, have a great day, people, and I'll see you on Wednesday,' says Miss Freebody.

Troy is out of his seat first.

Curious, I grab my bag and follow him.


He is fast, for a short lad, and I have trouble keeping up with him. It might be nothing, although something niggles at me about the notes he'd taken. In my mind, notes are generally taken for someone else's benefit.

Troy high-tails it from one side of the high school to the other in less than two minutes and I almost decide to quit until he disappears around the side of the sports block.

I slowly edge around the gymnasium wall.

The bottom drops out of my life with a loud thump.

*No way.*

The boy with the beautiful eyes is leaning against the cafeteria wall. His hair looks shiny or wet, I can't decide which. He catches me staring at him, his eyes inviting me closer.

Confusion comes first, then anger as I witness Troy handing him a note from his pocket. *His* note that equals *my* life.

Heat finds me again.

All of a sudden, my hands feel wet, although not enough to form puddles. The red plastic handles from my school bag are disintegrating before my eyes, coating my palms with a crimson-like glue. It's all stuck between my fingers.

The two boys return to their conversation and I take the opportunity to bend down and wipe my hands on the dewy grass. Heart thumping in my chest, my body comes alive with heat as I stand up, flames ripping my composure to shreds. I storm towards him, red hair flying around my head and a war-face that says, "geared for battle". Troy glances back, hearing my footsteps. His mouth stretches downwards as though he's about to vomit or burst into tears and scurries away before I can get to him.

The boy sees me coming too.

Confidence radiates off him in waves. His arms are folded casually across his chest as though he's been waiting for me. His eyes are as bright and as stunning as I remember them. It's far too late for pleasant introductions.

'What did Troy give you?' I demand.

I fight to keep the tremble out of my voice. It's hard, when every nerve, from my head to my toes, is being plucked by anger instead of fear. I feel giddy and out of my depth. More heat gathers, spiriting up from the earth's core, through the soles of my feet and into my bloodstream.

The boy shakes his head and puts both hands behind his back. 'I don't know what you're talking about. I don't have anything.'

I reach out to snatch the note, except he's super-fast. I lose my balance and fall towards him. He tentatively stretches one arm out to steady me and promptly retracts it as though touching me is against anything he believes in. He takes a measured step back, giving me space to recover. His eyes, however, never leave me.

'I saw him give it to you,' I say accusingly. 'Show me your other hand.' My fury rises. Heat increases. 'And why do you want to know when my birthday is?'

The boy ignores me and brings his other arm forward. He presents his palm. To my total amazement, it's empty.

'B-but, I saw him …' I freeze, replaying the moment over in my mind.

The boy's face is neutral, and his lips relaxed. 'I think you're mistaken.'

I'm sure I'd seen it. Positive even.

This strange heat is beginning to fry my brain. I have no evidence, and he denies having it. Like I said, introductions are far too late, leaving only one pathetic word left in my vocabulary to mop up with.

'Sorry,' I say tersely. Syrupy thick lava flows around my body as embarrassment shamelessly steps into my skin and slaps both my cheeks. Hard.

I turn to leave.

A sharp current, jolts inside me for a split second as he catches hold of my arm, like two live wires meeting, making me jump and squeal, although I'm not sure in which order. His eyes hold me prisoner again and his hand, resembling ice against my hot skin, sends cool waves surging beneath my flesh. It's calming, somehow, dissolving my anger and taming the volcano within. My eyes fall to his hand, staring in confusion at what I'm sure is nothing more than peculiarity at best.

The next words out of his mouth aren't what I'm expecting.

'Ember …'

Half dazed, I find his glorious face.

'Has anyone ever told you that your eyes are the colour of molten lava?'

I open my mouth to speak and promptly shut it.

I try again.

Nothing resembling audible words comes out ... more like a chicken clucking softly at the back of my throat. I'm left reeling. *Who says stuff like that?*

A shadow descends over me when his hand falls limply to his side. Coldness, like none I've ever experienced before, ventures into my skin and straight back out again like death had entered the wrong body somehow and then abruptly realised it had made a mistake. I know I should say something, anything, but I don't know where to start.

Too late.

I'm out of time.

His eyes float to the ground before he walks away, leaving me teetering for a moment, playing catch-up in a game I don't know the rules to.

The lunch bell rings, and I retrace my steps to F block, knowing I'd apologised for something I know in my heart I was not mistaken about.

# FIVE

'*RACH*, do my eyes look strange to you?'

Rachel glances up from her copy of Cosmo and gives me a quick once over. 'Nope.'

She continues to flip pages.

'What? Not even a *little* bit?'

Rachel lowers her imitation Ray-Bans and squints at me. 'No, not even a little bit,' she says, re-positioning her glasses. She pops the last of her mum's homemade quiche into her mouth and goes back to her magazine.

I exhale loudly, not satisfied with her answer. Typically, she has more to offer and the constant flick, flick, flick of pages adds to my growing frustration.

'What about the colour? Does the colour look different? Do they look bright, or dull to you? Look closer this time.'

Rachel huffs and lets the magazine rest against her thighs. She leans forward, pushing her sunglasses back and gazes into my eyes, giving me her full attention.

'I don't know what you're talking about. They're the same colour they've always been.' Her face is serious, for all of a second. 'The same murky hazel-brown you were born with, Ratface. Why?' Ratface is the nickname she gave me when we were toddlers. It had something to do with my pointy nose that turned up slightly at the end, and two bucked front teeth which naturally corrected themselves.

After my meeting with 'blue eyes', I went straight to the bathrooms to check. I had to see if my *eyes were the colour of molten lava*. I'd peered into the mirror, lifting my chin to form every angle I could possibly make, trying to see if the varying amounts of light made any difference.

They hadn't.

And if Rachel couldn't see what he'd seen, and I'd known her my whole life, then maybe he hadn't either. Maybe he was just being a twat to get out of handing over the note.

I rein in my thoughts. Rachel is still looking at me with one eyebrow half-cocked.

'It's … nothing.'

I pull out my compact and gaze into the small mirror for one final look, then dab my nose with a little powder.

'What's going on with you, Em? I've never seen you so worried about the colour of your eyes before.'

A cool wind sweeps across my face as the sun takes shelter behind a cloud. Two-thirds of the small courtyard falls into shadow. It isn't the reason Rachel's face has lost its lightness. I know exactly what she's about to say from the way her jaw and hands have clenched in unison.

'Was it *him*? Did he say something to you … because if he did …?'

I cut her off. 'It wasn't him,' I say soberly. The thought of defending him causes my skin to shrink back as muscle moves away from bone, blood from artery.

'Then who? Somebody must have said something. You don't get all flushed in the face for nothing. Something's up. What is it?'

Now I wished I hadn't brought it up.

I reach up and feel my cheeks. The fire had dulled some time ago leaving rose-tinted cheekbones. Confiding in Rachel about the boy with beautiful cobalt eyes, with the face I'd never get sick of looking at, and who is responsible for the warm and totally desirable buzz lingering in my skin long after his touch, is a bad move. She'd think I was nuts, especially as I've never talked about boys this way before, never indulged in dating or even window shopped, come to that. I know what will happen - the questions would start – how long have you liked him? What did he say? When are you guys going out? How much do you think he benches? She loves guys with well-defined shoulders. It's almost as ludicrous as melting wood and metal with my bare hands.

As much as I love my best friend, I can't tell her. Rachel is the only person in the world who makes me feel normal and, although the boyfriend side of things is as natural as bread and butter for most, the supernatural element that happens to me every time he is near, isn't.

'It's nothing, honestly. I thought they looked different this morning, that's all.'

Rachel's isn't buying it for one minute. Thankfully, the bell rings. I reach for my bag and sling it over my shoulder, forgetting about the recent modifications I made to the table.

Rachel spots the handprint straight away. 'What wanker vandalised our table?' She lines her hand up with the charred print. 'People get away with murder in this place. It starts off with something as simple as this, and the next thing you know, there is mayhem.'

I shrug, guilt trying to leak out of my pores. 'It could've been an accident,' I say.

Her eyes come back to me, the table forgotten. 'Are you sure you're gonna be okay?' Rachel softly tugs at my sleeve.

I nod unconvincingly. 'I'm sure. Don't worry.'

Her face relaxes a little. 'And if that fat prick comes near you tonight, accidently knee him in the balls. I guarantee you; he won't be able to piss out of that thing for days without it hurting.'

The door to my science class is already open. I head for the seat closest to the window on the back row and tuck my bag under the table. Mr Butcher is busily scrawling on the whiteboard about what he expects from his students. He is a colossal man in every sense – long, thick legs and torso, sturdy shoulders, and a massive balding head. Tufts of grey hair curl around his ears and carry on down his face in a scruff of a beard that has been long forgotten about.

A low grumble erupts from his throat and chatter ceases the moment he throws his red pen on to his desk. His presence alone commands authority, though his appearance lets him down a tad. His worn, black trousers could easily fit two of me inside them and are hitched up way too far with a belt that looks straight out of Braveheart. His yellowing shirt, sleeves rolled to the elbows, was perhaps found at the bottom of the washing basket this morning.

With a gentle brush of his tufty sideburns, from fingers long and fat enough to be sausages, he turns his attention to each one of us as though committing us to memory. When his gaze falls upon the only vacant seat left in the room, he pulls another pen from his top pocket and clicks it on and off in rapid succession, noticeably irritated.

The empty seat is as far away from me as it can be – front row, far right. Mr Butcher picks up his clipboard and walks over to the spot, tapping his pen against the board as he goes. Poor Katie Sullivan and the two rows in front of me, all jump at the same time as he brings his large hands down on to the desk with a loud slap

In mid-hunch, his eyes dart around the class again. A glimmer of a smile teases the corners of his lips. 'River,' he barks in a thunderous voice.

Several heads turn sideways, and shoulders shrug.

I look straight ahead.

Mr Butcher, as old as he looks, is lightning fast with his movements. His 'frying pan' hands fly to his hips as if his trousers are about to fall at any moment. He seems to be waiting for a response.

'River Fulton,' he says with a throaty growl.

His beady eyes, the colour of ash, shift from person to person at whirlwind speed and with interest. Still, nobody speaks.

Mr Butcher takes a deep, exaggerated breath and exhales. Backs and torsos straighten as he paces in front of the whiteboard.

'Does anyone know where River Fulton is?' Heads twist on necks to look at the person next to them or shake from side to side.

'Is it somewhere in Somerset, sir?' calls out a voice.

The boy sitting in front of me has the unmistakable tone of a drag queen. 'You boy, stand up,' says Mr Butcher. 'What is your name?'

The boys chair scrapes against the lino as he stumbles to his feet. 'Peter Capelli, sir,' he answers. I hear his exaggerated swallow from two feet away.

'Peter Capelli, you're an idiot. Sit down.' The stunned look on Peter's face as he glances around in confusion causes a ripple of laughter.

Mr Butcher claps his palms together with a thunderous thwack. 'River Fulton is not a body of water, you ignoramus. He is a body of matter.'

Not daring to make any sharp movements, I peek sideways through my hair at the row of puzzled faces.

41

Mr Butcher lets out another loud groan. 'Well,' he begins, clasping his massive mitts behind his back as he makes his way to the front of the room, 'if nobody knows where he is, we'll sit ... and wait ... until he gets here.'

No sooner are the words out of his mouth, the door opens and of all people, 'blue eyes' walks to the front of the class and hands the gigantic man a note. The boy steals a glance in one direction and one direction only, at me, as though he knows exactly where I'd be sitting.

Blood stops pumping.

Muscles freeze to bones.

Bones all break.

Paralysis sets in.

*I can't breathe.*

And, then the feeling is gone.

Mr Butcher scans the boy from head to foot. I see a glimmer of something change in his weathered face - a flash of something, I'm not sure what to call it. The boy's posture shifts ever so slightly most wouldn't notice. But I do.

'Well, well, well, if it isn't Mr Fulton, himself. Welcome, welcome, so good of you to join us. We were discussing your absence, weren't we ... class?' he says, directing his comment back to us, although looking straight at me.

Nobody answers.

'I apologise for my tardiness. It's my first day.'

Mr Butcher takes a second look at the note. His mouth twitches into a mocking smile.

'So, it seems. So, it seems. Class, I'd like to introduce, *Mr* River Fulton.'

Mr Butcher raises his chunky, grey eyebrows at Peter Capelli and Peter shifts nervously in his seat. More whispers and a giggle stop as quickly as they start. Cherie Bennett lets out a wolf whistle.

River Fulton looks unperturbed by Mr Butcher's shameful attempts at humour. 'Mr Fulton is new at the school and to the area. Isn't that right?'

'Yes,' says the boy in a flat, unimpressed tone. His arms hang casually at his side, his stance, relaxed. His chest rises and falls with ease and his eyes, still wondrously blue, are calm. As aloof and as confident as he is, he's like my favourite book that I just don't want to put down.

Mr Butcher stops to scratch his beard with his pen before jotting down notes on his clipboard. 'Because you are new, I will let you off with a warning.' He gestures to the only vacant seat with a severe wag of his finger, and River sits.

'However, that does not go for the rest of you. Tardiness, as so eloquently put by Mr Fulton, is a disease I hope to eradicate before I die,' he says between a chuckle that makes his entire body jiggle. 'Which brings me to the topic on the board.' He taps his pen against the whiteboard where he'd underlined the title three times. 'Rules of my classroom.'

I read the scrawl on the board for the third time.

1.    All assignments are to be handed in <u>on time</u> unless previous arrangements have been made with God, the devil or a social worker. Pets dying, eating, vomiting or defecating on homework are not acceptable forms of justification. Loss of limb will also not excuse.

2.    Tardiness <u>will be</u> rewarded with afternoon detention.

3.    Bullying <u>will not</u> be tolerated and those caught will face severe consequences –hanging, electric chair or guillotine are the favoured options.

4.    The unauthorised use of mobile phones in this class will earn you <u>500</u> lines – PRONTO.

It is glaringly obvious, that this isn't the type of class where you can get away with anything, regardless of Mr

Butcher's seemingly warped sense of humour. I hastily pull my books and pens out and push my bag further under the table.

'So,' he begins, 'let's move right along.' Mr Butcher rubs the list from the board, his arm resembling a giant windscreen wiper,

As if by some unwritten law, my eyes float upwards at the precise moment River Fulton turns around. Our eyes meet for a fraction of a second - long enough for me to see sadness, to see desperation. But, that's not all. I see desire.

Flames erupts in my throat, an inch from choking me.

I cough.

I swallow.

I cover my cheeks with my hands.

I'm really standing out like the weirdest person in the school right now … *and* without the help of gossip. That's *so* not me.

River Fulton frowns and turns back to face the front.

'This term, we will be studying a special topic on the four elements; their effects on each other, and the role they play on the surrounding environment.' Mr Butcher pauses as though what he's said is a monumental piece of information, holding significant meaning to each one of us. 'You will be split into four groups, given one element per group to study for the rest of the term, and the group with the best assessment will choose an excursion for the whole class to go on that corresponds to their designated element.'

My breathing behaves. My heart remembers its normal rhythm. The furnace dies down enough for me to think.

Elements doesn't sound too bad. Anything is better than the boring chemical equations we'd learnt last year.

'So, easy questions first,' says Mr Butcher, throwing his pen into the air and catching it. 'Who can give me one of the four elements?'

River Fulton is the first to put his hand up. 'Yes, a chance to redeem yourself, Mr Fulton. Nice to see your tardiness hasn't affected your reflexes.'

I want to see his face again.

I dare myself to want this.

I want to see if he owns a smile.

I squeeze my fists in my lap until they resemble the Rockies, willing him to turn.

'Water,' says River confidently, resistant to my incessant inner monologue.

'Apt …very apt,' says Mr Butcher with a grin. Someone giggles and it isn't until Jonathon King, a boy with a face like a Chihuahua, spins in his chair to face me, do I realise the laughter came from my own mouth. It isn't that I thought River's answer was funny; I simply knew he was going to say water before he'd said it.

'Another?' booms Mr Butcher.

My hand shoots into the air the same time Peter Capelli's does.

'Okay, Capelli. Here's your chance to prove you're not a complete moron.' Mr Butcher walks past the row of windows on my left and towers over Peter's desk, plunging him into shadow. 'Let's see if your brain has woken up from its little siesta, huh?'

*Don't say fire; don't say fire*, I repeat over in my head. *Fire is my word.*

'Earth,' calls out Peter.

A faint smirk crosses my face. It seems mind tricks do work on the weaker mind.

'Yup. Next? The young lass at the back of the class who had her hand up before.'

Heads swivel in my direction, including River's. Twenty pairs of eyes seek me out. Mine, however, are tractor-beamed diagonally across the classroom to where a certain pair of blue eyes devour me. I surrender happily as silence divides the room into dust particles.

The word *fire* is harder to say than I think and for what feels like the millionth time today, his glorious blue eyes hook me by the eyelids and draw me in. Another ball of fire makes a meal of my butterflies.

'F...f ...f ...fire,' I mumble.

Mr Butcher's acting skills are far too dramatic. He claps a colossal hand over his heart in an attempt to fake a gunshot wound. Those who aren't laughing sit rigidly in their seats. He looks my way and goes for his clipboard again.

'Ember Riley, right?' he says, tapping his pen against his notes.

I nod my head. *Shit. Now I'm on his radar.*

'It seems you and Mr Fulton share the same humour with your play on names.'

More laughter teeters around the room.

River Fulton does not laugh. Seriousness is woven across his face, and he rakes his hand through his dark hair once, before dropping his hands to the desk.

Much to my regret and relief, but mostly regret, he remains facing the front for the rest of the lesson. His back muscles constantly flex beneath his white shirt and a frequent stretching of his neck says he isn't as relaxed as he makes out. Even the way he rubs his hand across his forehead has me counting how many times he has done it. Ten, all up. He's intoxicating to watch.

Shianne Powell gets the last answer – air, and the rest of the afternoon is spent going through the fundamentals of the elements, taking notes and drawing symbols.

I am happy and sad when the bell rings, ending school for the day. I stuff my books into my bag and by the time I look up, River Fulton is gone.

# SIX

*WITH* Celeste at her boyfriend's house, I retreat to my room after tea and begin to write up my notes from today. By nine o'clock, I head downstairs and ask Rose if I can use the phone to call Rachel. It's against house rules for me to have a mobile phone. Nobody else, just me.

There was a time when Rachel had asked me to live with her and her mum, and I had almost turned inside out with happiness at the thought. The Burberrys were only meant to be a temporary placement until all the paperwork was finalised. A year has passed, and I've come to realise leaving was never on the cards.

Poor Rose had been on the verge of collapsing and wept for hours, begging me to stay, the only real emotion I'd seen from her. The Creeper, on the other hand, had crept into my room that night and threatened that if I ever left, he'd only have Aaron to keep him company. I have no idea how perverse The Creeper's demons are and I have no intention of ever testing that theory. Aaron is a sweet boy, and no amount of fear will *ever* make me put him second.

Then my world came crashing down when a letter arrived with the verdict. I was to stay here until I turned eighteen.

'You still there, Em?' says Rachel.

I haven't heard a word she's said. 'Yeah, sorry, I was miles away. What did you say?'

'I said, don't forget your towel tomorrow. You know how 'Lesbo Lindsay' loves us to have a shower after sport the first week back.'

A laugh lies in wait around my lips. 'Miss Lindsay isn't a lesbian. She has a boyfriend. I've seen them together.'

Rachel's soft laughter escalates into full-blown hysteria. 'God, you're so naive, Ratface. That's not her boyfriend. It's her brother.'

She's right. I am naive.

My brow lifts. 'Are you sure?'

'Of course, I'm sure.' Rachel lets out a nasal snort.

My eyebrows pull tighter together. 'Are you sure? Because I saw them kissing outside the fish and chip shop during the summer holidays.'

Rachel stops laughing.

'Em, I've been thinking about this a lot lately.' I brace for full impact as Rachel's shallow breathing filters through the earpiece.

'Thinking about what?' I get the feeling our conversation is about to take a downward turn.

'Your … um … situation.'

I remove the phone from my ear and close my eyes.

'Like I said earlier,' I finally manage to mutter. 'Leave it. I have. It's a no-win situation.'

Rachel clears her throat. 'Yeah, well I've been thinking about it, and I have this … idea. It's a bit radical and getting the *equipment* might be a bit tricky, but I reckon it would work.'

I don't like the sound of this. 'What equipment?'

'A mobile phone.'

I wince.

The idea cuts me open, leaving me to bleed out.

'Celeste's mobile phone,' adds Rachel hastily. My silence does nothing to deter Rachel. 'I thought you could sneak into her room and grab it, and then set it up near your bed and press record. When that disgusting pervert comes in, you will have all the proof you need, and the whole world would have to believe you.'

'I can't, Rach. I just can't.'

'Why not?' Her choked sobs toy with my words.

I hold fast.

'Everyone would see what a sicko he is,' she says between sniffs, 'and then you can come and live with us. You'll never have to see him again.'

*I cannot.*

Once upon a time I'd wondered why Family Services hadn't allowed Rachel's family to adopt me or at least foster me. The Creeper had told me that it was because Rachel's mum earned a minimum wage, although that never rang true for me.

'Because … it's not just about me. What if *He* got to Aaron? You think Aaron being his flesh and blood would stop him from being the monster he is?' My voice etches up a few decibels. 'He doesn't care, Rach. He doesn't care whether you're a child or a family member. He wants!'

A rush of fire-blood hurries to my cheeks. *I wish I had the strength to stand up to him.*

I inhale a long, hollow breath that goes right down to my feet in the hope to regain some control. 'Plus, it could go viral. What if *it* found its way on to the internet? How would *you* cope if something like that was out there? There are too many ways for it to go wrong.' The last words shudder their way from my lips.

The thought …

The image …

Out there for everyone to see …

Oh my god – my worst nightmare.

I can't bear to think about it. Going to school, everyone knowing my real life - everyone having access to it, talking about it, making fun of me, not believing me.

My brain shifts slightly.

Too much blood in my head.

Dizziness threatens.

Rachel hums her displeasure into the phone. 'I feel so useless, Em. I feel as though I should be telling someone. It feels wrong for me to sit by and watch you go through this.' Another silent pause ticks by before she speaks again. 'I wanna fucking kill him.'

More tears – hers not mine. I reckon she's cried more about this than I have. *Good old numbness*. All that aside, and for as loyal as Rachel is, it is *my* secret and no one else can know.

'Promise me, Rach. Promise me you won't say a word.'

After a few more sniffs, Rachel promises.

'All right.' I puff out an exaggerated breath. 'I'm going. Thanks for the chat, and don't forget your towel tomorrow.'


Rose Burberry stares vacantly at the television as I return the phone, Aaron curled up fast asleep on the sofa. I trudge upstairs with him, roll him into bed and pull the covers over him, amused by his random mumblings of velociraptors. I brush my teeth and change into my pyjamas before laying my own head on the pillow, ready for the many silent prayers to begin all over again.

I'm not in bed more than ten minutes when I hear Celeste screeching up the hallway, about why curfew should be changed to eleven on a weekday instead of ten. I couldn't agree more.

After three Kelly Clarkson songs, loud enough to shift my small crystal rocking horse across my dressing table – the last gift my mother bought me - the house becomes quieter than a morgue. I tiptoe across my room and lovingly reposition the horse back in its spot.

I lie back down, the frantic, erratic rhythm of my heart keeping any chance of sleep away.

Sleep. The one word that should bring comfort, sends waves of terror through me. The thought of waking up and seeing him standing over me again, or worse, is becoming more than I can handle.

The clock ticks by.

One hour, two, three. It's 2:22 before I finally feel myself drifting off.

Searing heat and wild, primal screams cut through to my bone and deeper. Screams that should be urging me to run. The sound of metal being cleaved apart forces more confusion into my mind. Where am I, and why can't I see anything other than orange and yellow clouds?

'Help me, someone …' I gag. Thick, murdering smoke steals my breath, kills my words. I cough as plastic and fabric fumes seep further into my lungs. I'm trapped. Oh God, I'm going to die. I'm going to die.

'Help …'

A deep rumble, much worse than thunder, trembles beneath my feet, splitting the earth wide open, folding the sky in on me. My ears ache from the explosion around me.

The screaming stops.

Silence takes a long, slow walk through the barren land that has become my mind. Sweet air filters in, and I turn my head, desperate for oxygen, for life. A whisper of a word blows in through the open door. 'FlameMaker.'

Then darkness takes me as its companion.

Something wakes me.

This is the same dream I've been having the last few months. But with a different ending. It's what happened on that fateful day when our car burst into flames and my parents were killed, except with a twist. With one addition … *FlameMaker*.

The bottom stair creaks, forcing my eyes wide open.

Then nothing.

51

Dreaded nothing.

I chance a quick, shallow breath.

Cool air tickles my throat.

My heart is sprinting the race of its young life. Hammering fast thuds pound against my chest, like a stone trying to break free from a cage, sweat gathering at my temples. Lumbering footsteps strike each step like intermittent thunder, the worn carpet doing little to dampen the sounds.

I find myself praying and counting - two squeaks left, and he'll be on the landing - o*h God, please let him be too pissed to think about me*.

My lungs ache, begging for more air. Invisible fingers press against my throat, tight, tighter, tightening reminding me I still have breath.

One squeak left – *please, please, please*. The peachy-pink colour of my hands disappears as I tighten the grip around the covers. I can't bring myself to watch the door anymore.

I squeeze my eyes shut.

'*Please, please, please, please …*' I mutter under my breath like some sort of chant. 'If you love me, you won't let anything happen. If you love me, you won't let anything happen. If you love me, you won't let anything happen.'

The stale smell of Indian curry, alcohol, and cigars reaches me before The Creeper does.

'My beautiful, Ems. Did you miss me?' I hear the familiar creek in his knees as he kneels beside my bed.

He strokes my hair back from my face, removing my veil.

Put me on the edge of a cliff and let me lean over until my body drops into the abyss. Let me fall. Let me fall until the ground finds my face, and body and smashes me into a million pieces. For this is where I am now. Not whole. Not in one piece but divided into slivers and slices of a broken me.

My eyes are closed, I think.

No daylight can get in, not even a crack. *Pretend to be asleep, pretend to be asleep*.

Tiny blue stars sparkle at me from behind my lids.

'I had to see you.'

Wandering, lost, alone in the dark, I reach to the heavens for help. My brain is trying to tell me it isn't his fingertips slithering down the side of my neck and across my shoulder. But the truth is, they are. There is no escape.

His touch sinks through each layer of my skin, driving poison deeper and deeper into my body, polluting my blood and stuffing every vacant space inside me with his worms and maggots.

He laughs softly. 'I knew you were awake,' he says as a low chuckle warbles in his throat. 'Open your eyes and look at me? I want to see you smile.'

I bite back the urge to cry and prise open my lids as stubborn as tombstones.

'Aahh, there she is.' There is a patronising tone to his slurred voice. 'My beautiful, Ems.'

I blink back hot tears.

His lips hover over mine, the smell <u>undefinable</u>. I stifle a cough.

*Don't, don't, don't.*

I force myself to swallow.

I can't do this anymore.

Too much fear.

Too much fear.

Somehow, I know I'm no longer in charge when my body decides it's time to take over. It knows what to do, even if I don't. Action needs to happen. Action that I am too numb, too paralysed to initiate.

'I can't stop thinking about you,' says The Creeper, whispering the words over my face. 'I've wanted to kiss you all day.'

I pull my lips closed and hold my breath, trying to suffocate myself.

NO! *Let go, Em. Let your body do what you cannot*, it says. *Fight and flight have come to your rescue.*

Without warning or permission, he crushes his mouth to mine.

My stomach lurches once, then twice. No way can I hold back. Not when I've become a spectator in my own body. One final urge takes over and I heave heartily and uncontrollably … into his mouth.

The Creeper draws back sharply.

I think he's gone into shock because it takes him a few seconds to realise what's happened. His face is pale and his jaw, slack, his mouth hanging gormlessly open. Slow-motion blinks pass over his eyes before he leans over the side of the bed and vomits violently on to the floor.

I can't believe what I've done.

I can't breathe.

I can't move.

I don't know what to say, if anything.

All I can do is stare at him.

He remains in that hunched position, with his hands resting on his thighs, looking down at the floor for what seems like a lifetime.

Time has become my friend and has pressed pause for me.

Time to think.

Time to think.

*Is this the moment when I beg for compassion? Or do I run like hell, leaving Aaron to a fate worse than the life I'm living?*

To be selfish or selfless, is the question stalling any escape plan.

*Think, Ember, think.*

'You ungrateful, little cow,' he growls.

The anger in his voice scares me. In his rage, he rips at my sheets, tearing off a piece to clean the inside of his mouth with before throwing it to the floor. There is a wildness in his eyes I've never seen before. His lips, no wider than a pencil line, tell me the worst is yet to come.

He seizes the tops of my arms so fiercely my skin puckers between his fat fingers. I feel my blood stop and then pulsate rapidly the second he throws me against the wall, my head smashing against the wooden headboard.

For three whole seconds, the room goes dark and then spins around in a crazy shape the moment I open my eyes. Ten thousand bees hum inside my skull as tiny blue stars speckle my vision.

Pain.

*Pass out, please pass out* I beg, so I don't have to live through this.

I hate you, I hate you, I hate you, begins my silent chant again. I close my eyes and pray harder, harder than I've ever done in my life.

*Save me, please ... save me.* Somebody ... anybody ... please.

I am beaten.

He has won.

*Do what you will. I give up.*

Unconsciousness is coming for me, about to become my friend. *Is this my saviour?*

I make one last silent scream out to the universe, begging for my life.

Startled, the Creeper scrambles to his feet as a smoke detector goes off outside my bedroom door. Voices and more footsteps gather on the landing as I drift into oblivion. The pain in my head now ice and nails.

My eyes close, my body on the brink, but I see them before I go – the beautiful blue eyes of River Fulton are waiting there to save me.

# SEVEN

*THE* next morning, I open my eyes to the rhythmic tones of a jackhammer inside my head. The thought of rolling over and skiving off school doesn't even compute. I can't wait to be out of this house.

I tiptoe to the bathroom.

Every muscle aches, as though I've been pulled apart and put back together without instructions. Blood has matted in my hair. I duck my head under the shower, the water turning pink. It stings and then is numb. I turn the hot tap on fully and stand there for twenty minutes, all the while wishing it was ten degrees hotter.

Looking in the mirror afterwards, I study the purple oval-shaped finger marks banding around the tops of my arms. The first thing that comes to me is relief.

Relief that he didn't kiss me again.

Relief it didn't go any further.

Relief it's autumn, and the long sleeves of my winter shirt will shield these bruises from Rachel's eagle eyes.

I slip on my uniform, tie back my hair and go down to breakfast like nothing has happened.

*He* is already sitting at the table when I walk in, jovially handing over two twenty-pound notes to Celeste.

'Thank you, Daddy,' she says in a whiny, baby voice, kissing the top of his head. She wafts the notes under her nose at me as she sits down.

He doesn't look up as I pass him to get to the kettle, which is another relief. Instead, he carries on talking to his daughter as though I don't exist. This is a welcome first.

More relief.

At last, an emotion I can cling to, other than the icy chill of numbness.

I walk Aaron to school as usual and drop him off at the gates, before heading up the hill to the high school. There are no blue eyes to greet me this morning. My heart notices the loss.

Barely beating.

Barely alive.

I have bigger problems to face – like perfecting my poker face for Rachel's morning interrogation.

Rachel, who should be a contestant on psychic TV, seems to know something is wrong before I have the chance to say anything, regardless of the length of my sleeves.

'What's with the hat? You never wear hats.' She yanks it off my head and I wince. 'What are you hiding?'

I glance down at my shirt, wondering if I'd accidentally written the episode across my chest in red pen and simply forgot about it.

'You're fucking kidding me.' She inspects the wound on my head informing me it probably needs stitches. She then paces back and forth, frowning a few times at my newly fashioned table art. 'Prick, prick, bastard, arsehole, prick.'

I tell her how I'd spewed into his mouth. Her delight doesn't surprise me, and she lets out a large squeal and hugs me tightly. My bones shatter and crumble, my muscles scream out as she unknowingly squeezes my shoulders.

'I wish I'd seen his face. I bet he was green. I don't know how you've lasted as long as you have. If it'd been me, I would've been serving time by now.' I think back to Rachel's comment about cutting off certain appendages. 'Or dead,' she adds.

The bell rings.

'I'll see you in sport,' she says, 'and, if I find out who the twat was that disfigured *our* table, they will get a good smack in the gob, too.'

I wave back half-heartedly, trying not to snigger.

On my way, I spot Troy Finnegan, the phantom note deliverer. I pull up in front of him and yank one of the wires out of his ear. His mouth drops open as though the two are connected.

'What the ...'

The look of shock on Troy's face makes me want to smile. I harness it real quick, clenching my teeth. I know he's heard the stories about me. Everyone has. How I killed my parents. How I set alight to our car. That I'm a witch who can't die. You name it, it's common knowledge around school. 'Didn't you hear me calling you? I want a word.'

He tries to brush me off until I throw my arm out to stop him.

He freezes in mid-step.

'Why did you give River Fulton that note yesterday, with my date of birth on it?'

'Who?' Everything about Troy is steeped in dumbness – his droopy eyes, mouth ajar, his orang-utan arms hanging limply by his side.

I purse my lips. 'River. Fulton. The guy you met behind the gym after English ... remember?'

58

Troy's gloomy expression lifts. 'Oh … him.'

I wait, shifting from foot to foot. '*Well*?'

Troy screws his face up. His freckled arms swing nervously. 'I'd never spoken to him before yesterday.' He pauses to scratch his head, 'and then he asks me all these weird questions.'

'What sort of questions?' Curiosity replaces anger.

'Weird stuff – like … had there been any recent car accidents in the area? Had anybody's parents died at the same time?'

I realise I'm frowning and make a conscious effort to soften my face. 'And what did you tell him?'

Troy shrugs. 'I told him that your parents … were … killed in a car crash a year ago.' He winces as though he's walking over hot coals.

A breath is stolen from me.

Hearing gossip is easy. The truth is harder to handle. Shockwaves rock my body the same way they did when I woke up in the hospital the day after the accident. My only memory, apart from the inferno, was of a tall doctor with kind eyes and a large mole on his cheek who told me they had died.

'And?'

Troy scratches his temple and moves on to his ginger hair. 'And, then he asked about …you.' I squint at him, waiting, momentarily wondering if he has nits. 'I told him your name and that you were in my English class and that's it.'

'So, why did you ask me when my birthday was?'

Troy's face turns an impressive shade of red, blending his speckled orange dots into one peachy-pink mass. 'He told me he'd give me five quid if I found out your date of birth. I didn't think anything of it …except the five quid of course.' He looks repentant.

I gasp. 'And my name? Did you tell him the story I told everyone in class?'

Troy looks down at his feet, even more embarrassed. 'He said any other information I found out would be worth my while too.'

Irritation washes through me, rinsing away any remaining curiosity.

'Why didn't he come and ask me himself if he wanted to know?' I growl between my teeth.

Troy takes a tentative step backwards. 'I dunno. Why don't you ask him that?'

'I will.'

Troy scarpers, and my mind scrambles for answers. *What does he want? Why me?*

I hang up my gym bag and slip off my shoes. Rachel arrives a few minutes later, and soon the room is flooded with a chorus of boy's names, music and swearing.

'Okay, girls. Listen up,' calls out Miss Lindsay, standing on one of the empty benches. She's a confident young woman with long legs and a high blond ponytail that swings wildly whenever she turns her head. 'This term, we're going to start off with a couple of games of either hockey or basketball, weather permitting, and finish off with tennis.' She pauses to tighten her ponytail. 'And, although I know a lot of you aren't going to like this,' she says, causing every girl's head to look in her direction, 'the headmaster, Mr Fisher, has implemented two compulsory sessions of dancing with Mr Martin's class.'

Groans echo around the room.

'With the boys?'

Miss Lindsay nods. 'I'm afraid so.'

'I ain't dancing with no boys.'

The room erupts with more cries of displeasure.

'*When?*' calls out someone.

'I bet I get paired with Vince Harrison. God, he stinks,' says someone else.

Miss Lindsay takes a deep breath and steps down from the bench. 'I'm not sure when. I'm guessing sometime during the middle of term.'

'Dancing isn't sport,' pipes up Eliza Campbell-Jones.

'And we never do sport with the boys,' chimes in Cherie Bennett.

'I'm sorry, girls, that's all I know.'

Miss Lindsay twirls the keys to the sports locker around her middle finger and points to the nearest two girls. 'Sonia and Emily, go and get thirty hockey sticks and bibs please, before we have a feminist rally on our hands.'

The two girls slip out of the room.

'C'mon then. Bottoms up and get moving or I can give Mr Martin a call right now.'

Slowly, bodies rise off benches, and those loitering near the toilets begin to form an orderly line to the door.

'The one good thing about dancing is pressing yourself against a few muscly bodies,' says Eliza. The tops of her ample breasts bulge over the neck of her t-shirt, leaving her with a cleavage that smiles at you every time you look at her.

A childish cackle whinnies out of Cherie's mouth. 'Yeah, I wouldn't mind getting my hands on the new boy. He's hot.'

My throat constricts. I wait for the next breath that should be there but isn't.

Eliza frowns. 'What new boy?'

Cherie copies the t-shirt act, minus the finesse. 'It's River something or other and whoa, is he gorgeous.'

That breath still hasn't arrived, and my lungs burn from the lack of oxygen.

'Em, are you okay? You look like you're gonna puke,' says Rachel. She has a hold of my arm, and yet the earth is still shifting crazily beneath my feet.

Blond locks whizz past my face in both directions. Eliza snarls her pouty top lip at me and drags Cherie away without a word. Physically, I feel fine, minus the air in my body, yet the thought of Eliza or Cherie with their claws around River's neck in a slow dance, scratches deeper wounds than Cherie could ever do with her fake nails.

I finally remember how to inhale and allow that fresh air in. Rachel squeezes my elbow for a second time, waiting for my reply.

'Yeah, I'm fine.' Deep down, I'm not. 'Next time they push in front of us … I give you full permission to bitch-slap those tarts.'

With sticks in hand, and not selected for the strongest side, winning for me isn't an option.

Survival is.

Eliza and Cherie aren't particularly good at hockey, yet they're brutal with the apparatus.

The first half of the game has me at the opposite end to where the action is. The second half, I have become Cherie's primary target.

In between the dull thwack of a ball coming towards me, accompanied by a high-pitched squeal, a huddle of boys vocalise their love of football, momentarily diverting my attention. One figure stands out among the lads. Black hair, tall, lean body and an arse Rachel would say is pinchable.

'Focus, Riley,' yells Miss Lindsay as the ball speeds my way.

I release my fingers a little from the hockey stick. Deeply charred fingerprints stare back at me, the rubber grip melted beyond recognition.

'Riley!'

I look up and make eye contact with Cherie as a ball hurtles towards me. I sidestep just in time. Rachel isn't faring too well either. Almost instantly, she cops a belt to the shins from Eliza.

'You bitch.' Rachel's face is bright red. 'You did that on frigging purpose.'

Rachel has never backed down from anything in her life. Already, they are nose to nose with sticks at shoulder height. A fight is imminent. Miss Lindsay takes off across the field in time to pull them apart and then calls time.

On the slow walk back to the changing rooms, I decide River Fulton has the body of a man, not a boy of seventeen. He runs past, shirt tied around his waist, sweat glazing a channel down his back. The rules have changed. I can't un-see now what lies beneath his clothes. I can't pretend any longer that what is there wouldn't interest me. He jogs away from me and just when I think I am safe, he glances back at me.

Fire ignites immediately.

It comes out of nowhere.

No warning. No slow heat rising.

Boom. Fire.

I fan my face.

'You ok?' asks Rachel.

I nod in a roundabout way.

'Give us that.' Rachel grabs my hockey stick, which I'm thankful for, before I reduce it to a pile of ashes. I don't miss her puzzled expression when she inspects the handle.

Make sure you all have your towels. I'll be counting heads,' calls out Miss Lindsay as she strides confidently up and down the length of the changing room, swinging her keys around her fingers. 'I don't want your teachers complaining this afternoon that their classrooms stink like mouldy cheese sandwiches because some of you girls conveniently forgot to shower.'

A few girls groan, and I overhear Alex Bartell telling Miss Lindsay that she didn't bring a towel because she has her period.

'Even more reason to shower, Alex,' responds the teacher and then raises her voice to everyone else, 'Excuses will not wash with me today, girls, nor will having your period. If you don't have a towel, borrow one. Every girl *will* have a shower.'

By the time I undress and wrap myself in a towel, all the single cubicles have been taken. The long communal shower with ten separate showerheads all draining into the same trough is all that's left. Nudity doesn't worry me; however, I am concerned about exposing the bruises on my arms.

I walk to the end of the shower bay and turn on the last tap. At least this way, I only need to shield one side of my body. Besides, everyone is more interested in getting in and straight back out again.

The rumbling of rusty pipework can be heard from the far end of the shower bay as taps turn on. Water splutters a little before spurting out in a thick, steady stream. The more water that flows, the louder the pipes complain.

'I hope you were going to tell me about those,' says Rachel bitterly, staring at my arms. A seriously disappointed look touches her face. I manoeuvre my body to hide the worst of them.

'Umm, yeah. I-I forgot.'

'You are *such* a liar.'

She's angry. 'I'm sorry, you're right. I should've told you. I didn't want to worry you.'

Rachel softens and shakes her head. 'If I didn't worry about you, who else will, and besides … it's my job now.'

'Hurry up, ladies, or you'll be cutting into your lunchtime,' shouts Miss Lindsay through the doorway.

'Stay close to me so that none of the others can see them,' I say as three girls take the showers next to us. I glance down at the trio of purple stripes wrapped around the tops of my arms.

Rachel sniggers. 'You could always say they're tribal tattoos.'

'That's all I need - more frigging stories going around about me.'

Rachel smiles as she turns her tap on a little harder. More girls now occupy the remaining empty showers and I duck my head under the same time Rachel does.

'Shit,' she yells, fiddling with the cold tap. 'It's boiling. Is your cold tap working? This one isn't.'

I hadn't touched the cold tap. 'My temperature's perfect.'

The steam billowing off me should be warning enough but Rachel runs her hand under my shower anyway.

She draws it back sharply. 'That's boiling,' she gasps. 'I don't know how you can have it so hot.'

I shrug – like I said … it was perfect.

Rachel steps out of the stream of water and splashes small amounts on her body, wincing at the heat. I tip my head back allowing the water to run over my shoulders and face. For the first time since my parents died, water is doing its job and soothing me. I close my eyes and lap up every glorious second.

When I eventually open my eyes, Rachel is not the only one standing out of her shower; four other girls are doing the same, complaining about the temperature.

A deep, throaty, groan rumbles from inside the walls. I turn and look at the small beige tiles as though they've spoken a language only I understand.

A feeling of dread, an omen of something awful happening, churns up from my stomach. Panic presses against my throat, restricting my breath. That need to protect, or voice my concern, which should instinctively kick in, is still turned off, the same way it's been inactive my whole life. The warning message that waits behind my teeth, urging everyone to get out, is waiting. All I have to do is open my mouth and say the words. I can even feel the syllables tingling against my tongue. But I'm unable to say anything. I simply can't, no matter what tragedy-in-the-making lurks in the mouldy recesses of this shower block.

I just can't.

Because how can someone know something is going to happen, before it *happens*?

A gut-wrenching scream shifts my premonition into reality. Then a second, high pitch squeal reaches my ears and a third, until the room fills with steam and pain.

Lots of pain.

# EIGHT

ANGUISHED cries for help, help that I am unable to give, have me rooted to the spot beneath a burning hot shower.

Fear.

My old friend has me right where it wants me.

I can't move. I can't breathe. I can't blink. I can't think.

My natural instincts urge me to stay put, not to run, not to seek help. The fight or flight thingy that was there before has abandoned me. Now, I'm lost, in a maze with too many options. Hedges grow around me in giant green walls of mystery, blocking my way out, blurring my path, feet scuff against the dirt, not sure which way to go, not wanting to make a decision that will end up making everything so much worse. My feet stop, and I remember I do have an option. The puzzle has been solved.

I can do what I always do. I can retreat into my shell, where life is safe. I immerse my head under the shower and do nothing.

Taking fleeting glimpses through the misty vapour, Grace Summer is perched on the edge of the shower bay, whimpering and cradling her arms around her knees. Her palms are spread wide, shiny and the colour of candyfloss. Guilt rises. I could've stopped this. I could've been somebody's hero.

'What on earth …?' Miss Lindsay pulls up short when she sees the two girls crying, one with her arm around Grace's shoulders.

'What's happened here ...?' *Her* fight and flight thingy has well and truly kicked in, as it should have, and she wraps a towel around each of the girls and escorts them away. The red welt, the size of a football, splashed across the other girl's back as she turns around, seals the lid on what a non-functioning and insensitive person I really am. And let's not even get into the word coward.

I hate myself for not warning them.

I hate myself for living through another event that could've been prevented - wounds that will still be raw in fifty years.

Rachel, and the other two girls, shiver behind towels regardless of the redness in their faces. A crowd has gathered around the doorway of the shower room to see what the commotion is. Thankfully, the mist is so thick, it prevents me, and the marks on my arms, from being seen.

I'm almost invisible … almost. Good old fear and relief. The two constants in my life, are by my side, as always.

Swirling hot vapours continue to drift upwards from the empty shower bays.

'Everybody out,' yells Miss Lindsay. 'NOW.'

The squeak of her trainers on the wet tiled floor reveals how slow her steps are. Her hazy silhouette stops in front of me and she turns her head. Her ponytail swings, cutting the burning fog like a knife.

'Ember, I need you to come out right now.'

Relief ditches me for a better alternative.

Exposing me.

Uncovering my secret.

Revealing my life.

All hope of anonymity circles my feet and tiptoes down the drain. I hear the shuffle of feet and the whisper of a thousand more rumours to come.

Miss Lindsay tentatively reaches out to test the water. Her fingers curl from the heat. 'That water is boiling.'

'It's not, Miss, honestly. Do you think I'd be in here if it was boiling?'

'But the other girls,' gasps Miss Lindsay. 'That water is hot enough to blister paint. Get out - now.'

Reluctantly, I emerge from my protective veil and turn off the water. The other six showers continue their cloudy downpour into the trough.

My body is pinkish, but no redder than it usually looks after a shower. I hurriedly dress, ignoring the horrified faces that look at me with a thousand questions on their minds.


Lunch is quiet. So is Rachel. And it isn't until the fifth period, when someone knocks on the door of my science classroom with a note requesting my presence at the headmaster's office, do I realise something is up. All heads turn to look at me, including River Fulton.

I knock on the fake wooden door of Mr Fisher's office and wait. Muffled voices and the sound of someone crying inside, falls silent. A moment later, a tall, thin man with curly brown hair opens the door.

'Miss Riley. Will you come in?' he says politely.

Mr Fisher makes no haste in securing himself back behind his desk while Miss Lindsay leans awkwardly against an overflowing bookcase. Her eyes are red and swollen, her first three fingers are bandaged, and a thick wad of gauze is taped to her palm.

I settle myself in for Mr Fisher's standard lecture about respect. Because that's why I'm here ... for answering back to Miss Lindsay, right?

Wrong.

According to Mr Fisher, the two girls involved were burnt so severely an ambulance had to be called. They were taken to the burns' unit of St Augustine's.

'Georgia Roberts is in a stable condition,' he tells me with a grave look on his face, 'and will return to school in a couple of weeks. We don't know about Grace, yet.' There is a slight tremor to his voice. 'She will have a long, slow recovery. They are talking skin grafts.'

'What?' I can't believe it. 'It didn't look that bad from where I was standing.'

Miss Lindsay whimpers again and I glance over as she blots her eyes with her uninjured hand.

'Well, I can tell you, Miss Riley, it was.' He pauses to take off his glasses. 'It's just ... we're having a little trouble dealing with ...' He polishes them on his shirt and replaces them.

He's stalling.

Part of me wants to see if he has the balls to ask if I had something to do with this. I know that's what's on his mind. It's what's on everyone's mind because I'm the only one who wasn't burnt, just like what happened with my parents.

Mr Fisher purses his lips. 'How is it ... that you didn't seem to be affected by it?'

I don't know what to say.

What possible answer can I give to him ... the truth?

I'd love to.

I'd love to see the look on his face as I reveal who I really am and what I'm capable of. His eyes would squint more, without the use of his glasses, because he wants to read my face better, look deeper, learn more. His bottom canine would appear, teasing and nibbling at his lip, deciding my fate. His hands would tremble more than they are now and a pen would tap against the desk as his anxiety works through his system. He didn't earn the nickname "frightened fisher" for nothing.

But what good will that do anyone – it won't make a difference to Miss Lindsay, and certainly not for poor Grace. Instead, I let my eyes drift around the room until they fall upon two oil paintings of poppies.

'Miss Lindsay said she couldn't even touch the water coming out of your shower because it was so hot.' I still refuse to look at him. 'And after you turned off the tap and left to get changed, she reached for the tap to see how hot it was.'

In my peripheral vision, Mr Fisher glances over at Miss Lindsay nursing her hand.

'Miss Riley, I don't think you understand the gravity of this situation. She was treated on site by a paramedic who told her she had second-degree burns. Can you see why we're …' Mr Fisher pauses again to rub vicious circles into his temples, 'concerned?' He then picks up a pen and starts to fiddle with it.

I nod, not trusting myself to speak.

My first incident with boiling water happened three months ago whilst making a cup of coffee. I'd looked out of the window to see The Creeper coming home, missed the cup and poured the hot liquid all over my hand.

Surprisingly, it didn't burn me. There was no blister, no red mark and no pain. Naturally, I was shocked at first. It was if all the nerve endings in my hand had been surgically removed. I'd simply put it down to the numbness I'd grown accustomed to.

'I don't know what to say.'

If I told him right here, right now, with Miss Lindsay as a witness, that my body has a natural affinity for searing hot temperatures, my skin turns metals into mush and my entire body has recently turned into a walking incinerator, they'd cart me off for more testing than a laboratory bunny.

Mr Fisher rests his head in his hands. He stays in that position a rather long time before looking up. 'I need to see for myself, Miss Riley. To satisfy my curiosity.'

I frown. *See what? Satisfy what?*

He raises his chin. 'Let me see your hands.' His face is slack and weary.

I hold them out in front of him, palms down. His eyes meet mine, clearly agitated. 'Turn them over.'

I slowly rotate my hands to reveal my usual peachy palms. Mr Fisher leans in to inspect them. Not one single flake of skin, not one scorch mark in sight. His shoulders sag as he rests his elbows against the desk and turns his attention to a piece of paper in front of him. My eyes momentarily fall to the gold photo frame next to it, of a small boy in red pyjamas with trains on them and similar curly brown hair.

'Do you know what this is?' he asks accusingly. He holds up the paper and I read the top line. It's a plumber's invoice.

I shrug. 'A quote?'

He snatches it away before I have chance to read the small print.

'It was written by the emergency plumber we brought in to cut off the water supply at the mains. He said that when the pipes to the school had been laid down thirty-six years ago, no thermostat shut-off valve had been installed.'

I sip a breath in through my teeth. 'And?' I know as much about plumbing as he does about living with a sexual deviant.

He throws up his hands, looking completely dumbfounded at Miss Lindsay.

'I don't know, then.'

Mr Fisher struts across the room to the coffee machine and pours himself a cup – black, no sugar. He drinks the entire cup in one go before refilling it.

'I suppose we take these kinds of things for granted these days,' he mutters to himself, more composed. He slurps down two more mouthfuls and sits back down. 'The plumber said that anyone exposed to heat of that magnitude would have fared better had they been in a fire. That steam was hot enough to melt skin from bones.'

Two pairs of eyes stare at me as though I am to blame. I need to leave.

I don't want to know what hot water or steam does to someone's body. The burns on Georgia's back and Grace's hands are reminder enough.

'Can you see where we're coming from?' Mr Fisher's tone, though somewhat perplexed, has softened.

Of course I can see. It's been obvious to me for some time that I'm a freak— a walking paradox, who has no explanation for why I am the way I am. I squeeze my knees together to steady my trembling legs. 'I'm sorry I can't help you.'

I take a quick look at Miss Lindsay and give her my best commiserating smile. If they are after a full-blown confession, then they've come to the wrong person. I can keep secrets like the best of them.

The two teachers briefly glance at each other and Mr Fisher shrugs his shoulders resignedly. 'You better head back to class then.'

I close the headmaster's door behind me and lean against the doorframe, letting out a huge sigh.

My secret is still safe … for now.

I stand for a moment, contemplating the worst that could've happened, unaware at first that Mr Butcher is sitting in the corner of the waiting room, staring at me.

'Not in trouble, I hope, Miss Riley?' he says, filling the room with his giant-ness as he gets to his feet. I crane my neck to look up at him.

'Not anymore,' I say with relief.

Mr Butcher frowns. 'Anything I can help with?' I stare at him as though he'd asked me if I needed help putting on makeup.

'No, it's okay.'

Mr Butcher narrows his eyes at me. He says nothing.

Walking to the Burberrys' that afternoon, with Aaron chatting happily beside me, I can't help reflecting on the accident that killed my parents. I try not to dredge up what little memory I have of those painful moments, however, the shower incident seems to have set a process in motion, triggering an urge to delve deeper into why I have such large gaping holes in my memory.

My life basically turned to a pile of shit the day before my sixteenth birthday.

The day started out much like any other with me coming down to breakfast to find pancakes already on the table. My father was reading the paper whilst my mother flapped around him, brushing crumbs from his shirt. She was a fusser ... always had been - always fixing collars or straightening pillows and net curtains. It drove me nuts.

I remember having the sulks that day. I wanted to go to Rachel's house instead of travelling three hours in the car to go and visit Aunt Cynthia and Uncle Reggie, my mother's sister and husband. To be honest, I hated going. They didn't have children, and constantly asked me if I was hungry or thirsty or whether I needed to use the toilet. They were also old – nearly sixty, and Uncle Reggie had a chronic heart condition.

I had sat in the back of the car for an hour with a sour face until Mum suggested we play 'Name that Rego'. It was a game she'd invented on our trip to London, the year before. You had to take the letters on the registration plate of the car in front and make an intelligent sentence. My foul mood soon ended when I came up with YCWH – you crazy warthog and Mum concocted TSLJ – toes smell like jam.

We were laughing so hard, and Mum was crying and dabbing the corners of her eyes, like she always used to do, that neither of us saw the silver body of a fuel tanker slam into the side of us.

But that's apparently what happened.

The details become hazy after that, and all I can remember is sitting on the side of the road, watching flames devour our two-year-old blue Vauxhall with my parents trapped inside. I'm confident I hadn't been thrown from the car because the windows were up, the car doors were intact, and I didn't have a scratch on me.

'Ember, what's up?' asks Aaron.

I shake off my melancholy and coax a smile from my lips.

'Nothing, honey.'

'Are you coming in then?' Aaron is waiting for me with the front door wide open.

I smile. 'Right behind you, Velociraptor.'

But something is up.

I'm ready to learn the truth.

# NINE

Rachel is waiting for me outside the maths block after registration the next day, and we take a deliberately slow walk to the sports' hall. The boys are already lined up along the wall when we arrive. The entire school knows what happened yesterday, and although Rachel keeps telling me not to worry, I find myself replaying the shower incident over in my head as more people than normally take their turn to look me over, take photos of me and text their friends about the witch who almost burnt a student alive.

'Co-ed sport. How gross,' complains Cherie. 'I don't want to be sweating and stinking around boys.' The changing rooms have been sealed off with red and white striped tape.

Miss Lindsay passes us with a box and DVD player under her arm. Her bandaged hand is well out of harm's way. 'Somehow, I don't think we're playing tennis,' I whisper to Rachel.

The sports hall is larger than four basketball courts and is as noisy as it is cold. Four rows of chairs sit facing a flat screen TV.

'Miss, are we watching *Bat*-man?' a boy calls out as he scoots down the first aisle of chairs to find a seat.

'Or how about Space-*balls* or Great *Balls* of Fire?' shouts another lad.

A soft rumble of laughter gets steadily louder.

Mr Martin, the boys' gym teacher, is still wearing his sports clothing. The man doesn't seem to own anything other than a pair of navy-blue shorts and an Adidas singlet.

'All right, settle down,' he says, closing the door behind him. His voice echoes off the metal clad walls. He doesn't look much past thirty, with dark brown hair and a rugged three-day stubble that never seems to grow out. He isn't what Rachel would call buff, but what would I know.

'I don't care if he uses a sunbed five times a week, I'd do him in a heartbeat,' I hear Eliza say to Cherie as they drool over him.

Out of sixty chairs, I can't imagine how we manage to find seats right behind *these* two? I huff out my frustration, knowing Rachel and I will be subjected to a running commentary on every little thing Miss Lindsay says and does, and the forever lewd suggestions about Mr Martin's hairless, slightly orange-tinged body.

'Due to recent events,' begins Mr Martin, 'Mr Fisher has decided to bring forward your first dancing lesson.' Heads twists on necks to look at me, and Rachel doesn't make it obvious at all ... much ...to snarl back at them, daring anyone to mutter a single word.

'To start with, I thought we'd look at the kinds of dancing you'll be learning this term. Miss Lindsay, can you load the first DVD?'

The lights flick off and we sit through two, fifteen-minute DVDs on English and Scottish country dancing. They are every bit as boring as I imagined them to be, and it isn't until all the chairs are stacked around the edge of the room and we gather in a large circle that I notice River Fulton standing directly across from me.

He catches me staring at him and I immediately deflect my gaze, blood rushing to my cheeks.

'Okay, divide yourselves into two groups of thirty, fifteen girls and fifteen boys and then arrange yourselves into two large circles,' says Miss Lindsay. The usual chatter erupts, and Mr Martin reinforces her words with a loud 'hey.'

Rachel and I skirt towards the left group, paying attention to Eliza and Cherie's choice. I see Cherie bump Eliza's elbow and point in River's direction. Eliza nods and the two trot towards him. A ripple of annoyance inches its way beneath my skin.

'I hope your dancing is better than your maths,' says Mr Martin after a quick head count. 'You guys have too many in this group, so I'll need a couple of volunteers to go into Miss Lindsay's,' he adds, addressing the small gathering assembled around Eliza. Everyone looks around, waiting for someone to offer themselves up.

'All right, we'll go, Mr Martin,' offers Eliza, fluttering her eyelids at him, enjoying the attention. I smirk as Cherie tries to pull her back. It's obvious she wants to stay close to River. There is barely a sliver of light between them.

'Sorry girls, step back. I'm actually after two boys,' says Mr Martin. The relief on Cherie's face is apparent and her thick pink lips pull apart with joy.

River Fulton steps forward immediately. 'I'll go,' he says, giving me a fleeting glance.

My heart thumps hard, twice. *Oh, heaven help me.*

'Great. That's one,' says Mr Martin, 'and, Seth, I think.'

I quickly look away as River draws closer.

*Control, Em, for goodness sake, apply some control*, my brain is saying, but my body is saying cut loose and enjoy the ride. It might be the only one we get.

The groups spread out into two huge circles, alternating girl, boy, girl, boy.

Miss Lindsay squeezes through two students to stand in the middle of the circle as Mr Martin does in his circle. 'This is where we find out who knows their left from their right,' she says.

'Everybody, listening?'

The huge room hushes, leaving nothing but the wind to harass the corrugated walls around us.

'The way this works is … everyone will turn to their left. When I say so, Shaun Gibbons.' Miss Lindsay tilts her head at the one person who turned prematurely. 'And then, we will move in a clockwise direction, weaving through each partner with your left shoulder to their right shoulder.'

'Doesn't sound too difficult,' I hear Rachel whisper to me from behind Daniel Frome.

We all turn ninety degrees to our left and begin threading ourselves through the line of people. I'm surprised at the number of kids who have difficulty with such a simple task.

But coordination isn't what's worrying me.

River Fulton is getting closer and closer. Every second or third person we pass has us trading stares. Three more people to go, two more people, one more …

'Stop, stop, stop,' calls out Mr Martin. He lets out a loud, frustrated breath and shakes his head before turning off the music. I stop.

River Fulton is right in front of me.

He is a full head taller, something I hadn't noticed when I was demanding to know about the note. He is also much broader, now that I'm standing so close. A spicy citrus tang hangs in the air between us and I breathe him in, debating whether it's his clothes or his aftershave that also has the undertones of lime and coconut.

My head feels as though it's been stuffed with foam and left to marinate for a month.

No words available.

No coherent thoughts forming.

I almost reach out to steady myself. *Get a grip, Em. Get a grip*.

I tilt my head back slightly, enough so his face comes into view. And those stunning blue lagoons have me questioning the definition of beauty. How can something so common, so simple, be so perfectly exquisite?

A breath slips from my lips and his eyes break contact with mine for a second to stare at my mouth. I follow his lead and look to his lips, which part and then press together. It's enough for my heart to begin it's mad, out of control rhythm again. Beating to its own drum.

Without warning, I am volcanic.

I am falling and soaring at the same time. I want to throw my arms around him and keep him at a distance. I want to lay next to him and ask him every question I've ever wanted to know the answer to, but not just any answers, his answers, that come from his lips, his thoughts, his heart.

'Okay, then.'

Mr Martin's circle has become more of an oval with a knot of kids down one end with too many partners, and a large space at the other where three students stand alone. Couples in our circle begin to chat as Mr Martin untangles his group.

We don't say a word to each other. I try to guess what he's thinking about, even though his face gives nothing away. What it does say is, I don't feel like talking ... otherwise he would ... right? But I don't care that he doesn't speak, and I don't care whether I do either. The stillness is just as intoxicating.

'Let's go again,' calls out Miss Lindsay. 'Can everybody return to their positions?'

Why do we have to move? Right here is so much better, I want to say. I begrudgingly make my way back to where we began with Flynn Roberts in front of me and Daniel Frome behind me.

I've never known Mr Martin to look so irritated. His hair is rumpled, like he's woken from a siesta in the staffroom. 'This time, if you can manage it, instead of bypassing left shoulder with right, I want you to pass hand over hand. It might be easier for you lot that can't tell your left from your right.' He glares at his group. 'You know, this isn't Mr Keneally's physics class.'

I look around my circle and count the heads until I come to River Fulton. Sixteen heads, which mean sixteen different hands until I touch him.

Something resembling nervousness takes hold of my body, although there's more to it than that. There's curiosity and excitement thrown in for good measure. I mean, who would've thought the thrill of touching a boy's hand could trigger so many feelings. The fact that I've never gone out of my way to hold a boy's hand before is irrelevant, apart from Aaron's, of course, and his is small and sometimes sticky from sweets, so that doesn't count. River Fulton's hand would be something quite different.

Miss Lindsay tries to whip up some enthusiasm. 'Okay, here we go,' she calls out.

Hand over hand, we begin again. Some cold, some hot, some sweaty.

Again, I'm down to three people to go, then two.

'Nope, stop, stop,' shouts Mr Martin.

He marches over to his group, who appear to be as uncoordinated as a litter of overweight pot-bellied pigs. He yanks apart a chain of hands.

I am one person away from River Fulton. I immediately release Emma Fitzgerald's hand and we exchange polite smiles. River does the same, and casually peers around Emma's shoulder. Fire and heat fill me from head to toe.

Mr Martin is confronting Kieren Patricks. 'Why are you having so much difficulty with this, Patricks? You play footy, don't you? It shouldn't be that hard. This is your left hand; this is your right. This is Natalie's left hand, this is her right,' he says, pulling Natalie Coombes into the debate. He spends a few minutes trying to teach Kieren the fundamentals by using a line of ten kids until it looks like he finally has it. The chatter amplifies to a level unacceptable for Miss Lindsay. She steals a glance at her watch before raising her hands and shushing us all again.

'I think we have time for one more go,' she says. 'Take your places, everyone.'

We all shuffle back to our spots.

'This time, concentrate,' groans Mr Martin and raises his manicured brows at Kieren.

The passing of hands starts again and the knot in my stomach grows tighter and tighter as River Fulton draws nearer. I see Emma coming closer, knowing River is right behind her. I give her a courteous smile as I pass her. I hold my breath as River Fulton's hand slowly and very deliberately slips into mine.

I let out my breath, the same way relief is released from the soul.

At that moment when our eyes lock on to each other and his thumb gently smooths the skin on the back of my hand, the loudest crack of thunder I've ever heard is unleashed from the heavens. Several people jump, including Miss Lindsay, and a surprised girlie scream would have split the room in two had it gone on much longer. Then silence.

Everyone has stopped, and I can only guess all eyes are looking upwards, sure the roof is about to fall in.

But not me.

My gaze is firmly locked on River's as his cool hand cradles mine. Wave after wave of heat and fire wash through my body, stirring up a host of emotions that have long been buried.

And then the clouds open.

Outside, rain pounds upon the tin roof like a thousand soldiers marching to war.

I am lost in the way his eyes ask me silent questions. I have trouble remembering where I am, who I am – lost in new feelings and old dreams - of hope and love and desire. And of strange images of open landscapes and plunging valleys. Of rock formations and bubbling lava, caverns and lakes and calm blue seas, rushing through my mind like the rain that spills from the sky by the gallon.

'Calm down, it's only a bit of thunder,' shouts Mr Martin.

I hear his voice.

His words mean nothing.

I couldn't calm myself if I tried.

Desperate breaths heave in and out of my chest in silent gasps. I am mesmerised by the expression of awe on River's face, and yet torment lives there too. I watch, unblinking, at the way his thumb brushes over my skin, time after time after time, like silk on silk. His eyes keep opening and closing, sometimes pinching so tightly shut its hard to know if he's concentrating or trying to block out everything. His cheekbones shift and bite every few seconds, and yet his lips are relaxed, inviting and slightly parted. The haunted look he wears, like this is somehow causing him agony, forms uneven fractures around my heart. I want to rescue him and tell him it's okay. It's almost unbearable to witness. But I can't stop watching. You couldn't pay me enough to stop.

And I want to close my eyes, and soak in this moment so that it's only the two of us, alone, away from the gossip and away from foster families and car crashes and I don't have to remember the horrors in my life, and all I can think of is, let me stay like this forever and never go home.

'Excuse me, Miss Lindsay, Ember won't let go of River Fulton's hand. I think she's gonna vomit or something,' says Cherie.

A sharp titter of laughter pulls me away from my glorious place. The realisation of where I am, of who I am and what I'm doing, swiftly dawns on me.

Painstakingly slowly, I peel my hand away from his, ignoring the stares and whispers that are as familiar to me as the clear, iridescent blue eyes of the boy in front of me. I give my eyes permission to wander over his face, committing to memory the slight curve of his lips that want to smile, and the jagged white scar on his temple that wouldn't be noticeable unless you were this close to him. His lightly stubbled jawline, the way his Adam's apple bobs up and down in his throat as though he's nervous. My eyes fall to something shiny on his neck – a necklace. I don't know why. He doesn't seem the type to wear jewellery.

I want to ask him if he saw the rush of images from before, that are now imprinted in my brain. Images of places we've been to and I'd seen with my own eyes - sands of burnt orange panning out as far as the eye could see, only to be washed away by the swirling waters of sapphire blue seas. I want to ask him if he can feel this second heartbeat inside my chest, his heartbeat, like I know mine is inside his, a connection that has waited a lifetime to come together. It seems so weird to even think, say, feel these things about a boy I've only just met, but its like reading a book for the second time and knowing how the story goes.

River stares down at our broken hands and the confusion and disappointment on his face lasts for no more than a second. He turns around slowly, by-passing the girl behind him, and strikes up a conversation with Harry Gates. He doesn't look my way again.

By the time we leave the sports hall, the rain has stopped and doesn't return for the rest of the day. The sun is barely out and all signs that water has fallen, is gone. The evidence that something magical just happened, has been erased.

All that's left, is the memory of a first touch.

# TEN

'DOES your mum know about the party tonight at the Garages?' I ask when we get to Rachel's house that afternoon.

'Course she does. As long as we are back by eleven. Are you up for it?'

'Sure. Who invited us ... exactly?' I don't mean to sound suspicious, but I've never been invited to an over eighteens party before.

'Can you believe it, Cole did himself.'

'*Really*?'

'Why do you sound so surprised?'

I'm not. She could get any guy she wants.

'I saw him hanging out near the year twelve canteen and he came right up and asked me what I was doing tonight. I told him that you were staying over, and he said both of us were welcome to swing by and wish him a happy birthday.'

My frown is back. 'How come you didn't tell me before?'

Rachel shrugs guiltily. 'I thought I'd give you all the time you needed to tell me about River Fulton.'

'Wha …?'

'C'mon, he couldn't keep his eyes off you in sport. And then you stand there, holding his hand. Why didn't you tell me you two had a …'

'We don't. I mean, he doesn't. I mean, I don't …'

Rachel cuts me off. 'I've known you a long time, Em, as long as you've known yourself. It's okay if you like him. It isn't a crime to feel something for …' her word hangs in the air, but I know she wants to say, 'a guy.'

'I don't know how I feel about him.' And that's the truth. He is fascinating and mysterious, but I know nothing about him. 'He could be a serial killer for all I know.'

Her eyebrow flutters. 'I was going to suggest you invite him along. It would be a great way to get to know him. Cole said you could bring someone.'

'No.'

The word is out of my mouth before I've had chance to think whether it was the right answer or not. I take a long, slow glance at my sleepover bag. From memory, I'd thrown in a couple of pairs of jeans, two tops and a summery dress in case the weather was warm, and a light jacket. Nothing that would pass for a first date.

'I-I didn't pack for a party.'

'When has that ever been a problem,' says Rachel. She opens her wardrobe and thumbs through her colour co-ordinated outfits. 'My clothes … are your clothes.'

We locate The Garages down a back street, lit up like Blackpool Illuminations.

'Not bad for an old youth-wing centre,' says Rachel, nudging my arm. 'I told you it would be classy.'

A hefty looking fella in a pink short-sleeved shirt and black pants blocks the doorway, his meaty arms folded across his chest. A large black tattoo covers most of one forearm and a barbed wire tattoo bands around the top of his other bulging bicep.

'Do we need *proper* invites?' I whisper to Rachel as we approach.

One side of Rachel's lips draws closer to her chin. 'I don't think so. Cole never said we did.'

The bouncer looks us up and down several times before speaking. The only part of him that looks friendly is his name tag, Greg. 'Evening, ladies. Names please.' His voice is much softer than I expect.

He glances down at his clipboard as Rachel rattles off our names. A weak smile scrapes over her lips as her fingers clench the strap of her bag.

'Sorry, girls, your names aren't on here. I can't let you in.' The blur of the tattoo, I couldn't make out before, is of a bulldog baring its teeth.

Rachel turns on the charm. 'Listen, Greg,' she says, sidling up next to him. 'Could you please check again? Cole only invited us this afternoon, which explains why our names might not be listed.'

The sound of a violin playing banshee screeches out of the main doors getting both our attention. 'What the hell are *you* doing here? This ain't no fucking kid's tea party.' The scratchy voice and foul language belong to Celeste.

I wilt. *Pour boiling oil over me and set me alight*.

'Cole invited us,' Rachel says boldly, taking a protective step in front of me. In or out of heels, she towers over me.

There's no pretence between Rachel and Celeste … never has been. The two hate each other and everyone knows it.

In that moment, Cole appears. His blond hair, almost halo like, sends a glow of reassurance to us. An inch taller than the bouncer, though not as wide in the chest; he walks towards us with slow, confident steps.

'That's ok, Greg. I did invite them,' he says to the bouncer. Greg drops his paperwork and waves us through.

'Do you have a problem with that, Celeste?' Cole asks, raising his eyebrows at her, 'because if you do, you know where the door is.' I holster the urge to smile as he loops his arm around Rachel's shoulder.

Celeste has that crazy look in her eyes that says I'm in for it when I get home. 'No,' she snaps, curling her lip at me. 'It's your party. You can invite whoever you like.'

'You're damn right I can,' says Cole.

Rachel flashes me a wink as she drapes her arm off Cole's hip and waltzes past Celeste, pulling me behind her. 'Close your mouth, Celeste, you look like a hungry old trout.'

To my own detriment, I giggle, knowing some time, in the not too distant future, I'll pay for Rachel's comment.

Rachel is right.

It is classy. Low lighting, tables draped in maroon linen tablecloths and laden with silver tureens of punch, rows of champagne flutes and food everywhere. Chairs and tables hug the outer edges of the room and, in the far corner, huge speakers are responsible for the thumping beat that fills every square inch of the place. On the back wall hangs a large sign with the words 'Happy Birthday, Cole' written in coloured glitter.

'Place is packed,' yells Rachel over the music. 'I wasn't expecting this many people to be here.'

Me either. I feel a little out of my depth.

Celeste brushes past me with all the grace of a gridiron player to join her group. They all turn and laugh in my direction. With so many people here, she is easy enough to ignore. Cole then hands us a drink and says he'll be back in a minute.

'Oh my God, can you believe it? He put his arm around me,' squeals Rachel, the second he leaves. Her hair is piled up on her head, curling strands soften her naturally flawless face, and the hot pink skirt she wears, shows off more leg than I would dare to reveal at the beach.

'You look great together.'

I scan the room again, identifying a few faces from my year. I groan the second I see Eliza and Cherie. Cherie is draped over some poor guy with his back to me. I gesture towards them and Rachel shakes her head.

'I suppose Cole had to invite sluts for the older guys who didn't bring dates.'

Rachel isn't talking only about Eliza and Cherie. She is staring down Celeste. I chuckle, and she wraps an arm around my waist. 'Anything to see you smile, Ratface.'

My laughter is short-lived.

The music dims, and the side-profile of the guy ensnared by Cherie talons, stalls my brain, dislodges my thoughts.

I'm not listening anymore. Not to the music or Rachel's small-talk. I'm not even looking at the way Cherie's arm circles his back or the way her hand rests over his shoulder, smoothing his jacket. All I can see are her hands on someone I never would have expected to be here in a million years – River Fulton.

Rachel hands me a second cup of punch and frowns as I down it in one gulp.

'What?' I ask. I am surprised my internal mercury warning system hadn't gone off like it's done in the past whenever he's been in close range. I hate to say it, but, I've begun to rely on it.

Her lips try to form the words that go something along the lines of 'are you all right?' except I answer for her.

'I'm fine. Stop worrying about me. Go and have a good time.'

She purses her lips, desperate to add something else.

'Did I show you my new tattoo?' interrupts Cole. He nods courteously at me and slides his arm around Rachel's shoulders. He pulls down the neck of his shirt revealing a bolt of lightning.

Rachel giggles. 'Did it hurt? My mum said I'm not allowed to get one until hell freezes over … whatever that means.' She threads her arms around his neck and pulls him in for a closer look.

*Turn me invisible.*

Each time Rachel and Cole move, I shadow them as best I can. I hear Rachel's hearty laugh thankful she's finally taken my advice and is having fun. What she needs now is some time alone with Cole and not to be worrying about me for once. What I need is oxygen and plenty of it.

'I'm going out for some air,' I tell Rachel. At least this way I won't have to avoid Celeste's death stares or watch Cherie fawning all over River.

'Want me to come with you?'

'S'okay. I won't be long.'

I weave my way through the frenzied quartets of girls wearing skimpy clothing, too much bronzer and eyebrows the same shape, colour and thickness, all the time wishing the door was closer. Salvation is within my reach and I can taste the teasing flow of fresh air through the doorway. Six feet of diamond patterned carpet is all that stands between me and freedom.

'You're not leaving, are you?' Familiar fingertips settle on my arm. An electric bolt charges through me, sending the empty cup out of my hand and straight into the air. A muffled squeal escapes my lips. My arm prickles with equal quantities of blazing heat and frost-biting chills and I stare at my fingers, wiggling them, encouraging some feeling back.

River is in front of me, trapping me in mid-step, blocking my path. His eyes drill through me, his face showing no emotion, just like before. I wonder if he knows how to use his lips, or if he knows what a smile feels like. Even in the dim lighting, the wondrous depth of his eyes, hold me completely at his will.

I regain my ability to speak, but before the word comes out, I can tell my tone isn't going to be polite. 'Pardon?' This stupid relentless heat is doing zero for my love-life.

My heart skips more beats than I can count as he steps closer to allow someone to pass behind him. His jacket brushes against my shirt. His brow wrinkles ever so slightly and his eyes become two round, sorrowful millponds that I would willingly drown myself in. In an instant, my mood shifts into calmness and, if I'm being truly honest with myself, a little sadness too. Anything he wanted from me, right now, he could have.

'I said, you're not leaving, are you?' His voice is as smooth as chocolate and just as sweet.

My brain is on overtime. Sifting through a few possible responses, I finally come up with, 'I need some air.' The word, 'why?' that follows is something, I hadn't planned on saying.

River opens his mouth to answer when Cherie burrows under his arm and slides her tentacles around his waist. He glances sideways and although a light smile appears on his face, his eyes tell another story.

'There you are, handsome. You promised me a dance,' she says in a whiny baby voice. She ruffles her hair and seductively bats her false lashes at him. I feel instantly nauseous.

Her smitten eyes veer towards me, now manifesting fury, ready to take me apart in slow, steady blinks. 'What are *you* doing here?' She leans in closer to River and rests her face against his jacket, claiming him. My lips twist in deliberation, unsure whether I want to retaliate or retreat.

Cherie spins River around to look at her and places her hands against his chest. She runs her fingers along the edges of his jacket. Retreat is a much better option. I take my only chance and sneak through the door.

I let my breath out slowly, ignoring Greg the bouncer as he tilts his head to one side at me. I turn away from him, indicating my need to be alone. I have no idea what I'm more flustered by, River *actually* talking to me, Cherie trying to steal him away or the heat that is smouldering beneath my skin … AGAIN.

I am thankful for the cool air though. It revives me and stills the pounding in my chest. I draw it into my lungs in long, fulfilling breaths, feeling instant relief as the fire that had abruptly ignited, slowly begins to fade.

The small paved patio, I hardly noticed when we arrived, is decked out with wrought iron tables and chairs and bathed in a soft orange light. I walk over to them and stand with my back to the windows, resting my hands against the back of a chair. The cold iron sends a not-so-welcome chill through my body. Rachel's skirt, desperately clinging to my thighs, is doing little to keep the wind out, and her thin, crepe blouse isn't helping much either. Tiny goose bumps ripple across my forearms in a matter of seconds and I shiver. I withdraw my hands, rubbing my arms vigorously.

'Are you cold?' a voice whispers from behind me.

My body locks into position and no matter how much heat rockets up from my feet, my body trembles. I'm about to say no, I'm not cold, when a soft, warm jacket is placed over my shoulders. The weight falls across me like a pair of comforting arms. His arms. The smell alone makes me want to draw it up in both hands and breathe it in until I have no breath left in my body, and the warmth radiating out of it, makes me want to curl around it and go to sleep. Never has an article of clothing meant so much to me. I want to keep it, forever.

I close my eyes and gingerly lean my head to one side, unable to control the impulse to smell the lapel of his jacket. The fabric brushes softly against my cheek and I fill my lungs with him. His unique aroma saturates my senses, bringing about hints of sandalwood, and a sweetness that overpowers it, like the smell of a summer's day at the beach, long wading strides through cool, salty water; the smell after it rains; skiing in the Alps; fishing in the Lake District; smells that come back from my childhood. My legs are first to feel the impact, trembling uncontrollably, convincing me Rachel's thick stilettoes aren't such a great idea. My vision goes in and out of focus as the burning ramps up, discovering all the new places in my body it hasn't touched yet.

I am lost and I am found.

A cool breeze cuts across my face. I awaken to find River no longer standing behind me. He's less than two feet away, his head leaning questioningly to one side. My gaze falls to his feet and slowly pans upwards. He's dressed in faded jeans and a t-shirt and his black hair, normally spikey, is smoothed down.

'Thanks,' I say, ignoring the heat that tints my cheeks.

We stand in silence.

Our eyes take in our surroundings, somehow always meeting at the same time. The occasional burst of laughter coming out of the doorway and the thud thud thud of the bass are barely noticeable. The clouds have parted, revealing a startling clear sky, yet my head remains foggy. So many questions prevent my rambling brain from deciphering where one ends and the next begins. I want to ask for a time-out, so I can persuade my thoughts to stay put for a moment while I catalogue them into audible sentences. I want to make sure the clutter is clear and that important points won't slip through my radar.

The filmy haze disperses, leaving four standout questions that beg for answers. Why did he want my date of birth? Why did he say those things about my eyes? What happened in the sports hall, but most of all, why did he sound so sad when he thought I was leaving tonight?

River takes a measured step closer. I chance a look at him. Bad move ... his eyes make me forget everything I was about to say.

'How do you do that?' he whispers to me. Hollowness echoes through his voice, like he's been lost for such a long time.

'Do what?' I answer breathlessly.

'Hold me in the palm of your hand like that? Like you ...' He hesitates. His brow creases, and the turmoil returns to his eyes. 'L-like you can make me do anything you want.'

*What? No! He has it all wrong.*

'Me?' I gasp.

He doesn't seem to hear me and his eyelids lower, leaving semi-circles of tropical oceans to stare at me. 'Your eyes are ... mesmerising,' he murmurs softly.

*No. No. No. This is all wrong.* These are my questions, my thoughts. Floundering in disbelief, I grapple for something ... anything to claim my right to my own observations.

'My eyes?' I say, my voice pitchy and a little out of control. 'Your eyes.'

His frown becomes heavier and his face stern. 'What do you mean - my eyes?'

One solitary second is all it takes for us to realise we're both in the presence of something neither of us has a rational answer for.

Raucous voices behind us halt our conversation. A girl with long brown hair and a face of black makeup, and a guy with two piercings in his lip, are a few feet away from us, screaming in each other's faces. It isn't difficult to hear what they're saying, and I certainly didn't want to be the blond girl from inside who had apparently tried chatting up this girl's boyfriend. No less than two seconds later, Cherie marches towards them, swinging her arms furiously. She stops short when she sees River and I together.

'Oh ... River?' Cherie is clearly flustered. 'I didn't know you were out here ...' She pauses to examine River's jacket on my shoulders and then immediately averts her eyes before finishing her sentence, 'with *her*.'

The corners of my lips tingle as I resist the urge to show her how pleased I am at her reaction.

'I wondered where you'd got to. I thought we were going to have that dance you promised me.'

Irritation, the kind an annoying mosquito might create, flickers across River's face and his body takes on all the characteristics of a marble statue. I wonder if he feels as uncomfortable as he looks.

'Is that her?' screams the girl with the long brown hair, pointing directly at Cherie.

Cherie turns ninety degrees. Her hip juts out as she folds her arms across her chest. 'Are you talking to me?'

'Yeah, I'm talking to you, Barbie. Where do you get off, chatting up my boyfriend?'

I step away, trying to remove myself from the situation. To my surprise, River copies, closing the gap between us to less than a foot. All I want, is for Cherie to disappear so I can find out what River was about to say. Instead, she glares at his jacket again as though it's hers, as though I've stolen it. Her top teeth chew aggressively at her lip.

'Oi, I said, where do you get off …?'

'I heard what you said, Goth,' snarls Cherie. 'I can't help it if your boyfriend finds me more attractive than you?'

Before the girl can get remotely close to Cherie, Greg the bouncer steps in. He escorts the girl off the premises as she squeals profanities, mostly at Cherie, whilst her boyfriend trails behind her, shaking his head.

'So, River …'

River stands tall and offers her an apologetic smile. 'Can you give us a moment, Cherie? I was in the middle of asking Ember something.'

My heart skids to a stop.

'… asking *Ember* something? Fine.' With a swish of her hair, Cherie struts back inside.

My endless inner monologue is off and running again and so are the nerves. The air of confidence I'd come out with has gone, along with the steadfast questions. I can't tell him about the first time I saw him … how I felt as though I couldn't walk past him without his permission. How hypnotising he is. And there is no way I can describe

95

the heat that's swelling in my body right now, when I don't even know why myself.

'You mean to say, you don't see the flashes of reds and oranges when you look in the mirror?' he asks, confused.

I raise my eyebrows at him. For some reason, his words irritate me, more so this time than the *first* time he'd said them. 'No, and neither can anyone else, it seems. Anyway, who tells someone their eyes are the colour of molten lava?'

He appears to find my comment amusing. One corner of his mouth tips upwards, setting my heart off at a gallop. It's the first time I've seen any real flicker of emotion other than seriousness. 'You actually asked someone after I said that?' he says, one eyebrow lifting higher in surprise.

His smile widens, and I lose track of words, my thoughts, my mind. The universe stops. Everything inside it stands still, except for my heart and breath and pulse raging within and I know right then, I will do anything and everything I can to see that smile again. This boy has come to life in front of me. And, I think I am falling for him.

He is still waiting for me to speak.

'Yes, no ... I mean.'

He folds his arms across his chest. His eyes are light and teasing, and a mock smile plays around his lips. 'What *exactly* do you mean?'

'I don't know,' I mutter as the heat rises inside me, dulling my ability to think. 'Forget I said anything. Most people do.' Instead of bringing the conversation to an end, so I can crawl back to the party and die from embarrassment, I manage to open a barrel load of questions.

'That's not what I've heard,' says River. His serious face is back, although his tone is soft and curious. 'You seem to be on everyone's lips recently.'

The second he's said it I can tell he wished he hadn't. His jaw clenches over and over again. Even the huge sycamore tree swaying at the edge of the car park manages to steal his eyes away from me. For me, that comment is the end of our conversation, gorgeous smile or not.

Reluctantly, I remove his jacket and place it over the back of the chair. 'Thanks, but I don't need this anymore.'

His face drops in an instant and his head shakes from side to side. Although I haven't even begun to figure him out yet, I sense the internal beating that is going on inside him.

As I turn to leave, he grabs hold of my hand. 'Please don't go.'

A rush of volatile energy, ten times, no a hundred times stronger than in the sports hall, surges through my arm, creating stars across my vision and tiny bubbles in my blood. The same beautiful landscape and scenic images replay over in my head, more vividly, as though I've just returned from these distant places.

Spots of rain continue to land on our hands. I want him to release me, except I can't find the words to ask and don't want to ask, because I want to stay like this forever. We are oil and water, compatible yet fighting for our own individuality.

Thunder rumbles in from the east. River looks up with a frown and I instinctively mimic his expression. The few splashes of water become many, dissolving into my skin the moment they land.

Water! Here, to ruin everything.

Party poppers explode one after the other like gunfire, startling me back into reality. He is still holding my hand and I begrudgingly uncurl my fingers from his, one at a time. The coolness from his touch still lingering.

'Tell me you saw that?' gasps River, his wide, hypnotic eyes frantically searching mine for answers.

Feeling as freakish as I've ever felt, I let out a long, controlled sigh. 'I saw nothing,' I say, unable to meet his gaze. I head back inside, the lie smouldering against my tongue.

And yet, something *is* different.

97

A tiny fissure has opened, freeing me, if only a little, from this hell on earth, from fear and darkness and despair. At the end of a very long tunnel, I see a light, something to work towards. Numbness ebbs away, giving way to desire, and hope, and maybe one day, happiness.

I want to open myself and experience everything. It is time to discover me all over again. It's time to let the girl I used to know have her voice back, a voice River Fulton knows better than I know myself.

Sweeping my hair out of my eyes, I catch a glimpse of myself in the mirror. Public toilets are fast becoming my refuge.

*Freak*!

I hang my head over the sink. 'Pull yourself together. You saw nothing … *he* saw nothing.' It's then I notice what's left of the collection of cheap bangles I'd begrudgingly borrowed from Rachel. The tiny coloured diamantes have congregated in a mess of uneven rows where the gold has congealed into one solid mass of misshapen metal.

With effort, I slip it off my wrist and drop it into the waste bin. It lands with a dull thud. 'And how are you going to explain that to the world?' I mumble to the bin. I cut my conversation off as the door swings open.

'Are you okay?'

My answer comes out clipped and dismissive. 'Yep, I'm fine.'

The girl places a hand on my shoulder. 'They're all bastards,' she says, looking sideways at me in the mirror. She has a tired, lived-in look that is all too familiar to me. We both stare at each other for a second until she heads into a cubicle, leaving me to question the lolly-pink walls.

My eyes return to my recently naked wrist. This flurry of heated episodes and metal melting ability is getting out of control. I take another look at my reflection. My eyes glow more vibrantly than before. I peer closer until my nose almost touches the glass, trying to convince myself it's the fluorescent lighting and nothing to do with River Fulton's "molten lava" theory. My thoughts race back to his "tell me you saw that" remark. *Was he referring to the rain, or the images I could see in my head?* This is all too much for my sensitive fragility.

I need to leave … now.

That night as I snuggle down into sheets that smell far too good to simply lay on and ignore for twelve hours, I am certain of two things. One – I will sleep soundly tonight without any unwelcome visitors and, two, River Fulton, as hard as it is for me to say, is every bit as strange as I am, if not …stranger. His words won't leave my thoughts, even during Rachel's obsessive babbling all the way home about Cole and what a great kisser he was. There is no way he could have seen those images in my mind … *no way*. As much as I want to cast him and his curious, outspoken analysis of me out into the dark, I find myself clinging to them as though they are the last fragments of normality left in my life. All I want, is to be normal. Live a normal life.

Irritation sets in and I roll over and bury my face deeper into the pillow. Of all the nights I can sleep ... of all the nights I can relax, every time I close my eyes River Fulton's face is waiting, stuck inside my head.

# ELEVEN

*IT* isn't the sound of a lorry lumbering up the road that wakes me the next morning, or the sweet chirps of Rachel's mum's budgies outside in the aviary below our window. It's the sweet, smell of butterscotch pancakes. I stretch my arms and legs down the bed, deliriously happy. Mmmm, I love pancakes.

*Wait a minute.*

I sit up so quickly my head spins.

Rachel's mum *never* makes pancakes. She is more the warm cream cheese, apricot compote and fresh brioche type.

Rachel's bed is empty and already made. Her second dressing gown, the one with the tiny bumblebees on it, has been left on the bottom of my bed and I slip it on and wander downstairs. I open the kitchen door and step back in surprise.

'Morning, darling. Sit down and I'll get some lemon and sugar for you.'

My mouth is unattractively agape, and I begin to say something, except the words I search for won't form in my mind. My mother, with her chequered pinny on and her luscious wavy brown hair, tied back in a simple tortoiseshell clip, fetches something from the cupboard, while my father, a tall man with emerald-like eyes and a smile that makes you want to smile yourself, is sitting at the table strumming on an old guitar. He's wearing my favourite blue shirt with the sleeves rolled to the elbows.

Confused, I gaze around the room.

Dark, solid oak cupboard doors line the kitchen, an avocado coloured bench top with matching two-toned double sink and the collection of china thimbles on the shelf near the dining table, are as familiar to me as my own skin. This isn't Rachel's kitchen. This is my old house on Clarks Road.

'Sit down, poppet, or your pancakes'll get cold,' says my father. He winks and the fine lines around his eyes crease. The very sight makes me want to burst into tears. I've missed seeing that … so much …and I swallow down a sour cocktail of pain, regret and resentment. He looks so vibrant, so alive, exactly how I remembered him. This can't be happening; my parents are dead.

I drop down into the seat opposite my father, staring wide-eyed at him. 'H-how ...' I squeak. It takes a few slow blinks and several squirts of maple syrup on my father's pancakes to realise this must be a dream. One of those "got to be real" dreams.

My mother bumps down a plate in front of me and sits down with her toast and honey in one hand and a collection of multi-coloured vitamins in the other. 'We've got a busy day today, lots of things happening, Em. Eat up or we're gonna be late.'

A blanket of thick grey smoke descends over me, shutting out my beautiful mother and the arms I long to have around me again.

When it finally clears, I don't find myself sitting in the car going to Aunt Cynthia's and Uncle Reggie's place, like we'd done on our last day together. I am standing on the pavement, alone, waving them off in my pyjamas and bare feet.

'Don't go,' I scream at them, but they continue to wave. 'Please come back.' I know what waits for them. They drive to the end of the street, make one left turn and are gone forever.

I walk up the street, strangely aware of how dirty my feet are getting. I stop in front of a large glass shopfront where thousands of miniature rocking horses gently sway back and forth. One particular rocking horse draws my gaze – the same delicate crystal one I have on my dressing table.

Usually, I feel nothing other than peace when I look at it, but right, now an icy breath, far too real to be a dream, starts at the back of my neck, navigates through my body to my feet, bringing every nerve to life.

'Look at me,' I hear a voice in my head say.

I feel myself frowning. *Just a dream. It's just a dream.*

I peer further into the window, past the rocking horses to the unmistakable reflection of a man, staring at me, from across the street. Long straight hair, smooth and unbound, and reminding me of wood ash, hangs limply over his shoulders to his waist.

Without giving my body permission to move, I swivel to find myself facing him. His bony white finger, encased in a thin layer of flesh, beckons me closer as he lifts his hand. Curiosity and an unusual lack of fear urge me to step off the pavement.

Out of nowhere, a hand clamps hold of my arm. I pivot on one foot to see who it is, only to find I'm standing alone.

My reflection shocks me.

Two fiery copper orbs burn brightly, bathing everything I see in an orangey light.

River was right - eyes blazing like molten lava.

102

I was right.

I am a freak.

'Have you figured it out, yet?' His voice is familiar, and empty, like a stone inside a tin can.

'What?' I shout back even though I heard every word he'd said.

'Have you figured it all out, yet?

I have no idea what he's talking about. 'Figured *what* out yet?'

My words anger him, and he sweeps across the road like an irate spectre, his feet ten inches off the ground. His pale, gaunt skin and colourless eyes halt inches from mine. Speckles of neon blue light shines through the cracks in his skin, dividing his flesh into small uneven triangles.

'HAVE YOU FIGURED IT OUT YET?' he screams at me.

My body bolts upright for a second time, my heart pumping wildly as though it's only just learnt how to beat. The sudden urge to vomit passes as my breath returns in strangled gasps. I remove the fresh beads of sweat from my cheeks and forehead with my sleeve before massaging my fist into my chest, pressing back the urge to cry. The image of my mother and father is now marred by some creepy, irate wraith. The thought of seeing their faces again, unleashes the dam. Tears fall freely.

'Bad dream?'

Rachel is leaning on her elbows, her blue eyes searching every inch of my face.

I nod. 'Something like that.'

'Prick,' mutters Rachel under her breath. 'He'll get what's coming to him. I'm sure of it.'

Rachel is so far off the mark it isn't funny. I don't correct her, instead, I muster a weak smile.

'You believe in karma, Em, I know you do. We've spoken about it before.' She pauses to clench her teeth. 'I would pay the devil himself to witness that low life prick copping his shitload of it.'

103

I'm two days pure and that's all I care about. Two months ago, I started to count the days in between The Creeper's visits. I call these my pure days – when life is that little more liveable, that little more *normal*.

After filling up on a breakfast of muesli and toasted bagels, I take my time in the shower. A pair of jeans is standard dress code for me, but the long-sleeved shirt is a deliberate choice, purposely hiding the bruises that are taking their sweet time to fade.

The 1940s puce coloured terraces thin out the closer we get to town and bungalows begin to line the streets backing on to the shopping centre. Rachel is still going on about what a great party it was and how wonderful Cole is. I nod and throw in the occasional "yeah" and "cool" although I'm only half listening.

'I still reckon that cranberry punch was spiked though,' Rachel says, pressing her fingers into her temples. 'I only had three glasses and yet my mouth tastes like I drank from the toilet all night. Hang on a minute ...' She stops to rummage through her bag. 'I'm sure I've got a couple of pieces of chewing gum in here somewhere.'

My eyes fly across a freshly mowed lawn to a signpost staked in the middle. At first, the words don't register, I mean, who cares about hypnotherapists? But after reading *Sylvia Banks – clinical hypnotherapist*, a few times, a light bulb goes off in my head and the edges of a plan starts to form.

What do hypnotherapists do?

They hypnotise you, of course.

Maybe this is a way to access memories about my car accident - memories that should be vivid and hard to forget instead of non-existent or, at best, vague. A sense of Deja vu prickles over my skin. This feels right. It's never felt so right.

I look past Rachel, still elbow deep in her bag, to the brown coloured cottage with its dark mahogany porch and leadlight windows. Lavender bushes in full bloom spill out onto a winding path.

'Ember Riley, are you listening to me?'

'What?'

'I said, do you want some chewing gum or ...' Rachel's voice trails off and her gaze skates across the grass to where I'm looking. 'Oh my God, you're so right.'

I frown. 'About what?'

'About getting that fucking prick hypnotised.'

A smile passes over my lips. 'Actually, I was thinking about going to see if she had any appointments ... for me.'

'What? *Now*? *Why*? What about our shopping spree?'

'It'll only take an hour. I can meet you over there.'

'I don't know, Em. What about that TV programme last year where that bloke hypnotised a bunch of people from a studio audience into believing they were chickens. You might stay one forever.' Her naivety humours me. 'What if she scrambles your brain?'

'It's not only used for party tricks,' I say. 'It must be legitimate otherwise she wouldn't be allowed to practice.'

'But you don't know anything about this *Sylvia Banks*. What if she's a nut job?'

'Only one way to find out.'

Rachel zips up her bag, the same time her smile disappears. 'You shouldn't mess around with your mind.' I want to tell her it already is messed up, but I keep my mouth closed.

She's not ready to give up without a fight. A fight I need to win. 'Why don't you wait for me at the Tulips cafe and ...'

Rachel interrupts. 'I'll come with you.'

I wince.

'Just to be on the safe side.'

My shoulders sag.

How ironic? Every day I go home to a practising paedophile and yet Rachel is fretting about me spending an hour alone with a woman who has a bird feeder hanging from her tree.

'I need to do this myself, Rach. If she can't fit me in, I'll come back straight away. Promise.'

'But, Ratface ...'

'Please.'

Rachel's lips are still set in two straight, thin lines.

'*Please*.'

'Okay, but I'm going to be watching the clock. If you're not back here in an hour, I'm calling the police, the fire brigade and an ambulance.'

I exhale rather obviously. 'Fine.' Rachel looks back three times before reaching the end of the street.

Feeling slightly awkward, loitering outside Sylvia Bank's house by myself, I finally make my way to the front porch. The leadlight glass catches the sun, and for a moment, I'm positive I see the long-haired man from my dream standing behind me. I spin around, and in the time it takes me to blink, he morphs before my eyes into a balding man in a beige raincoat, who hasn't sprouted hair in fifty years. The presence of a cool, icy breath on the back of my neck is unsettling. I adjust my collar and reposition the strap of my handbag before mustering the courage to open the door.

'Can I help you?'

Startled, I leap into the garden bed, squashing something woody and pink beneath my feet. A woman with bleached blond hair, twisted into a French knot, stands in the doorway with an inquisitive look on her face.

'Oh, shit.' I wince as I remove my foot from what used to be a pretty, flowering shrub. 'I mean, sorry. I'm sorry.' The woman has a soft face that doesn't falter at my limited vocabulary.

'I'm sorry, dear. I didn't mean to scare you. Were you here for an appointment?' I turn back to the old man in the raincoat.

He's gone.

'Sweetie, are you okay?'

'Yes, sorry,' I mumble again. 'I mean, no, I don't have an appointment although I would like to make one.' The woman reminds me of an older version of Rachel's mum.

She steps into the sun and offers me her hand. I'm going quietly mental, I think, as I follow her inside.

The small reception has low ceilings and equally low lighting. Three walls are painted a deep violet and the wall behind her desk is clad in fake timber panels.

'My name is Sylvia,' says the woman, 'and I'll be taking you through your treatment. I'm fully booked today, but do you have a particular date in mind?'

My first reaction is disappointment. 'I can only come on a Saturday because of school,' I say.

Sylvia thumbs through a few pages in her appointment book and grimaces when she stops at a blank page. 'I'm afraid all my Saturdays are booked up for four weeks, my love. My first available appointment is the fifteenth of October.'

Coming face to face with the events that caused my parents' death, events I've consciously or is that *subconsciously* stricken from my mind, has me feeling light-headed and no longer eager to find out. The big brave me from yesterday is gone.

'Suits me perfectly', I say, relieved. 'How much is it?'

The woman smiles sweetly. 'It's seventy pounds for an hour and a hundred for an hour and a half.'

'An hour will do.' If I manage to pluck up the courage to come back, an hour should be sufficient time. *What would Sylvia Banks find? And oh God, please don't let her say it's somehow my fault.*

Money is and isn't a problem.

I have plenty of it, or I will have when I turn eighteen.

Presently, it's tied up in a trust fund. After my parents died, Rachel's mum suggested an amount of £300 a month be deposited into a bank account for me, for incidentals as she put it. All this had changed after I moved in with the

107

Burberrys. Now, any money I need, I have to ask *him* for, though The Creeper doesn't know about my post office account that has five hundred pounds in it. I keep the book at Rachel's house, for emergencies and, although hypnotherapy can't exactly be considered an emergency, it may be my lifeline to better days.

Reece's Mall isn't the kind of a place you can buy silk stockings or diamond tiaras, but the dress and shoe shops are abundant.

I pass Tulips.

Rachel is not there.

My next guess is La Bella Forever.

Jackpot!

Sparkles, sequins, beads and satins make La Bella Forever look like the inside of a firework. The reds, oranges and pinks of the shirts, skirts, tops and pants scream at you from every rack and hook. Rows of silver and gold chiffon dresses adorn mannequins, and scarves blending from the deepest aqua right through to shamrock green are splashed across the walls. Where clothes are concerned, it's the shop from heaven.

I find Rachel rubbing a pale pink shirt between her thumb and finger and gazing longingly at garments on a rack close by.

'That was quick,' she says, picking up a blue jumper dress with silver threads running through it. She jiggles it at me.

I scrunch up my face. 'She was all booked up,' I say.

Without looking at me, Rachel continues. 'So, that's it?'

'Mmmhmm,' I murmur. 'Pretty much.'

Rachel turns sharply and stares right in my face, waiting. 'And?'

*God, I hate that she knows me so well.* 'And ... I made an appointment for a month's time.' I mumble the last few words.

'Are you serious? What do you need to see a hypnotist about?'

I roll my eyes. 'Er, everything.'

Rachel's face softens. 'I didn't mean it like that, Ratface. I mean you should be seeing a counsellor or therapist or something. Not a circus act.'

My smile takes work to form. 'I really think this will help.'

Rachel puts the dress back on the rack and gives me her full attention. She reaches up and puts her hands either side of my face. 'How? By erasing the events of the last twelve months? That's not healing, honey. That's hiding.'

I have no alternative now. I have to explain. 'I want to remember what happened the day of the crash.'

Rachel opens her mouth to speak, and I jump in quickly. 'Don't you think it's odd that I have no memory of the accident?'

'That's why they call it trauma,' she replies. 'Because you found it too hard to handle so you've shut it out …so you can deal with it.'

'*Exactly*. I *did* shut it out. And now I need to know what I've shut out because I haven't dealt with *anything*.'

'But why do you have to do it alone?'

I want to tell her it's because of the heat and burning issues that have plagued my thoughts, except I can't. I don't think she'll understand, and more than likely she'd suggest a psychologist rather than a hypnotherapist. I can't be seen as mad, as a freak, not in her eyes. She's my rubber ring to normality.

'Because I do. End of story.'

Rachel lets out a loud, exaggerated breath. 'All right.' She deliberates for a second. 'Still, it's a shame you couldn't get that disgusting pervert an appointment, too. I would buy front row tickets to see her hypnotise him into thinking he was a used-up prostitute with a scorching case of herpes.'

My sudden irritation is smothered by laughter and the snort that comes out of my nose immediately defuses any tension between us.

# TWELVE

RETURNING to the Burberrys' on Sunday night, I become "un-normal" again.

The air, uninviting and thick, clogs the back of my throat as I inhale, the second I open the door. Ten thousand bricks seem to automatically press against my chest, making it difficult to breathe, difficult to feel, difficult to see. I wish it was to do with the smell of burnt toast and unwashed floors, but it isn't. It's the horror of what's to come. Of what, and who lies in wait.

I feel physically sick.

'Ems, is that you?'

My chest is glue, my breath less than a vapour. Blood pumping around my body slows to a pathetic dribble. His voice echoes from the lounge room and I tentatively walk down the hallway and poke my head around the door. He's lying on the sofa in the same vest he's had on since Friday and pair of boxer shorts. The remote control to the TV balances on his bulbous stomach, rising and falling with his breath.

'Yep, I'm back.'

Celeste grins maliciously from the armchair. 'You're in trouble,' she mouths. My moment of payback has arrived.

I'm dead meat!

The Creeper groans his way into a sitting position and points to the empty chair. 'Sit.'

I do as I'm told.

A smile teases at his lips. It isn't because he's happy to see me. That smile I know well.

'Celeste tells me you were quite the "party animal" on Friday night.'

*Hardly*, I think, but it isn't a question. He taps the arm of the sofa, waiting for my answer. It takes everything I have, not to stare at the baked bean stain sliding down the front of his vest.

There's no use lying. 'Yes, I went with Rachel. Her mother gave us permission ...'

Like an axe against my neck, the sheer volume of his voice cuts the words from my tongue in one swift strike. 'But *I* never gave you permission,' he booms back at me. Spit froths at the corners of his mouth.

It's obvious The Creeper hasn't let the vomiting incident drop, not that I expected to get off that easy. I've learnt too many times that the silent treatment isn't in his nature. 'And you didn't think to ask *me* if you could go? I am, after all, *your legal guardian*.' A joyous smile bursts from his pudgy face as though he loves those three magical words more than his own children.

I drop my head to my chest. My eyes glaze over as I stare solidly at my fingers, twisting and squeezing every ounce of blood out of my hands. When the arguments start, and when punishment is warranted, it's a foregone conclusion that my pure days will drop back to zero.

'I'm sorry.'

Sometimes, apologising works.

'Sorry isn't good enough, and look at me, girl, for Christ's sake.'

112

My neck crackles as I raise my head. Only once had I thought I'd seen a scrap of guilt in his eyes, but I was mistaken.

Remorse doesn't live here.

It never has. It's never seen the wallpaper peeling above my head or the scorch marks on the carpet in front of the fireplace. Remorse wouldn't even get an invite because in all honesty, there isn't room. Only pure evil lives here.

'You're grounded.'

'*What*? For how long?' I gasp, momentarily forgetting my place. The shock of having to spend entire weekends with my neurotic 'family' pushes me closer to my favourite cliff. The freedom of falling, the quickness of a pain-free life is as tempting as it is despicable.

'For as long as I say so, Missy,' he snarls. 'And if you think Cinderella had it hard ... just wait and see what I've got in store for you.' His piggish eyes devour me.

Celeste giggles childishly and the desire to get up and thump her in the mouth springs up out of nowhere.

So does the fire growing in my belly. Not quite volcanic proportions, but like a pot on the stove, gently simmering, hearing the pop of occasional bubbles as warmth begins to exchange places with cold. It's the comforting hand of a close friend on my shoulder.

Except, I don't know what to do with it.

I take a second to revel in its warmth, to milk what little strength is there, hoping to learn from it. For the first time in my life, I start to wonder if it's there on purpose.

'So, you can start by getting upstairs and stripping off that cesspool you call a bed.' He glances over at Celeste. 'We had to close the door for the entire weekend because your room stunk so bad, didn't we, love?'

Celeste nods enthusiastically. 'Yeah, you really need to shower more Em-*bar*. Other people do live in this house too. It's not all about you, you know.'

The harder I clench my fists, the more my body fires up.

God, I want to wipe that smile off her face permanently ... with a cricket bat.

The words are like a battering ram inside my head, trying to knock down a wall that's been up for far too long. Flames leap higher into the gaps between my bones and joints, flooding my palms with heat.

I feel like I'm capable of doing it.

'I can't believe it, Ems. I take you in, feed you, clothe you and you ungratefully won't keep your room tidy. How much more do I have to do?'

The words, "keep your hands to yourself," scratch against my tongue. Memories of him touching me, kissing me, controlling me, edge closer and closer, toppling my confidence, and making themselves right at home again. Fear remembers the way in, and tucks itself safely back into my heart, dousing the fire instantly.

I wait a few seconds to be sure he's finished and then push myself out of the chair. I creep around the door, fighting back tears as I go, ignoring the sinister smile that snakes its way across Celeste's face.

The next few weeks of house arrest are the worse they've ever been. The Creeper came to my room every night, whispering venom into my ear, touching my hair and face, and anything else he wanted to do. And every morning, I retched until my stomach muscles were useless and scrubbed my skin so hard, you could almost see through it. I wondered if I'd ever know what normal felt like again.

I keep telling myself, it can't last forever.

And it can't.

It has to end.

One day, I'll be eighteen and then, legally, I can leave, and perhaps take Aaron with me. Poor, sweet Aaron, who has no idea who his father is and how dangerously close he is to becoming a victim.

Chores had tripled, which I could handle. The upsurge of mental abuse I can't. The games … the threats … the Mr nice guy act … the angry drunk. Fifty personalities rolled into one fucked up loser. His unpredictable state of mind, swinging me from manic to panic, are starting to take their toll, drawing on my already bottomed-out reserves.

Even school hasn't been the relief I'd hoped for.

More fatigue has set in than usual, and the desire to retreat into a matchbox and live there forever until the sun dies out and the earth becomes a crust is driving a wedge between River and I. The first week he had followed me from class to class, trying to make conversation, without much success, but by the end of last week, he'd given up completely and now stares at me with concerned eyes from across corridors and open doorways. He continues to intrigue me with his bold comments and yet the determination I'd once had to find out, has all but disappeared.

And it isn't *just* him.

The gossip about me has reached epidemic proportions too. Cherie went on a rampage after Cole's party telling anyone who would listen that not only am I a freak and murdered my family, but I'd slipped River hallucinogenic drugs to lure him away from her, and then had sex with the bouncer in the park. My life is a pile of shit. I've even found myself avoiding Rachel on some days, just so I don't have to see the sympathy in her eyes.

Three weeks of walking a tightrope, walking the plank, walking on eggshells has broken my spirit and shattered anything else left over - my penance for going out and having a good time, and not hurting a soul.

I put the last dish away and pack my lunch into my school bag.

It's Friday.

Walking to school alone, and not have to keep up the pretence with Aaron that everything's all right, is something I've been looking forward to all week. Only yesterday he asked me why I looked so sad. I told him I missed my mum and he gave me a hug that meant more to me than any hug I'd had since they'd died.

I stand in my usual corner of the kitchen, as far away from The Creeper as possible, and sip my tea.

'You look a little tired, Ems,' he coos. A flicker of worry passes over his face.

I stand tall, squeezing the muscles in my thighs so tightly the numbness overrides any sensation that tries to push through.

I will not let myself feel anything for him.

I can't.

Not understanding, not sympathy, nothing. It's a self-preservation thing.

'I think it might be time your punishment ended. You can stay at Rachel's house tonight, only if you promise not to go to any more parties.'

I slowly raise my head, peering through him to the chicken tiles on the wall behind. 'Thanks,' I mutter lethargically.

A certain amount of joy should be felt at having my restrictions revoked, though it fails to register. I sullenly throw my bag over my back and pull the door behind me.

I'm alive ... that's all.

Morning fog swirls around my feet as I step on to the street. I haven't even passed the neighbour's fence when I hear footsteps behind me. I peek over my shoulder to see River Fulton jogging towards me. His hair has grown a little and his eyes cut through the dense mist, reminding me how much I've missed seeing them. For the first time since being grounded, I feel semi-happy to see him.

He matches my pace, ensuring an arm's width between us. I hold back the smile I want my lips to make as I gaze into his soulful blue eyes. *Why do they always calm me?*

116

'Do you mind if I walk with you?'

I shrug. 'It's a free country.'

We walk in silence; the torment on his face constantly switching places with indecisiveness. A dilemma of some sort seems to be going on behind his eyes because he keeps frowning and then not. And then frowning, and then not. But I don't care to ask. It's nice to have company, to feel someone walk next to me because they want to, because they bothered to ask if it was okay, but that's it. That's all I need right now.

'Do you have a study period this afternoon?' he eventually asks as we approach F block.

I nod once, stunned that he's finally spoken.

'And you'll be in the common room for that then?'

I roll my eyes. Where else did he think I'd be? 'Actually, I'll be on the roof.' River glides over my sarcasm.

'Good. We need to get a few things straightened out. I'll meet you there after lunch.'


The first half of the morning is a total waste of time as far as learning is concerned. The left side of my brain, apparently responsible for logic, language, critical thinking and reasoning, has packed up and disappeared on holiday, leaving me with poor right-sidedness – who isn't capable of threading a simple sentence together if my life depended on it.

When I arrive for science, Mr Butcher is pacing militantly at the front of the room. His head jerks in my direction and nods once. My chance to ask River what he meant, ebbs away when he takes his seat at the front of the class. I find my chair and stare vehemently into his back, wishing he'd turn around and give me a clue as to whether it's good news or bad. I'm expecting bad. He's probably conjuring up an excuse why we can't hang out together anymore, or something like that. I can't blame him really.

Several times I think he's about to turn around, only he stops in mid-twist and abruptly faces the front again.

Keeping his eye on the clock, Mr Butcher continues to strut back and forth, throwing up his pen and catching it. 'Not a second to spare, Mr Higgins,' he says, addressing the last boy and gesturing to the only vacant seat left in the room. Darcy drops into his chair without a sound.

Mr Butcher picks up his trusty clipboard and waves it about his head.

'Anyone know what this is?' A smile skims over his face, resting in his eyes.

Peter Capelli's hand is up straight away.

'Don't say a clipboard, Capelli.' Peter promptly lowers his hand.

Mr Butcher flicks his gaze from the clipboard and then back to the class. 'Need another clue? Okay, it's the day you've all been waiting for.'

No one moves.

'C'mon, it's not a trick question. Someone must know.'

Peter Capelli inches his hand halfway up and I hold back a smirk as Mr Butcher's shoulders slide down his back towards his tawny brown belt. He lets out a wistful sigh.

'All right, Capelli, give it your best shot.'

Peter Capelli shuffles nervously in his seat and glances sideways at his peers for reassurance. 'Christmas holidays, sir?' he says with a hopeful smile.

Mr Butcher shakes his head in disbelief. Even I can't believe he's said it. 'The correct answer is ...' Five long seconds pass. 'It's the day when you'll be sorted into your designated element groups. So, when I call your names out, you will pick up your own chair, take it to the assigned areas and sit in your groups. Everyone got that?'

A hum of answers ripple across the room. Mr Butcher proceeds down the list, calling out names in no particular order, thumbing students into their groups. When he gets to my name, he pauses.

'You, Miss Riley, I think would favour … f-f-f-fire.' I look over to see who else is in my group. I groan noticing Cherie Bennett is.

Only three names are left that haven't been called out. River is one of them.

'James Jenkins, you're in earth, River Fulton …' Fire and water are the only elements left to choose from. 'You are in …water and Josh McTavish is in fire.'

I'd be lying if I said I wasn't disappointed River wasn't in my group. I was counting on bringing up his 'straightening out' statement which will now have to wait until later. And now, thanks to my brain finally beginning to fire on all cylinders, there's another downside to this situation - Cherie, soliciting herself to him in such proximity, is going to be more than I can stand.

I reach for my pencil case and take my frustration out on the zip, forcing it open and closed in quick successive bursts. In the time it takes Mr Butcher to turn and face the board, the zipper has come off in my hand and melted against my thumb and forefinger, leaving behind a smudge of silver-like paint. I peer through the veil my hair makes to see if anyone saw it happen and quickly drop my hands into my lap.

Mr Butcher is busy writing hints on the board about how the tasks should be divided, whilst the rest of the class set about organising who is responsible for what.

'Why do I have to list all the ways fire can destroy or generate,' groans Cherie to our group. 'Everyone is doing way cooler stuff. How come I get the shit topic?' I sigh, peeling the metal off my skin now resembling candle wax. *I wish someone would destroy her.*

'Well, you bunch of hotheads are certainly in the right group. Don't you think so, Miss Riley?'

He makes me jump, and I narrow my eyes at him. *What does he mean by that? And why does he keep directing those questions at me all the time?*

By the end of the lesson, I'm totally deflated, and our group hasn't accomplished a thing. I stuff my notes into my bag, surprised to see Mr Butcher and River Fulton deep in conversation as I leave.

After lunch, I make my way to the common room of F block. It's a bland room where *Danni loves Scud* has been scratched into the cream walls so frequently, it passes for wallpaper. The lino, the colour of Scottish kelp, is disgusting too, but I've seen worse. The floor in D block has tiles missing and an over-sized penis has been drawn in permanent marker.

I find River sitting by the window.

He looks up as I walk in, his eyes gliding over every inch of me. A sprinkle of goosebumps shimmers beneath my skin. I feel almost giddy.

He slides his books to one side without looking at them. The pages are blank and the lid to his pen is on.

'I'm glad you came,' he says. His voice is a soft, cosy blanket.

A gentle spark ignites inside my chest, inside my stomach, my heart, my head. Warmth begins to build. It's not like the fire and flame I'm used to. It's much better. It's a sensual bath with bubbles and candles and soft sweet music lulling me into a blissful sleep. I wait, preparing for the overwhelming heat to take over, yet none comes. He gestures to the seat opposite him.

I unconsciously pull my books from my bag and set them on the table too. 'It sounded important,' I murmur in a low, flat tone.

He lowers his eyes and I'm glad to be momentarily released from their spell. I wonder if I'll ever get used to them. I draw in a breath and my head clears somewhat. I grip the back of the chair and ease it out before sitting down. I fold my arms onto the table so he can't see my hands shaking and wait for his response.

River relaxes back into his chair. 'I don't know about important, but I do think that maybe we've got off to a shaky start. I thought … we could rewind and begin again.'

His head is cocked, his eyes focused and clear. His lips look good enough to kiss. *I can't believe I'm even thinking that.*

'So, this *isn't* about the colour of my eyes again then?' I blurt out unexpectedly.

River risks one quick glance at me and averts his eyes. 'You're very astute and my answer is both yes and no.'

I open my mouth to ask what he means except he jumps in before I have a chance. 'I figured because we have something in common, we could be … well … umm friends.'

*What could we possibly have in common?* I angle my head to one side, my lips twitching with curiosity. 'And that is?'

At first, he doesn't speak. His stony expression vanishes, and his eyes glaze over, making them more alluring than ever. His jaw clenches beneath his skin, again and again. 'Your parents were killed in a car crash, weren't they?'

My heart thuds uncomfortably in my chest. That was the last thing I expected him to say and my breath catches in my throat, trapping every word with an invisible net. *Why my parents? Why start a brand-new friendship with an old hurt? Maybe I was wrong. Maybe he is like all the rest —out to get the latest scoop.*

I deliberate for a second, feeling a rush of heat come up from my feet. I want to close my eyes and shut out any influence that might sway my decision. I feel the rumble of an argument waiting in the wings. I hear the whisper of tender words I'd hoped he'd say, getting lost on the cool currents that drift above my head and out through the open window.

I want.

I need.

121

I feel.

Unable to decide what approach to take – whether to tell him to mind his own business, get up and leave, or ignore it – I opt for choice number three and sharply nod my head once.

The depth of his eyes stuns me as I look up. 'My parents are dead too.' His voice is barely a whisper, his jaw taut. 'They drowned two years ago.'

I clear my throat, my brain unable to form a response. Everything about him is unpredictable; leaving me stranded each time he speaks. I understand his pain because it matches my own. It rolls off him in waves, taking me back to that sterile, beige hospital waiting room I've tried so hard to hide from … and forget.

River's face is void of emotion, as though he's vanquished not only the memory of their death but also the memory of their life. A chain reaction begins in my brain and travels down to my wrist. I tentatively reach out to take his hand, to comfort him, and then think better of it. Instinctively, I withdraw my arm and fold my hands back into my lap. River, however, is still staring at the empty spot on the table where my arm had laid for him.

A long minute passes. 'I'm sorry for your loss,' I finally say, offering him a sympathetic smile. My thoughts drift to my own "family" life. 'Who do you live with now?' My voice crackles.

'My dad's cousin and his wife,' he says without hesitation. 'They lived an hour away from us when we were up north, and my mum and dad stated in their will that if anything ever happened to them Terry and Annabeth were to be my legal guardians.'

I can tell by the look on his face he's going through the motions.

The same way I did. Those few rehearsed responses I said for nearly twelve months was my mechanical backup whenever I wasn't up for dealing with it.

'And you like them?'

I wince, when I realise I have no idea what made me ask that.

River frowns but doesn't look angry, more curious. 'We don't always see eye to eye but they're family and they've been really good to me.'

I'm glad he fared better than I did, and my relief obviously shows.

'What?' he asks pensively.

Circles of aqua beauty look right through to my core, not with greedy pickaxes to uncover my secret, but with tenderness. I fight against the urge to open up. 'So, why did you move here then?'

'Terry got transferred down here with his work so, rather than commute, he decided it would be best if we moved here and made a new start.'

'Oh,' I say. It sounds so *normal*. 'Whereabouts?'

The concentrated look on his face disappears. He almost looks engaged. 'We moved in a few streets away from your friend, Rachel.'

My brain goes into overdrive. First, how does he know who Rachel is or that we are friends or where she lives? And second, if he lives across town near her, what the hell was he doing walking behind me today?

I stare out the window, waiting for the answers to questions I haven't even yet asked. Okay, he could have followed behind Rachel one afternoon and seen her go into her house ... that sounded reasonable enough, but that still left query number two without a logical explanation.

My eyebrows dip towards my nose, my forehead instantly heavier. 'Then what were you doing ...?'

'Hanging around your place this morning?' he says, finishing my sentence.

'Yeah.'

His lips turn into a full-blown smile and I fall apart, all dizzy and bubbly, like too much energy has been injected into my veins. *Where is the pause button of life in moments like these?*

'Like I said, I thought we needed to iron out a few wrinkles.'

A light smile flickers over my lips as I realise he was waiting outside for me *on purpose*. I replay his words not once, not twice but three times, allowing them to tip-toe across my thoughts. They're not words anyone would forget in a hurry because he doesn't speak like the boys do from around here, not that I speak to boys on a regular basis, unless of course I'm accusing them of deceitfully gathering information about me. He has a whimsical way about him – not quite old-fashioned, more well-read or cultured – like he's been to an all-boys prep school all his life or an expensive grammar school or something. I'm aware my vocabulary is letting me down, and 'oh' or 'yeah' is fast becoming my only response around him.

'What do you think? Does that give us enough grounds to be friends?'

Blood rushes back to my cheeks and I return my gaze to the window for confirmation before looking at him once more. More questions throb inside me. I need to know more about him before I can commit to calling myself his friend, but in that flash moment, with him leaning forward, his fingers gripping the edge of the table, I can think of none.

'Friends.'

I hold out my hand as a gesture of alliance.

It comes more naturally to me a second time because I know our touch has boundaries. He didn't accept my hand before when I offered it, therefore, I know our relationship is not going to be based on the idiotic feelings of a mushy romance like I'd imagined or hoped or feared.

We are friends. Just friends. He said so himself. River draws his hand into his chest and hesitates for a moment, confirming my previous suspicions, before weaving his hand into mine.

In the distance, thunder rumbles, gradually getting louder until a splintering crack rips through the sky directly above us, causing the building to shudder.

A blinding white light fills the room.

I stare at my fingers as they glow and mould into River's skin like they are one and the same. The harder I try to pull my hand away, the firmer they remain. His hand grips tightly to mine, charging my body with heat, growing hotter and hotter every passing second until I'm sure I'm about to self-combust.

I glance over at River, only to find it's no longer him sitting across from me holding my hand. It's the silver-haired man from my dream.

His eyes resemble two hard boiled eggs except for the burning blue flames inside them, and his hair flies about his head in Medusa-like tendrils.

'When will you challenge me, FlameMaker?' The skin around his lips puckers when he smiles, revealing jagged white teeth bathed in cobalt fire.

My lips tremble. 'What. Are. You?'

The apparition laughs a sinister, wicked laugh, sending signals to my bladder that it's okay to pee myself. I wrench my hand away from River's and run from the room.

'EMBER?'

I hear my name being called and know its River's voice, but that doesn't stop me from running, regardless of the confusion and concern that hangs on every syllable of my name.

# *THIRTEEN*

*IN* my panic, I find myself in another bathroom.

Open mouthed and reeling from shock, my fingers tremble against the cold enamel. I examine my reflection in the mirror, hardly recognising the person staring back at me. My eyes transform from the fiery coppery-red orbs, I can't stop staring at, to a duller, more hazel brown.

It *is* there, like River said. He wasn't lying.

Out of control and wavering on the brink of insanity, I splash my face with water until the front of my shirt is wet and my hair clings to the sides of my face in thick red ropes.

'What the hell was that? … What the hell was that?' I mumble to myself. 'What the fucking hell was that?' I yell louder at the mirror this time. I have to force every breath into my lungs, making each one longer than the one before, until I feel light-headed. I sink to the floor and drop my head into my hands. I'm really losing it.

The pamphlet Rachel had covertly stuffed into my bag recently, warning about the detrimental effects of long-term stress and family trauma coming out as depression or psychotic episodes now seems not only real but logical and possible. *Was that what was happening to me? Am I delusional – seeing and hearing people who don't exist? Am I creating an alternate world to hide from because I desperately wish to escape from the one I'm in?*

Maybe I am.

All the signs are there.

All I have to do is put my hand up and say I'm in dire need of a lobotomy, or at the least a visit to the nearest psychiatric ward for a stretch of time.

I stretch my fingers out in front of me and gaze into my palms, expecting to see hair sprouting or some other sign that I'm crazy. My hands are as smooth as ever and no longer clammy. I run the back of my hand across my brow that thirty seconds ago glistened with sweat.

It too has evaporated.

They're coming for me. Those people in the white coats … they're coming for me … it's no longer a matter of *if*, it's *when*.

But, and there is a huge … but.

I can't admit to lunacy.

I can't, because deep down, much further than even The Creeper can penetrate, I don't feel mad or psychotic or delusional.

In truth, I've never felt saner.

The cold tiles soaking into the backs of my legs, sends a wandering chill up my spine. If I can still feel hot and cold, I know my name, and where I am, then I can't be completely bonkers, plus waiting here until the bell goes, although a favourable option, isn't a mature one. And I still have questions for River, if he hasn't thought I'm the craziest person in the school by now.

My breath comes back to me and I stand up and straighten my shirt. I stick my head under the hand-dryer to dry my hair and sneak a glance at the semi-presentable girl with the flushed cheeks. At least I look *normal*, regardless of how I feel.

Tentatively, I make my way back to the table and slump back down into the chair. River's face is pale and his customary taut jaw hangs slightly open. Lines of worry are etched across his forehead. Abashed with guilt, I focus my attention on the open page of his book, drawn to the wave-like patterns he's scribbled over and over until the entire page is filled with wiggly blue lines.

'What was *that* all about?'

I can't bring myself to look at him. 'Sorry.'

He notices my sudden interest in his book and discreetly closes it. 'I ask you to be friends and you run out looking like you're going to throw up.'

I don't know what to say.

'Way to go, River. You sure know how to make an impression,' he grumbles under his breath. He is irritated about something, although from his tone, it's not me. It sounds like this isn't the first time he's said those words to himself.

He lets out a long, held-in breath, and at the edges of my vision, I watch his hair spill over his fingers as he rakes his hands over his head. I am transfixed by his every move, even to the sound his shirt makes as his arms stretch upwards. He leaves his hands resting on his head and although I am desperate to witness the way his biceps arch and the way his shoulders might look, I can't. I'm too caught up on that same unexplainable aroma of seaside breezes that drifts towards me, stunning me, and making me want to close my eyes and breathe him in until the long years of my life are over, and my last breath runs out.

'Seriously though, you scared the shit out of me.'

His words blur past me like a fast car.

'Sorry,' I mutter again, still stumbling along in dreamy town. Wow, I've gone from a two-word vocabulary to one. At this rate, I might pass with the intelligence of a goldfish. 'If you want to take back your offer of friendship, I'll understand,' I finally manage to get out. My lips strain to make a smile as I chance a glimpse at him.

His eyes have an extra sparkle to them. 'No way. I think things are just starting to get interesting.' A hint of humour touches his voice. 'It's certainly one way to get a guy's attention. Do you normally do stuff like this?'

I can tell he's trying to lighten the moment, but I lower my eyes and answer with a soft 'no.'

I haven't prepared anything in the way of an excuse and River is still waiting, his eyebrows cocked, waiting for an explanation. I could say I had a migraine or that I was going to be sick, but I don't want our friendship to start with a lie, so I say nothing. Instead, I need a diversion, and proposition him before I change my mind. 'What are you doing tomorrow?'

River looks as surprised as I am for asking. 'Tomorrow? Umm … nothing, I don't think.'

I can't back down now.

'Do you want to hang out?' I can't believe what I'm saying. Sure, it's a better alternative to explaining what happened but it doesn't stop me from squirming in my seat. I count back from ten, waiting for all the reasons he can't be seen out with a total lunatic.

A smile touches his eyes and yet his lips remain in neutral. 'All right, sure. What did you have in mind?'

Now I've blown it. I have nothing planned.

A few scenarios flicker across my open gaze as I wrack my brains for something cool to do. Boys didn't shop or go out for ice cream, not that I knew of, and from the look of his taut shirt sleeves, he's the type of guy that's used to something a little more athletic rather than reciting *A Dream within a Dream* to me in the park.

I say the first thing that pops into my head. 'How about grass skiing and tobogganing?'

River Fulton's lips break into a wide smile. I'm loving this look a whole lot more. If his eyes are breathtaking, then his smile is the wind that blows me away.

'Wow,' falls out my mouth.

'What?' he casually asks.

'It suits you,' I say shyly, captivated by it.

River looks down at his shirt, checking himself.

'The smile,' I say, using my finger to paint an imaginary smile back and forth on my face.

Now *he* looks embarrassed. 'You should try it too. You know, it doesn't hurt as much as you think.'

'Some days it hurts too much,' I say grimacing, but I'm not just thinking about The Creeper. River nods, like he knows what I'm talking about. 'Sometimes it feels like I'm betraying them, like I've forgotten who they were and the things they used to say,' I add, my words spiralling off on a tangent of their own. I find myself shamelessly staring into his eyes. I'm a rabbit caught in headlights.

'I know what you mean,' River mumbles.

His eyes stare back at me, unwavering, unblinking, as though he's caught in the same net I am. I have no idea how long we sit for - powerless to move and incapable of speech. I'm not aware my eyes are watering or that my breath is so shallow my chest hardly rises. I'm only aware of the meditative state I'm falling into. Soft lapping water surrounds us, filling the room, until I can see nothing but clear oceans of sapphire blue in the distance. The warm water caresses my body and soothes the ragged emotions of sorrow that have become my existence.

The sudden sound of a chair falling over draws River's gaze to the other side of the room, severing the images from my mind. Although I'm relieved to be released, I'm filled with more emptiness than ever before.

'What did you say?'

River looks equally embarrassed although he recovers much quicker and with more grace than I do. 'I said, I'll come to yours about ten, then?'

'No,' I snap much too quickly. I don't want River within a hundred yards of the Burberrys' house.

River jumps, his eyes wide.

'I mean, it's a twenty-minute bus ride away, so how about we meet outside the fish and chip shop on Grange Road and then we can catch the bus from there.'

I watch the confusion dissolve from his forehead as River reins in another smile. 'So, it's not a date, then?'

*Date*? That's the furthest thing from my mind, even though I secretly want it to be. 'No, it's not a date. I thought we were going as *friends*.'

River drops his head and sniggers. 'Well, I'll meet you at ten unless you have any more objections.'

The bell rings and I try to ignore the mocking smile playing across his lips as he packs away his books. This is a new side to him - a side I really like ... much better than the marble statue with the personality of a pebble. I throw my bag on to my back and am ready to leave, when ...

'Is it okay if I call you Em from now on?' I open my mouth to protest but stop when he raises his finger in warning. 'And one other thing.' I close my mouth. 'Your eyes only burn the colour of molten lava when I lose myself in them and not all the time now. Maybe I'm finally getting used to them.'

His wide, pleasing smile stuns me all over again and although I'm sure I've been taught to read, write and speak English, not a single word forms in my mind.

He walks away with strong, confident steps, his head held high, his shoulders back. He gives me one quick wink from over his shoulder before heading down the stairs.

I sigh.

I am jelly.


River Fulton isn't your average geek, sports buff or rebel. He's far more complex than that and therefore requires an expert. With my sanity at stake, and my reasoning skills and general communications at an all-time low, I have no choice but to finally confide in Rachel.

I wait for her at the gate, like we'd arranged, but as she comes into view the peculiar look on her face tells me my questions will have to wait.

'Sorry, I'm late,' she says. The collar of her school shirt is askew, one long strand of her hair is stuck to the side of her face and the dusky pink nail varnish she wears, normally pristine, is chipped and unsightly.

My eyebrows draw together. 'What's up?'

She looks up and down the street three times before she speaks. 'Is there some weird hippie fest in town at the moment?' Her bottom lip trembles on the word 'weird.'

'No, I don't think so. Why?' She seems reluctant to move. I link my arm in hers, encouraging her to take the first step of many towards her house.

'Well, Cole and I ducked down to the paper shop during study period for some "alone time" and as we were making our way back to the school gate on Carlton Avenue ...' She pauses and her mouth stretches downwards as she takes in a lengthy breath. 'This creepy guy came out of nowhere, wearing a long dress thing and baggy trousers starts following us all the way from Breckon Street. Cole kept saying if he didn't get lost before we got back inside the school grounds, he was gonna deck him, no matter how old he was.'

'Maybe he *was* a hippie and he'd had one too many bongs,' I add, chirpily. 'Plenty of them about these days.'

'But he was really creepy.' Rachel gnaws on her thumb nail.

'How so?'

'His face. Oh my god, I'll never forget it as long as I live. It was eerie and like, so pale I could see through it.' She pauses. 'He looked like a ...'

'A ghost?'

Rachel's mouth quivers again as I say the word for her and this time, her teeth plunge into her bottom lip. Her eyes fill with water. 'But you don't believe in ghosts,' I say.

'*Didn't*,' she says abruptly, '*didn't* believe in them. And another thing, he seemed to be ...' She hesitates and takes another look around her. I do the same.

'What?'

'I can't believe I'm saying this ...'

'*What*?'

'He seemed to be ... floating.' Her voice is a shadow of its true self.

'Your joking, right?'

'No, I'm not joking, Em. Do I sound like I'm joking? Have you ever heard me talk about stuff like this before?'

No, I hadn't. She sounds down right nuts, oh wait, she sounds just like me.

'He didn't seem *real*. And he had this long grey hair and ...'

My knees jerk at the same time as though the joints have forgotten how to work. Anxiety works its way through my blood until I can barely stand. My mouth pops open, though no words follow.

'Are you all right? You look like you're going to be sick,' asks Rachel.

I recover enough to ask a simple question. 'D-did he say anything?'

She shakes her head. 'No. Just stared at me.'

A slight drop in temperature has me rubbing my arms. Well, I think it's a drop-in temperature. The air around me has grown cold. I scan my immediate environment.

'What did you do?'

'I couldn't do anything. My feet wouldn't move. Cole had to drag me into school and when I turned around the hippie had vanished. All that was left was this spooky blue mist, you know, like the stuff you get on the big playing field early in the morning. It was the creepiest, weirdest thing I've ever seen.' There was that word again ... *weird*. I thought I was the only one qualified enough to say that. 'You do believe me, don't you?'

Tiny, ice-coated needles prickle over every square inch of my body. I thrust my hand into my mouth and bite down on my knuckles. A soft strangled cry still manages to make its way out.

Rachel spins around so fast I don't have time to erase the panic on my face. 'Oh my God! Have you seen him too?'

Yes, yes, I have, but I can't tell her that. I can't tell her I had a dream about him. That's even weirder than seeing him in the flesh ... or spirit, or whatever he is. I can't tell her I saw him outside Sylvia Bank's place the other day when he transformed himself into a bald man in a raincoat or that he showed up in the common room less than an hour ago and spoke to me. Not when I can pass him off as some random who is acting a bit strange. I have to think fast.

'Someone was talking about a weirdo hanging around the school·gates in science this morning,' I say, clenching every muscle in my body to stop myself from peeing. 'It's probably some old fart testing out his Halloween costume.'

It works and Rachel's face softens a little. 'Well, somebody should report him. What if he's around when school breaks out? Some of the younger kids walk home alone that way.'

I wish I could reassure her that he isn't after younger kids. He isn't interested in following them home either.

He is after me.

What had he called me again ... that's right – *FlameMaker*? What does that mean? Who does he think I am? By my calculations, this goes way beyond random sightings.

A frightening fact dawns on me. I can no longer put this down to madness or sheer consequence and it isn't my imagination either.

He is real.

# FOURTEEN

$A$ patchwork of grey clouds hangs low and meddlesome by the time I turn into Grange Road. River is waiting at the bus stop, just like he said he would be, in black jeans and a hooded jacket.

Out of uniform, he looks much older. His face is relaxed and there's no hint of regret, like I thought there might be. The nervous knots began the moment my eyes opened, condemning me back to a one word greeting. Hello, is all I manage to get out, creating a moment of awkwardness, of silence and polite smiles. I stare intently at my fingers twisting a loose cotton on my shirt until the bus arrives.

The bus is almost empty when it finally turns up and River walks to the middle and sits down, leaving me with a choice to either sit next to him or to take the empty seat in front. I choose the latter and slide along the seat, swinging my body around to face him. He doesn't appear surprised.

I casually glance over River's shoulder as the bus pulls away, and the gasp that hisses at the back of my throat and clenches my heart into a tight ball, makes River frown. He casts his eyes over his right shoulder just as the metal rail I'm holding onto, attached to the back of my seat, bows beneath my scorching grip. The rail flattens in one small spot with definite finger impressions embedded into them, just like my parent's headstones. I release the rail immediately.

'Someone you know …?' he starts to ask, his attention suddenly diverted to the newly modified rail. He stares at it for a few seconds, frowns and looks at me. I sense the blood emptying out of my face, and I collapse back into my seat.

The man with the long silver hair is standing at the bus stop.

'Not exactly,' I mumble into my hand. I force a tight smile, which River isn't convinced by.

'Em?' He pauses as though savouring the taste of my name against his tongue. 'Now that we're friends and you're not trying to vomit on me.' I open my mouth to speak, ignoring the smirk playing around his lips which never quite erupts. His eyes, serious. 'I want you to know you can talk to me about … anything.'

River follows my gaze as I peer through the dirty bus window to see if my ghostly stalker is still there. He's gone – like I knew he would be, and I only hope to God he won't unexpectedly materialise a few seats down from us. That would warrant a scream I won't be able to talk my way out of.

Getting back to River's offer of opening up to him, I revisit my mental inventory from last night and strike a line through every one of my idiotic concerns. None seem to be the right topic to bring up, let alone to casually discuss on a bus. The old woman opposite me looks up, sucking nosily on a hard-boiled sweet before returning to her book.

Now is not the time. 'Thanks, but I'm okay.'

River appears to be genuinely put out and his tone conveys that. 'It's up to you, of course.'

Shit. I'm ruining this day, simply by being me.

I drop my hands into my lap and stare out the window. Trees, trees and more trees hurry past and I pretend to be enthralled by their long elegant limbs and feathery fronds rather than risk looking at River's face. The tension between us widens by the mile.

'I'm sorry,' he mutters. 'Of course, you're entitled to your privacy. It's just, I …'

My eyes lock on to his as he struggles to find the right words. I notice his cupid's bow is a little off centre and the scar above his eyebrow has turned silver as sunlight finds his face through a crack in the clouds.

I wait until I can't wait anymore. 'You …'

His eyes, momentarily clouded, gradually clear. 'I don't know when to mind my own business, that's all.' He focusses on something in the distance.

Unconvinced by his answer, I turn back to face the window. I get the distinct impression he's hiding something from me.


A huge billboard with a picture of a grassy hill and two bright red toboggan runs snaking around it in a figure of eight have GREENACRES SKI-TOBOGANNING written on it. We head up the gravel laneway.

I try to rekindle our conversation. 'Have you ever grass-skied before?'

'Not since the Olympics,' says River around half a smile. His humour inches to the surface and I shake my head, glad we're getting back on even ground again.

'Yeah, right,' I scoff. 'Is that where you scored that gold medal from?' I gesture to the gold disc hanging around his neck. I'd seen it once before, half-hidden beneath his sports shirt.

River tucks the chain back into his t-shirt. 'It was the last present my parents gave me.'

My heart thumps loudly against my ribs. 'I'm sorry. I didn't mean that … I know how precious it is. My mother gave me a beautiful rocking horse before …'

'It's okay,' he says, jumping in quickly, but I can tell I've upset him … for a *second* time. His face loses any smidgen of excitement and cold grey eyes replace his tropical oceans of blue. The idea of cancelling this so-called 'friendship' date is getting better and better by the minute.


Standing at the bottom of an enormous, man-made hill, I inhale a shaky breath. My throat dries immediately. What the hell was I thinking? I can't believe I'm going to go through with this.

It isn't the speed or the height that worries me although, as I take another petrified glance up, maybe the steep descent is a little daunting. It's the adrenaline that will flood my body as I wait at the top, anticipating the rush and fear on the way down.

That's what I'm dreading most.

I hate adrenaline. And there's only one situation in my life where liquid fear comes into play and, today of all days, I don't want to be reminded of The Creeper or the nausea he brings with it. Most of all, I don't want to be afraid when I should be happy.

We pay for the hire of the skis and poles, not uttering a single word to each other. I bend down and run my fingers over the artificial grass. It prickles my skin and I have visions of carpet burns and grazed knees.

The skis are heavy and cumbersome. After testing them out for a few minutes, I reluctantly follow River, who is already waiting for me at the beginning of the drag-lift.

The slow build-up of adrenaline as the mechanical arm drags me up the hill triggers a chant in my head. 'I can do this, I can do this, I can do this.' It begins to fill me with courage, smothering the low murmur of the, 'please don't do this, please don't do this'. Dark scenes slide across my vision, trying to trade places with the good memories I'm trying to create. I keep checking my fingers are gripping the black rubber handle of the drag-lift and not the polka dot print of my duvet cover.

I then make a crucial mistake.

I close my eyes.

Just for a second.

And in the space between sipping in shallow breaths and letting them go, I see *his* face.

The Creeper.

I am a lifeboat again without survivors.

I am both adrift and aground.

My hands throb with a steady rhythmic pulse, urging me to let go. One by one, my fingers, stiff and white, peel away from the handle to reveal less and less of the black rubber that is now becoming a sticky mess in my fingers.

'You okay?'

River's shout jolts a fierce shock through my hands, making me flinch. Without thinking, my fingers automatically curl back around the handle, keeping me safe. More heavy lines ripple across his forehead as he turns to check up on me.

'I'm good,' I say, keeping my gaze fixed upon the rapidly approaching summit.

River lets go of his draglift and I know I'm next.

Fear races around me, affecting my ability to think, feel, hear or see. My breath and heart gallop together, one trying to outdo the other.

My fingers let go with a sharp jerk and my legs wobble as I stand unaided. The drone of a thousand bumblebees vibrates inside me, bringing with it the urge to vomit.

'Steady, Miss. They can be tricky the first time,' says a red-haired attendant now supporting my arm. I nod my thanks and scrape together something resembling a smile.

I can't be positive, but as I glance over at River, poised and sure-footed and looking like he's done this a thousand times before, I swear I see him wipe the remnants of a smirk from his face. I grind my teeth together and half-walk, half-stumble over to him.

'Something funny?' I ask. The pole's soft grips mould into my hand the harder I squeeze. Heat is surfacing and my nose picks up the distinct aroma of burnt rubber.

'That depends on what you think has piqued my humour?'

I frown at his choice of words. Again, there is that fancy grammar school air that mocks my public-school intelligence.

'Perhaps you'd like to fill me in then.' The three-foot-long rollerblades, with a mind of their own, keep sliding at odd angles trying to bring me down.

River holds out his hand as if to steady me. 'Em, for Christ's sake, you look petrified. We don't have to do this if you don't want to.' His eyes challenge me.

I gather every ounce of courage I can muster, wishing it would filter through to my shaky voice and legs.

'Are you saying, I couldn't beat you in a race?' I ask.

He stifles a laugh. 'Oh, I know you can't beat me,' he says confidently. 'I don't want you to hurt yourself trying.'

'Really?' I huff in a condescending way. 'Would you like to bet on that?'

His cheeks are a little flushed from the wind and his eyes shine with some kind of excitement in them. His smile is back too, and I couldn't imagine being anywhere else. 'Are you sure you're up for this?'

I wobble on my skis again. 'Not scared, are you? Not frightened of a little competition?'

River drags his hand across his chin and lips and up to his cheek, removing another smile.

'All right, you're on. How about, the last one to the bottom has to answer a question from the winner … honestly.'

I squint at him. He's serious about the question, but more serious about the quality of the answer. Honesty to him, I figure, is like trust is to me.

I think it over for a full three seconds. I can't back down now. 'Deal,' I say and with that I push hard with my poles. 'Go.'

I take off before him and hurtle down the hill, hearing his groans of 'cheat' as I go. Going fast isn't nearly as wobbly as standing still or going slow, and the exhilaration I feel surpasses anything. Adrenaline channels in different directions, coursing through my muscles, ridding my body of anxiety and fear and giving me the kind of speed and freedom, I'd never dreamed of. The wind tousles my hair and I steal a glance behind me to see River gaining on me.

I dig my poles harder into the ground and bend my knees to gather more speed – not daring to think how I'm going to stop these things or where the brakes are, or what is going to happen to me as the kiosk and dining tables below grow rapidly closer. I continue to slalom this way and that, determined to shake River and not let him pass.

But he's too good.

With twenty yards to the finish line, he flies past me and skids his skis in the dirt, sending up a shower of dust.

I copy his manoeuvre and to my surprise, the skis obey. I managed to stay on my feet and although I lost the bet, my integrity remains intact.

'Cheats never prosper,' he says smirking.

I scowl as I suck down breath after breath. It's nice to see him enjoying himself but I'm annoyed that he'd won and looks so damn smug about it.

'Double or nothing,' I say determined.

River's lips widen, his eyes playful. 'Okay, but it's your funeral.'

I rise to the challenge and take off up the hill like a woman possessed, the draglift posing no problem for me a second time around.

I stand at the top, composed and not a wobble in sight.

'Go,' he yells.

I push off hard. River appears to be enjoying this game, glancing over his shoulder and waving casually as he passes me yet again. He doesn't even seem to be trying, and when he welcomes me in at the finish line for the second time, clapping, I'm ready to explode. Fire erupts inside me.

'Again,' I growl.

After six runs in all, River winning four and me only two, which I'm sure he let me win, I sit at the bottom and glare up at the colossal green hill and huff out my annoyance.

'I think we'd better get some lunch before you kill yourself, or me,' says River, 'the questions can wait … a while.'

We remove our skis and the young lad behind the counter frowns at me as I hand in my grip-less pair of poles. 'What happened to these?'

I shrug. 'Hot hands, I guess?' Part of me wants to laugh.

We cross the paved area to a small café.

'I didn't think you were that competitive,' says River, placing his salad roll and apple on the table before pulling out his chair. 'Or that competent.'

My eyebrows rise. I agree with his assessment of my competence, regardless of the cheap dig that accompanies it, but the competitiveness is something new, even to me.

'Well, now you know,' I reply smugly. To be honest, I've never felt competitive before. I never cared about winning or losing, playing sport for medals or striving for the dizzying heights of a taut, lean body and all the honours that go with it. I drop into the chair opposite and unwrap my sandwich.

'So, what's it going to be …?' River says amused, 'the rack or the guillotine?'

I go for the sourest face I can muster.

'They're only questions, Em. I'm not asking you to streak across the grass in your birthday suit.'

142

I frown at first and then realise what he means – with no clothes on. His words cause my lips to tingle. River leans forward. 'Shit, that's not a smile hiding under there, is it?'

'Is that your first question?' I ask, not able to contain a straight face anymore. My lips stretch against the corners of my mouth, dulling the hotter than chilli feel within and replacing it with warm treacle pudding and custard.

River sits back in his chair, his eyes feasting on mine. He doesn't speak. Self-consciousness sinks in when his gaze refuses to release me. He stares until embarrassment washes off my smile. 'I'm not very good at letting people in,' I offer.

The lightness from his face fades a fraction. 'Who is?'

I want to ask him what he means by that, seeing as how we have our 'friends' hats on, except the guy from the kiosk is hovering close to our table and it isn't the sort of conversation I want to share with strangers.

'Do you guys need anything else?' he asks in an accent I don't recognise. It isn't *what* he says but the agitated way in *which* he says it that causes me to stop eating. River looks up too.

At first, the boy doesn't look real – way too gorgeous to be *just* a waiter, especially in this part of England; maybe on the French Riviera. Blond hair, streaked white, copper and gold, and grey eyes like silver coins left to smelter in the sun are what catch my attention. His curious expression flicks between River and I with quick repetitive movements, confusion edging its way into his brow.

A voice calls out to him from inside the café. 'Skye? If you've finished with your social life, maybe you could come in here and restack the Coke machine?'

'What the f…' He turns to us once more and then storms back towards the café, flicking his cloth like a whip.

River sneers at him. 'Where were we?'

My sudden need to feel grounded is paramount, and I take a bite of my sandwich. River is still staring at me, his eyes showing how desperate he is to read my mind.

'First question, then.'

The cloud covering his eyes evaporates, snapping his attention into first gear. 'Yes, questions,' he says, taking a bite of his roll. He waits until his mouth is empty and then tosses his head from side to side, thinking.

'I know. What happened during study period that made you get up and run away?' He sits back and folds his arms across his chest. His eyes never leave me.

I swallow hard.

I had a feeling this was going to be one of his questions.

I graze my teeth against my bottom lip. 'I don't know how to explain that,' I reply.

An encouraging smile waits patiently on his lips. 'Try,' he says. His eyes plead.

I put my sandwich down and sip my coke. Oh God … how am I going to explain this without tangling myself up in lies?

'I don't even know myself.' River remains silent, waiting for me to continue.

What's the worst that could happen? He could tell everyone what a freak I am, creating a little more gossip … I can live with that. Or he might think that I'm too crazy to talk to anymore and this will be our last conversation. I'm not sure I could live with that.

In truth, I do want to be his friend. I want him to be someone I can talk to and rely on. Someone, other than Rachel, who will pick me up and lift me out of this misery and remind me how much fun life can be. Remind me that I'm only seventeen and that this nightmare will be nothing more than a shadow in years to come. It's a big ask, I know. But I have to believe I am capable of having more than one friend.

I swallow another gulp of air and scrunch my toes into my shoes until I feel my bones crackle. 'Would it be weird if I told you I thought I was psychic?' River raises his eyebrows as I fold my head into my arms, embarrassed.

I want to die.

I want to evaporate into thin air.

I squeeze my eyes shut and hang on to my breath. I don't want to hear his answer, but I know I must.

'No,' he says flatly, 'it wouldn't be weird at all.'

Slowly, I lift my head. I'm afraid to find his expression amused, but his face shows no signs of judgement. I have no idea if I am psychic so technically, I'm not lying but I have no other explanation to give him apart from my insidious ramblings of madness. Psychic sounds so much better than lunatic. I find the courage to continue.

'I had this vision of a man, who sat right where you were sitting.' I leave out the FlameMaker part or what he'd said to me. 'It scared me, and I ran.'

'I believe you,' he says. His voice is soft and understanding and my heart eases its frantic pounding. 'And, as the bus pulled away?

'The same man,' I say without any hesitation.

'And you've never seen him before?' he asks, leaning forward, interested.

'I had a dream of him once,' I offer. I'm not thinking of my answers, only counting the questions until he's done. That is question number three as far as I'm concerned.

'Mmm, dreams,' mutters River. 'They have a lot to answer for.' His eyes pierce through me, holding me as though he desperately wants to tell me something.

I frown when he finally looks away. 'And your last question is …?'

River's mouth drops open. 'How do you figure? It's still the same question.'

'Last question,' I insist.

His shoulders heave with his breath. He thinks for a moment, then says, 'what date were your parents killed?'

I'm shocked he has asked this. I can't begin to understand what difference it will make to him to know such a personal yet trivial piece of information.

'Why?' My voice quivers.

'Is that one of your questions?' he asks. I want to say touché, but don't.

I nod. That leaves me one.

He searches my face. 'You answer me first, and then I'll tell you why.'

I concede. 'It was the day before my sixteenth birthday – 22 August.'

River is up and out of his seat, bumping the table in his haste. It judders against the pavers with a clunky sound, prompting curious glances from those around us. The boy with the grey eyes is one of them. River stands with his back to me, but I can't mistake the deep breaths that inflate his ribs in long drawing gasps. He clasps his hands over the back of his neck, his shoulders tense and his posture stiff. The impact my words have on him, aren't what I'm expecting.

I'm not sure if I should speak.

The young waiter appears at my side. 'Is everything all right here?'

River doesn't budge.

'Yes,' I say, taking a fleeting glimpse at him. 'Everything's fine.'

With slow hesitant steps, the boy leaves.

Not wanting to attract any more attention, I tentatively open my mouth. 'Now, can I ask why?'

River leisurely turns and rests his hands on the back of his chair. His clenched fingers blanch into the white plastic.

'My parents died exactly the same day.'

I blink and blink, deciphering his words to make them mean something other than what they do. *Why would he lie about that?*

'It's a coincidence, yes, but please explain to me what it means to you?'

This isn't the question I was going to ask, but after hearing his answer I know I have to have this mystery solved.

'We share the same birthday, too,' he offers hopelessly.

I exhale until all the air is out of my body. I don't want to breathe in because that will mean I'm alive and that this is really happening. Sharing the same birthday – lots of people share the same birthday but having your parents killed on the same day too is more than a double fluke. I can't convince myself it's nothing.

'Tell me I'm not imagining it, Em. Tell me, it means something ... that maybe we were brought together ... for a reason.'

I know he's right. I felt it the first time we met. I still haven't figured out the 'why' part.

'I don't think you're imagining it and yes, I do think it means something, as idiotic as that sounds, though I have no idea why ....' His eyes darken one shade and anguish thins out his full lips. '... do you?'

River shakes his head. 'Just when I think I've figured it all out, its as though someone has pressed delete.'

I give a grim smile, 'One thing I am certain of, is if we have been brought together for a reason then whatever is coming, I'm sure we're going find out soon enough.'

River nods in agreement and the anxiety magically slips from his face. He shrugs. 'Suppose no use worrying about it until then ...' His gaze disappears over my shoulder to the 500 yard toboggan run meandering behind me. 'And no point in wasting the rest of this glorious day,' He gestures with his chin. 'How about we tackle those and leave the future where it belongs?'

His words blow towards me, instantly easing the tension from my body. The sun touches my skin, driving away the cold. 'Sure. Why not?'

River smiles. 'I'm glad to see you're not consumed by it,' he says surprised.

'Believe me.' I sigh. 'This is nothing compared to what I've been through.'

# FIFTEEN

*THE* clouds blow over, revealing an icy blue sky, and River and I spend the remainder of the afternoon racing each other down the twin toboggan tubes, glistening like red jelly snakes basking in the sun. I haven't had this much fun in … well … forever. It's so easy to be myself with him, no barriers and no walls of fear to hide behind. I'm free to be me.

My body slumps off the end of the run and onto the grass matting and I puff out an exaggerated breath. I laugh from the abruptness, and the fact that River is still trailing behind me on the adjacent run.

'You have to be the biggest cheat in the world, Riley,' he says incredulously as he stands and picks up his mat. I laugh again and River laughs with me. I push my hair out of my eyes, leaving one strand for River to curl back behind my ear. His eyes lower and embarrassment leaks through his skin. I check my watch. 'I reckon we can get one more slide in before it closes.

I race River to the top of the run and throw down my hessian mat. He glances sideways at me.

'Last chance to redeem yourself,' he bellows. 'And without cheating this time, if you can manage it.'

I scowl at him and seize the front of my mat as I push off hard. It takes a moment to pick up a decent speed and I crouch lower to gain maximum velocity. I keep River in my sights as I careen down the straights and fly around the sharp bends. But as I take the top of one of the curves, the sensation that someone is watching me is too great to ignore. I look left and then right.

My heart stops and starts, stops and starts like a rusty old engine left for scrap. Adrenaline that has hidden itself so well injects into my body by the bucket-load. I feel the urge to vomit and pee and frankly pass out. The man with the long silver hair hovers a short distance away.

'When will you challenge me, FlameMaker?'

His voice booms at me and like thunder, I close my eyes from the sheer terror of it. He is thunder – earth-cracking, quiver-under-a-blanket, thunder. I realise my fate has arrived and I greet it scarily and blindly from the inside of my eyelids.

What happens next, happens in slow motion. My fingers seize up of their own accord. The mat is reefed out by some unnatural force, causing me to veer sideways into the wall of the toboggan chute. I cry out in agony. A hot stinging sensation sears through my chin and cheek in a way I've never felt pain before. My arm trails behind me on the hot red slide, scorching a burn into my flesh seven inches long. At first, I don't hear River calling out my name as I roll about in the cut-out tube like wet washing in a dryer. What I do know is that I have never hurt in so many places at once.

When the dizzying momentum stops, I find myself at the bottom of the run, disoriented and lying face down in the dirt. River is already at my side as I raise my head. Open mouthed, he scours my body that stings and aches everywhere at once. I spit a mouthful of dirt and blood on the ground. 'Oh my God, Em, what happened? One minute you were flying and the next ...' His face could double as a tombstone, in colour and personality. He seems to be deliberating whether to help me up or ring for an ambulance.

I ease myself on to my elbows and slouch against a wooden planter box. Twisting to gaze back at where the man had stood, aches more than the flu I had two years ago. Of course, he's performed his traditional Houdini act.

'Em?'

The concern in River's voice brings me back, alerting me to something warm and sticky running down my neck. I send my curious fingers up to explore.

'Don't,' says River softly, reaching for my hand.

He doesn't touch me, but his action alone is enough for me to see my hand is covered in dirt.

Blood streams from the open wound on my chin and my arm bears a superficial graze running from my elbow to my wrist.

A handful of serviettes appears out of nowhere and is thrust against my chin. I grimace as the added pressure makes the wound pulsate.

'I don't think it'll need stitches,' says a confident voice. The hand belongs to the waiter. He withdraws his hand and inspects my chin before finding my eyes. The blood slows a little. 'Those corners can be a little tricky.' He hands me a fresh wad of napkins and I change them over, wincing again at the pain that follows. 'I've never seen anyone do a kamikaze roll like that before. You were awesome.'

My lips break into a wide smile, which I immediately regret. The wound on my chin splits open again and begins to throb in time to the music coming from inside the café. In my turmoil, I decide this grey-eyed model is confident, cocky and cute; something inside me likes him instantly. River on the other hand, seems not to, and his face is darker than death.

151

'Well, I think you're gonna live,' says the boy. He takes a snapshot in River's direction and grins cheekily. 'And it looks like you've got a handle on this, champ. I'd better get back to work.' He stands up and leaves, checking backwards twice before disappearing inside the café.

'Hey?' I sing out to River, slightly amused by his longstanding glare in the boy's direction. His eyes come back to me and they are as soft and as tantalising as they'd ever been.

'That looks sore.' His face is full of empathy at the huge carpet-burn like mark on my arm. 'I'll go ask for a wet towel.' He marches off in the direction of the café and in the time it takes for him to return and for me to inspect the damage, the searing hot pain of the burn is gone, the redness reduced to nothing and the open wound completely healed, leaving behind the remnants of a light graze. I almost snatch the towel from him and press it to my skin so he can't see how abnormal my freaky healing powers are.

'You don't want to risk an infection,' he says, gently lifting my dusty hand off and replacing his hand over the towel. The tips of his fingers rest casually against my hand. No electrical current shocks me this time, no splintering white flame engulfing my body. It is warm and caring and utterly desirable.

I close my eyes for half a second and breathe him in. When I open them, he is still staring at me in a way that incites more than a nervous tremor in my body.

His top lip twitches ever so slightly and I lift my eyes to meet his.

A moment is about to happen. Everything in my body tells me that this is a moment. A time stalling, unbelievably deliciously, precious moment. My heart spikes. A simple yet intimate touch is the prelude. Tiny, out of control heartbeats go berserk inside my chest. I may never catch my breath again.

A pause.

A look.

A breath.

Without warning or permission, River leans in closer, slow and controlled, and kisses me. His lips are gentle and part enough for me to taste the sweetness of his breath. He tastes like apples. Sweet, mouth-watering, apples.

In that instance, the amount of rain that falls on us in those few seconds of passion, is like God turning on a high-powered hose, soaking us both to the skin.

'Why did you do that?' I ask softly. I try to cover myself with my arms, my shirt desperately clinging to my flesh. 'I thought we'd agreed we were going to be friends?' My brain is scrambling for answers.

River sits back on his heels, his chin falling heavily to his chest. 'We were ... I mean, we are. I'm sorry, Em, I couldn't stop myself.' Turmoil swim circles in his eyes. 'I shouldn't have done that. Please forgive me.'

I do forgive him, and part of me wants him to kiss me again, and perhaps not stop quite as fast as he did. *Is it wrong to feel this way?* A haunting memory of Blue Stratos fills my throat and The Creeper's face torments me as I close my eyes to think. I want River's lips to kiss me whenever they want, and yet, at the same time, I am repulsed by the act. These conflicting emotions tear at me, and, brick by brick, a fortress rises around me.

'When I said, I don't do well letting people in, what I meant to say was, I don't trust anyone. Please don't become one of those statistics.'

River drops his head even further, his shoulders hunch. 'I really am sorry. Is there anything I can ...?' I raise one finger to stop him. He drips of remorse and if his eyes could tell the saddest tale, they would, and I would believe him, in a heartbeat and accept his apology unequivocally. But I notice the disappointment too. It doesn't seem to be because of my rejection of him, rather failure in himself.

I heave a sigh. 'Next time, wait until I say so.'

The waiter comes back as I dab the last serviette against my chin. His puzzled face pitches between River and I, and then upwards, confused. 'Did it rain?'

River scratches his head. 'Apparently.' He scoops up the collection of bloodied serviettes. 'I'll get rid of these.'

'What's got up his arse?' asks the boy, straining to hold back his smile as he watches River leave.

'My first impression would be, a lot,' I answer offhandedly and then wish I hadn't. It must be the shock setting in.

'How's the arm?' asks the boy, watching River continue his search for a bin.

'It's good,' I reply, getting to my feet.

'You can take that towel with you, if you want. They won't miss it,' he says, peering back through the café window at a young woman wrapping knives and forks in paper serviettes.

'Thanks.'

His head tilts to one side, sizing me up with his eyes. 'Do I know you from somewhere?' His voice fades to nothing.

I snigger.

'No, really. Your face is familiar, that's all. What school do you go to?'

'Hudson College.'

He gestures to River with a nod of his head. He seems irritated. 'Is he your boyfriend?'

'No. We're friends.' What a strange question to ask. I wondered if he'd seen us kissing. 'I have to go,' I say, keeping the towel pressed firmly to my arm, 'and thanks again for the towel.' I'm pretty sure my arm wasn't burn at all, but all the same, it seems to be healing much faster than my chin and I don't need anyone who witnessed it to start asking questions.

'No worries,' he smirks. 'See you around.'

154

This time, the bus is full, mainly men in business suits and women with bags of shopping.

'Is there something else you want to tell me?' I whisper, shuffling into the seat beside him.

He checks his surroundings. 'It can wait. How's the arm?'

'It's okay, for the twentieth time.'

He grins. 'Do these kinds of things happen a lot to you?'

What? Ghosts appearing out of nowhere, sending me on a collision course with death …? 'Not until recently,' I say, my smile coming more naturally this time.

Explaining to River that not only did I see the strange man from my dreams again who was, without a doubt, stalking me, but he'd managed to burrow into my head and demand that I challenge him for a second time … and because I hadn't acted on it, he had taken control of my body, causing the accident. It sounds totally preposterous and as much as I know this to be the truth, I can't say it out loud. The next time I see that long-haired freak, I will confront him and demand to know exactly what he wants from me.

'I like it when you smile,' River says, frowning at his loose words.

I take it as a compliment and nothing more. 'Being around you makes me want to smile more,' I tell him.

Mrs Curtis used enough Dettol on my wounds to kill a small dog, but I still love her for it. Mum was just the same It's a haunting reminder of what I miss most in my life. Which brings me back to the worst part of my week, Sunday, the day I return to the Burberrys. I hate leaving Rachel's house to go home to misery and depression and when I push open the front door that afternoon, an eerie silence invites me in.

I screw up my nose at the smell, and creep into the hallway, my old friend, fear, right beside me.

The TV is off and no loud music thumps down the stairs from Celeste's room. The happiness I feel in those few seconds of being alone is ripped away the moment I hear The Creeper's voice.

'Ems, can you come in here. I need to talk to you.'

*'Please don't let him be here alone, please ...'* I beg from behind the kitchen door.

I find him sitting at the dining table dressed in a disgusting short-sleeved lemon shirt and dirty tracksuit bottoms. His head is cradled in his hands. For a blink, it looks serious, and my first thoughts go to Aaron. That is until The Creeper lifts his head and smiles at me with the hungry eyes of a predator. Thoughts of his fingers creeping over my skin shuts down my ability to think straight.

He rises quite nimbly for a man with a tonne of weight to lose and charges at me with all the bravado of a rhino. He begins to say how much he's missed me when his words choke off.

'What happened to your face?' He ventures closer, forcing me into the corner so that my back presses into the sharp edge of the dresser. It digs in, piercing the skin, but I'd rather be impaled than have him another inch nearer. I hold my breath as he traces his plump, girlie-soft finger over my chin. It slides across my skin like an oil slick. 'Who did this? Was it that boy I saw you walking to school with the other day?'

My heart comes to a screeching halt for two whole seconds before pumping frantically beyond its natural capacity. I can't catch my breath. He'd seen me with River? I thought he'd already left for work that morning.

'I fell over,' I say, deliberately evading a discussion about River.

'You're lying.' His stubby fingers disappear into the apples of my cheeks as he squeezes viciously, making my jaw throb worse than any headache. His breath reeks of old fish as his mouth hovers close to my lips. 'And you know what happens to naughty little girls who tell porky pies, don't you?' His spit lands on my lip. Slobbering like a ravenous pig, he crushes his mouth to mine.

My body locks into position.

I don't resist him. Warm liquid dribbles down my chin as the new wound tears open again.

My eyes water.

I taste blood.

I stand strong and wait for him to stop. This time, there is no fear. Only disgust. Whether it's from a single moment of defiance, or leftover courage from yesterday, making its way out of my veins, I'm grateful for it. I breathe it in and it fills me with hope. With fear gone, it paves the way for something new, something stronger. Timid, and a little unsure of what it's capable of, a relatively new emotion arises.

Fury.

I feel it in my teeth every time I clench. I feel it in my hands each time I make a fist and envision it slamming through his face and coming out the back of his head, all bloody and free. I feel it in every follicle of my hair as he yanks it back from my skull. I feel it in my arms as he forces them behind my back just because he can do that. I hear it in the voice inside my head telling me to squash this insect and be done with it. Anger rises, gaining momentum and power, creating unseen images in my mind as The Creeper fills me more and more with his poison.

Fire spawns up from the soles of my feet, through my thighs and chest, and straight into our point of contact - my lips. I want to look down to see if my feet are alight because they feel like they are. With my eyes closed, my body frozen, my lips molested, the rumble of something happening inside me has me suddenly afraid. My body momentarily goes limp before … A release of some kind – fast, jolting, surging, escaping out of me, immediately breaking the contact between us.

The Creeper reels backwards, stopping only when his back strikes the kitchen cupboards on the other side of the room. His eyes are wide and unblinking, his mouth agape. He tentatively reaches up to touch his lips, then baulks when the two meet.

'What is this?' He rubs his mouth vigorously over his sleeve, gawking at me in horror. I stare back, puzzled.

'Have you put chilli on your lips?' he demands as he thrusts a tea towel under the cold tap and pats it gently against his lips.

'What? No. I don't like chilli,' I say, blinking through my confusion. 'You know that.' It's the truth. I don't. It has nothing to do with the hotness; it's the flavour I dislike.

'My mouth is burning. What did you do?'

I go all meek. 'I don't know what you mean.'

His lips are swelling rapidly and small, round blisters forming around his mouth, heavy with pus, are getting bigger by the second. All I can do is stare at him. Black, dead and insane are the only words I can use to describe his eyes.

As though a menacing storm approaches, the panic fades from his eyes and is replaced with something far more formidable.

I'm in trouble, serious trouble.

I've never seen him so angry.

I don't see his hand reach out for me. One minute I am still; the next, my whole body is lifted off the ground as he swings me around by the hair. My cheek slams into the wall.

'You're gonna wish you'd never been born, pulling a stunt like that. You think rubbing chilli on your lips is going to stop me? I haven't even begun to show you what I'm capable of. I need to pull you back into line.'

One of his hands grips the back of my neck while the other fumbles feverishly for the entrance of my jeans.

Fear floods in, swamping the anger.

He kicks my legs out wider. The button of my jeans yields under his groping digits and the sound of my zip buckling under the pressure has me on the brink of tears. His hand goes south. I squeeze my eyes shut.

Then voices clatter up the hallway as the front door bangs shut. The Creeper steps away in time for me to see Aaron's smiling face and Rose Burberry coming in with two bags of shopping.

Saved … saved … I want to kiss Rose Burberry in that moment. I send up a silent pray to whoever seems to be watching out for me.

'What happened to your mouth, Dad?' asks Aaron staring. Rose Burberry isn't the slightest bit inquisitive. I artfully blot my freshly opened wound against my sleeve.

'Nothing, nothing,' he growls and tears out of the room. A few seconds later, I hear the bathroom door slam shut.

'Is everything okay?' asks Rose Burberry as she unpacks the shopping. I wonder if she means with me or with her husband. I choose not to respond, not that she's waiting for an explanation.

A dull light at the back of my mind becomes that much brighter. This new revelation is not a coincidence I tell myself.

This is real.

I have a power, although to what extent, I don't know.

Yes, my body can withstand boiling water and I can heal burns faster than anyone else on the planet, and wood can be reduced to ashes but to go as far as burning others and causing them pain is something entirely new. And if I'm being truthful, exciting. What other mysteries are hidden inside me? What else have I suppressed? The word FlameMaker interrupts my thoughts and the question of 'who am I?' flashes in pink neon letters inside my head.

Only one person can answer that question – Sylvia Banks, the hypnotherapist.

# SIXTEEN

*THE* Creeper stayed away for a week after the lip burning incident. The swelling subsided, and the blisters healed, but he hasn't tried to kiss me again. And that in my world, is something to celebrate.

I am back to being *one* day pure though. The kissing may be over, but he's found other ways to torment me. Last night, I woke to find him standing over me, watching me sleep, talking to himself about all the things we could do if we were alone. The worst part was, he was getting aroused. I tasted bile when I woke.

River hasn't been at school all week either. He briefly mentioned he had some family stuff to deal with, and apart from him joining our fire group instead of the water group in science which he gave no explanation for, not much has happened. I do, however, sense something else is hanging between us.

Now, I find myself in Sylvia Bank's reception area, fiddling with the clasp on my bag.

'Ember, love, would you like to come through,' utters the soft voice of Sylvia Banks. The waiting room is smaller than I remember and smells of antiseptic this time rather than roses. This day hasn't come quick enough. I click the clasp on my bag shut for the final time and loop the strap over my shoulder as I stand.

Sylvia gestures me into a semi-darkened room with soft shell-like lights on the walls. Two comfy chairs sit either side of a heavily draped window.

'Now, Ember, take a seat. Don't look so scared, dear. There is nothing to be afraid of.' *For you … I think.*

Sylvia places a set of earphones over my ears and picks up a microphone from the table beside her chair.

'You will be able to hear everything I say,' she says, pummelling a sandy coloured cushion before sitting back. 'And if you have any questions, I'd prefer it if you left them to the end, please.' Her voice softens and she smiles. 'Okay?'

'Sure,' I reply. I take a fleeting glance around the room, swallow once, cross and uncross my legs twice, kicking my bag over in the process, weave my fingers into a tangled mess and drop them into my lap.

'Relax, Ember,' she says soothingly. 'Everything will be fine.'

I inhale a long breath through my nose and my shoulders sag as I breathe out.

'I'm going to tape the session so you can take it home with you and have a listen for yourself.' I feel myself frowning, and Sylvia's eyes lower and the corners of her mouth slowly lift with some unknown, unseen tranquillity. 'I find that some clients don't necessarily believe the things I tell them they've said, so this way, you can be sure you are hearing it, not only from me but, more importantly from you. Now, is there a problem that is troubling you or maybe an addiction you need help with?'

'Addiction?' I say firmly. 'No. No. It's nothing like that.' Sylvia presses her lips together. 'It was something that happened just over a year ago that I can't …'

'Aaah, trauma then,' says Sylvia knowingly. 'Does it involve you or someone else?'

'Both. I was in a car crash with my parents.' A lump erupts in my throat, as I knew it would. 'They didn't survive.'

Sylvia's face drips in sympathy. 'I'm sorry to hear that, dear, I really am. So, you're wanting some closure then?' she asks.

I don't say anything. It's not closure I'm after. It's answers. I've accepted my parents' death, but I can't ask the question I want to.

Sylvia senses my apprehension. 'We'll see what comes then. Okay?'

I nod.

"Now I want you to relax," are the last words I remember hearing before Sylvia removes the headphones.

'How do you feel, dear?' she asks, stepping back to give me some space.

'It's *over*?' My eyebrows draw together. A mysterious cloud fills my head, telling me I've been here an hour and have no recollection of it.

Sylvia smiles warmly at me. I have to admit, I do feel great, like I've had the best sleep of my whole life.

'How did everything go?' I ask.

Sylvia Banks tugs on her lip before answering. Keeping her hand over mine as she speaks, she hands me a disc. 'Go home and listen to it. You may find things you can relate to, and there will be others that frankly make no sense at all. A few … umm… *issues* did come up, dear, that … might need another couple of sessions to work through.' This is the first time I see her frown.

My heart flutters in my chest. 'What kind of issues?'

Sylvia's frown dissipates and her practiced clinic face reappears. 'Listen to the disc, Ember, and if you want, you can call to discuss anything you don't understand. Then we can work out if you'll need another appointment. My number is on the back.'

I have no intention of going back to the Burberrys' to listen to it. I own a CD player from way back, but my headphones are probably in the same place as my comb. No, I'm going to the library where I can listen to it in peace.

The icy breath that now resides down the neck of my shirt and treads on the heels of my shoes as I turn left on to Cedar Crescent is as present as ever. 'Becoming accustomed to it' is one of the weirdest thoughts that has ever entered my head. I hurry along the street, on full alert for my spooky stalker, ready at a second's notice to test my martial arts on him. It's of no great comfort that I only took four lesson at the local hall for karate.

The library is on the opposite corner to the bingo hall and although the building was only renovated last year, chairs remain empty and the hum of silence inside has nothing to do with the "Please Be Quiet" signs on the walls. I push the glass door open, overpowering my sense of smell with a million, musty pieces of paper.

Tucked away behind the section on religion, I locate the computers.

'Can I help you?' asks a young lady from behind a wooden counter. Stacks of books, piled high, block my view of her body.

'I'm here to use the computers,' I say casually, trying to see around them.

'One moment, please,' she says politely and scoots half the books to one side and then half the other, leaving two bookends towering protectively around her. I can now see her pale blue blouse, with a frill on the collar and a black name tag which says Melinda Garson, Head Librarian, on it.

'You said you wanted to use the computers. It's two pounds fifty for the internet for twenty minutes ...'

'I don't need the internet,' I interrupt, producing the disc and waving it in the air.

The woman smiles. 'Okay. Then it's three pounds for an hour.'

I hand over the money and head to the first available computer. I sit down and place the headphones over my ears. Lastly, I load the disc and wait.

'Now Ember, I want you to relax,' I hear Sylvia say. 'I want you to listen to my voice. I want you to close your eyes and breathe deeply, filling your lungs and then slowly releasing it.' Sylvia's voice is as relaxing as I remember and sitting here listening to her is as hypnotic as being in her clinic. Several times I have to shrug off sleepiness that threatens to take me under.

'Do you feel relaxed?' asks Sylvia.

'Yes.' I hear myself let out a long, slow breath.

It doesn't sound like me, but I know it is. Rachel and I used to tape ourselves when we were younger, and we would laugh at how strange we sounded.

'Okay,' says Sylvia in her melodic tone. 'I want to take you back to the day your parents died. Is that all right with you?'

'Yes,' I murmur again. I find myself mouthing the word 'yes' as I listen to her.

There's a brief pause.

'Can you tell me where you are?'

'I'm sitting down to breakfast. Mum is making pancakes, but I don't want to eat them.' My lips turn upwards at the memory.

'Why not?' asks Sylvia. I can hear a hint of a smile in her voice.

'I want to go to Rachel's, but Mum says I have to go to Uncle Reggie's house because he's sick.' I force down the urge to laugh as I listen. The words bear all the tone and defiance of a cranky fifteen-year-old.

There is more silence.

'Now what's happening, Ember?'

'We're in the car, going to Uncle Reggie's' says fifteen-year-old me. 'Mum's trying to cheer me up with a stupid game but it's not working. I still want to go to Rachel's house.'

Another pause, much longer this time. I press the earphones firmly against my ears.

'What's wrong, Ember?' asks Sylvia. 'Why are you frowning?'

'Somebody else is in the car with us,' I hear myself say.

My heart jerks fiercely.

Exploding.

Gathering speed.

I've never recalled another person in the car. Icy fingers tickle the back of my neck and fan out across my back and down my arms, spreading a blanket of goose bumps across my skin. What the hell!

'Who's in the car, Ember? A hitchhiker? Has your father pulled over and given someone a lift?'

'No,' comes my reply. 'He appeared out of thin air. He's sitting on the seat next to me.'

'No!' I cry out, wrenching the headphones off. A pulse throbs in my ears and cheeks as though the truth is trying to hammer its way into my head, or is that, out of my head. I stare at the blank screen, watching the reflection of me dragging my hands through my hair. The horror I see on my face is too much to look at. It can't be … it just can't be.

The librarian peers over the mountain of books, her eyes cautious and her hand resting on the telephone. 'Are you all right?'

I nod, but I'm not all right. *I might be going into shock?* Sweat gathers at my armpits and I keep trying to breathe in faster and faster but it doesn't feel like any air is getting in. The world spins one way and then the other, my whole body breaking out of its natural rhythm into this uncontrollable mess. I can't believe what I'm hearing … a fourth person in the car. Why would I say that if it didn't really happen? Why would I have deliberately blocked that out? Unless the memory was purposely erased by someone else. Surely, I would have remembered? It was only a year ago.

One of my hands grips the edge of the desk while the other remains flat against my chest. My breakfast shifts. The melamine coating on the desk starts to yield under my fingers, turning it to play doh. A lump comes off in my hand and I stare at it, wondering what the hell to do with it. I press it back into the desk, re-moulding it as best I can with fumbling fingers and too much speed.

'Are you sure?' repeats the woman.

I can't move.

*Did she see me?*

More beads of sweat gather on my forehead and I brush them back into my skin with the back of my hand. *Get a grip, Em. You can do this.* I reposition the headphones. My finger hovers above the key before I push play.

'He is sitting on the seat next to me,' I say for a second time.

'Are you frightened?' asks Sylvia. I can hear her concern. 'Has he hurt you?'

'No. He's smiling at me.'

Stillness filters into the earpiece until Sylvia clears her throat. 'Do you know him? Have you ever seen him before?

'I think I had a dream about him once but I'm not sure,' I say. I sound hazy.

More erratic heartbeats throb against my ribcage.

'I see,' says Sylvia. I wish I could've seen the expression on her face so I could gauge her reaction. 'What does he look like?'

Fifteen-year-old me speaks again. 'He has long grey hair, longer than mine and his face is white like snow.' Hearing this isn't as much of a shock as I thought it would be; some part of me already knew it was going to be him.

'Is he saying anything to you? Can your parents see him?

'No, they can't, but he is talking to me.'

Sylvia's voice raises a few decibels. 'What is he saying, Ember?'

'He is saying he will come for me soon and that when the four Elementars rise, the forces of nature will become one and he will reign over the earth.'

'Who is he?' asks Sylvia.

My ears pound against the silence as I zone in with concentration.

'He says his name is Ra-Mon.'

I hear the sound of rustling paper and a bird chirping, probably from outside Sylvia Banks' window.

'What else is he saying?'

'He says water seeks out fire, air seeks out water, and earth seeks out air. It is the order of evolution.'

'Do you know what he means, Ember?'

'No.' My lips trace the word even before the *me* on the disc has spoken.

I gasp and cover my mouth as the piercing scream of a child, of fifteen-year-old me, reverberates through the headphones. My heart picks up its tumultuous pace again and simply breathing through my nose isn't enough. I open my mouth to take in more oxygen, consciously aware I'm on the brink of passing out.

Sylvia sounds panicked too. 'What's happening now, Ember?'

'A petrol tanker is heading for us. It won't stop. It's going to hit us.'

Another scream sounds on the disc and then silence.

'Ember …?' says Sylvia softly.

Heartfelt whimpers cross the boundary between unconsciousness and consciousness.

'The car is on fire. My mum and dad are screaming and can't get out. The flames are all around us. We're trapped. We're going to die.'

Tears hurry down my cheeks and I fall apart as bouts of uncontrollable sobs rack my body. 'I don't understand why it's not hurting me. My skin isn't black and burning like theirs is and the seat I'm on has burnt right through to the metal. Why am I not catching on fire?' My heart is stabbed over and over, torn to shreds, ripped to pieces, burnt and incinerated and trodden into the ground like it has never beaten before. Like it is worth nothing. Been part of no one.

I squeeze my eyes shut, reliving each second, each horrifying, gut-wrenching second. Tears soak my lashes.

'Please help me – I don't know what to do. I need water. Lots of water. Please find some water to help me put out the fire. Please let it rain and save us. Please God, make it rain. Make it rain. There's fire everywhere, all around the car, around my mum. Water ...pleeease. She's reaching her hand out for me, but her seatbelt is on and she can't get any closer. Help me! Mummmmm! What should I do? I don't know what to do.'

I now understand where this deep hatred of water has come from. It wasn't there when I asked for it. It didn't save my parents.

Sylvia interrupts, calming and soothing. 'It's okay, Ember. Relax. Feel your breath filling your lungs and calming you. You're safe.'

I hear myself taking deep breaths as the bird in the background continues to twitter.

'Better?' asks Sylvia.

'No. My parents are dead.'

My throat constricts and pain resonates from every molecule in my body as I listen to myself crying. It's a sound nobody should ever have to listen to.

'What's going on now, Ember? Is the man still with you?' asks Sylvia.

'No. He's gone. The door is open, and I am walking to the side of the road. I can hear a siren.'

'What can you see?'

'Nothing … except wait … A beautiful woman is coming towards me,' I say. The sheer amazement in my voice stuns me. 'She's a rainbow of fire, all different shades of reds and yellows and oranges. She is putting her arm around my shoulder and telling me everything is going to be alright. Her name is Nuria.'

The quietness continues, and I know that I've come to the end of my session.

I remove the headphones and stare blindly into the black screen. It doesn't sound real but there's no reason I would make that up, to be honest I'm not that creative, and it makes perfect sense to me.

FlameMaker, I wonder …

# SEVENTEEN

*THE* next few days have me testing everything that's hot and anything that causes a spark. I'm not sure why at the toboggan park my arm looked burnt one minute and not the next. Perhaps it was a different kind of injury or because it was caused by supernatural force because now every time I pour a whole kettle of boiling water over my hands or strike matches over my skin, or even extinguish the gas ring on the stove by cupping my hands over it, it makes no marks on my flesh at all. I come to one conclusion … my skin is fireproof, resistant to flame and totally unaffected by heat. But Ra-Mon called me Flame-Maker, which must mean I should be able to create fire. Except I have no idea how to do that.

Ra-Mon, if that's his real name, hasn't appeared since the tobogganing accident, much to my horror and delight. I want to ask him how to conjure flames, who or what the four Elementars are, and the forces of nature becoming one, not only sounds dangerous but detrimental to the planet. I try to follow the advice I had given freely to River

– whatever is coming, worrying about it won't make it happen any faster.

*Easier said than done.*


'Settle down, settle down,' calls out Mr Butcher. 'I said, get into your designated groups … quietly.' The scraping of chairs and muttering of voices softens as we descend into the four corners of the science classroom. 'Every group will have twenty minutes to use the computers and then I'll come around and assess your findings.'

'Come and sit next to me, River,' purrs Cherie, sticking her chest out as she pats the chair beside her. 'I'm so glad you got moved to our group. Now we can hang out like we did before.'

River bites his lip as he throws his bag on to the table. 'I'm good here thanks, Cherie,' he says, pulling out the chair and sitting down next to me. 'But thanks anyway.' Cherie makes a funny giggling sound at the back of her throat. He shoots me a look which says 'help'. So, I sarcastically preen my hair and flutter my lashes at him.

'You're incorrigible,' he mutters under his breath.

'And then some,' I answer.

The earth group flocks to the computer and students start pulling out their phones to google stuff, including Cherie, although I don't know what Adele's latest song has to do with fire.

Mr Butcher approaches, his body casting a mighty shadow over us, his eyes coming to rest on me.

'We're having a little difficulty, sir, with who does which topic,' I say. 'Could you offer some suggestions?' River's gaze switches straight to Cherie. She winks seductively at him.

'Who's the eldest?' asks Mr Butcher.

'I was born in December, the tenth to be precise,' offers Cherie. 'I'm a hot-blooded Sagittarian and you know what that means.'

171

Mr Butcher throws her a look that borders on confusion and disbelief.

'Yes … well. Simone Kennedy, when were you born?'

'September the fourth, sir.'

'That counts you out,' says Mr Butcher moving on to Dante Fisk. 'And you?

'Nineteenth of October.'

'Way off. What about you, Mr Jenkins?'

'November,' he mumbles.

'That leaves only you two,' says Mr Butcher wearily.

River speaks before I can open my mouth. 'That's too bad because our birthdays are on the same day in August, sir.' A curious twitch begins in Mr Butchers left eyebrow.

'Is this correct, Miss Riley?'

I sigh and nod, still unable to believe it myself.

'Well, surely you couldn't have been born at the same time.' Mr Butcher's brow has grown heavy and if I didn't know any differently, I would say he looked to be holding his breath. 'What time were you born?' he asks to nobody in particular.

'Eleven minutes past eleven,' we both say in unison. We swing around and stare at each other in total shock.

'You were born at eleven minutes past eleven,' I gasp. 'Are you joking?'

'No, I'm not joking,' says River indignantly. 'Why would I joke about something like that?'

'Why would anyone joke about something like that,' injects Mr Butcher. The thick grooved lines on his brow smooth out and he shrugs his massive shoulders.

'So, Ember,' he says, moving right along. 'Since we can't decide who the eldest is, I will designate the first two tasks. Yours is to locate the history behind the four elements.'

'The history?' I groan, craning my neck to find his face. 'I thought this was science.'

'It is, it is, but history and science fit together like bricks and mortar. There cannot be one without the other.

I'm a bit of a historian, myself,' he says proudly. 'Philosophers and historians have their own views on where and how the four elements were created and the influences they have on the world, Miss Riley. I suggest you start there.' I let out another noisy breath. 'And you, Mr Fulton, can break down the different capabilities of fire.'

River has a less than enthralled expression on his face than I do, and Cherie comes to his rescue without hesitation.

'Doesn't fire just burn,' she says defiantly, slipping him another sly wink. 'I've got your back,' I hear her whisper. 'I reckon you should come and sit next to me. He'll only end up picking on you more if you're next to Ember Riley. She has the worst reputation, you know?'

Heat billows up from my feet, fuelling my fury. Immediately, I withdraw my hands from the table. I don't want to touch a table or a pencil case zip or anything, but the chair I'm sitting is getting hotter and hotter beneath me. I stand, hoping not to damage it further. 'How dare you ...' I say explosively. The chair kicks out behind me, the legs getting tangled around River's chair.

Cherie shrugs and her mouth and eyebrows copy. 'You're delusional if you think you'll ever have a chance with him. He's way too good for you.'

Red covers my vision. 'I'm gonna scratch out your beady little eyes?' I growl, totally upending the chair this time. River catches it before it falls. I press my palms into the table and lean across to face off with Cherie.

Heat smoulders up my legs, driving through my body with all the force of a fully loaded rocket. It builds in momentum, second after second, owning me and taking over, filling me with an energy that rivals any tactical force. Images of breathing fire over Cherie, charring her body to resemble something you might find in the bottom of a fireplace, makes me smile. I can almost taste the crunchy black ash against my tongue. That is, until I sniff. A fumy, plastic smell wafts upward from my hands.

I don't dare check because I know what I'll find.

'Everything all right down there?' calls Mr Butcher from across the classroom. He raises his chin at me.

As swiftly as the fire inside starts, it stops. I discreetly slide my books over the baked-on handprint that will remain on the table forever and draw the chair up and sit down before anyone notices.

But I think River did notice. He'd glanced at the warped seat, the legs slightly buckled, and can't seem to draw his gaze from my "molten lava" eyes. He doesn't say anything, although his face has all kinds of questions over it.

'Em, are you okay?' he mumbles, 'it's only Cherie.' My body tingles from the best sugar-rush like feeling I've ever had.

'Yeah, just a bit tired,' I say, rubbing my hand over my forehead.

River frowns, his head turning left and right, before reaching over and lightly dusts his hand over my forehead. A chalky grey residue coats his fingers.

Alarm bells ring out in my head and I hastily drag my sleeve over the last of the evidence.

'The computer's free,' calls out Shianne Powell. 'Why don't you use it first, Ember?'

'Thanks,' I say, grateful to be out of Cherie's line of sight and off River's radar.

I make my way over to the computer, with River close behind, aware of her death stares corkscrewing through my back.

I sit down as River hesitantly drags a chair closer. I type in, 'history of the four elements' and up comes a page full of sites. I click on the first one and read it aloud.

*The invention of the four-element theory of matter (earth, air, fire, and water) is credited to*

*Empedocles (of Acagras in Sicily) 492-432 BC,
who was a philosopher and poet. He was
regarded as a materialist physicist, a shamanic
magician, a mystical theologian, a healer, a
democratic politician, a living god, and a fraud.*
He doesn't sound as boring as I thought he would.
*Empedocles' philosophy was that the world was
in a cosmic cycle of eternal change in which two
cosmic forces, Love and Strife, engaged in an
eternal battle for power. He believed in the
travelling of souls and claimed to be a divine
being who was banished from the immortal
gods. He was forced to suffer many
reincarnations through the different orders of
nature and elements until he achieved the
perfect human state and was reborn as an
immortal. It was believed that he possessed
magical powers including the ability to bring
back the dead.*

*His death is reported to have occurred in
several ways: that he fell overboard from a ship
and drowned; that he fell from his carriage,
broke his leg and died; that he hanged himself;
or the most famous account was that, when he
felt he was shortly to die, he leapt into the crater
of Etna. In this story, the hoax was unfortunately
discovered when one of his bronze sandals was
regurgitated by the volcano.*

I glance down at the next few sites.
'No way.'
My breath catches first, almost choking me. My mind
is overflowing in thoughts and I can't think, and my brain
is working too fast for me, and words want to tumble out
of my mouth, but I can't remember what a word is or how
to say it, how to pronounce it. Second, my body locks into
position, almost paralysing me. And my arms and legs

have become timber posts, and I can't feel the seat I'm sitting on, and my chest is squashed and useless and I'm a jumbled mess of words and actions. And I think I want to laugh and cry and faint all at the same time.

The word on my tongue I can't say.

The word that I read is "Elementars".

Ra-Mon had used that word – 'when the four Elementars rise, the forces of nature will become one and he will reign over the earth.' Hesitantly, I click on the site and begin to read.

> *The Four Elementars are separated into fire, air, water and earth. They can replenish themselves by absorbing more of their own element if needed: For example, the Water Elementar may enhance his powers by absorbing water from a lake or by walking through rain.*

River coughs.

I turn to him.

'Sorry,' he says, 'carry on.'

> *The Fire Elementar is flame resistant, can withstand extreme heat, can command fire and manipulate flame. Elementars cannot reproduce with humans as they are magical beings. However, the saying goes that during the War of the Chosen, Elementars were able to join with other Elementars, doubling their size and power. None can say if the creation of Elementars actually happened. And most knowledge has fallen into myth, but the saying goes, if several Elementars were produced at the same time, the consequences could be catastrophic.*

The mouse crashing to the floor has everyone staring in my direction. The possibility of fainting is now a reality. My vision distorts, sloping sideways and diagonal, sending me in and out of blackness. And air has abandoned me, just like water did, emptying my lungs until I am a brittle shell, waiting to be recycled.

I can't believe what I am reading.

Logic tells me it can't be real.

It can't be true.

Because if it's true, I am not nuts, not crazy, not weird.

'Do we have a problem over there, Miss Riley?' says Mr Butcher.

I still can't speak. Air sneaks in, I don't know how, it just does. And I am floaty and not in my body, but somewhere else where fire doesn't exist, and reading doesn't matter and answering a question has run off to some far away world where it can't be pestered.

My thoughts are still stuck on the 'Fire Elementar is fire resistant, can withstand extreme heat, can command fire and manipulate flame'.

'I-I'm a …I'm a …' I babble incoherently.

'Miss Riley,' yells out Mr Butcher for a second time. 'Is. There. A. Problem?'

I swing my chair around, the brush of cool air on my face still not tempting the words from my mouth.

'She's fine, sir,' River answers on my behalf. 'I accidently knocked the mouse off the table,' he lies.

'Well, hurry along then. You only have five minutes left. The next group want to get on there.'

I slowly turn my chair back to face the desk. I can no longer see the words on the screen, no longer hear the hum of the computer. My mind is scrambling for understanding and reasons, for truth and fact. But what other explanation is there. I can do things the average human being can't.

It all makes sense.

I have the same traits as the Fire Elementar.

I have been reincarnated.

The rest of the day passes in a blur of fiery images. Certain aspects of this new revelation comfort me and help confirm the ambiguous questions that have bothered me into fits of wakefulness. Dots have been joined and parts of the puzzle solved, and yet instead of easing my mind, I've been given permission to peek inside a whole new bag of questions.

Who are the other three Elementars?

Will they seek me out?

The text said Water will seek out Fire.

Is Ra-Mon good or bad?

And regardless of which side he's on … when will he come for me?

Days go by without me saying more than a handful of words to anyone.

# EIGHTEEN

'*HAVE* you got your period?' barks Rachel.

'Excuse me?' I'm off on another mental excursion.

Rachel tuts, the same way Mum used to when she pressed me for information.

'What's going on with you, Em? First you say you're feeling a bit vague, *then* you say you have a lot on your mind and now you're not even listening to me. If you want a new best friend, all you have to do is say so … don't string me along until I get sick of the silent treatment.'

Confusion sets in. 'What are you *talking* about? No, I don't want a new best friend … and *what* silent treatment?'

Rachel raises her eyebrows at me and says nothing.

'Forget it,' I snap. I'm no angrier at Rachel than I am at River, who asked me the same thing only yesterday, *twice*. How could I go to either of them with …? *I am the element of fire and I think something dreadful is going to happen soon*? Sure, Rachel would be my first choice to confide in, but she doesn't do *weird things* well. Her visit with Ra-mon a classic example.

179

River at least has an inkling about my psychic side, although getting him alone for more than five minutes has been hard. He's always the first one up after our science lesson and gone before I can follow him outside. And he must play sport at lunchtimes because his hair is always wet from the showers. One thing is sure, I have to tell someone before I explode. It's too much for me to handle alone. Maybe if I can tell River how my skin reacts to fire, rather than show him like I would Rachel then perhaps he'll believe the rest of what I have to say.

'Does that mean you're coming on Saturday night?' asks Rachel a little softer this time. I am guilty of not listening for a second time and, after defending myself, how can I admit to missing what she'd said?

'I said I would, didn't I?'

I have no idea what I've signed myself up for now.

Walking home that afternoon, I realise what Rachel was talking about – Bonfire Party. Two boys, no older than ten, are outside the corner shop with a stuffed Guy Fawkes in a wheelbarrow and a large cardboard sign.

'Penny for the Guy?' Two pairs of grubby hands hover around my knees.

I smile apologetically. 'Sorry, boys. I don't have any money on me.'

I only hope this party isn't taking place at her house. Her father, who'd travelled all the way from Glasgow last year, almost burnt down her backyard and the fire brigade had to be called. I'm holding out for the traditional firework party at the canal, which is where we normally go.

'Penny for your thoughts?' says a voice in my ear. River smiles in between catching his breath, and his blue eyes gleam at me as though they're made for me, and only me.

'Where does the colour come from?' I say in a slow dreamy voice.

His comical frown casts shadows over his eyes, releasing me from their bind. 'Where does what colour come from?'

Realising that I'd voiced my thoughts aloud, I have no alternative but to follow through with my question. 'Your eyes? What side of the family do they come from?'

River lets out a surprised laugh. 'Neither, would you believe? Both my parents had brown eyes and so did their parents. It was a standard joke in our house that there'd been some kind of mix-up at the hospital and I'd gone home with the wrong parents.' A moment of sadness creeps over his eyes and then vanishes. He recovers his smile. 'What about you? Where do eyes of molten lava descend from?' He chuckles and I smile with him. He seems to read my mind. 'You don't laugh much, do you?' There is concern and genuine care in his voice.

'Haven't found much to laugh about recently.'

River's eyes darken and his brow is heavy. 'What happened to you, Em? People I've spoken to say you were always happy and now ...' He hesitates for a second. 'Parents die all the time, and yes it's hard to forget them, but you also have a life.'

'It's not *just* them,' I say vaguely.

River's brow lifts with curiosity. 'Then what?'

I opt for the diluted version. 'My home life sucks.'

River hums under his breath.

No other words are needed to get my point across, adding finality to the subject.

A few awkward moments pass. 'My mum had blue eyes and my dad, green,' I offer, shrugging.

'We are the oddest couple, aren't we?'

I throw him a quizzical look and his eyes widen.

'I didn't mean couple as in *couple*.'

My lips spread further until the beginning of a laugh pops out. It's fun to see him squirm for once.

Saturday, Guy Fawkes Day, comes around all too soon and another gloomy, overcast morning slides through my curtains reminding me that summer is still a long way off. The Creeper is in Bristol for work, and I snuggle down beneath my sheets, contemplating what kind of a day it might be. It is already looking good.

Some of what River said the other day has started me thinking. Yes, I have a shit family life. Yes, The Creeper makes my life hell. Yes, I am a phenomenal fire freak with unique powers, but the rest of my life is *semi*-normal. Why can't I live like other teenagers do and let my hair down? I'm ready for some festivity. I deserve some fun.

My bedroom door flies open and Celeste barges in.

'Where have you put it, you little cow?' she snarls. She reefs open the middle drawer of my dresser, turfing my clothes onto the floor. My little bubble of pleasure pops instantly.

'What have I supposed to have taken *now*?' I mutter, rolling onto my tummy and pulling the covers closer to my ears.

'Get out of bed, you fucking bitch and find it. I know you've got it.'

I ignore her … something I've never done before. Even though I know it won't make her leave, there is a certain amount of satisfaction to it.

In one swift action, Celeste throws off my covers and jumps on top of me, trapping my arms by my sides like worthless flippers.

'Get off me,' I yell, but my muffled pleas dissolve into the bed as Celeste pushes my head further into the mattress.

'I hate you. I hate you,' she continues, basket-balling my head into the pillow until my vision blurs. 'I've always fucking hated you. Nobody wants you here, Ember Riley. Even my mum hates you. And don't even think about trying to talk your way into my dad's good books, because it won't work. He hates you too. You've ruined our family with your bad moods.'

'Me?' I moan into the sheets. I wince as Celeste's nails gouge into my cheek, my face pressing further and further into the bed. Another realm, a dizzy one, climbs further into my skull. 'I can't breathe,' I yell out, pins and needles rippling over my body as a lack of oxygen starts to take hold.

The door slams shut, and Celeste jumps up, giving me a clear view of The Creeper. I gasp down several breaths to find him standing in the doorway, wearing his usual striped pyjama bottoms and no singlet. His hair is sticking up on one side.

'What in blazes hell is going on in here?' he yells.

'Oh, Daddy, you're home. I didn't think you were going to be back until tonight.'

The Creeper isn't listening to his daughter. 'I said, what the hell is going on in here?'

'She stole my new shirt. The one you bought me, Daddy,' Celeste says, turning on the sad, sweet eyes for her father.

*His* eyes tell me he's ready for violence, but his voice is composed. 'Give it back, Ems. We don't steal in this house. If you need a new shirt, all you have to do is ask for it.'

I try to sit up but he's right next to the bed. He turns to his daughter, giving me the chance to take in a fresh breath. He stinks of bed sweat and dirty ashtrays. 'Go on, honey,' he says soothingly, 'I'll deal with this.'

Painstakingly slowly, Celeste closes the door behind her. The cruel smile on her face has me praying she'll never be able to conceive children of her own.

He waits until the door is fully closed before pointing his finger right into my face. 'You know what happens to thieves in this house, don't you?'

I have a fair idea ... the same thing that happens if you lie, come home late or if you do nothing at all.

At first, I think I'm safe.

He heads for the door and half a breath makes it out of my lungs until he drags my heavy chest of drawers across the floor, blocking any access in or out.

Panic sets in.

I hear a scream somewhere in the back of my mind, somewhere in the darkest recesses when no light touches, where love is a stranger and happiness has never felt at home. A silent scream that doesn't have the courage to show itself.

'You have forgotten your place recently. Is there anything you want to tell me?'

I shake my head. 'No,' I murmur.

His top teeth tease at his bottom lip, rolling and rolling it. 'Something has changed. You're not my little Ems anymore. Have you found someone to replace me?'

My thoughts go to River.

I say nothing because I can't say the words he wants to hear.

'Then maybe I need to jog your memory,' he says, sauntering towards me like a dog on heat.

'Don't touch me,' I warn assertively.

The words are out.

Words I've wanted to say forever ARE. FINALLY. OUT.

I want to say more and tell him what I really think of him, and how he has made my life come apart and utterly useless and not worth living, and that I've thought more of dying in the last twelve months than I have about the small things in life that make you smile, and bring you joy and peace, and that it's all his fault, and he should pay for his crimes and be miserable for the rest of his days for all that he has done to me.

His eyes change into black, lifeless discs that seem to suck the life right out of me. 'Don't threaten me, little darlin', or you'll never live to see tomorrow.'

My dear old friend returns.

FEAR.

It returns with its suffocating hold around my throat, blocking any air in or out. He leans towards the door, hearing a sound on the landing, and I slip out of bed and back up until I feel the window behind me.

'I can make it look like an accident or perhaps a suicide.' He gestures to the window. 'I deal with this shit every day. Another little wayward girlie won't make much of a ripple in the system.'

Something is different.

I'm waiting for his usual moves - his mouth crushing against mine, spit finding is way around my mouth, his pudgy, stinking fingers defiling my skin, that once touched, I can't bear to live inside it, and I want to peel it from my bones and scrub it with bleach and soap before I feel clean again, and then hang it in the sun so any trace of him has been scorched away.

So, when the swinging arm that comes out of nowhere, smashing me into the wall, rattling my brain inside my skull until my body slides down into a heap, it takes me completely by surprise. My head hits the corner of the bedside table on the way down and darkness falls over me.

When I wake, the chest of drawers is back in its usual spot. Blood has dried on my cheek, from Celeste's tantrum, while my temple has that fresh, salty smell of rust to it. My pyjama top is ripped open, exposing my breasts. I can't begin to think what happened whilst I was unconscious.

I won't let myself go there. I can't.

I tentatively push up into a sitting position, ignoring the pain in my head and sit there for a few minutes, gathering what little strength I have. I pack my weekend bag.

I need to leave now.

If it wasn't for Aaron, I would never come back. There's no point in taking him with me. I have no legal right over him and with the way The Creeper works; it would take less than twenty-four hours to get a court order advising me to surrender him. It isn't worth putting the little chap through it, despite what I feel is right, plus it's obvious he adores his father. What excuse could I give him that won't leave *me* looking like the monster?

Rachel throws her arms around my neck the minute she opens the front door.

'I'm gonna kill him,' she screams between clenched teeth. 'I'm gonna fucking kill him.' I've no doubt, if she could get her hands on a gun, she would follow through with her threat without thinking twice about it.

'Rach ... please. I just want a shower and a cup of tea.' I put a hand on her arm, staring into the face of helplessness. Tears stain her cheeks. She acknowledges me with a forced nod.

I peek around the bannister of the staircase and into the kitchen. 'Tell your mum it was another tobogganing accident,' I whisper as she shuts the front door.

'She's gone shopping,' says Rachel flatly, tilting her head to get a better look at my temple. She sucks a breath in through her teeth. 'You have to leave, honey. Before he kills you.'

Rachel's words sear into the back of my head as I trudge upstairs and into her bedroom. I drop my bag down and gingerly sit on her bed. 'I can't. What about Aaron?'

'Fuck Aaron! What about you?'

'I can't Rach, I just can't. If anything happened to him, I'd never be able to forgive myself.'

'Report it to the police then. They have to follow up a charge as serious as assault.'

'I've thought about that too, but it won't work. He's a lawyer. He'll know how to get out of it and then when he gets off, it'll all fall back on Aaron ... or me, and to be honest I don't have the strength for that. You don't know what he's like. You don't know how low he would go to *have* me.'

'Em, please ... you need to ...'

A flicker of heat ignites. '*Don't* tell me what I need to do, Rach ... *please*. I've made my decision. Now, can I use your shower or not?'

Nothing more is said on the matter.

'Is Cole going to the bonfire party tonight?' I ask, submerging beneath my second bubble bath for the day. Rachel mum's corner tub is the best part of her house. Rachel sits on the toilet with two slices of carrot cake in her lap, feeding me between questions.

'Cole sch-mole,' she says irritably. I raise my eyebrows. 'He's the biggest wanker, ever.'

A smile lingers at the corner of my lips. 'Since when?'

'Since he told me he wanted to see other people as well.'

I blow into the foamy bubbles. 'What did you tell him?' I ask, amused.

'I told him to go fuck himself.'

'And has he?'

Rachel sniggers. 'No such luck.'

'So, we're in for an interesting evening then?'

Rachel hums something under her breath. 'You should be okay, though, with River being there.'

I have to admit, he's been my sole focus today. Waiting to see his face tonight, watching the corners of his eyes crinkle now that he's found his smile, the way his hand grazes over his chin when he finds something funny in what I've said, lapping up each glorious second and minute with him, waiting for him to *maybe* want to kiss me again, and whisper that he wants me to be true to him and just him. It's what got me through today as I raced up the road, bag slung over my shoulder, praying that The Creeper wasn't behind me, ready to barrel me into his car, roll me in some dirty Persian rug and throw me in the canal.

I'm ready. In jumper, boots and jeans, I'm ready for Guy Fawkes Night.

# NINETEEN

AIR, cold enough to be snow, uses zero effort to penetrate my jacket and scarf. Shadows of night surrounds us as we turn onto an un-made road. Thankfully, orange lanterns on stilts guide us in, leading us to a bonfire that unashamedly sets the sky alight with its brilliance, boasting her supremacy to the remnants of a stuffed guy on top. Huddles of dark human forms can be made out where lanterns intermittently chase away the blackness. The aromas of jacket potatoes and hearty oxtail soup hangs heavily in the air competing with the charcoal taste of wood smoke.

'It's only six o'clock. Should we be drinking this early? Do you feel like a cider or mulled wine? I'm getting a cider?' says Rachel.

'I hate mulled wine,' I say, taking hold of her arm. Well, I think I do. I definitely don't like the smell. 'What's with you? I've never seen you like this before.'

'Oh God, there's Cole,' says Rachel. 'Shit and he's seen me. Shit. He's coming over.' She takes off in the opposite direction, leaving me alone.

'Would you like a drink?' asks River, startling me. He offers me a plastic cup.

I sniff. 'What is it first?'

'Cider.'

I peer into the darkness, seeing others walking around with cups.

'Did you buy it here?' I ask incredulously.

'Yeah, why?' He seems confused.

'You're not eighteen, that's why.'

'When has that ever stopped anyone from buying alcohol.' He laughs. 'Anyway, who the hell can see us?'

I relax and bring the cup to my lips. The sharp yet sweet taste makes the insides of my cheeks tingle.

'Looks like your friend's busy,' says River, staring over my shoulder. In the romantic glow of the firelight, it's not difficult to see Rachel and Cole facing off. 'You wanna walk around for a bit, to keep warm?'

'Yeah, why not? I wouldn't wanna be in Cole's shoes anytime soon.'

'Let's go sit over there,' says River, pointing to a couple of large tree stumps placed closer to the fire than the rest.

We sit, awkwardness settling in right beside us. I place the cup between my knees and hold my hands out against the warmth.

River mimics my actions.

This is the perfect time to bring up my own fire issues. 'Can I ask you a question?'

River turns to me. 'I knew something was bothering you. What is it? Does it have anything to do with what we were talking about at the grass skiing place?'

I suppress a shy smile, picking the cup up and twisting it in my hands. 'Sometimes I think you can read my mind.'

River disregards my response and carries on with his own line of questioning. 'So, is it?' he persists.

'Kind of.'

River shuffles close enough I could lean my head on his shoulder, if I was game. I may need to, after this confession.

'A lot of things have happened to me in the last few months. Things that defy logic and stuff that's … well … too hard to talk about.' I roll up my sleeve and dangle my arm in front of him, exposing the area that had been burnt at Greenacres.

River frowns at first, and then realisation opens his eyes wider. Checking in with me first with his eyes, he trails his fingers over the area that should still be healing or at least have some sign of scarring. A loud crack echoes around us, just like when he'd touched me during country dancing, and at the grass skiing, and his fingers leap off my skin.

'Sorry, sorry,' calls out a male voice. 'I had to let one firework off as a test run.' A guy wearing a high visibility shirt comes running towards us. 'Didn't frighten you too much, did I?' My eyes follow him to a van, where he loads up a few more boxes.

River's eyes return to my arm. There is nothing but two moles, pale skin and the residual feeling of having warm chocolate drizzled on my arm. 'I don't understand. I saw it. There was a carpet burn the size of my hand. I saw it.'

'It had healed before we'd even got on the bus,' I say gravely.

'But your lip,' he says. 'That took at least a week to heal.'

His eyes devour every inch of my face, lingering mostly on my lips. I feel deliriously faint. I fight against the urge to close my eyes because I don't want to miss anything he sees, and then his gaze sweeps up to my eyes. He turns my cheek and gapes at the swelling on my temple 'What the hell happened there? I don't remember that happening at Greenacres.'

My beautiful little bubble bursts.

'It didn't. I fell over this morning.' It's a weak lie and suspicion extends across his face. 'I can't help it if I'm clumsy,' I add quickly. He doesn't challenge me.

'Besides, I can't heal cuts … only burns apparently.' I wince as I say the last word and River, who is almost sitting in my lap now, promptly sits back. 'And there's a reason for that.' I inhale, shutting out the image of me sitting in the corner of a padded cell wearing a white hospital gown and playing with my jelly cup. 'My skin is fireproof and heat-resistant.'

Listening to his silence is worse than any taunt.

'Really?' I wait for the laugh that accompanies his smile. His lips tighten when he sees I'm serious.

'I've spent the last week testing it out,' I rattle on before he can stop me.

River's eyes are wide and unblinking. 'Do you realise what you're saying?'

My head falls forward a little. 'I know,' I say soberly. 'It sounds so … unbelievable, doesn't it?'

I glance up as River nods. 'You have to show me,' he mutters. His face contorts as though the words have soured in his mouth.

'I thought you were going to ask that.'

I take a quick look around before dragging a small branch away from the fire and sit back down. Lucky for me, the crowds have gathered on the other side of the field, jollying for a good spot for the firework display.

Small flames lick the charred wood and, before River can stop me, I reach for the end that's glowing bright orange and extinguish the flame quicker and more efficiently than a fire blanket.

River winces, expecting me to scream out.

I smile wearily and toss the stick back into the flames.

River takes my hand and prises back my fingers. Black ash lays crumbled in my palm and he blows away a few larger pieces before brushing off smaller bits with the pads of his fingers. He draws my hand right up to his face, at first awestruck by my unburnt skin and then confused.

He looks back at me. 'Em …' he whispers. 'How the hell …?'

'I know,' I mumble. 'Weird huh.'

'Not weird … amazing. Have you told anyone else?'

'Yeah, I posted it on YouTube last week,' I say sarcastically. 'Of course, I haven't told anyone else. I still can't believe it myself.'

The second River mumbles his apology, my body softens. This time it's me who shifts closer.

I am a broken engine, of no worth and left to rust, left out in the cold and no use to anyone, ready for the end, and then …our thighs touch. He is the shock to my system, recharging battery and my lifeline to living and breathing and happiness and desire, restoring me to my former glory. Currents of fizzy energy run through my body.

'There's more,' I mutter.

I unfold the piece of paper I printed from science and hand it to him. His eyebrows come together as he angles the paper towards the light. I didn't think he could look any more shocked. His face convinces me otherwise. He looks at me, wanting to say the words that seem too insulting to what is going on in his head.

'River, I'm an Elementar. It all makes sense, and the man I told you about who keeps hanging around the school, visits me in dreams and visions. He told me I have to challenge him.' I pause, not sure whether to say anymore. The lid of my self-induced coffin comes smashing down on me. I swallow. 'He's coming for me.'

I choke off the urge to cry.

Casually, but gentlemanly, River threads his arm around my back and my head instinctively falls on to his shoulder. 'I won't let him hurt you, Em.' If only I wasn't so emotional, I could enjoy this moment for what it is - being comforted and held and tenderly soothed by the most amazing guy in the whole world.

We sit like this, staring into the flames, until all the fireworks have disappeared beyond the stars and the bonfire's magnificence has dimmed to a petite roar. The wild and ruthless dance of the orangey-red flickers makes me think of my parents last moments.

'I was in the crash that killed my parents,' I say, my voice little more than a whisper. At first, I think I hear him say, "I know", but when I can't be sure, I continue. 'The car was full of fire and while my parents burned, I opened the door and got out.'

'That wasn't your fault, Em,' he says soothingly. 'You didn't do this. No more than it was my fault my parents drowned. You have a power that needs exploring and I will be with you every step of the way.' I glance up at him, the reflection of the fire dancing in his eyes before I rest my head back down. His cheek rests against my head.

'It's beautiful, isn't it?' I say as flames soar against the black backdrop.

'You're beautiful,' he softly whispers into my hair.

The sound of my heart beating out of its natural cadence is not that unusual to me anymore, so I let it beat as hard as it wants and for as long as it wants as we sit watching the fire. I wonder if he sees what I see - the beauty and simplicity of something so vulnerable yet so powerful. For a moment, I see myself as the fire – the image of my face engulfed by flames, my naked body scooping up handfuls of searing hot embers as though it's water. The urge to get up and walk into the middle of the bonfire is like a desire I've never felt before. Maybe that is how I could learn to manipulate the flames – by taking in what I need to use, like the water element did by walking in the rain. Maybe I have to walk in fire. Had there not been people here right now, I would have done so.

'I want to tell you something,' he says. I turn to look at River. His face hints at a hundred different stories. 'I'm not sorry I kissed you that day.'

My heart flutters, then pounds, then races, and finally slows into a deep, thumping pattern. 'I'm not sorry that I let you,' I admit.

He removes his arm from my shoulders and picks up my hand. There is no buzzing now, only warmth. I think of my parents again. They would have approved of him.

River's touch doesn't feel anything like when The Creeper touches me, but regardless my body is tainted. *He* has spoiled me. This is all *His* doing and in that single moment the hatred I feel for him flows like soured milk inside my veins.

'I'm going to kiss you, so if you don't want me to, now is your chance to stop me.'

I close my eyes to think.

A mass of emotions criss-cross inside me, telling me one thing, warning me about another, saying yes, saying no, saying keep away you'll hurt me, saying hold me close and protect me. I open my eyes, ready to push him away but something in his eyes stops me. His lips hover inches from mine as though he's waiting for me to come to him. Something inside me breaks free, gives in. For the first time in my life, I willingly kiss a guy.

His lips are warm and soft and custom-built to fit mine, and the definite sharp, tartness of apples from the cider is there again to remind me of our first kiss. His tongue tenderly searches for mine, his breathing coming a little faster, making my heart race and soar and hit the dizzying heights where I might faint and collapse or even die all at once and I don't care, because this kind of death would be the best death in the world. My mouth aches in the same way my body had when he'd first touched me, like the wires beneath our skin are somehow connected, aching in a way that makes me want to reach inside his jacket and under his jumper so my fingers can explore the beautiful contours of his body, so I can see what he feels like to *me*, and not what I imagine he would feel like.

His hand softly traces the cut on my temple and then drops to my jawline where his thumb outlines the pale white scar on my chin, reminding me it's *me* that has let him in this time and not the other way around.

Our lips part for an instance. The heavens open and the fire hisses beside us as juicy-sized droplets fall from the sky.

'One thing I don't understand,' he says with a snigger. 'If you're the fire element, why do you make it rain every time I kiss you?'

I tilt my head back and close my eyes as he kisses me again. My hands reach for the stubbled texture of his cheeks, both dying and coming alive at my first touch of him. The rain, no longer my enemy, no longer abandoning me, no longer punishing me, now tickles my face as the sounds of panicked squeals and rushing feet, head for cover. Shrieks from surprised people everywhere pale in comparison to what is going on inside my head. All I know is ... it's the most perfect kiss, ever.

I open my eyes, expecting to see the same reaction on River's face, but I'm so off the mark, it isn't funny. His eyes are dark, grief-stricken and horrified. His fingertips first trace his bottom lip, and then the top. I try to pluck the thoughts from his head as he stares at me in silence.

'Who kissed you last?' he asks breathless.

My heart picks up its tempo. 'What are you saying?' The bubble of ecstasy I fashioned around myself, detonates. I am rolling and spinning and falling. 'You were the last one who kissed me.'

Then I remember.

It wasn't River.

It was The Creeper, the day after I had returned from grass skiing and I'd burnt his lips.

River shakes his head. 'I don't believe you, Em.'

'I ...I ...' Cleaved in a thousand shards, I scramble to pick up the pieces of my heart and force them together, force them back into my chest where they belong, praying that they stay there because the thought of being alone again, of being broken again, of never having River look at me the way he had before he kissed me, will splinter me into a trillion pieces that will never find their way back together again.

'I saw a man … a much older man, kissing you.'

My world stops turning. My life stops living.

The crowd hushes as does the wind. All I can hear is the erratic beat of my heart. Stop beating, *please* … stop beating and I won't have to explain, I won't have to witness the pity, the disgust, in his eyes. Falling … falling … falling. I can't stop myself. No, no, no … My broken world has cracked wide open and my secret is ripped from under me. I'm naked again and vulnerable.

My eyes sting as they fill with water.

'Please …'

My voice ebbs away taking with it three new friends - desire, hope and trust.

I have nowhere to go.

I have nothing to offer as proof.

All I am left with are the memories of a dead mother and father and the screaming nightmares of a life gone wrong.

The Creeper's hold over me, tightens, squeezing any chance of love from my life.

I have nothing.

I drop my head into my hands and cry alongside the rain bleeding over me.

# TWENTY

$\mathcal{MY}$ tears appear to be gone, on the surface, dried by the warmth of the fire, and yet a monsoon continues to rain down inside of me. The invisible streaks that I still feel on my face, tightening my skin, seem determined to leave a scar and I try to wipe them away, embarrassed by them now. River keeps looking at me as though I might fall in a heap at any moment.

The empty plastic cup in my hand has been a welcome distraction, but as the crowds dwindle and the wind blows colder, I know it has served its purpose.

'I'm going to find a bin. You want me to take yours too?'

River holds out his cup. I take it and disappear, glad to have a few minutes to myself. It's a good chance to scout around for Rachel too. This night, which started out with such high expectations, leaves with me nothing more than a hole in the heart and a tangle of trouble.

The smoky aroma of fireworks lingers in the air and I stop in front of the only bin I can find, ready to dispose of my ~~life~~ ... our cups. 'I thought I recognised you. You were at Ski-Tobogganing a few weeks ago, weren't you?' I turn to see the blond waiter who had brought the towel for my arm.

'Oh, hey,' I say. 'How are you?'

'Good thanks. Great firework show, huh?' A set of white teeth break through the darkness as he smiles.

I want to say yes but I'd spent most of the time gazing into the palms of my hands, wondering if the tears that had fallen onto my skin were ever going to dissolve. I'm not in the mood to chat, I do, however, pick up his strange accent again.

'My name's Skye Buchannan.' He offers me his hand.

I've had enough of touching for one night and casually toss the cups into the bin and shove my hands into my pockets. 'I'm Ember Riley.'

'Ember? What sort of a name is that?' His cheek lifts in humour.

'What about Skye? Isn't that a girl's name?'

'Fair point,' he says and sniffs.

'Where are you from?'

'The accent, huh. Dead giveaway, right?' I don't say anything. 'In a small place outside of Sydney. That's in Australia, in case you don't know.'

'Of course, I know where Australia is. We discovered the bloody country,' I say tersely. My lips stretch down. I take a moment to breathe. 'I'm sorry. That was rude of me.'

He doesn't seem to care. 'I moved here last year,' he says with a twang.

'With family?' I don't know why I asked that.

'Yeah ...kind of.'

His head turns left, then right.

'Are you here with someone, or do you need me to walk you home?' he asks, raising his eyebrows.

'No, I'm here with a friend.'

'That same guy you were with before?'

I'm surprised by his question. 'What's that got to do with you?' I blurt out.

'Nothing … I suppose, if you like that type. Bit of a dead shit, if you ask me. I've seen more life in a can of baked beans.'

His words puzzle me. 'And how would you know?'

His light blue jacket lifts towards his ears as he shrugs. 'I know his kind. But listen, if you get sick and tired of Mr Personality and feel like having some real fun, I'll be around.'

He walks off without waiting for my reply, leaving me reeling in his wake. I circle back, hoping to find Rachel. What I'm not expecting to find, is Rachel and River together, talking in low voices. I use darkness as my ally and sidle up behind the van they're standing in front of.

'Clumsy? You got to be bloody kidding,' I hear Rachel say. 'You obviously haven't seen her on the balance beam in gym then. She's as sure-footed as an alley cat.'

'I thought so,' mumbles River. 'And the bruises …'

'That's not for me to say,' says Rachel. In the dim light, I can make out River shifting uncomfortably from foot to foot.

'She told me her family life sucked.'

Rachel again says nothing.

'I'm worried about her. I don't think she's living in a safe environment,' he says warily.

'That's the fucking understatement of the year,' blurts Rachel. 'Prick.'

I wonder if she growls this between her teeth.

'Is he violent?'

Please, Rach. Please, don't tell him.

'You haven't even skimmed the surface of that putrid family, but if you can get her to listen to you and get her out of there, you'll not only be my hero, I'll be forever in your debt.'

I know deep down, they're both looking out for me. But now my secret is out. I'm not looking for sympathy, and I

199

don't need anyone else telling me all the reasons I should leave. Through River's eyes, the only innocence I had left has been extinguished. The next time he looks at me, all he will see is a gutless, broken down nobody.


Two days later, walking back from maths, a hand reaches out and pulls me into the dark alcove under the stairs leading up to the science wing.

'You scared me,' I say, punching his chest affectionately.

River blocks my exit. 'No use trying to avoid me now … your secret's out,' he says with a playful smirk. My first thought is that he knows more about The Creeper, that is until he waves my school timetable in his hand.

He closes the distance between us. 'I've been reading up on some stuff I think you should look at.' The smell of him makes me dizzy, like I forgot to eat lunch. 'I reckon the reason you can't throw fireballs is because you're suppressing your natural aggressiveness.' *How does he know I can't? I never told him that.* My mind is elsewhere, deciding if he is going to ask me to be his girlfriend or maybe kiss me again.

'My *what*?'

'I pulled this article off the computer yesterday, and it says all four elements live within the balance of nature and within their own balance. Fire is both destructive and cleansing. It can act positively as well as negatively.' He stops to check in with me before continuing. 'So, my theory is, you're not letting your emotions out, which is holding you back and not igniting your inner candle.' He sniggers like he can't believe those words have come out of his own mouth. 'It sounds strange, but I think you should give it a go.'

What do I have to lose?

'So, I have to get mad or something?' His starry eyes dazzle me.

'Only one way to find out,' he says, taking a tiny step towards me, 'and, yes, I do want you to be my girlfriend.'

*Girlfriend*? How did he …?

He turns to walk off when I seize a handful of his shirt and pull him back so fast we collide with a bump. Instant heat radiates over my body. I look down to see his hands on my hips, casually thumbing the fabric of my skirt.

His eyes glaze over. 'A compromising position and yes, very tempting, but not here.'

I had no intention of kissing him. I want an explanation. Suddenly, my head doesn't feel like it belongs to me.

'Can you read my mind?' My teeth are so tightly cemented together I barely squeeze the words out. 'This little trick you have going on, has happened way too many times and I need to know the truth.'

'Of course, I can't read your mind. You're the one with the freaky sideshow act, not me. It was just that …you had this look on your face and I thought I'd clear it up once and for all.'

The amusement in his eyes causes me to back down. His hands exert the smallest amount of pressure against my hip bones and I almost turn inside out.

I want him to kiss me.

'Wait for me at the gate and we'll finish this discussion in private,' he says, turning to stare down some girls who have gathered a few yards away. He leans in and gently brushes my lips with a kiss. For two tiny seconds, the tiles fall away from my feet and I am floating in the clouds, free to wander, free to love and free to be anyone I want to be.

I let go of his shirt and he pulls it down to straighten it.

'Oh, and try not to burn down the school; you know how everyone would love that. You don't want to become everyone's hero.' He traces his thumb over the scar on my chin and walks away without looking back.

When I arrive at English, the class is waiting outside, and Miss Freebody is counting heads.

'What's going on?' I ask.

'The headmaster has called an assembly.'

The auditorium is at full capacity and teachers congregate in small clumps near the stage displaying all the symptoms of a bunch of over-anxious parents. Mr Fisher looks particularly well-dressed today. His curly hair is brushed straight and his fawn coloured tie matches his shirt.

'Let's have some hush,' he calls out. He waits until everyone is settled. 'Reports have been made over the past few days of a person loitering around the school gates.' Rachel and River turn to look at me and each for their own reasons.

'I am therefore requesting that, until further notice, no child is to walk home alone. Your teachers will organise designated groups or pairs if you can't do so yourselves. The police have been notified and parents that could be contacted, have been. Everybody else will be given notes today that will need to be signed and returned tomorrow. If students need to leave earlier, alternate arrangements will have to be made.' He pauses and ruffles his hair, untaming a few curls at the sides. 'Under no circumstances are you to talk to this man if he approaches you. Report it to a teacher immediately.'

Mr Fisher and Mr Butcher exchange concerned looks.

A student's hand waves above a sea of heads. 'What does he look like?'

I don't recognise the voice.

'The only firm description we have is that he has long, grey hair and occasionally wears sunglasses.'

Ra-Mon.

Mr Butcher finds me in the crowd. He stares as though, somehow, he knows I'm involved. I look to Rachel and she offers me a commiserating smile.

'I'm sorry. I had to,' she mouths.

'So, you're my new escort then?' I ask accusingly. I'd been waiting all day to ask him that. 'Funny how you knew before the headmaster told us.'

'Yeah, funny,' he says offhandedly.

I stop walking.

I'm not buying it for one second.

'You accused me of being a liar the other day and, okay, you were right. But now, I'm accusing you of lying. I don't believe it when you say you can't read my mind. It's happened way too many times to pass it off as a coincidence. So … if you value me as a friend …'

'Girlfriend,' interjects River.

My brows rise. 'If you value me as your *friend* first, you'll tell me the truth.'

River's shoulders droop. 'All right.' He pauses before letting out a much pent up sigh. 'I'll try to explain.' He points to the park across the road.

The park. *My* park.

It's where I go to read in the summer to escape the soul-sucking hole I'll never call home. Where children play and squirrels hurry about their business. Where a hundred birds come to gossip and where lovers lay in the clover, tickling each other with grass. Where my dreams come alive and are shattered all in the same instance. It looks dark and bleak in there now.

Another foggy, drab day. Another day almost at its end. English Oaks and Beeches try their best to flaunt their thick canopy of Autumn foliage, but they are fighting a losing battle. The ground has become a mosaic of fiery shaped leaves that would blaze with colour if they didn't look so sodden and past their glory days. The wooden bench, River points to, is damp and mossy. Not my first choice of seats. Under the oak tree on the other side of the park is my favourite place to sit, but I don't have the luxury today. It's this or the ground.

It takes less than a second to feel the chill penetrate my skin and find a home amongst my bones. I bounce my knees in anticipation, and to keep the cold away as River treads the grass deeper and deeper into the mud in front of me.

His mouth twitches from side to side. 'I swear to you, Em. I cannot read minds.'

'But ...?' I add, waiting for the rest.

He presses his lips together. 'I have this weird *thing* ...' He stops speaking, yet his pacing back and forth is making me dizzy. I look him over, confused.

'*Thing*?'

'It's more like an ability that somehow lets me read ...' Again, he stops mid-sentence.

'People's minds ...?' I offer sarcastically.

His head flicks up and his eyes drill into me. 'No, not minds ... emotions.' He cringes as he says the word.

'And you never thought to mention this when I was spilling my heart out to you about being some freakish fire-child.' Keeping the irritation out of my tone is tough.

'No,' he mutters, biting his top lip.

Finally, he sits beside me, staring blindly into the unknown. The wind picking its way through the treetops, makes me glance upwards. A crown of burnt orange leaves sway to its own tempo, unaware I want answers as much as River does. I turn my attention back to River and I soften when I see the turmoil plaguing his normally placid eyes.

Guilt leaks out of me any way it can.

He hadn't judged me when I'd told him what a freak I was, and it isn't fair of me to do that to him now.

'How does it work?'

A forced smile appears on his lips. 'I don't know. When someone is down or nervous or excited, I get flashes of images or certain words in my head. Love and hate are the easiest to read but anxiety or jealousy are a little more difficult.' His words break off. 'I've had it since I was a child.'

On cue, the park comes to life. A sliver of sunshine peeks through the clouds, landing at my feet. 'Give me an example. What am I feeling now?'

He holsters a short laugh. 'It doesn't work like that. I can't switch it on and off like a kettle. It only happens when the emotions are true and in their rawest form.'

'Example?'

River seems to be lost in thought. His face tells a story his mouth can't convey.

He takes my hands in his, the muscles in his jaw working overtime. 'I called you a liar because I saw you with an older man. I saw your pain and his pleasure. I saw your fear and his desire.'

I lower my head.

'I'm right, aren't I?'

I can't look at him. The slight nod of my head causes River to fall to his knees in front of me.

I want to die.

I want to scrub this memory from River's mind with bleach and hot water so that no residue can be found, so that it never was. I want to drive a steak knife through The Creeper's heart for who he is and what he's done and everything he stands for. I want to run and hide, and curl in a ball, and pray and pray and pray until my brain runs dry of words and my life becomes a desert island where talking doesn't exist. An ache which has no limits, and can't be measured, fills my body until I become nothing more than a vessel to dump sadness into. My eyes burn with fresh tears.

A hundred more tears follow.

Slowly, my eyes find his. He runs his fingers over my temple as if to wipe away my pain, his jaw clenching and biting beneath his skin. 'He'll never get away with it. I will see that he pays for everything he's done to you.'

His arms circle my waist and his head presses against my lower ribs. I hold on to him, my body quivering. Seconds stop. Minutes freeze. Time melts away.

When the wind blows a little harder, the clouds darken to twilight and the temperature drops, I know we've been given what we needed – time to lay our cards on the table.

'I should get home,' I say with a weak smile.

'I'll walk you,' he says firmly.

I could object but I don't want him to go. He fills an emptiness that not even Rachel, her mum, or my own parents could. I realise, in the scope of everything that is going on in my life, I'm experiencing some form of love. It's a love that has its own rules, its own limitations, and its own trust.

He puts his arm around me as we walk and I snuggle deeper into his jacket, allowing my body to soak up everything that is good about him.

'My life is so much better with you in it,' I mutter without thinking.

I feel his jaw tighten again as he smooths his cheek against my head, but he says nothing. Instead he draws in a breath that makes me think it's a sigh. I don't understand it. I don't understand him.

I straighten up as we come to the corner of my street, fear dictating my actions. The Creeper might be watching.

We stop a few doors up from the Burberrys' house.

'I want to meet him,' says River. There's a look of determination on his face.

'That's not a good idea. Anyway, he's probably not … home.'

'Then it won't matter if I come in and meet this Aaron you're always on about.' I hadn't realised I'd even mentioned Aaron.

I tussle with the idea of letting him in. I'm sick of being afraid. I'm sick of living my life by someone else's rules, and okay, in some morbid way, I want to see what The Creeper will do if I bring River home. Will it stop him from coming into my room, knowing someone new is around to protect me? Or will it simply make everything ten times worse? It's a gamble but one I'm willing to take.

'Em, relax. You're even making me feel sick,' says River, smiling. He kisses the side of my head, his lips lingering longer than they should.

I don't mind one bit.

The front door creaks as I close it behind us and River's smile strengthens me that much more. Voices echo down the hallway from the kitchen, one in particular.

'Ems?'

I hesitate as I turn the handle.

The sight of The Creeper, dressed in his usual blue suit, leaning over the sink and looking out of the kitchen window, steals my breath.

He *was* watching us.

He glares at River as though he wants to choke every breath from his body. Rose Burberry is stirring something on the stove that smells like gravy and Aaron is at the table building a house from Lego.

'I was about to send out a search party for you,' The Creeper says as River and I stand in the doorway. His eyes spear through me and then switch back to River. His voice, although light, is every bit as calculating.

'Sorry I'm late. A weirdo has been hanging around the school and the headmaster advised all students to walk home in pairs until further notice.' The Creeper squints as though he doesn't believe me. It's then, to my surprise, and *his*, that Rose Burberry steps in.

'I had a phone call from the school today about it.' Her eyes flicker in my direction but fail to meet me.

The Creeper's face clenches even tighter. 'And does it take you two hours to walk home?'

What can I say to that – we dawdled? We stopped at the park for a chat? We got milkshakes? It doesn't matter what reason I come up with, it isn't going to be the right one. Keep it simple. 'No.'

'And does your knight in shining armour have a name?' I glance over at River who looks to be having a hard time trying to remain calm and stay in one spot. Despite his recent tan, his face is pale, and his lips have lost their pinky plumpness.

'This is River. He's my ...' I'm about to say my friend from school when River jumps in.

'Boyfriend.'

I freeze, and so does The Creeper. The room grows smaller by the second as egos silently battle each other. If I don't do something soon, blood will be spilt. Then River does something I don't expect. He drapes his hand across my shoulder and whispers in my ear.

'I think you're right. If I don't get out of here in a minute, I'm going to rearrange his face so that even his own mother won't be able to recognise him.'

All the while, I'm watching The Creeper's eyes fall to River's hand as it tenderly cups my shoulder. Insanity in a bottle is all I can think of – ready to explode at a moment's notice. Thank God for Rose Burberry.

My eyes widen as River gently kisses my temple, the temple *he* had hurt.

'I'm sorry I can't stay any longer. I have to get home,' he says to no one in particular. He directs his next comment at Mr Burberry. 'But I'll be back real soon.'

There is that dreaded silence again and I don't know what makes Rose Burberry turn around at that precise moment. I'd like to think she knows how to defuse the situation. 'Nice to meet you, River.'

'And you, Mrs Burberry. By the way, the food smells great.'

From the corner of my eye, I swear I can see a tiny smile appear on her lips before she mutters a soft goodbye.

'And, I'll see *you* tomorrow, Princess,' he says into my hair before leaving.

The front door opens and closes, leaving me speechless and unable to move.

# TWENTY-ONE

*THE* next morning, I can't face anyone at breakfast, not even Aaron. I'm only half listening as he chirps away about today's school excursion to the fruit markets, my attention … elsewhere. Three glances later, I see River loitering around out front. I dash outside without saying goodbye, dragging Aaron behind me.

'Hey,' says River as I pull the gate behind me. 'I hope that little stunt of mine didn't ruffle too many feathers yesterday.'

'It's okay,' I say soberly.

I try to keep my tone light. There are always repercussions. I am naïve to think otherwise.

River remains silent while Aaron skips in between the cracks of the pavement in front of us.

'And don't try and use your emotional telepathy on me this morning either because it won't work. I'm good … honestly. I didn't sleep well, that's all.'

His eyes lose their usual vibrancy. 'It's too late for that, Em,' he mutters grimly. 'The game's up.'

I swallow.

'The fear is dripping off you.'

*Shit, he's good.*

'I'm sorry. I shouldn't have insisted on meeting him.'

Too ashamed to look at him, I spend the next ten minutes watching my shoes appear and disappear as I walk. I will never tell him about the bruises on my back The Creeper inflicted last night with the back of his fist or the cruel and nasty things he'd whispered to me if I ever utter one word. He's getting smarter, hiding the evidence of his handy work, which I realised this morning in front of the mirror makes him even more dangerous. I would gain nothing out of re-telling River, and he'd only feel worse for knowing it.

We both speak at the same time.

'Go on,' he urges.

'You're mad at me for not telling you, aren't you?' I ask, after we drop Aaron off at school.

'No … well, yes. It never feels good to be lied to …'

I grimace.

I fold into River's embrace the second his arm slides across my shoulders. 'I'm sorry,' he whispers against my head. I feel his lips moving in my hair. 'I had no right to pry.'

'Forget it … really. What were you going to say?'

Darkness touches every facet of his face. 'Being able to read emotions isn't as cool as it used to be.'

His riddle stirs my curiosity but, from the look in his eyes, this isn't the time to ask.

'So, when do you want to test out this new anger management theory of yours?'

He frowns. 'Anger management? … I didn't say anything about … oh …' His confusion lifts. 'I didn't say anger management. I said we needed to bring out your natural aggressiveness.'

'And how *exactly* do we do that …?'

River grins. 'Easy. We need to find out what makes you angry?'

I know what frightens me and what makes me happy. Anger on the other hand is difficult. I don't feel anger towards Celeste, even after the catfight the other morning. I feel sorry for her that she's been brought up in a family with *him*. I recall the slight irritation from Cherie Bennett although I wouldn't call it true anger. The only time I've felt remotely cross was when The Creeper had threatened to hurt Aaron.

'I think I know what might trigger it,' I say, grinning. 'When do you want to put this little stunt of yours into action?'

'How about this weekend?' The quicker I learn, the less nervous I'll be about facing Ra-Mon again. If he challenges me, at least I'll stand half a chance.

'It couldn't come sooner for me. Where did you have in mind?' Indoors is a definite no-no. Setting fire to someone's lounge suite, or God forbid someone's house, is an exercise I can do without.

'How about behind my house? There is an empty field, surrounded by trees?'

I shrug. 'I suppose.'

'It's not totally private, but at least the people from the housing estate won't be able to see you burn down the neighbouring cornfields.'

'Ha-ha.' I scowl at him.

'Em … I'm joking.'

He may be, but me … I'm not so sure I can be trusted. I am a box of matches in the hands of a five-year-old.

'Okay then. Sounds like you've got it all figured out,' I say.

'Nearly,' says River and laughs.

Three days later and three days pure, I find myself sitting in the corner of the field behind River's house, trying to get mad.

'It's not working,' I yell to him. River is standing a sizeable, safe distance away.

'Are you thinking about Aaron?' he shouts back.

'Yes, and I get this heat flowing through me, but then it fizzles out.'

River holds his hand out in front of his body. 'Don't do anything … I'm coming closer.' I suppress a laugh as he gingerly walks over as though at any moment, I'll breathe fire at him.

He scratches his chin. 'I didn't want to say anything before, but I thought this might happen.'

I laugh. 'When did you suddenly become master of the elements?'

'Very funny,' he says, bending down and stealing a kiss. 'I've been thinking. It might be similar to how I sense emotions.' I cock my head, momentarily dazed, dreamy, floaty, not yet used to the way his lips make my whole body go limp. 'You have to be right in the thick of it to provoke a reaction. I reckon simply recalling it as a memory won't be strong enough.'

'And you know this … because?'

He shrugs a shoulder. 'Because memories never work for me. Every time I tried to channel into how you said something, or why you ignored me, it never worked. Maybe you should think of something I could do to … get you fired up.' He pulls a face at the pun.

I think for a few seconds. 'You don't make me angry; in fact, you have the opposite effect. You stifle it.' Why can't I channel fear? I have shitloads of that.

'How ironic,' he mutters, shaking his head. 'The one person who gets it, and I can't do a frigging thing to help.'

'Let me try again on my own,' I suggest. River backs up, never taking his eyes off me.

'If you promise not to incinerate the field, I'll go and make us some lunch.' He turns and points to a massive two-storey house with leadlight windows. 'That one's mine. I'll be back in ten minutes.'

'Fine,' I yell back.

I wiggle my bum into the grass to get comfy, and focus. I can do this; I know I can.

I close my eyes and think about the most spiteful and malicious thing ever, willing the anger with everything I have.

'The only way you will gain that kind of strength is if you are pushed to your limit,' says a voice.

Ra-Mon!

His presence alone tells me he's standing less than a foot away and isn't simply a voice in my head. My eyes now *very* open, my heart a loaded freight-train. Dressed in a long black cloak, his eyes shine white against his long silvery hair.

'You will never be a worthy opponent if you don't learn to focus on who you really are. Just this once, I will show you how.'

I see Ra-Mon glance over my shoulder as River returns. Instinctively, I know what is about to happen. Anyone hurting River would send me into a rage I'm not sure I could come back from.

Shards of blue lightning spew out of Ra-Mon's hands, hitting River square in the chest. The two lunchboxes he's holding, take to the air, time slowing their descent. His confused, horrified expression as he falls backwards, clutching his ribcage, rips the sanity from my bones. Fury falls in its place.

I let loose a frantic yell. 'Stop!' His body bucks in pain, fingers spread and unnaturally stiffened, as he writhes on the ground, clawing at the grass. His face, looking to me for help, for answers, totally helpless, is a memory that will torture me forever.

Ra-Mon continues his torment. 'You have the power to stop this at any time, FlameMaker.'

I wilt. 'I don't know how to. Please! He has nothing to do with this. I beg you. Stop.'

'He has everything to do with this.'

213

I open my mouth to speak.

'Find the fire. Feel the flames rising in your body. He only has minutes to live. If you do nothing, you will be responsible for killing him.'

Desperation circles my body once, before dissolving.

Anger is all that's left.

I hold my breath and let it consume me.

A heat, rivalling any that's previously visited me, burns up inside me like a flare gun, igniting my muscles into ropes of fire and my bones into blazing iron bars. The flames of hell are nothing compared to how the blood boils beneath my skin. I dust a finger over my hand to discover my skin is cool to the touch. My body is a thermos, taming a raging inferno within.

The furnace in the pit of my belly, hotter than Satan's lair, springs to life. My hands are the first to experience this new power as, with surge after surge, my body convulses rhythmically as the intensity begins to build.

I slowly rise to my feet and glance over at River.

He isn't screaming anymore.

His body is still, and his blue, blue eyes, that tell me so much, are now silent, staring trance-like up at the clouds.

I glance at my hands, aware of a delicious tickling experience. I am shocked beyond words to discover they are totally engulfed in fire. I can't move. Flames dance in figures of eight around my fingers, and then spin faster and faster, making me dizzy. I've no idea how I'm doing this or how to make it stop All I know is, I have a job to do.

I focus all my attention on Ra-Mon.

A molten ball of whirling heat grows and grows until it's the size of a basketball. Again, I don't know how I'm doing this, and I want to take a moment, to feel how it responds to my will and yet I can't. I have no time. River needs me.

Moving my arms, no more than an inch, sends a fireball hurtling towards Ra-Mon. It slams into him, turning him to nothing more than pollen-like particles drifting on the cool currents above my head.

My brain ceases to process this miraculous phenomenon.

*Whoa. I did it.*

I run to River.

His eyes, glowing neon blue, stare into space. I drop to my knees and lift his head into my lap.

'River, oh my God. Please, be all right. Please be all right.'

My heart leaps as he mumbles something along the lines of not happy about being my guinea pig anymore. My lips find his, and I kiss him until I feel his arms around my neck. He pulls me into him.

'Aargh,' he whimpers immediately, rolling me over so he's on top. His heart, beating wildly against my chest, should calm me, except it has the opposite effect. It races alongside his. I eagerly kiss him again and again, my fingers catching in his hair, my body moving in a way it's never known before. He holds me tighter as though I'm about to disappear, as though I'm the last thing he'll ever touch.

Intensity!

Whoa!

I can't conjure any words, and as much as it's exciting and what I've dreamt of since I first met him, something scary creeps inside me and waves a little white flag. I ease up a little and he responds straight away, loosening his touch.

'Anger really does become you, Em,' he says when I pull away. 'You should've told me from the start that I had to nearly get killed to get you to kiss me like that.' I thump him hard on the shoulder and he groans in feeble protest.

'I thought you were dead,' I say, still overwhelmed by his face, which is glowing again in its usual vibrant way.

River rolls off and lays on his back for a few minutes, massaging his chest. Warily, he pushes up into a sitting position, clutching his ribs. 'But you did it though, didn't you? He's gone and we're both still in one piece.'

'Only just! I think it was a test to see what I had, and yes, he's gone … for now. But he'll be back.'

My gaze floats over to where Ra-Mon was hovering. 'It was all too easy and yet the way he said something about me being a worthy opponent, I got the impression our next meeting would involve less telling and more showing.'

'I wish I could've seen you,' River mumbles as he brushes the grass from his jumper. I open my palm and a small flame flickers in the centre of my hand. I close my fist around it and then reopen it. The flame reappears like the click of a lighter.

'I have to focus hard to do it, but I reckon it's like learning to drive a car.' River's brow wrinkles. 'There are lots of things going on in my head and body, which happen in a series of actions. It's difficult to decipher whether I check my mirror, indicate or turn the engine on first.'

River laughs and pulls me closer. 'God, you're the coolest chick I've ever met.'

'And don't you ever forget it.'

I spy the lunchboxes River had put together and reach out for them. 'Let's see how cool I am.' I smile as I prise off the lid. Inside, the contents are a little shaken but bear a vague resemblance to a Caesar salad.

'No, bacon?'

'Nah, I don't like it. I can go and put some in if you want.'

I grin as though he knows my secret. 'It's perfect the way it is. I'm a vegetarian.'

'Same,' he mumbles under his breath.

'You're a vego?' I ask incredulously.

'Don't tell anyone. It doesn't do any favours for my reputation.'

I laugh. 'What reputation?' You've only been here a few months.'

'Exactly. Keep 'em guessing.'

'And what about me? Am I allowed into the strange and wonderful world of River Fulton?'

River smiles but it doesn't touch his eyes. 'Come on. I think we've had enough for today.'

# TWENTY-TWO

CHRISTMAS is coming at me from everywhere, and it isn't even December yet. Wreaths of holly adorn front doors; the street I live in has come alive with chains of fairy lights going from one window to the next, and shops smell of wrapping paper and orange chocolate. It's all just a horrible reminder that this is my second Christmas without them. And to make matters worse, and on cue as always, Autumn disappeared overnight taking with it the only colour in my life. One thing for sure, is, I won't miss those rainy days.

I pull my scarf around my face and blow warm air into it as the wind snaps at my cheeks. It's been over two weeks since Ra-Mon's appearance in the field and only twice have I managed to conjure a five-second flame before it dies out. There's no doubt I am a FlameMaker. I just *wish* I came with a set of instructions.

I start walking, surprised and a little concerned to find River isn't waiting for me at the end of my street. We'd agreed a week ago it was a much better rendezvous point than outside The Creepers favourite window.

I look up and down the street, pushing away the panic that's determined to set up house for a bit. He must have a good reason, although what he said about keeping tight-lipped about his personal life, won't leave my thoughts. It's just not like him to be late or not turn up at all.

I decide to go on without him. It's too cold to stand around and wait. Winter has definitely set up camp and the iciness, chilblains and foggy coldness are my only company until two year seven girls, with their heads into the wind, speed up to overtake me. It just happens to be at the entrance to the school gate, which now seems to have some kind of unwritten curse over it, and nobody wants to hang out there anymore because of Ra-Mon.

I hurry into the school grounds, wishing more blood would flow into my toes and get me there quicker, when the sound of a car door slamming makes my head snap up. I blink several times, trying to convince myself I'm not witnessing two teachers arguing in the middle of the faculty car park.

'Are you calling me a liar?' Mr Butcher towers over Mr Fisher's tiny frame.

'Yes ... yes, I am ... because I remember you ... as clearly as you are standing in front of me now,' Mr Fisher bellows back.

I pull up short and stare at the two men, the wind whipping water from my eyes.

Instinctively, the two men stop. 'We'll talk about this later,' mutters Mr Butcher as he turns to look at me. 'Off to class, Miss Riley, before the bell goes.'

I give him my best curious look as he and Mr Fisher take off in opposite directions, exchanging tense expressions as they go. Something is going on between these two and although it isn't my business, somehow, they've managed to make it mine. I hightail it to registration trying to come up with a way to find out what their deal is.

Two more days pass and still there's no sign of River. I decide it is time to pay him a visit.

'So, tell me again, why you're going to his house?' asks Rachel. We stop at the corner of her street. 'I feel like I've missed out on so much.' Rachel has spent the last three weeks in Morocco with her mum.

'We have our science presentation tomorrow and I want to make sure he's going to be there for it.'

'What do you care?' she asks offhandedly. It's a fair point, considering I haven't even told her we're an item. The fact that I hardly know anything about River, and haven't even been to his house, is beginning to show. My palms are sweaty, and an inner tremble is working its way down my legs.

'It's a group presentation thing and …'

'Sure, Em. Listen, if you wanna go and see him, you don't have to make up excuses. I know you, remember. It's ok to have the hots for a guy.'

Heat presses deeper into my cheeks.

'Go! And bring me back all the juicy details.' She cups the apple of my cheek and winks at me.

Alone, I continue down the next street. It narrows slightly giving the trees either side an excuse to touch in the middle. Half a mile down, I stop short of a beautiful Victorian-like manor, set back from the road.

Surely this can't be it?

The flat, ashen stonework and dark grey roof are what I remember from the day in the horse's field, but I had no idea that a sweeping horseshoe-shaped driveway, manicured gardens and hedges, arched gables and white painted windows by the dozen, all portray the most spectacular picture from the front. All that's missing is the horse and carriage.

Instead, a shiny black sports car is parked in its place.

Not that it matters, but I had no idea River came from such a wealthy family. Money has always been in short supply, even when my parents were alive. I suddenly feel totally out of my depths.

A huge willow bows down to me, daring me to set one foot on the cream pebbled driveway that looks recently raked. I grimace at every crunch my feet make, glancing back several times to make sure I'm not leaving footprints. In the porchway, a long golden rod dangles beside a brass bell. I have never seen anything like it. I pull on it gently, hearing a soft ringing from inside. The door swings open and a middle-aged man with black hair, greying at the sides and wearing a black shirt and pants, appears.

'You must be Miss Ember,' he says, lifting a thick, black eyebrow.

I am relieved. 'Oh good. I have the right house. Is River home?'

'Master River has been expecting you.' *Master* River?

'He has?' I ask, shocked.

'My name is Walter Bryson, but you may call me Wally if you like.' He extends his hand to me and I almost expect him to be wearing white gloves. I nervously shake it.

Awkward!

'Master River seems to prefer it too. A little less formal, don't you think?' He smiles, putting me at ease instantly.

'It's nice to meet you, Wally,' I say, stepping into a huge foyer where gleaming white tiles spread across the floor like a crisp December morning.

Forgetting myself and my manners, I turn in a circle, mouth wide open, admiring the chandelier above my head. 'Wow. This is an awesome house. I feel like I've stepped back in time.'

Walter Bryson smiles. 'You'll find Master River down the hallway, second door on the left.' He stops at the foot of a wide elegant staircase that disappears upwards into a spiral.

He gestures in the direction to take.

221

'Oh, right … thanks.' I push open a glass-panelled door.

The hallway is long, and white, and I follow it until I come to a set of stairs leading downwards. There are no other doors, let alone any on the left, and I begin to wonder if I'm going the right way. I turn a corner and see the first door. Relief breaks through my chest as a second door on the left appears.

I knock on it gently.

No answer.

I knock again, louder.

I wait.

Still no response.

Gritting my teeth, I seize the handle and turn clockwise. The door is unlocked. I shoulder it open a little, puzzled by the echo and the sterile smell that wafts through the door. Then I hear splashing.

I let the door swing wide and find myself in a monstrous terracotta coloured room with a thirty-foot swimming pool in the middle of it. The glass wall on the far side is all steamed up.

River is alone but hasn't noticed me.

I close the door quietly and stand at the edge of the pool, waiting.

Effortlessly, he powers through the water with strong arms and little splash. Two laps later, he finally looks up. I'm stunned at how blue and gorgeous his eyes are.

'I thought you'd be here today,' he says, shaking the water from his hair.

I'm still mute and I want to speak, and I want to ask questions, but his eyes steal the words from my lips. I can't stop staring at the way his mouth curls into that breathtaking, familiar smile as though he knows exactly what I'm thinking, and the way the water ripples off his neck and shoulders and runs down his chest makes me want to reach out to him to make sure he's real and not a dream because this is too magical a moment to exist in my world. And if it's real, if he is real, then I'd be happy to live in this moment for the rest of my life.

I blink hard a few times, trying to get the neurons in my head to communicate with each other. I clear my throat.

'So, did your *butler*, apparently,' I reply with a curious grin.

River swims to the side closest to me. Effortlessly, he half pulls his body out of the water and rests his arms on the edge, looking up at me, expectantly. 'I haven't seen you for three whole days, and the first thing you ask me about is my butler. Is there anything you've forgotten?'

I bend down and kiss his wet lips. My eyes run over his face, checking for reasons he hasn't been at school.

River smiles and winks at me and throws himself backwards. I step away to avoid the splash.

'You don't look sick,' I say. I'm finding it difficult to keep my eyes above his neck.

He laughs. 'That's because I'm not sick,' he replies, floating on his back.

'Why weren't you at school then?'

'Would you believe me if I said I wanted to swim more.'

I'm confused by his response although not surprised. The house surprised me, so had Wally the butler, and this strange room I'd found River in, but not what came out of his mouth anymore. His "I can read your emotions" line has become number one on my list of topics to bring up with him.

'If you can get away with it, then power to you but I came because we have our presentation tomorrow. Will you be there?' At that moment, Wally comes in carrying a jug of lemonade. He fills two glasses and hands one to me.

'Will you be taking yours in the pool, Master River, or shall I leave it here for you?' he asks in a casual manner. River waves him over and takes the glass from him. 'As I thought,' mumbles Wally with a tight smile. He places the tray under his arm and shuts the door.

223

'He's great, isn't he?' River says, draining the contents in one go and reaching over to place his glass as far from the edge of the pool as possible. I spy a long wooden bench and sit down.

'Yeah, he is. What's his story?'

'He came with the house.'

'What?' Lemonade fizzes up my nose as I swallow.

'When Terry and Annabeth bought the house, he came as part of the deal.'

I frown. 'Yeah, because I always buy my servants with the house I purchase. Do you wanna get out so we can talk properly?' I'm now on a mission to ask some of those questions that Rachel will require answers to.

'I'm not done yet,' he says with a smirk.

'What are you? A cake?' My newly acquired temper is getting a workout.

'Come in and join me if you're that keen to talk. The water's perfect.' Water is never perfect. It's hot, warm, cold, wet, or non-existent, especially when you need it the most, but never perfect. And yet the tranquillity of the room, and how it oozes off River, is a temptation too irresistible to knock back. I haven't been swimming since I went to Greece with my parents five years ago.

Reality jumps forward and stops me in my tracks. 'I don't have any bathers,' I say gloomily.

'Who needs bathers?' He pats the water. 'I promise I won't look.'

'Yeah, right,' I mutter under my breath. 'I'm not going in starkers, if that's what you're thinking.'

I think about the underwear I'm wearing. If they match, it wouldn't be any different than a bikini. I take a quick glance down my shirt. My bra is white with little pink polka dots on it. The only question in my head now is … did I think to put on the corresponding knickers. I ignore River's laughter as I turn around and pull my skirt up to have a look. Yes. A harmonised pair.

'Turn around, and don't you dare look.' I wait with hands on hips.

He complies.

I unbutton my shirt and step out of my navy-blue pleated skirt and slip into the water without a splash. I porpoise beneath the surface and swim all the way to the end. River is already right beside me as I pop up at the deep end. It takes six laps of freestyle before the embarrassment is washed off my face.

He's right … the water is perfect. I can't believe I'm saying it. Water has never had this effect on me. My rising temper is all but gone, the rampage of thoughts and questions I wanted to ask has grown quiet and every nerve in my body has been to the spa and back.

I scoop up a handful and let it run through my fingers. 'This is amazing. How long have you been in here?'

'Since this morning,' he says, swimming over to me. Normally I would have called him on it but the feeling the water gives me, I can believe it. 'It seems to … recharge my batteries,' he says behind a smile. I understand exactly what he means and the long intense stare he gives me, as though he wants to say more, or ask more, doesn't go overlooked.

He also hasn't answered my question from before. 'So, are you coming tomorrow?'

'I hope so,' he says vaguely. I don't know what kind of an answer that is and decide not to go there for now. The water has a way of dissolving my questions so that I don't care about anything.

River looks as comfortable in the water as he does walking, or breathing, and we swim about, racing each other up and down the pool until my legs tire. And boy, can he hold his breath a long time.

He surfaces super close to me and I gasp as he wraps his arms around my waist and pulls me closer. His skin touches me in all the places I want it to. His chest heaves in shallow breaths like mine is, and my heart is trying to

225

out-beat his, and when he brushes my hair from my face and cups my cheek and kisses me so slowly, so softly, I think I might fracture into a tiny million pieces in his hands.

I hear a courteous cough and River still doesn't let me go when Wally appears. He collects the empty glasses and leaves us with two fresh towels. 'Will Miss Ember be staying for dinner?'

Darkness had fallen without me noticing.

'No, but thanks anyway. I have to get home.'

I hurriedly swim to the side.

'Stay for dinner. I'm sure Wally will chauffeur you home,' says River, switching his gaze between Wally and me.

Wally gives a stiff bow. 'I can do that for you, Miss.'

'Some other time. I really have to go.'

Wally nods and excuses himself.

'Em, wait. You can't walk home by yourself.'

I'm already out of the pool and towelling myself down. I slip my skirt and shirt back on and tie my hair back.

River is beside me now but there's a reluctant look in his eyes as he stares back at the pool. He hasn't dried off and there are no clothes in the room.

'It's okay, honestly. It'll take you ten minutes to find your room in this house and in that time, I'll be halfway home.' On a good day, it takes me twenty-five minutes to walk from the Burberrys to Rachel's. River's place is five minutes closer.

I don't give him chance to speak. 'I'll see you tomorrow, okay?'

I kiss him on the cheek and the sound of a large splash as I close the door confirms my suspicions. River seems addicted to water.

I retrace my steps into the foyer, where Wally is already standing with his hand on the front door handle, waiting.

'Thanks, Wally. I'll catch you next time.'

'Goodnight, Miss,' he calls after me.

It must be close to six.

I am so late.

The Creeper will be home already. The conversation about where I've been, is one I'm not looking forward to, and with the damp chill in the air, my wet hair will be a dead giveaway.

I pull the sleeves of my jumper over my hands, wishing I owned a pair of gloves, and hug the only coat I own around me as I walk. It's thin, and two sizes too small, allowing winter's icy fingers to slide down the back of my neck as I free my wet hair from beneath my shirt. What I wouldn't do for a hat! At this point, hiding the evidence and drawing in a little more heat, I would consider trading my precious rocking horse for it. Almost, consider it.

The faster I hurry, the more my legs tingle, the louder my teeth chatter. If I was any good at being a FlameMaker, now would be the perfect time to power up and curl my fingers around a flame.

The street is almost deserted, apart from a lady and her husband walking a large brown dog. They cast me a sideways glance as they pass as if they know my secret.

Tables packed away and shutters down, I barely notice the shops and cafes on the corner, where River and I caught the bus. I quicken my pace. There is a still, eerie personality attached to this evening, and it has nothing to do with the dank night air.

I feel as though I'm being followed.

In fact, I'm sure of it.

My instincts never let me down. I felt it the second I left River's house. My senses tell me it isn't supernatural. What I mean to say is, it doesn't feel like Ra-Mon. It feels human, a person walking in the treads left by my shoes.

I look behind me, positive I hear breathing, and then footsteps.

Nothing. Nothing but the wind and the dark.

I continue on.

I hear a cough.

This time, I stop and glance backwards, straining my neck, my eyes, inspecting every hedge and alleyway, every window and doorway. My heart responds with a succession of unruly beats, urging my legs to go faster, faster, faster. Relief washes over me when I finally turn on to my street and then gushes out of my body when I catch sight of a hulking black figure sitting on the wall ten doors down from my house.

My body is on full alert. My palms prepare for action. Pins and needles flutter across my skin.

Five houses away and I still can't see his face. The new moon is doing me no favours tonight and I send up a quick prayer to whoever it is that loves to keep me in the dark, *literally*, to cut me some slack.

In the space between blinks, when lights go out and a million and one possibilities can happen, a large hand clamps onto my arm. A noise I didn't know I was capable of making, punctures the darkness until ...

'Mr Butcher? Is that you?' I didn't even see him get up or come towards me. The large man drops the hood of his sheepskin coat. His concerned face looks up and down the street a few times before he speaks.

'You shouldn't be walking around alone, Miss Riley, especially in the dark.' A faint smile lifts beneath his beard.

'I'm almost home,' I say, pointing down the street. 'That one's my house, right there.'

'Then we share the same street,' he says. This time the smile touches his eyes. 'I live right at the far end with the yellow door.' I don't normally venture down that end of the street, but I know which house it is. It's the only house in the street with a door the colour of vomit.

'Well, I won't keep you. I'm sure you want to get *home*.'

'Were you following me?' My tone, somewhere between rude and curious.

He smirks. 'We are all following *someone*, Miss Riley.'

Mr Butcher steps aside and I pass him with a nod of my head. By the time I push the key into the lock, he is halfway down the road.

The house seems to be holding its breath as I gently close the front door behind me. A strange humming emanates from the top of the stairs. I've never once called out, 'hello, I'm home,' although a part of me wants to right now.

Something doesn't feel right.

A sense of dread anchors my feet to the ground in the same way it says run for your life. The air, thick and gluey, clogs my throat, slows my steps. I start up the stairs. My legs heavy, urging me to turn back. The buzzing sound gets louder.

*Where is everyone?*

My bedroom door is open, the light on.

'What's going on?' I ask, and then pull up short. The Creeper is kneeling down, cordless drill in his hand, fixing a bolt to my door. My eyes widen in horror as I realise it's on the outside of the door instead of the inside. A nightmarish grin spreads across his face as he takes in my wet hair. 'You've been with him again, haven't you?'

The dull thump of the drill dropping to the ground as I race for the stairs, frantic, scared for my life, matches the thud I feel on the back of my neck. The cream walls dissolve around me and the darkness that lives in this house is there to greet me again.

# TWENTY-THREE

WHEN I wake, it's morning, I think.

I'm just guessing because there's no daylight cutting through the crack in the curtains, like it normally does. Instead, my alarm clock beeps annoyingly beside me.

An alarm I never set.

The idea, that the whack on the back of my head is all a dream, disappears the second I try to reach up to brush my hair from my face.

My arms won't move.

Neither will my legs.

I half expect to see thick ropes around them, pinning me in place.

There is nothing. The heaviness even radiates to my chest every time I take a breath in, and yet my mind and vision aren't altered. I try to lift my head, but the blanket might as well be made from concrete. The sound of the lock opening freezes me in my tracks, my eyes instinctively close.

'Wake up,' he growls. I slowly open my eyes. He is dressed in his business suit and light blue shirt.

'Why can't I move?' I ask, trying once more to raise my head.

'It's an insurance policy,' he says, turning his back as he fiddles with something on my dressing table. I can't make out what he's doing until he turns around with a bottle of pills in his hand.

'F-for what?'

'In case you try to escape when I go to work.'

*Escape!*

What did he mean? Am I in a prison? Does he mean to keep me captive?

I dig deep for my fire. It's not there. Not even a flame.

Fear rips through my chest. 'Where are Rose and Celeste?' I utter. A picture of Aaron's innocent face sweeps into my thoughts like a soft breeze. 'What about Aaron?'

'They've all gone to Rose's sister's place at the coast. A well-deserved holiday, I think.' He seems to be reminiscing because the light fades from his eyes.

My teeth grind together, forcing down the bile I know is coming. 'And me?' I whisper. 'Where am I?'

'Oh, you're with them too. I notified the school yesterday that you wouldn't be back for at least two weeks.' Though my muscles are useless, and my body controlled, I turn my head to one side and vomit over the sheets.

That disgusting noise at the back of his throat is back. That disgusting chuckle that makes my skin crawl with ants and spiders and bugs. 'You'll have to sleep in that for the rest of the day,' he says, checking his watch, 'because I have to go to work. And don't bother calling out to anyone - they won't hear you.'

He takes a couple of steps towards me and sits down. He clamps his fingers over my nose until I open my mouth and then fires a pill towards the back of my throat, jamming my jaw shut until I swallow. 'Not that you'll have any chance of getting up. I have also taken the liberty of boarding up your window because the next-door neighbour's son apparently hit a cricket ball through it yesterday, the little tyke, and I couldn't very well get it repaired, not when the glaziers are busy for the next fortnight.'

I'm appalled by how deep his lies run and how far he's gone to set up this cosy little soiree.

'You're a filthy, fat pig,' I spit as soon as his pudgy fingers are away from my mouth.

Evil finds his eyes. 'And you'll pay for that comment tonight.'

I hold my breath.

'Are you done?'

I blink once. 'Careful, Ems. Aaron is only a phone call away.' He brushes his hand across my face. 'I have a few special ideas for him.' Anger screams through my veins as I search for my fire, willing it to flare up inside me so I can give this disgusting excuse of a human being exactly what he deserves except …

There is no fire. Not even a flicker.

'It's amazing the perks of being a medical malpractice lawyer. So many drugs that needs to be disposed of that the medical profession can't recirculate,' he continues to brag. 'A few favours later, and hey presto.'

Whatever he's given me is beginning to take hold. I can't stay awake and my body is getting heavier, my bones turning to lead, pressing into my muscles, pressing me further into the mattress. And my arms don't work, my fingers turn numb and I cannot lift them and each blink hurts and I don't want to sleep. I don't want to sleep. I don't want to disappear.

I feel groggy when I wake for the second time. As hard as I try to concentrate, nothing comes into focus. My room is a blur of colours as I drift in and out of wakefulness. Nightmarish screams call out to me from Aaron; the

Creeper drowning River in a pool of black water; Celeste scratching my eyes out.

By the time I open my eyes again, my mind feels more my own.

I turn to look at the clock but he has spun it around so I can't see it. Just another aspect of control he enjoys. I have no idea whether its afternoon or evening, the boards at the window doing a fine job of keeping time from me. My fingertips tingle and prickle, like they somehow know they are meant for movement and not the useless sticks of bones they felt like this morning. My arms are still numb, my legs feel amputated.

My eyes sink back into their sockets as the front door slams. Footsteps up the stairs, fifteen steps to be precise. I've counted them in my sleep. I hear him whistling and the sound of his trousers unzipping. The dense stream of water, only a man can make whilst urinating, echoes from the bathroom.

There is no begging now. There's no use. The inevitable is going to happen. Begging simply makes me more fearful. The door to my room swings open and he walks in with a smile that cuts his stupid, round face in half.

'How's my favourite princess, today?' The pet name River had given me loses its lustre the second it comes out of The Creeper's mouth and I cringe, begging for the word to be stricken from my vocabulary. But, it's not that which strikes my face like a sharp slap. What did he mean when he said 'today'? Wasn't it only this morning that he'd left? He is speaking like I've been here for days.

His plan is to use me whenever he wants, not kill me, otherwise he would have done so already. The question I haven't yet found an answer for yet, is how will he explain all this to his wife when she returns?

Then a horrible thought.

What if he's told the school, the neighbours that the rest of the Burberry's are away on holiday … when really, he's chopped them up and hidden them beneath the floorboards or weighted their bodies down and dumped them in the canal. It wouldn't be the first time a floater had washed up on the bank.

I need a strategy; one I won't enjoy. I need to lose the attitude and adopt a different tactic. I need to play smart and be what he wants me to be. My stomach curdles at the thought of having to speak kindly to him, but I also know if I ever want to get out of here, I must do whatever I have to. I lower my lashes and smile.

'May I have a drink of water, please? My mouth is so dry.'

His eyes light up as though I have complimented him. He returns thirty seconds later and lifts my head. I smile my thanks, and he reaches over and puts the glass on the bedside table. The bed sags as he sits, resting his hand on the other side of my body.

'You look positively beautiful today,' he remarks, unable to take his eyes off me.

There's that word again ... today. I pretend to look embarrassed. 'I was wondering ...' I say timidly. He leans forward, eagerness clouding his vigilance. 'How many more days before the rest of the family returns.' His lips break into a smile, a smile too creepy for me to look at for long.

'I told you yesterday that she's staying a few extra days, silly. Apparently two weeks isn't long enough for the sour old cow.' Bile climbs up my throat. 'Did you forget that already? I did tell you yesterday.'

I titter a soft, fake laugh. 'So, today is ...'

'You really have been sleeping a lot. I'm not surprised. We have been indulging in a little too much fun,' he says with a girlish giggle. 'It's Wednesday, the fourteenth.' It takes everything I have not to throw up.

If this is true, then by my calculations, I've been here two weeks and yet I have no recollection of getting up, going to the toilet or eating. There are no tell-tale signs that my body has been active because numbness occupies every inch of me. I can't remember what I did yesterday because as far as I know, yesterday hasn't happened, nor the day before that or the day before that, yet somehow my body does feel stronger. Maybe whatever he is giving me is having less effect. Maybe my body is beginning to fight back. Fire, I sense, is simply resting, waiting for the right moment. If I play this right, it means I have three days left before …

I refuse to think about what might happen after that. I play my trump card, hoping to hell it won't back-fire on me. 'Do you have to go into work tomorrow?'

'I already told you, Sugar. I have a tough case on this week. I won't be home until after six, that's why I've come home early tonight, so that we'll have more time together.' Vomit regurgitates up from my stomach and into my mouth. I hold onto it. 'And don't let me forget to leave some extra food for you,' he says, lifting me upright and propping me against the headboard. I feel my body starting to slide sideways and he props me up with a pillow. If my mouth wasn't full, I'd ask him how I'm supposed to eat when I can't even raise my hand.

Now that I'm sitting up, the room looks like a commercial kitchen. Empty plates, and trays of half-eaten food are stacked up one on top of each other, all lopsided, food spilling onto the carpet. Crisp packets and chocolate wrappers and dozens of bottles of water intermingle with clothes strewn on the floor that I can't remember wearing in the last few months. And glass after glass of half-drunk milk line my dressing table, and *even* my footstall. I search my memory for the taste of leftover food. Nothing registers with me.

The Creeper leaves, bolting the door behind him. I spit the contents of my mouth down myself and close my eyes. I am tired.

I wake to sounds of birds twittering outside my window.

Now I know it is definitely morning. The little buggers are the reason I can't sleep in when The Creeper is away for work. I'm relieved to finally have some semblance of time and normality and doubly thankful my mind is not hidden behind a veil of distorted images. Whatever pills he was supposed to give me last night didn't happen, I don't think, and I don't think I ate either. In fact, I'm sure I didn't.

Maybe that's how he's drugging me? Force feeding me when I am out of it, followed by more meals or snacks to top up the dosage. My arms and legs are heavy and useless but the tips of my fingers and toes tingle again, remembering once upon a time they could feel.

I hear him throw back the bolt, cursing under his breath. This is my day.

I do what I can to make myself appear meek.

It isn't too difficult …a mirror of the face I've been wearing the last twelve months is in place as he enters. He stares and stares at me, minutes ticking by. He has a lost, gormless look about him, his jaw hanging, his tongue almost panting. Pathetic is the first word that comes to mind. I feel the urge to dry reach. He's just standing there, catatonic, staring and staring, giving me the shivers, *if* I could feel my body. It doesn't look like he has any intention of moving or leaving and I wonder if he's going to stand there all day. I need to hurry him along.

'Didn't you say you had a big day, today? Tell me about this important case.' My voice trembles.

The Creeper's eyes open wider. 'Christ,' he yells, checking his watch. 'Thanks, honey. I don't know what I'd do without you.'

Fresh vomit finds its way down my t-shirt.

He heads for the door 'I'm so sorry,' he says, gesturing to my recent mishap, 'I am running so late. That will have to wait until I get home.'

In his haste, he forgets to lock me in.

Any other time, I would have been out of bed, down the stairs and out on to the street, racing as fast as I could to River's house. Why I think of River first, rather than Rachel, comes as a surprise. I suppose it's because he would know where to find me at Rachel's. Different areas of my body tingle sporadically where the drugs have worn off.

I hear the shower shut off and the Creeper whistling again. I'm holding on by a very thin thread. His happiness seems to seep through the walls at me, trying to attack me, infect me, mould me into something so unlike me I won't recognise myself. There are parts of me now resembling a thousand shards of glass, never eroding, never decaying, just being broken forever and totally alone. I just want this to be over. It feels like an eternity before he returns with a tray of food. I smell toast and honey … and pancakes.

He's in an exceptionally good mood. If I can keep him talking and not thinking for long enough, he might forget to feed me or forget to give me the pills from the bottle that rolled off the dressing table last night. I can see the red cap peeking at me from under the leg.

I look under my eyelashes at him.

Vomit threatens again.

'Perhaps when you come home,' I say sweetly. The fork, loaded with fluffy pancake, slowly lowers. 'Maybe we could have some …champagne.' I see the words forming on his lips, but he seems too love-drunk to say them. He nods in a vague manner and lifts the fork back to my mouth. 'I saw some at the back of the food cupboard.' The fork lowers for a second time and he props the plate up on the bed.

'And I'll get a takeaway,' he says doe-eyed. 'What do you say to Chinese?'

His eyes shine.

The voice in my head is back … *last time, this is the last time he'll ever come near you. Hold on Ember, it's nearly over. We're almost there.*

237

He crushes his mouth to mine. His hands go wherever they want, up and down my body and neck, through my hair and over my breasts, and yet all I want to do is scream out my gratitude to the drugs that blunt his touch and anesthetise my skin. I find another place to be, a place so far from here, somewhere he will never find me. I am with River. He is holding my hand, and we are laughing. I am safe and happy and the love I feel is real.

The alarm goes off.

He pulls away and looks at the clock. 'Bloody hell, I've got a client in fifteen minutes.'

It's eight-thirty.

He takes a long pensive look at me and then around the room as though he's forgetting something. I hold my breath as he moves to the door. I will him to forget. I beg for him to leave. He takes one more look, and then bolts the door behind him.

I wait until I hear the front door slam before unleashing enough tears to fill an eggcup. The fact that I'm lucid, and pinpricks of feeling are coming back into my body, gives me hope.


By midday, sensation has returned to my feet and fingers and I can partially lift my body off the bed. Even if I could get to the door, I can't open it.

My only hope is the window.

At the rate, my body awareness is returning, I guess by around five o'clock, I should have enough strength to break the window and kick the boards out. It's cutting it fine but it's the only plan I have.

Then I will run until I reach River's house. For once in my life, I have to think of me. For all I know, Aaron might be dead, or perhaps The Creeper doesn't go for young boys and that it's the only leverage he has over me. I must put myself first, for once.

Two o'clock. I'm lying on the bedroom floor, pushing pieces of cold toast down my throat. Starvation is the only thing stopping me from going any further.

It might be drugged but you need to keep your strength up, I keep saying to myself. Unfortunately, it doesn't stay down for long when I come across an empty condom packet. My first reaction is to curl into a ball and rock back and forth in the corner of the room, crying until my eyes bleed dry, until I disappear from the world, but I can't let myself go there.

Survival comes first. I have to get out of here.

I drink the lukewarm milk in one gulp and freeze in mid-swallow. The distinct trill of the doorbell has me leaning against the bed, my ears straining for the slightest noise.

'I'm up here,' I scream out. 'Help me.'

I gasp at the pain in my throat from muscles that haven't been used in a while.

Silence. Then hope shines again.

The bell rings and a loud knock raps on the door.

'Help me,' I scream even louder, tasting blood at the back of my throat. 'Someone, help me!'

The quiet hums in my ears, distracting me from listening to real noises. Then a real lifeline.

'Em? Are you in there?' It's River's voice and it sounds as though he's shouting through the letterbox.

'River,' I scream as loud as I can. 'Help me.' More tears on my cheeks, navigating unchartered territory.

I grit my teeth hard and drag my useless body over to the dressing table. It's the heaviest item in my room. I yank out the bottom drawer and empty my clothes on to the floor. I prop myself against the wall and raise the drawer over my head. With all my might, I throw it towards the window.

It misses. NOOOOOO!

The drawer bounces off the windowsill and comes hurtling back at me. It lands with a dull thud against my leg, splitting the skin wide open on my shin.

I don't scream out in pain because I feel nothing. I simply watch as the blood flows out, spilling on to the cream carpet.

It's bad and definitely needs stitching but I don't have time to worry. Sure, there's a slight chance I might slowly bleed to death but the possibility that I could be murdered outweighs everything.

I pick up the drawer again and hurl it into the air. This time it hits the window and a small crack splinters up the pane. The problem now is that the drawer is stuck up high and I can't access it. Turning sideways, I heave another drawer out and turf its contents beside me.

'C'mon,' I whisper as I throw again. This time I hit the pane that doesn't have a crack in it yet. The drawer tumbles off my chair and into the corner of the room, out of my reach. My technique sucks, and at this rate, The Creeper will be home and find me hidden under every item of clothing I own and in a pool of my own blood.

I stop what I'm doing.

Footsteps crunching outside on the pebbles beneath my window has my heart leaping for joy. I thought he'd given up. 'River,' I scream. 'I'm locked in here.'

I double my efforts. I drag out another drawer and launch it at the window. It makes contact and I cringe as a loud crack pierces the air. The floor becomes a minefield of jagged glass. My body, racked from starvation and no sleep, is beginning to feel the effects as lethargy, and unconsciousness begin to take over.

'River,' I scream again. My last-ditch effort. 'Hurry, please hur ...'

At first, I think I must be dreaming, my eyes closing longer now than staying open. And then the most beautiful sound I've ever heard.

'I can hear you, Em. I'm coming.'

# TWENTY-FOUR

*I* wake up in a bed I don't recognise.

The sheets are soft and luxurious beneath my skin and I smooth my hands over them, relishing the touch beneath my fingertips. I shuffle a little, getting comfortable and that's when I realise, I can move my arms freely without that weighty feeling in them.

I test out my legs next; curling them and stretching them back out. Such a simple action fills me with hope, yet pain tarnishes the pleasure. I can't exactly pinpoint where the pain is coming from because I hurt everywhere *equally* – the screaming headache, the slicing, throbbing in my leg, my muscles aching from lack of use and then too much exertion, my stomach gnawing away at itself, starved and force-fed, my lips, bruised, and the core of where my life began is shattered, maybe beyond repair.

Someone clears their throat and I sit up.

'Easy there, Miss.'

It's Wally.

'I'll go and fetch Master River and let him know you're awake.'

The light mauve of the walls reminds me of the underside of a mushroom. Tranquillity seems to have been added into the paint, quietening my heart and soothing my emotions. Lighter and darker shades of the same colour are used in curtains, sheets and duvet covers, and the massive bed I'm lying in hardly takes up any room at all. The elegant chest of drawers and designer paintings, all purposefully placed, are on par with the perfect bedroom.

There's a knock at the door.

I don't get chance to respond as the door opens. River stands in front of me for a full five seconds, staring, his fists knotted into tight balls, before he finds a spot on the end of the bed as far away from me as possible. I wonder how long it's been since he slept. He looks terrible.

My hero sits before me, his face a mixture of relief and self-loathing. I want to kiss him and keep kissing him until my lips run out of love for him, for rescuing me and caring enough to risk everything.

'Em ... I,' his voice trembles as he speaks. My heart melts at my name. 'I'm sorry I didn't get there sooner. I only found out two days ago and I rang the doorbell and knocked every few hours ...' He massages his grazed knuckles before pulling the sleeve of his jumper over them. 'I only found out because I overheard one of Celeste's girlfriends talking about what a crap time she was having on holiday.' Surprise stains my face. 'And she never mentioned you once, so I sweet-talked Cherie into finding out who was with her because Rachel said she was sure you were with them and wouldn't be back for a couple of weeks.' River takes a deep breath. 'Cherie told me Celeste was with her mum and brother and that you had stayed home at the last moment because you had an important assignment to finish.' His face darkens and his eyes take on the colour and depth of an abandoned well. He drops his head low. 'I'm so sorry.'

I blink several times, confusion spinning its way through my head. 'Why are you apologising?'

He continues to speak into his lap. 'I shouldn't have let you leave that night. I should've gone to school, and then you wouldn't have felt the need to come and check on me.'

My temples pulse. 'River, why are you saying this? You couldn't have avoided this, any more than I could have. It's not your fault.'

Dry and raspy, I cup my hand to my throat to relieve the pain. River hands me a glass of water and makes no haste in resuming his position. I drink slowly at first, wincing with every swallow. The rest goes down with ease. I hold on to the empty glass until he rises again and relieves me of it, cautious with his eyes and even more cautious with his touch.

'Thanks.'

His gaze drops to the floor.

I hold out my hand to him. I want to touch him to convince myself that he's *really* here and that I'm not stuck in some god-awful nightmare where The Creeper is waiting to smash through the door and kill us both. He looks up and shakes his head slightly, refusing my offer.

'Please ...' I say softly. He reluctantly shuffles up the bed, still unable to look at me. I lift his hand and lay it against my cheek. He closes his eyes ... first lightly then much tighter, as though he's purging God knows what out of his head. 'Tell me what happened ... when you found me?'

River's body crumples as if the recollection alone will break him. His face tells me he'd rather not say.

'Please ... I need to know.'

His fingertips knead small circles into his forehead. At first, I'm not sure he is going to answer, and I'm about to ask for a third time ...

'I knew something was up,' he says, through tight lips. 'Something inside kept telling me to go back and have another look. Have you ever had that feeling, Em, when you've lost something and you keep searching in the same place for it because you're sure it's there and yet, each time you look … it's not, but you know you're right?'

I nod.

'That's what it was like with you. I knew you were stuck in that house. I knew it. Everything told me you were, and yet I left the first couple of times telling myself I was over-reacting and jumping to conclusions, and then I heard your voice …' His prominent Adam's apple almost disappears as he swallows hard. 'I didn't care what I had to do. I had to get you out. I contemplated kicking down the door, but it was too risky with neighbours already peeping through their curtains at me as I thumped on the door. I didn't want them to call the Police. Then I heard the window smash and I ran around the side of the house to see the window had been barricaded. By the time I had come up with a plan, Wally had arrived with the car and a ladder.'

I start to fiddle with the corner of the sheet. 'Did I say *anything* to you?' I murmur, having no memory of seeing him.

'Not much. You were pretty much out of it. It was more nonsense than anything. You kept repeating my name over and over, and you mentioned something about the toast tasting off, which I thought was strange.'

'How did you get me out?'

'Wally helped. I couldn't have done it without him. He was brilliant. He was the one who patched up your leg, too.'

The hazy image of the drawer falling on me triggers the pain again. I push back the duvet to look and then pull it back over myself quickly.

'Who dressed me?' I am wearing a clean pair of pyjamas, and although I can tell I haven't showered, my face, neck and hands smell like … *freesias*.

A tear falls from River's eye. 'You were in a bit of a mess, Em. I couldn't leave you like that, and I swear I had my eyes closed the whole time.' I'm not so much embarrassed about him seeing my nakedness, but rather the condition he found me in. I knew I must have reeked of urine, vomit and sweaty bed sheets, and God knows what else. I can't imagine what River was thinking.

I reach beneath the sheets and slide my hand up the leg of my pyjamas until I come to a wide crepe bandage.

'You have six stitches.' River informs me as I run my fingers over the dressing. 'Wally was a paramedic for nine years, so he knows all about that stuff.'

Reality is shuffling past at a fast pace. 'I need to ask you one more thing,' I say, biting my bruised lips. River glances up. 'Did you inform the police?'

'No, I didn't.' The look on River's face suggests there's more to it than 'no'. Guilt and shame smother him.

'Does anyone else know I'm here? I mean, apart from Wally.' I can't relax just yet.

River frowns. 'No …'

'Good,' I interrupt. 'That's the way I want it to stay.' I know The Creeper wouldn't dare call the police when he'd found me missing.

River opens his mouth to speak and I immediately cover it with my hand. 'Don't. You wouldn't understand.' His lips brush my fingers, a hint of a kiss, and he places my hand back down.

'The bathroom is in there,' he says, pointing to a panelled door. 'I wasn't sure what you'd need. I couldn't grab much.' Until now I hadn't seen my sleepover bag on the floor by the window. 'You need to rest now. We'll talk more in the morning.'

I lay back down, staring at the ornate ceiling with its rose centrepiece and plump bold leaves, certain that sleep will never take me again.

I am wrong. A peaceful blackness, without demons and nightmares, finds me and cradles me into unconsciousness.

It's still dark when I open my eyes again.

I can't decide if having little to no memory of what went on in that room for two weeks is a curse or a blessing. If there were horrors, I've decided there will be no trips to Sylvia Bank's place to revisit them. They will remain in the shadows, where no-one can find them. All I want right now, is a shower and to start the first of many pure days to come.

The room is warm regardless of its high ceilings and I peel back the duvet and swing my legs over the bed. My feet come alive with pins and needles as I wriggle them into the rich mauve carpet.

I wobble to my feet. 'Whoa, head spin,' I mumble as I test my balance.

I take my time with the eight to ten steps to my bag, slowly bend to pick it up, and slip into the bathroom. Sparkling gold taps, large glossy tiles that match the colour of the bedroom decor, a corner spa that has been sunk to floor level and the biggest, fluffiest plum coloured towels I have seen, means I've found my new heaven.

I turn the lever on the bath allowing water to gush out from a rectangular spout. Lifting the lid on one of the three gold canisters close by, I smile to find the culprit behind the delicate floral aroma clinging to my arms and hands - freesia bath oil. I pour in an extravagant stream and return to my bag to see what River has put in.

I pull each item out and lay them on the floor, nodding at the pair of jeans, a few shirts, and two jumpers. It isn't a bad combination, for a guy, and I can only imagine the panic he must have felt, throwing any item he could get his hands on into my bag. I do, however, grimace at the two bras and three pairs of knickers stuffed into one corner. A hairbrush, the pyjamas I'm wearing, a pair of ballet flats (that won't go with my jeans) and a bottle of perfume are the last of the articles.

I re-pack them back into my bag.

There's only one item I can think of that would've been top of my list to pack – the crystal rocking horse my mother gave me. The thought of it in such proximity with The Creeper, brings back my mother's words. On my twelfth birthday, she'd said … "Though you may find yourself on rocky ground; always keep your eyes on the road in front of you". Until now, I had never fully understood what she'd meant.

A sandwich and a fresh glass of water is waiting for me on the bedside table as I enter. I devour it in a few bites as I drop my bag in the corner and turn on the bedside light. The curtains have been closed too, and the duvet has been smoothed out with the top half turned down for me. It doesn't bother me to know what day it is or what the time is. I'm happy to be alone and safe and free.

The door opens a crack as I pull the covers over me. River appears hesitantly from around the corner.

'Feeling better?'

'I am … much better. Thanks for the sandwich. Wally, right?'

'Actually … that was me,' he says, venturing in a bit further. I smile, encouraging him closer. As soon as he sits down the sharp, tanginess of chlorine hits the back of my throat.

'You've been swimming again?'

His hair is wet and the colour of coal. 'Have to keep fit some way,' he says with the remnants of a smile still on his lips. He shakes his head and chuckles as though it's a private joke.

I stare into those eyes, sure that I can see every emotion and feel every feeling that swims deliriously around and around in them. I blink and straighten my posture, determined not to go to sleep. I try to recall the last lucid days before I was incarcerated. Being at school is the only thing I remember.

'Did you end up doing the element presentation?' I ask.

'Are you kidding? After all you've been through, you're worried about that?' says River exasperated.

'I'm not worried about it,' I reply coyly. 'To be honest, I don't want to go back to sleep, so filling me in on what's happened since I've been out of it, kinda takes my mind off … stuff.'

His eyes, mouth and cheeks mellow. 'Okay. Yes, we did the presentation and we got a B plus for it, missing out on an A minus because you were absent.' I screw my face up as though I'd tasted something sour. 'And Cherie insisted on reading out your notes as though she'd written them herself.'

'Doesn't surprise me,' I chime in. My shoulders wilt. 'So, we came …?'

'First as it happens. The earth group were close with a B minus and the other two groups got Cs because they hadn't answered all the criteria.'

'That's brilliant.' I wish I'd been there. 'And, the reward?'

River's eyes shine. 'You're never gonna believe where we're going?'

'Where?'

'North Western Fire Brigade. Mr Butcher said we are going to be part of a cadetship program for the day.'

My heart plummets to the bottom of my stomach. Am I safe to be let loose around fire with a class full of my peers watching my every move? 'When?'

'The first week back after Christmas holidays. We get to put out fires on the training pad, complete a walk through the notorious smoke house, and even get to demolish a few front doors.'

'Sounds like he's got it all figured out,' I murmur to myself.

'Yeah, Mr Butcher reckons we were lucky to get in. He said they're normally booked out for months.

'Yeah, lucky,' I say. I feel as though I'm on an assembly line with no brakes, and yet the people watching me go past know exactly where my destination is and what is going to happen. The word mushroom comes up again, although it has nothing to do with the colour of my room. Being kept in the dark is beginning to feel more like home to me.

'And under no circumstances are you allowed to show off with your new skills.'

I throw him a look. 'As if?' That is something I'll have to keep in check.

The mild excitement in River's voice dies down and his hands wind themselves in knots in his lap. Not only is he deliberately keeping his distance from me, but his whole demeanour towards me has changed. He doesn't appear to have any feeling for me, other than sympathy. And he reeks of it.

I stare at his arms, wishing he'd wrap me up in them and hold me – if only to shut out the demons that whisper to me that I'm actually back at the Burberry's and that this is all a dream.

I'm about to ask him when River laughs aloud. 'And what have you said to Mr Butcher?'

My train of thought switches tracks. 'Mr Butcher? Why?'

'He sounds like your new best friend or something.'

My eyebrows pull closer together. 'How do you mean?'

River rolls his eyes. 'He keeps asking every day whether I'd heard from you, whether you were back from your holidays and I keep saying no. He sounds kind of ...' River pauses and looks so directly into my eyes I gasp with pleasure.

'Kind of ...?'

His mouth stretches downwards. 'Worried. I thought the school knew that you were supposed to be on holiday with your family.'

'They did,' I say incredulously, 'well ...at least that's what *he* told me he'd said to them.'

My gaze wanders around the room, searching out items I haven't yet noticed. A question burns on my lips but I'm too afraid to ask it. River seems to anticipate my torment.

'What?' he asks pensively.

'Do you know if they're home yet?' My voice trails off to nothing.

River's face darkens. 'I didn't see Celeste at school two days ago. Did they say when they'd be back?'

'No,' I whisper. My eyes fall back to my hands as I twiddle with the sheet again.

'You don't think he'd come looking for you, do you?'

That is the worst of my fears … that The Creeper will find me and drag me back to that life without a life. 'He is my legal guardian, so I suppose he has every right to make me go back.' My voice is thick and I fight back tears. 'What kind of person does this?'

'Someone with a sick take on the world and someone who had better not cross my path again,' he says furiously. His jaw is set like stone.

He gets up to leave. Apprehension radiates off him in waves. 'I'll let you rest.'

I pat the empty space beside me. 'Stay.'

He reluctantly folds at my request and half lays half sits next to me, stiffly propping himself up against the headboard. The space between us could fit a small child lengthwise. I roll towards him and rest my head against his chest. His heart is pounding in a frenzy of unsure beats.

'You won't break me,' I hear myself saying softly to him. I loop his arm around my neck, desperate for comfort. Desperate for reassurance. Anything to chase away the demons.

River tenderly brushes the hair from my forehead, his caress warm and so sweet. 'I'll never hurt you, Em. I promise.'

They are the last words I hear him say before I drift off.

# TWENTY-FIVE

*RIVER* looks much brighter this morning. The dark circles have almost disappeared from under his eyes and his skin glows as if he'd bathed in candlelight all night. 'I thought you might be hungry,' he says.

I am.

The smell of chlorine follows him in, as usual, and he sets the tray down on the spot where he lay only hours before. He lifts the tray onto my lap, careful not to spill the glass of orange juice. I'm thankful no pancakes or toast are present, instead the tray is laden with pastries, muesli, fruit and yogurt.

'I didn't hear you leave,' I mumble.

'Eat. You must be hungry.'

My words sail over his head. 'Have you eaten?' I ask, going for the pastry first.

'Yep.' He waits a few moments before he speaks again. 'Would you like to swim this morning?'

I demolish the pastry in three bites and lick the blueberry jam from my fingers before reaching for the

251

orange juice. 'I think your mind-reading ability is back. I was about to ask if we could take a dip.'

River smirks. I down the entire glass and then start on the banana. 'Only emotions, remember,' he says as his smile grows wider. 'And don't worry; I won't make you swim in your underwear this time. I had Wally go and buy you a bikini yesterday.'

'You didn't *make* me,' I say firmly, trying not to look embarrassed about a middle-aged man picking out a bikini for me. River hands me a bag from the bottom of my bed.

'And I apologise if it's not to your taste, but Wally has never been asked to purchase such an item before, plus there are a few other things that I thought you might need.' That is two for two in not acknowledging me.

What other things would I need? The question running through my mind seems to be haunting River's as well – how long would I be here for? If today is Sunday, then by all accounts, I should be returning to school tomorrow. River gets up and leaves and is back a few minutes later with another two full plastic bags.

I push the empty tray away. 'Glad to see you've got your appetite back. I'll leave you to get dressed. Come down when you're ready,' he says courteously. 'I'll be waiting in the pool.'

I rub my stomach as he pulls the door behind him. I've eaten too much, and too quickly, and my belly gurgles in protest.

The bags, however, are too enticing not to consider. I edge my way down the bed. The first bag contains every item of school clothing I need, including shirt, skirt, shoes and blazer. This little package wouldn't have been cheap. In the second bag are a red bikini, a pair of trainers, two pairs of tracksuit pants and a sweatshirt. Wally has done well. Apart from the school shirts that look to be one size too big, he has bought everything in the right size. The image of the two of them going through my thrown-together bag from Friday, ascertaining what size I was, makes me smile and cringe at the same time.

I go into the bathroom, wash my hands and face, brush my teeth and wriggle into the bikini.

I find myself staring at my reflection in the full-length mirror. No hint of molten lava eyes this time. Instead, my ribs look sparse and thinly clad, and my hips protrude a little more than they did a few weeks ago. The skin across my abdomen looks a little tighter too. My shin is patched up and a multitude of bruises dance across my skin ranging from purple and red to dusky blue shadows. My skin lacks that certain vitality that comes from being active and in the sun. I remove the dressing from my leg and take a closer look at the wound. Six well-manicured stitches fasten together a two-inch cut.

I can't put this off any longer. I wrap myself in a gorgeous fluffy towel, open the door and head downstairs. The tiles are cold beneath my feet as I stand in the main foyer, expecting at any moment to run into Wally, but instead, I find him sitting on the wooden bench near the pool, talking with River. He is wearing his customary frown.

The two separate quicker than oil and water when I enter, and Wally rises and bows in a gentlemanly fashion.

'Sorry, Miss. I didn't see you there.' He smiles stiffly. 'Will you be requiring anything else, sir,' he says, turning to River.

'No thanks, Wally. I'll give you a holler if we need anything.'

For the first time, I look at River with doubt. Something doesn't feel right.

'Right you are, sir,' says Wally, taking his leave.

I don't waste any time getting into the pool. The same calmness soaks through my skin, layer by every sore layer. I swim several lengths, reminding my muscles they were meant for movement and not a sedentary lifestyle and by the time I stop to catch my breath, the questions and responses have begun to unravel in my head again.

'Thanks for the clothes,' I say, looking down at the red bikini rippling beneath the surface.

'You're welcome,' replies River. He smiles, his face wet and shiny.

'But, surely you don't expect me to return to school tomorrow, do you?'

River sighs. 'That's why I had Wally buy you the clothes, in case you wanted to.'

Going to school, on the one hand, has a normality to it that I crave. But with *normal*, comes problems - problems in the form of Celeste returning to school, or of The Creeper turning up to apprehend me.

I swim up and back a few more times hoping the calm waters will wash away all the complications in my life and present me with the right decision. I can't define how the water makes me feel. It has all the elements of soaking in a hot bath with ample helpings of cleansing salts, and an invigorating spa – tipping the balance between vitality and lethargy. On the last turn, I hear River call out my name.

'You know you can stay here as long as you want.'

I nod and offer him a brief smile. I know that, but I also know I can't hide away from my life forever. Not only is The Creeper looking for me but so is Ra-Mon. Running from either of them isn't going to end their desire to find me. It'll only increase it, causing me and those around me more harm than good. I have no choice.

'I will go back tomorrow,' I say firmly. River's eyes widen and yet he doesn't look overly surprised.

'Are you sure?'

I grin. 'I can't spend all day here swimming, like some …'

'No, you have to be a real water-lover for that.' We both laugh.

The rest of my day is chock-a-block with things to do. After two back-to-back movies with popcorn and lunch in between, three different board games and an hour of Twister, I haven't an ounce of energy left. A clever plan, on River's behalf, and one I'm not afraid of telling him I'd discovered as I slip into bed that night.

'That wasn't my intention at all,' he says defensively. For a moment, I almost believe him until his smile gives him away. 'No ... really,' he begins. 'It's fun to have someone to spend time with.' His casual remark sparks questions I'd forgotten to ask when I woke up in what reminded me of an adult's bedroom.

'Where are your father's cousin and his wife? Do they know I'm staying here?'

The question is easy enough, yet I can't decipher the frown on River's forehead which looks deeper and darker than usual.

'Oh yeah, they know. They said it was okay. Luckily, they're on a photo shoot up in the Lake District and won't be back for another few weeks.'

A few photos *are* dotted around of River as a baby, and several he'd deliberately pointed out of his parents, but not one of his guardians. Not even a wedding picture of them. 'What are they like? You never speak about them.'

He shrugs in an offhanded way. 'Not much to tell really. They spend a lot of time away, which is why Wally was such a find. Built in babysitter, if you know what I mean.'

I'm not taken in by it.

'Well, sleep time. Back to the old grindstone tomorrow,' he says with an encouraging grin.

I guess our conversation is over. I watch him walk towards the door.

Our day together has been nothing more than a couple of friends hanging out and not the beginnings of the budding relationship I remember from a few weeks back. It began first thing this morning on the sofa as we watched movies - the distance between us large enough to accommodate two extra people, the formal manner in which he addressed me as though we'd only met yesterday, instead of the few times of intimacy I was getting used to, ending up with a cold indifference every time I reached out to touch his hand.

'River?'

River slowly turns, his hand on the door handle.

'Will you kiss me goodnight?' I ask shyly. It's a big ask, I know, but I need to find out if everything in that department is still okay between us.

His face becomes taut. His jaw clenches.

And unclenches.

And clenches again.

At first, I think he's going to leave without saying anything. Instead, he hesitantly retraces his steps and stands next to the bedside cabinet.

I tilt my head back, excited, impatient to feel his lips against mine - the only lips that bring my body to life instead of the alternative.

His eyes consume me, his breath warms my face. I am one step away from heaven itself.

He lifts his head and kisses my forehead. It isn't a kiss that says, 'I don't feel that way about you anymore', or 'I'm sorry, this feels awkward.' It's a long, intimate kiss that says, 'I miss you, I miss you so much and you need some time'. It's a kiss I never want to end, will never tire from and never get used to. I close my eyes until finally his lips peel away from my skin. Part of me wants to cry.

'Goodnight, Em. Sleep well.'

Looking up from my cereal for the fifth time, I catch River's anxious eyes staring at me from across the dining table, but he's the least of my worries today.

I still have to face Rachel. She will have her standard repertoire of questions … why didn't I go to hers? Why aren't I at hers now that it has all blown over? Aren't we friends anymore? I have no idea how I will answer, even though I know she deserves the truth.

An icy wind bites at my cheeks as River and I trudge through the slush to school. I am hyper aware of how close he is to me at all times, never veering more than a few inches away. It's kind of cute, in a fairytale sense, but I am not in Wonderland or Hobbiton, and the threat *He* might find me is very, very real. Nervous knots are forming, and I'd be lying if I said I wasn't having second thoughts on whether this was such a good idea now. There are only three days left at school for goodness sake. I'm sure no-one would miss you, says my rational brain, but the thought of hiding away, like I've just been hidden away against my will for two whole weeks, scares me more. I need to feel and see the world, to tell myself that I am free.

'Thanks for the loan of the parka,' I say with a shaky breath, pulling the furry lined hood around my face.

River's nose is glowing. 'I know it would've looked a bit awkward, but Wally could have driven us.'

'A *bit*,' I retaliate, failing miserably at maintaining the calm and steady-like tone I practiced before we left. I'd said no the three times he'd brought it up and I meant it; besides, who gets chauffeur-driven to school unless they attend Eton or somewhere even posher. There's enough gossip about me already. Turning up hand-in-hand with the enigmatic new boy would give them morsels to chew on for weeks, so imagine pulling up in a car worth more than their parents' average yearly income, complete with chauffeur, would do. I might as well serve myself up on a platter and ask them to dig right in.

'I'll see you in science, then?' he says with a pained look. I start to walk away. 'And, Em ...' I stop. River suddenly looks nervous, like he's about to do something he isn't sure he should. He plunges his hand into his pocket and pulls out a phone. 'I want you to have this.'

My eyes water, forgetting to blink. 'I can't possibly accept ...'

'It's just on loan,' injects River, before I can answer. His face pales as I contemplate rejecting it for a second time. 'In case you need …' His helpless smile is adorable. I take the phone and his face brightens in an instant. 'I've added my number. Press six and it'll come straight to me.'

Overwhelmed by his genuine concern, I smile. 'Thanks.' River's smile grows wider and he looks down as he weaves his fingers through mine for the shortest time, before releasing them. He then walks away with his head hung low.

After English and maths, I find Rachel *inside* F Block for once, brushing her hair and reading a magazine. River is already there, watching me from the opposite end of the room. He nods and raises his hand in a static wave but doesn't move out of his seat.

I take a deep breath and tentatively slide into the chair next to her.

She jumps. 'Where the bloody hell have you been?' she says, yanking the cord out of her ears and flinging her arms around me. 'No phone call, no email … nothing. I have been going out of my mind. First River said …'

This is exactly what I was afraid of. 'Nice to see you, too, honey.'

Rachel sits back in her chair and folds her arms stiffly across her chest. Her lips twitch to one side, her eyes examining every movement I make. 'Why didn't you tell me you weren't living with the Burberrys anymore?' Her voice is much louder this time, enough to catch River's attention. The anxious look on his face is back.

'Keep your voice down,' I urge, looking left and right.

Rachel leans in closer. 'That spiteful prick said that when you got back from holiday you were upset about something and had taken off and that they hadn't seen you since.'

'And you believed that bullshit?' I growl under my breath.

'Of course not, but what else was I to think? No phone call, no email ...' I hold up a finger for her to stop. 'You need to get yourself a mobile phone.'

258

I reach into my pocket and shake the phone River had given me in her face.

First Rachel sighs, then her eyes widen. 'Great, but a little too late, don't you think? When he'd said you'd run away and you hadn't told me, what was I supposed to think? I went and knocked on the door and searched the place myself.'

'You did *what*?' The thought of Rachel being in that house, *alone,* makes me sick right down to my feet. I reprimand her without thinking. 'Well, that was stupid.'

Rachel purses her lips. 'What would you have done? I have to check for myself. What if he had locked you in a room with no food?'

Fresh tears sting my eyes.

'Em?'

I shake my head, my hair becoming a waterfall of red.

'Em?' whispers Rachel again. This time her voice quivers and I feel her hand on the back of my neck. 'Please don't tell me I'm right … *please*?'

The energy it takes to lift my head has me gasping for breath. Two wet streaks follow the course of my nose to the corners of my lips. At the edges of my vision, I see River out of his seat, his eyes never leaving me. I gesture for him to stay where he is, and he deliberates for a moment before sitting back down.

Rachel glances over at River and my eyes find him too. 'He rescued me, Rach. He rescued me.'

I relive the whole despicable event, or as much as I can remember, with Rachel going through half a packet of tissues. Witnessing Rachel go through her own battle of guilt and regret is as bad as when River went through his.

'Oh my god,' sobs Rachel when I finish.

I don't *want* to ask what she saw when she was there. I *have* to ask. 'What did it look like, when you went in? Was anything out of sorts?'

Rachel pulls a face. 'Paint. First thing I noticed was the smell of paint. But I didn't think anything of it, especially when he told me to be careful of the walls up the stairs because he was in the process of sprucing up the place as a surprise for when you guys got back.'

'What else?'

'Your door was slightly stiff when I opened it; although I'm sure there weren't any signs of a lock on it. I would've noticed that.'

I consider the possibility that The Creeper had brought a new door, hung it and painted it, and then, knowing the smell would have lingered, covered his tracks by repainting the hallway.

'And what about my room?'

'It was like it normally was … tidy. There was a board up at the window because he said one of the neighbour's boys had thrown a cricket ball through it. I could see a big hole in the glass, so I took it as that's what had happened.' Rachel continues shaking her head from side to side. 'I'm sorry, Em. If I had known …' Her eyes are the violin, playing soft, sad music while her lips are as tight and as thin as the bow that works the strings. 'He needs to be punished,' says Rachel fiercely.

'I agree,' injects River, now standing beside me. Rachel offers him a smile that radiates gratitude. His fingers brush my cheek as I look up.

I set my jaw firm. 'I've told you both before. This is my life and I don't want anyone to know. I can deal with the fear and all the shit that goes with it. What I can't live with is the humiliation of everyone knowing. Do I make myself clear?'

River nods but Rachel holds fast.

'Rach?' The look on her face says if she had access to a gun, she'd be incarcerated in under an hour. 'Rach?'

'Okay,' she growls.

I hug my friend as the bell goes, and her last squeeze is so much tighter, I feel my ribs creak.

'You know you can come to mine any time you like,' she whispers into my ear.

I smile. 'I know and normally I would. But it would be the first place he'd come looking for me. If it's okay with you, I'll stay at River's until …' River clears his throat. 'Well, for as long as it takes.'

Rachel takes off across the quadrangle to history and River and I head through the tunnel into the science block. I peek into the classroom, relieved to see Mr Butcher isn't here yet.

'I'm going to use the loo before he gets here.'

River's lips tighten. I can tell he's previously thought of, and fought with, certain boundaries that he can't infringe upon, and that aren't up for discussion, like unscheduled toilet trips.

'I have my phone,' I say light-heartedly.

He disappears into class.

I peer into the mirror to inspect the damage. Wearing no makeup has its benefits - no black panda eyes. They are red and a little puffy, nothing that can't be fixed with a few splashes of cold water.

I open the door to leave, when an arm adorned with gold sparkly bangles, materialises across my face, drags me out and pushes me into the lockers.

'I can't believe you have the fucking nerve to show up at school after everything you've done.' Celeste's forearm presses against my neck almost choking me.

'Get the hell off me,' I spit, unbridled fury sinking deeper into my veins, charging my body with what seems like an endless supply of power.

Celeste hasn't slackened her pressure in the slightest. 'My dad said you'd better get your frigging arse home before he sends the police out looking for you.'

I shove Celeste away, anger turning my blood into hot, soupy lava. Fists tighten, without me telling them to, and heated white peaks rise across my knuckles. 'You can tell him from me, I won't be home for Christmas or anytime soon, and if he has a problem with that then I'll be telling the…'

'Are you threatening my father, you little bitch.' Celeste claws at me again but I block her, sending her reeling face first into the wall. She clutches protectively at her arm.

'You're going to pay for that, you cow.' She lunges at me a second time and I step aside at such a speed, I'm not even sure it happened. In fact, I'm confused I moved that fast. So is Celeste, and she slams into the lockers, wailing out her annoyance. Blood trickles down her hand, her long talon ripped from its temporary home.

'Look what you've done,' she says spitefully. Her top lip curls up. Part of me wants to recoil, knowing the next words out of her mouth are going to sting. I straighten my back and look her in the eye. 'Even your mother and father probably topped themselves to get away from you.'

Any self-control I thought I had, has now left me. Heat and more heat masses in my bones. Eager flames soar and plummet through my flesh, twirling and dancing in all the other places in between. Revving up and then slowing down but building always building, climbing higher and higher, bringing with it an awareness that surpasses any joy, enhances any pleasure and amplifies my every expectation. My body trembles as I try to reign in the raging energy powering up from my feet. It aches inside me, wanting to be released, wanting to be free.

Celeste backs away, slowly. 'What are you doing?' she finally mumbles unable to draw her gaze. I have become the predator, not the prey. And she knows it.

Lava courses down my arm, resting for a second at my wrist. I casually open my hand allowing a small flame to flicker away in the centre of my palm. I toy with it, opening and closing, opening and closing my hand, making it appear and disappear at will.

Like a trapdoor, Celeste's mouth drops open. 'H-how are you d-doing that?'

'Do you have any idea how much danger you are in right now. I could destroy you, just like that,' I say, clicking my fingers. The flame wraps itself around my palm in a spiral of burnt orange and then vanishes.

Celeste wobbles as she turns.

Then she runs and doesn't look back.

I take my seat as Mr Butcher brings the class to order. I know River is looking at me. Every fibre on my body is acutely wired in to his visual antenna. I fiddle with my bag, so I don't have to acknowledge him.

'Now then,' says Mr Butcher, pacing. 'Considering we've come to the end of term and I know as much about any of you as you do about me and that *Miss Riley* ...' I look up and catch Mr Butcher's eye, 'has made it back from her holidays in one piece ... I'm going to change today's lesson of revision to one of fun. So, in two hundred neatly printed words, I want you to write down everything you like and don't like about your new science teacher. It can be as descriptive as you like ... no holds barred. It will not be graded or looked at by another teacher and remember ... honesty is the key.'

Mr Butcher writes the question on the board. 'You may begin.' With slow measured steps, he walks around the class, hands clasped behind his back.

When he gets to me, his brow creases. 'Where are your books, Miss Riley?' River spins around. I can see in his eyes that he can't believe he forgot to buy them.

'I left them at home, sir,' I say.

Mr Butcher glances under the desk. 'And your bag too, it appears. Somebody who has returned from holidays, Miss Riley, should be revived and ready for action, despite the fact we only have two days left of school.'

'Yes, sir,' I mutter.

'Well, lucky for you that I enjoyed your piece on the history of elements. Empedocles was an interesting man by all accounts, although I wouldn't put too much faith into his demise in which you have explained in great detail.

263

I found his death to be highly exaggerated,' he says with a hearty chuckle.

'It was … interesting,' I rebut, 'but some still believe that he didn't die at all but was, in fact, immortal.'

'Indeed, indeed,' he says, scratching his beard. A light dances in his eyes, a light I've never seen before. His neck disappears as his monstrous shoulders heave. 'But who would believe you?'

I watch as he moves on to the next few people, peering over their heads as they write. He glances back at me every few minutes, unsettling me. When the lesson ends, he pulls me to one side as everyone else is leaving. I suspect it's more about not bringing my pencil case with me.

'Miss Riley, may I have a quiet word?'

'But it's lunch, sir,' I groan. River hovers in the background.

'It'll only take a few minutes, I promise.'

I usher River away, ignoring his customary frown. A few options run through my mind. It's either to give me homework for the work I've missed, or it's to do with the argument I saw him and Mr Fisher having, or maybe he was going to tell me why he was loitering outside my house. I'm certainly not expecting him to say what he says next.

'I know everything, Ember. I know where you've been these past few weeks and I also know what has happened to you and by whom. So, my question to you is … can you accept me knowing this, without me having to tell you how I've come to learn of your predicament?'

Total horror comes first. Panic rattles around my body like a train with no destination. De-railed … off the tracks … heading for certain destruction. Then shock that my secret is out. Then confusion. It sounds like he's covering for someone.

Four people know what happened to me, and two of them have been warned, for the *second* time, *and* only this morning. The torment of which one has lied to me ties my stomach into knots. *Who can I trust?* I've known River a short while, not long enough to gauge where his motives might lie, yet there is genuine feeling for me. I'm not wrong about that. It whispers to me in every word he says, in every warm caress and always when his eyes meet mine. Whereas Rachel, my best friend, who knows everything there is to know about me and who has listened, sympathised and stood by me all this time has also threatened on more than one occasion to disclose my secret. One of them is lying. One of them has betrayed me.

I can only answer Mr Butcher's question with another question. 'What do you want? You wouldn't be telling me this unless you wanted something.'

His lips form a grim smile. 'You're very intelligent for a girl your age. Has anyone told you that?'

I note he is playing the same game I am – question for question. I huff out my annoyance. 'This isn't going to get us anywhere, is it? You answer one of my questions and then I'll answer one of yours. Deal?'

Mr Butcher maintains his smile. 'All right, however, my first statement still stands.'

'Fine,' I growl irritably. 'What do you want?' I repeat.

Mr Butcher paces again, not far away, enough to muddle through his thoughts. 'I don't want anything.' I roll my eyes. 'Except, to keep you safe.'

I exhale softly 'I don't understand. Why should my safety matter to you? How does it affect you?'

His mouth twitches to one side. 'It affects all of us, but let's say, as your teacher, I have a vested interest in your well-being.' As far as I'm concerned, he is still talking in riddles.

'My advice is - not to come back to school until next year. You need to take some time to gather your strength and be ...' He pauses to scratch his head. '... you.'

He is trying to tell me something without *actually* telling me. I feel as though I'm on that damn assembly line again. 'What kind of an explanation is that?'

River pokes his head around the door at the precise moment Mr Butcher opens his mouth to speak. 'You ready, Em.' I turn towards River annoyed and then look back at Mr Butcher, one eyebrow raised, still waiting. 'The canteen will be packed if we don't leave soon.'

It's a clever ploy on River's behalf, especially as his anxious face tells me he isn't even hungry. The separation looks *almost* torturous for him.

Mr Butcher's voice is softer and full of compassion. 'I'm sorry, Miss Riley. It's the only explanation I can give you.' With that, he passes me and nods to River on his way out.

'What was that all about?' asks River as we walk to F block.

'I'm not sure. He said something about gaining strength and being myself.' My face darkens as I recall what else he'd said.

'And?' adds River inquisitively.

I wanted to wait until later to ask him if he'd let anything slip to Mr Butcher, but my curiosity isn't prepared to let me wait that long. 'He knows about what happened to me; everything that's happened to me. But he refuses to say who told him.'

I pause, swallow, blink once and then twice, grit my teeth and swallow again. 'I'm going to ask you once, did you …?'

River's eyes lose their dazzling glow and delayed shock works its way into his features. 'Are you serious?' he says angrily. 'You think I said something? Well, that's great. After everything that has happened …'

He doesn't finish his sentence. I grimace as he speeds off ahead of me.

# TWENTY-SIX

*THE* end of the day comes quicker than I'm ready for.

The dress rehearsal apology that had changed more times than a Vegas girl, continues to stir trouble in my head. It's pathetic really, because I should be an ace at saying sorry. I've had enough practice over the last twelve months.

I spy River a hundred yards from the front gate, his arms folded stiffly across his chest. It doesn't take a genius to tell his mood hasn't improved, making my apology all the more difficult to come forward. He hasn't seen me yet, the grey slush gathering in the gutters, seems far more interesting than keeping a sharp eye out for me. A vast contrast from this morning.

I stop in front of him. 'About what I said earlier …'

'Forget it,' he says, refusing to make eye contact.

'I'm sorry, I really am. Mr Butcher said he knew everything about the last few weeks and because you and Rachel are the only ones that know, I jumped to the wrong conclusion.'

'A very wrong conclusion.'

I wince as he forces his hands into his pockets. 'It's cold. We'd better get home.'

I don't notice the lofty frame of Mr Butcher striding towards us until he almost mows me down. His mission: two year-eight boys smoking behind the bush inside the school gates. I smirk as they hastily butt out their fags and stuff a handful of mints into their mouths.

'You two, up to the headmaster's office. Now,' he orders. The miscreants pick up their bags and march back up to the school.

I turn back to Mr Butcher, ready to ask him if he was serious about me *not* returning to school this year, when my body locks into place, breath absent, logic becoming a million grains of sand in my head. I can't believe what I'm seeing.

Ra-Mon and Mr Butcher ...together ... talking, like the last two people in the world you'd expect to meet. It's like watching the Queen and Osama Bin Laden crocheting together.

The icy cold air adds another dimension to my ability to move, and it takes all my strength to grab hold of River's coat sleeve and yank him into the bushes. I can feel the slow, jarring motion of my mouth trying to form words, my throat trying to create sound. The blood must drain from my face because River's mouth pops open the second before he catches me around the waist.

'Em?' He follows the direction of my gaze, the pair now deep in conversation.' He sharply inhales. 'Is that who I think it is?' He whispers into my hair.

I force my head to move – in what direction I'm not sure. 'Yes,' I mouth. My first instinct is to drag River further into the bushes that still somehow smell of cigarettes.

'How do you suppose he knows him?' River mutters.

'How the hell should I know,' is the only response I can come up with. Branches dig into my coat as I push him deeper into the bushes.

'What are we doing? Setting up camp? Because I forgot to bring my tent,' whispers River. 'We can't stay here forever.' I growl a non-verbal response. 'What's he going to do in broad daylight? I'm not afraid of him.' Lacing his fingers into mine, he pulls me back onto the path, my heart thudding at a million miles an hour.

I half-hide behind River as we head down to the gate. Mr Butcher and Ra-Mon, who somehow looks less spook-like and more scungy hippy-like, stop in mid-speech when we reach them, their expressions, a perfect Kodak moment. It's a strange interlude that I couldn't describe even if I had a hundred years to think of the answer.

'Em, hold up. I do walk this way home too, in case you forgot.' It's Rachel. She comes running straight for us, severing the invisible bond from Ra-Mon. 'Are you going to stand here all day? I'm bloody freezing.' I wait for her to freak out over seeing Ra-Mon again and yet for a reason stranger than any I've had recently, she can't see him, standing there, in front of us, his eyes glowing electric blue. I can't help wondering if Ra-Mon's presence is interchangeable depending on his company.

We head out of the school gates, words scratching at my lips to come out.

I grit my teeth. 'Mr Butcher knows.'

'I swear on my life, Em. I didn't tell him, or anyone else, about what happened,' are the words that comes blurting out Rachel's mouth before I can finish my sentence. 'Although, I'm not going to lie to you. I'm glad an adult knows,' she adds.

Frustration screams inside my head. Somebody must have said something, and the only way I'm going to find out, is to go to the source. Mr Butcher requires a home visit and that means walking back down my old street.

River dumps his bag on the floor by the old grandfather clock. 'I'm going for a swim. You can join me, if you want.' I can tell he doesn't want me to go. He is just being polite.

'No, it's okay. I think I need to chill by myself for a bit.' River shrugs and receives a stern look from Wally for it.

'Suit yourself. You know where I am if you need me.'

I do need him.

I do want to talk to him.

I want to tell him about the fight with Celeste and how the flame appeared again, and how she ran off faster than I have ever seen her move before, and how good it felt to have finally stood up to her.

Mr Butcher's words ring in my head, "I know everything". He can't possibly know about me being a FlameMaker, surely, and yet the rest of his sentence, "you need to gain strength and be yourself," suggests he does. Gain strength – meaning I needed to practice. Even I realise that. Maybe practicing will make me stronger, make me more … *myself*?

I fly upstairs to my room, head straight for the bathroom and shut the door. I still marvel that this room matches the size of my bedroom back at the Burberrys'. I figure there are fewer things in here to catch on fire and, in case something happens, water is on hand if I need it. I fold the three fluffy towels and place them outside the door. Now … to practice.

The heated tiles are a godsend as I sit cross-legged in the middle of the room. I close my eyes and concentrate, even though my brain chatters noisily with questions and theories. After a few breaths, the voices still until all I can hear is the soft plink, plink, plink of the dripping tap. Outside, the wind howls too, not distracting me but simply offering its breath of encouragement. The last few times, I recall, anger has been the key to drawing the flame up from the core of my body, erupting like some aggravated volcano, spewing forth a desire to desecrate everything in its way. Surely that can't be the only way. There has to be another trigger - a calmer, more controlled method. An amazing revelation came to me this morning after one of my old science books fell out of my locker and opened to a page on volatile and non-volatile charged particles. This power seems to be a natural and integral part of me. I should be able to harness it somehow without becoming an irate banshee.

I focus all my attention, tapping into my inner self. Each inward breath is softer than the one before, each breath out, more controlled. Conjuring fury when I'm not even remotely angry is a challenge. Over the last year, fear has been my dominant emotion, and I have done nothing to stop it from infiltrating bone and slithering through my arteries. More than ever, sitting in my quiet, peaceful pose, I'm positive it is the reason for smothering the fire in the first place, fire that flows as native to my body as oxygen is to my blood.

Time seems to slow as I reach deeper inside myself, desperate to discover what my purpose is, willing locked-away traits to reveal themselves. With my eyes still firmly shut, I picture the fire in my mind, burning, using my body as its source of energy, using me as I am using it in return - a fusion of two trusting partners. I visualise a blaze of bronze and copper, of blistering heat far exceeding boiling, and yet as cool in my hand as this evenings chill that waits outside with slow patient breaths.

I raise my chin a fraction and open my eyes. I know a flame is there before I see it; my body tells me it is, the same way an itch waits to be scratched or a headache begs to be rubbed. A single flame waits in my hand – waiting for orders … my orders. Placing my other hand above it and widening my arms, I can somehow stretch the flame longer, lengthening it until it resembles a fiery red spear. The pointed end tickles my palms. I smile proudly, surprised it wasn't as difficult as I thought it would be.

With my arms in the position of six o'clock, I rotate them ninety degrees to quarter to three, holding the flaming orange bar at arm's length. Slowly, I push my hands together, compressing the flame. The velocity increases tenfold until it begins to circulate between my hands into a mass of swirling fire. I have created a fireball. My first fireball.

'Cool,' I mutter, catching a glimpse of myself in the full-length mirror behind the door. It's about as surreal a scene as I've ever witnessed, sitting with a ball of fire spinning in my grasp. I bring my hands together, cupping one inside the other, extinguishing my new ally for a moment and then opening them. The small flame from before bobs about in my hand. I laugh out loud.

'Em, you've been in there for ages. Is anything wrong?' comes River's worried voice, followed by a sharp knock. 'I'm coming in,' he says firmly.

There isn't a lock on the door and even though he knows, and has seen me perform something similar, the fact that I am playing with fire in *his* house, and without his permission, suddenly makes me nervous. I close my hands but the flame refuses to leave. I open and close them, open and close them, willing it to go out.

The door handle twists.

I shake my hand frantically. The door starts to open, and, in my desperation, I extinguish it the only way I know … I blow on it.

Wow. It was *so* the wrong thing to do.

As River pushes the door open, a roaring flame rips from my hands and flies past his face. He jerks away in time, although the door doesn't fare as well. A black scorch mark arcs across its shiny, cream paintwork.

'What the …' shouts River. The door slams shut, and silence fills every available space except for the plink, plink, plink of the tap. I can't move, horrified by what I've done … and what I nearly did.

A tiny voice and a soft knock echo from the other side of the door. 'Em,' he says meekly. 'Can I come in? I'm not mad at you anymore.'

Yeah, not now, I think, amused. Not now that I tried to trim your eyebrows with a flamethrower. I still cannot find my voice as River cautiously opens the door, apprehension oozing out of him.

My body slowly recovers.

'Are you okay?' His voice is thin, his concern thick.

I jump up and fling my arms around his neck. 'Oh God, I'm so sorry, I'm so sorry,' I mutter into his chest. His hands circle my waist and one hand pats the middle of my back. I hold on to him, fearing if I let go, he'll crumble to ash. 'I didn't know that was going to happen … honestly.'

He soothes me. 'It's all right. I'm still here – minus a few strands I didn't need.' I screw up my eyes and hug him tighter.

'I could've killed you,' I mumble. River lifts my head and I stare into his glassy blue eyes.

'Nah, I'm stronger than you think.' He moves closer to me, inch by inch, my breath quivering as I inhale.

'Even now,' I whisper, closing my eyes.

'Even now,' he whispers back. He hesitates and I wait for his lips to find mine. They don't; instead, he kisses each eye tenderly.

Later, after dinner, and after a few more laps of the pool, I curl up in front of the open fire in River's formal lounge room, admiring the recently put up Christmas decorations and tree, Wally's doing, no doubt. It has never felt so like Christmas. The twelve-foot tree shimmers in gold and silver baubles and matching tinsel, and wall decorations adorn the ceilings and fireplace. At the Burberrys', a two-foot artificial tree is usually propped up in one corner, only for Aaron's benefit, and the house is shrouded in 'bah humbug'.

I tell River all about what happened with Celeste, adding that I don't think she will be bothering me any time soon.

River laughs. 'I would have given anything to see the look on her face.'

273

I suppose it was funny. Celeste's face was the colour of powdered chalk and her eyes rolling back into her skull is an image I won't be forgetting in a hurry.

A new interest dances in his eyes.

'What?' I ask.

'You have to show me,' says River eagerly. 'I'm dying to see you in action.'

And that is the point! He'd almost died both times I had conjured the flame. Am I prepared to risk it a third time? 'I'm not sure that's such a good idea,' I say, trying to find a smile for him. 'The times you've been there have somehow left you too incapacitated to watch.'

'Hmm,' says River. He doesn't look convinced, so I turn the conversation back to Celeste.

'And I hope you don't mind. I told her in no uncertain terms that I wouldn't be home for Christmas either.' This pleases River immensely and he joins me on the floor in front of the fire. Auburn flames, competing with the colour of my hair, lick at the charred brickwork as they jump and transform into pointy russet fireworks. River gazes into the fire.

'I know you can touch it, but can you pick it up and hold on to it?' he asks without removing his eyes from its flickering dance.

I stretch my hand towards the heart of the fire and scoop up a handful of flames. They leap into my palm like a playful pup.

'Freaky,' gasps River as I hold my hand over the hearth.

'Yeah, it is a bit, isn't it?' I withdraw my arm, making sure I haven't collected any embers with it. Although my skin is fireproof, my clothes and his uncle's soft furnishings most definitely are not. River sits in awe as the soft, compliant flames float in my hand like water.

'Will I meet your family when they come home for Christmas?' I ask, casually tickling the flame with my other hand.

River scratches his head nervously. 'Actually, I was going to talk to you about that.'

'Oh,' I say, curious.

'Yeah, they're not going to be able to make it home after all. Something went wrong with the shoot and they've got to stay for another few weeks.'

Maybe it is the way his voice rises a few octaves as he speaks, or the tiny twitch in his left eye, that gives him away. All I know is … I'm not buying it anymore.

'Really,' I say, one eyebrow arching. The flame is weaving its way through my fingers like a game. His disturbed frown makes me smile.

'Yes, really,' he says, less convincingly this time.

'So, show me a picture of them.'

Just then, Wally comes in with two mugs of hot chocolate. I slap my hands together to distinguish the flame, startling the poor man who quickly recovers the wobble from his tray.

I smile him an apology as he places the tray onto the table.

'Wally, where's the photo album?' asks River. Wally walks over to the large cream dresser, opens the glass doors at the top and pulls out a navy-blue album.

'Here you go, Master River,' he says, smoothing his hand over the cover, even though I see no signs of dust.

River flicks through the pages, one by one, showing me pictures of him and his parents at this castle and that fair, but all the photos were taken when he was small. When I ask if there are any up-to-date shots, he says his 'guardians' got too busy and hadn't found the time. I find this even more difficult to swallow, considering they are supposed to be photographers.

I yawn loudly.

I will get to the bottom of it but now I want to sleep. I decide to take Mr Butcher's advice and not go to school for the remaining two days of term. River walks me to my room, which I don't find strange anymore, to find the bed already turned down and the bedside light on.

'His blood's worth bottling,' I mumble to myself.

'And then some,' replies River with the same air of gratitude in his voice. He traces his finger from my temple and along my hairline to tuck a loose strand behind my ear. I want to lean into his hand, feel the warmth against my cheek. Something holds me back. Maybe it's the same something that prevents me from initiating the first move to reach out and touch him.

My arms remain at my sides as River cups my cheeks. Everything tells me he's about to kiss me like he's done before, but in that moment when I think he will, his single peck on my lips is over before it begins.

'Goodnight.' His voice is soft, leaving me wanting more of it.

He turns to leave and then stops. 'We need to visit Mr Butcher soon. Something about him bothers me.'

Relief floods my brain that I don't have to walk past *that* house by myself. It takes a long minute of looking at his face, inspecting the shadow across his cheek and the way his lips are so full they look like they might burst, before I finally mutter a goodnight.

As I lie down, knowing I am four days pure, the reality of my situation dawns on me. There is one Christmas present The Creeper isn't getting this year – ME. Never again will I lie in bed and pray to whoever is listening. Never again will I have to endure his breath in my mouth. Never again will he touch me. I sigh heavily, bringing with it one last burning tear.

Never again …

# TWENTY-SEVEN

$\mathcal{A}$ secretive smile appears and disappears on those full lips every time River looks at me from across the breakfast table the next morning.

'All right … I give.' I finally ask him, pushing my empty bowl away. 'What's with the smirk?'

River slides a lumpy looking gift along the table to me. It has all the airs of a rushed Sellotape job. 'I thought we'd head into London today for some Christmas shopping,' he says, still grinning. My throat fills with joy and sadness and I want to run around the table and kiss him, except his arms are folded so tightly against his chest, he doesn't look up for it. Every Christmas, my parents and I would spend the day in London, shopping. I sit for a minute, contemplating whether to laugh or cry.

'Aren't you going to open it?'

Colour floods my cheeks. I rip the paper to see something cream and woollen inside. It's the first gift anyone has given me since my crystal rocking horse.

'They're lovely.' I partially ignore the label saying they were made in Paris. I slip on the gloves, relishing the softness. There's also a matching scarf and hat.

'You'll need them,' says River, glancing out of the window. 'It's freezing outside.' I follow his gaze to see delicate snowflakes, falling effortlessly.

I race upstairs to get ready, and on my return, find River leaning on the bannister, ready to leave. Without allowing my brain to come up with all the reasons why I shouldn't, I reach up onto my tiptoes and kiss his cheek. 'Thanks.' I tell myself his jaw clenching beneath my lips is all in my head.

The immaculate, pebbled driveway is hidden beneath a thick carpet of snow until Walter reverses a black car out of the garage. He pulls up in front of us as we stamp away the cold. 'What do you reckon?' River gestures to the car.

'It's shiny,' I say, seeing my reflection shrug back at me.

River looks flabbergasted. 'It's shiny! It's shiny!' he gasps. 'This is an Audi S8. It goes from zero to a hundred in four seconds.'

'*And*?' It shows that I know absolutely zilch about cars.

'It's the coolest thing on four wheels.'

'Right, an Audi S8. I'll commit that to memory,' I say sarcastically.

River opens the door and, as always, is waiting with a reply. 'Well, unless you want to run behind it, I suggest you get in.' I can tell from the second I slide across the leather seats it isn't your average family car. There's a built-in iPod, mobile phone and DVD outlet in the rear of the car *and* a button to heat/tilt or massage the seats, tinted windows to keep out the nosey parkers and the cup holders contain a bottle of water for each of us.

River grins.

Something I knew before but am even more aware of now is that River's family were extremely wealthy.

Wally pulls over at the top of Oxford Street to let us out and makes no song and dance about telling River to phone him every hour on the hour, so he knows where we are and that we're safe. I don the scarf and hat but leave the gloves in my bag. River throws his gloves on to the back seat, and we have barely walked a few minutes before his hand slides cosily into mine.

The first stop is to buy a coat. River's Parka, although warm, is way too big for me and twenty minutes later, I ditch my old, thin coat for a three-quarter length bottle green woollen coat that I got for a steal. The hat and scarf look gorgeous with it, and my reflection in the shop windows, dangling with pastel fairy lights, says I could be anyone I want to be.

London is the best place to be at Christmas. But being here comes at a cost ...memories. The smell of pine, and roasted nuts waft out of shop doorways and the delicious aroma of sweet cinnamon and treacle pudding reminding me of when life was easy, and I wasn't an orphan. Sadness creeps into my heart as snow lands softly on the shoulders of people in front of me, most head down into the wind, carrying brightly coloured gifts under their arms or in bags. My parents met in Carnaby Street on a freezing December evening outside a roasted chestnut van, and it had become a tradition for them to re-enact that same day every year. It then became *our* special day. I glance across to the park, remembering the adorable snowman we'd built when I was seven. My eyes prickle at the edges with tears.

River squeezes my hand as though he knows and sends me one of his adoring looks that I don't ever think he'll know what it does to me ... physically, emotionally and spiritually. 'Are you hungry?' He points to a place across the street that has a sign out the front saying, "Eat-All-U-Want - VEGGIE Christmas Dinner."

I nod.

The bay windows at the front of the restaurant remind me of a house from a Charles Dickens movie, although I wouldn't know which one or when I'd seen it. Snow has piled up in little crescent moons along the edges of each individual windowpane.

It's so toasty warm inside and I shrug out of my coat and woollies immediately. We are shown to a seat near the window and a young girl takes our drinks order. Christmas shoppers scurry about in the snow and I lose myself for a moment until River's voice brings me back. 'You must be hungry. I'll wait for our drinks.'

I head over to the serving stations and load up my plate. On my return, I notice River on the phone and figure it must be Wally checking in. Gazing out of the window, he is oblivious that I'm standing right behind him.

'No. I haven't seen any sign of him. Have you?'

I'm confused.

River falls silent for a few seconds. 'Good. We must have given him the slip.'

My knife and fork accidentally chink against my plate, and River looks up at me in surprise. 'Yeah thanks, Wally. We'll probably do a bit more shopping. I'll phone you when we're ready to be picked up.' He hangs up.

I sit down, unable to take my eyes off him.

'Wow, you were hungry,' says River. There is a nervous tremor to his voice.

'Gave who the slip?' I ask. The food can wait.

'What?'

'You heard me, River Fulton! I said, gave who the slip?' Just then the drinks arrive.

'Ember?' A hollow, unexpected voice speaks. 'Is that you?' I'm concentrating so hard on River I hadn't seen the young guy turn up with our drinks.

'*Skye*?'

'You *remembered*,' he says, flattered. It isn't the *only* thing I remember about him. His pewter coloured eyes glow at me, erasing my line of 'what are you doing here?'.

River's head is going back and forth between us. I notice the recollection in his eyes, but if I had to put money on it, I would say it is more irritation than plain curiosity.

'River, you remember Skye from Ski-Tobogganing, don't you?'

'And the bonfire,' chips in Skye playfully.

I hadn't told River about that.

The cloud lifts from River's face. 'Yeah, how ya going?' he says flatly.

'Better now, champ,' he says as he winks at me.

I blush.

'Well, I'm going to get my food.' River gets up to leave and pulls Skye to one side. 'Don't be here when I get back,' I hear him say.

Skye simply laughs and nods.

River turns back once and scowls as he heads towards the food station.

'What was that about?' I ask as Skye places our drinks on the table.

He smiles so widely people on other tables stare at him. His streaked hair falls perfectly into place as he runs his fingers through it.

'Your big, bad boyfriend feels threatened by me.' He puckers his lips. 'Don't blame him though; you're worth duelling over.'

I let out a laugh. 'Did you say duelling or drooling?' He's so full of himself, I can't help liking him.

His straight, white teeth gleam from behind a pair of pale pink lips. 'Both work for me. Let me give you my number in case you get sick and tired of Mr I'm-about-as-exciting-as-frozen-dog shit.' He pulls out a small pad from the pocket of his apron and scribbles something before handing me the note, leaving with a cute smile as River returns.

'See ya handsome,' Skye calls out over his shoulder to River.

River slumps down and shovels forkfuls of peas into his mouth.

'You don't like Skye?'

'What's to like? The guy thinks his shit doesn't stink.' River attacks his food as though he hates every mouthful as much as he hates Skye Buchannan. I try making small talk, although the exuberance from before seems to have dried up. It's then I remember my question. This time, I need a little more tact. I reach across the table and trace the lines on the back of his hand until finally he looks up. His face softens.

'River, what did you mean about giving someone the slip? Who were you talking about? Does it have anything to do with me?' My first thought is The Creeper.

River places his knife and fork down and takes a gulp of his Coke as if deliberately prolonging the moment. 'I didn't want to say anything to you before. Not after all you've been through ...'

I feel the blood drain from my face. 'About what?'

'Someone has been following you.' The words hang in mid-air. I go through the list in my head ... could be The Creeper, could be Ra-Mon, or perhaps ...

'It's Mr Butcher,' says River grimly. Strangely enough, he was going to my next guess. 'He's been hanging about out the front of my house for days now. I didn't wanna freak you out, but I've also seen him loitering outside your old house, too.'

'I know,' I say as I recall him sitting on the wall three doors down from the Burberrys'.

River's face darkens. 'What do you mean, you know?'

My brain is still fuzzy from the two weeks of amnesia and I'm not sure if I'd told River about the encounter with Mr Butcher or not. 'I thought he was waiting for someone or taking a rest,' I explain. River mumbles something about how he should have said something before. I weave my fingers into his hand. 'Again, you're blaming yourself. Just stop, okay. Stop.'

River nods unconvincingly.

'Can we carry on with our day and deal with this when we get home? I just want to spend one day where I don't have to think about fire, or me ending the world. I mean, he can't be any more dangerous than Ra-Mon, right?'

'Sure,' replies River. And we finish our meal in silence.

It's well after three before we leave the restaurant and the snow clouds have grown thicker and heavier bringing daylight to an end. We shop in virtual silence until the streetlights come on, Oxford Street coming alive in colours of blue, red, green and amber.

I thread the last of my carry bags on to my wrist. 'Do you want to give Wally a ring to pick us up? I'm all shopped out.'

'OK,' says River, 'but we're not going home just yet.'

I glance up, curious.

River's face comes to life again. 'I have something special organised.'


'Is everything going to plan?' asks Walter from over his shoulder as we bundle into the back of the car.

'Yeah, Wally. We have fifteen minutes. Do you reckon we'll make it in this traffic?'

Walter laughs. 'Have I ever let you down, Master River?'

River pats the man's shoulder. 'Never, Wally. You know I wouldn't have got through this without you.'

Walter chuckles. 'You flatter me, sir,' he says, weaving in and out of cars.

River and Wally seem to have a friendship way beyond a master and servant relationship. Their familiarity is obvious, and I add it to the ever-growing list of anomalies in the secret world of River Fulton.

Some nine minutes later, the car pulls over to the side of the road.

'Hyde Park?' I ask. 'What are we doing? Having a picnic?' I can't help the sarcasm.

'Nah. I thought it would be too cold.' River smirks. 'How about Winter Wonderland? I've booked an hour on the ice rink too and then we can go and see the ice sculptures and the Christmas circus and rides if you want to.'

Tears spring from my eyes and I leap across the seat and hug him. 'Want to?' I gasp. 'I'd love to.' It's the one place I visited every year with my parents.

'I'll call you,' River says to Wally as he shuts the door.

While we queue for our skates, I wonder if River actually knows how to skate. He's a gun grass skier, but ice is totally different. Rachel and I used to go ice-skating every weekend until my parents died. I haven't skated since.

I stand poised at the edge, mesmerised by the net of twinkling lights hanging above us like a web of glow-worms. A thirty-piece orchestra, sits in the middle of the ice rink, spiralling out the sounds of *Santa Claus Is Coming to Town*.

'Are you going to stand there all night and watch?' asks River, an eyebrow half cocked. I wait for a break in the traffic and then confidently zoom out into the middle, glancing over my shoulder to see River closing in on me with all the pace and agility of a speed-skater.

I roll my eyes and turn around so that I'm skating backwards. River immediately copies my move.

'So, you're an Olympic swimmer, downhill skier and a rough-as-guts hockey player. 'Is there anything you can't do?'

'Nope. I don't think so.' He grins. For the first time since we've met, he actually looks happy. I spin around and thread my hand into his.

'Did I ever tell you that you're the coolest chick, ever?'

The icy breath of winter stings my face as I smile. 'Yeah. You did. But I'll never get tired of hearing it.' He smiles and hugs me closer. Our hour is up and, as always, far sooner than I want. I force my boots off, and River takes our skates back while I put my shoes on.

I blow into my gloved hands and glance up in time to see Mr Butcher staring at me from across the other side of the ice rink. My mouth drops open as our eyes meet, before he disappears into the crowd. River hurries back and I discard all traces of panic from my face. He doesn't need to know, not when he seems more relaxed and is finally beginning to enjoy himself.

We make our way into the Magical Ice Kingdom where bears, foxes and rabbits and a whole range of woodland creatures, including reindeer, have been carved out of ice and set in amazing scenes that have kids oohing and aahing as they walk around. I say no to the Observation Wheel, which is a huge Ferris wheel overlooking the whole of Winter Wonderland. Instead, we walk around the amusement rides that either shoot up in the air at warp speed or spin so fast they make you sick.

Snow gently swirls around us as we stroll through the outdoor markets, sipping hot chocolate and eating warm sugary donuts. Christmas novelty gifts and handmade crafts decorate every table. Jewellery, crystals and clothes stalls adorn the paths and walkways, and a jolly Santa sits in his giant gold chair, waving and smiling to children as they look on in awe.

I loop my hand through the crook of River's arm. 'This is the best day I've ever had. Thank you.'

'You're welcome,' he says, tenderly brushing snowflakes from my nose. 'Now, would you believe me if I said I have nothing left on my agenda?'

I smile. 'There's one thing I'd like to do before we go but I have to find it first.'

River's marine blue eyes narrow and his lips twitch to one side. 'What are we looking for?'

'I'll tell you when I find it,' I tease. We walk for another half an hour with River asking every few minutes or so 'can you see it yet?' and me shaking my head. It must be here. Christmas isn't Christmas without it.

'If you tell me what we're looking for then …'

'You'll know when I find it.' This is killing him. I'm sure the moment I tell him I'm looking for mistletoe, he'd point to it straight away. No … I need to find this myself. We circle around the ice rink and stop at the spot where I'd seen Mr Butcher, hours earlier.

'There,' I point excitedly.

I drag River behind me. He is still calling out, 'where, I don't see anything?' I stop in front of the Star Tavern, a quaint looking building that has been made to look old with its white rendered walls and thick black crossbeams. The stained-glass windows and thatched roof give it that extra walk back into history. Handfuls of people, drinking mulled wine, occupy the wooden benches outside and yet all I can smell are mince pies.

I pretend to sound surprised: 'Oh look, mistletoe.' A beautiful bouquet hangs over the doorway. It hasn't escaped my mind that River hasn't kissed me since I was captured. A kiss would be such a perfect end to a perfect day.

'Is *that* what you were looking for?' River says with an incredulous look. I'm grateful for the cold that nips at my cheeks, hiding my blush. I could also put the icy temperature down to the reason my teeth are chattering and not the nervous rumble in my stomach, wondering if he's about to kiss me again. I saunter over and stand beneath the magical kissing plant, woven into a wreath threaded with ribbons and dried berries. River follows behind me, his face twisting with all kinds of anguish.

He takes a deep breath. 'Look, Em. It's not that I don't want to kiss you … I do. It's just that I …'

'It's him, isn't it?' I mutter the words to my feet.

'Yes and no.'

I lift my head, my eyes finding his, my jaw set firmly. 'That's not an answer. Either you want to kiss me, or you don't. Don't use him as an excuse for how I might feel or react. If I want you to kiss me, then it means exactly that. Nothing is hidden beneath my words and nothing ...'

River pulls me into his arms and kisses me fiercely at first, almost desperately, totally oblivious of who is watching and what people might think. It's as though he's held off for as long as he can and now, he's free and he can't stop, won't stop, doesn't know how to stop. It's so unlike him, so out of control, and yet exhilarating beyond measure. The urgency in his touch is wild and a little scary as though I am the drug he has been holding out for. The heavy pulse in his neck throbs beneath my fingertips, and I would pay the devil himself to have a lifetime of this. His hands are cold against my skin, but I don't care, because we are one again. I want him so badly, and kiss him back just as hard, fuelling his hunger for me, un-taming myself in the process, desperate to know this part of him that wants me more than he can tell me. He responds, more excited, more reckless, his hands wandering over my body, his tongue searching for me.

An inferno erupts.

Not totally from me, rather than between us. Flames leap from him to me and back again, sparking my own internal firestorm. Blazing hot fire thrusts out of me, anxious to extinguish his cool, calming demeanour. His breath turns hot in my mouth, increasing my need of him and when my hands find the contours of his cheekbones, they are slick with sweat. There seems to be a battle going on and I gasp for air as his lips move to my ear and then to my neck, his hands full of my hair.

And then stillness. Total and utter nothing. No heat, no passion. No longer competing, now compatible, harmonious as if an agreement between our bodies has been made and an understanding reached.

'Sorry,' he whispers breathlessly into my neck. His torment eases, his hold loosens, his mouth softer as he comes back to me, kisses now slower. His lips shape themselves around mine, like they are made for me and only me. His eagerness settles and I fall into him, my life in his hands, my future running parallel with his, my heart always belonging to him. This is the boy I know. The boy I love.

'Why are you sorry?' I manage to ask when he leans away to look at me.

'I shouldn't have. I can't …' Very softly, he dusts his thumb across my chin and then over my lips.

'Can't, what?'

'Never mind. I thought you needed time to … heal,' he says, grimacing as he overly pronounces the last word.

I run my fingers from his temple to his jaw. 'You heal me, River. You. Heal. Me.'

His lips are full and soft when I reach up and kiss him again and with all the sounds of Christmas, the chatter and laughter from within the tavern, the wind blowing around us in caressing bursts, the high-pitched screams from the fairground rides and the snow that continues to fall, I have never known life to be so peaceful.

# TWENTY-EIGHT

*It's* well after three when the car finally pulls up in front of his house. I sleepily refuse his numerous offers to carry me in and feel immediate relief when I open the door to my room. There's no bedside light left on, and the bed hasn't been turned down like I am used to. I now understand what River means by not getting this far without Wally. He makes life a little sweeter.

River flicks on the light, chasing away every last remaining shadow. His face abruptly turns to stone and he strides past me to the bedside cabinet. Leaning against the lamp, is an envelope with my name on it.

My heart thunders when I see it - adrenalin ripping through my body, ridding me of sleepiness. I walk over and pick it up, debating whether I have the courage to open it. River, stares at it, no doubt wondering how someone has managed to infiltrate his home, which has more locks and security systems than Wormwood Scrubs.

His voice nudges me out of my daze. 'Open it.'

I slide my finger beneath the seal and pull out the contents.

The note is brief and to the point: 'It's time you knew the truth.' It is signed by Mr E Butcher.

'Looks like someone's up for a visit sooner than we thought,' says River.

I'm thinking the exact same thing.


The sterility of chlorine coaxes me from my sleep the next morning. River's hair, it's usual colour of wet coal is as familiar as the gentle kiss on the lips and the bucket load of guilt lingering in his eyes. I still don't understand what his apology was for, and I don't suppose I ever will. Getting him to open up is fast becoming a problem.

'Are you getting up today, sleepy-head?' He yanks back the curtains and I stretch out my arms and glance over at the clock. I groan. It's eleven thirty. 'Wally has breakfast ready.'

Still groggy with sleep, I shower and head downstairs, trying to ignore the nervous tremor growing inside me.

River looks up. 'Em, it'll be all right. It's only Mr B.'

My eyes follow the cream dining table to its end, amid racks of toast, ceramic pots of condiments and butters, to see River leaning over his plate, anxiety replacing those wonderfully romantic blue eyes from last night.

I purse my lips, struggling to find a smile. I want to say I know, but I can't entice the words out. I *don't* know. Every time life is good and sweet and coasting along nicely, something always happens.

River pushes his plate away. 'I'm going for a quick swim before we leave. You should join me. I think you need to wind down a bit.'

My eyes find solace in the chairs, the walls, the dresser. 'You go. I'll meet you there.' River hesitates a moment before pushing his chair out. He disappears before I can add anything else.

I chase my eggs around the plate a few times before giving up and settling on a piece of toast.

'Not hungry, Miss?' asks Wally, appearing out of nowhere to clear the plates.

'Sorry, Wally. I'm sure they're delicious, but I don't think I can face anything this morning.' I frown at the word *anything* and wonder whether Wally picks up on it. He says nothing and yet, for a fraction of a second, I see a glimpse of someone more than a butler – a friend, a brother, a father, a man who has been there for River come hell or high water and who is now there for me too. A saviour, who helped River drag my unconscious body into the car in whatever state I was in, and yet still able to look at me with respect and integrity. A shot of sympathy flickers across his gaze and vanishes just as quickly.

'Thanks, Wally. For everything.'

He removes the remains of my breakfast. 'I'll get these out of your way.'

I sit for ten minutes, contemplating joining River for a swim. In truth, I don't want to feel calm. I don't want to wash away the one feeling that has kept me alive, and sane, and alert. I can't give up my inner warning system, not when I need it more than ever. I need to channel this and use it to my advantage.

I slip down from the table and follow the long, cold corridor down to the pool. River is still swimming, and I press my back into the wall and wait for him to stop.

'Aren't you afraid of what he has to say?' I ask after he finishes his last lap.

'No. I told you, he doesn't scare me. Anyway, I've taken care of everything.'

I have no idea what he's talking about and it isn't until we are standing at the front door ready to leave, that he tells Wally if he doesn't get a phone call by six o'clock at the latest, he's to send the cops around to the house with the yellow door at the end of my street. I don't ask what would happen if we leave that house, forced or otherwise.

291

'Maybe Wally should drive us?' I say as the reality of walking past the Burberrys revisits my thoughts.

'I won't let *anyone* near you, Em,' says River.

I know my fire will protect me and that I have better control over it, but what if, when it comes down to it, when I'm under pressure, it fails to work? I have yet to put that scenario into practice.

It's way after three before we set out. My pace instinctively alters to match my heartbeat as we reach the top of my street. Three inches of snow piles up around our shoes as we walk, hindering the speediness of my legs as the Burberry's house comes ever closer. I whisper my apology for crushing River's hand and finally let out that much needed breath once we pass.

The yellow front door of Mr Butcher's house is all that stands between fear and knowledge. The curtains are haphazardly drawn across the window and I knock as though I don't really want to disturb him. The door swings open the second I withdraw my hand and the formidable figure of Mr Butcher stands before us, his hulking frame filling most of the doorway.

'I'm glad you came,' he says, smiling first at me and then looking over my head at River. 'Come in, first door on the right.' River and I are ushered into what I can only assume was once a lounge room.

My first observation is how sparsely furnished his house is. There are no pictures up, no photographs, not even curtains on the back window. A single brown chair in the corner snuggles up close to a coffee table, leaving the rest of the room bare. Mr Butcher, being new to the school and the area, surely owns more than a few pieces of scrappy furniture, especially a man of his age and education. I glance into the kitchen to see no dining table, no clutter and no lived-in mess.

Mr Butcher gestures me to sit in the only chair. He disappears for a few minutes and returns with two metal dining chairs with red leather seats, layered with a decade of dust on them.

'You don't expect me to believe you *actually* live here, do you?' I say, surprised.

Mr Butcher grins. 'Like I said, one of the smartest I've come across, and no, I don't live here. It's more like a … halfway house.'

Halfway to what, I wonder. 'At least you're starting off with the truth.'

'And straight to the point … I like that,' replies Mr Butcher, smoothing his wiry beard with the back of his hand. 'It will help later on.'

With my hands clasped in my lap, palms damp, I wait … poised.

'I suppose I should get right down to it then,' says Mr Butcher. He rises and offers me his hand. 'I would like to *re-introduce* myself.' I frown the same time River does. 'My name is Empedocles.'

I let out a laugh, but River looks puzzled. 'Who?' he says.

'You're not honestly going with that, are you?' I say, shaking my head and waiting for the smile to slide from his face. 'However did you manage that?'

Mr Butcher is neither delirious nor joking. His lips tighten. 'I am also immortal,' he says.

'Right,' I say, 'of course you are. And I'm Cleopatra.'

River's face contorts in confusion. 'Would someone like to fill me in?'

Mr Butcher raises his bushy eyebrows at me. 'Are you going to tell him, or shall I?'

I sigh. It will sound better coming from me. 'Do you remember when we were researching the history of the four elements?' I wait until he nods. 'Empedocles was the man, born in 492 BC mind you, who supposedly founded the four elements and who is now standing right in front of us … in the flesh.'

River stares at Mr Butcher, who shrugs with a sheepish grin. 'You expect us to believe that?'

Mr Butcher cuts him off and turns back to me. 'Why is my story any less believable than yours, Miss Riley? I know you're a FlameMaker. How would I know that if I wasn't who I said I was?'

'You must have overheard us,' River butts in.

Mr Butcher gives a weary shake of his head. 'I know about Ra-Mon too,' he says.

'You could've seen us together,' I add hastily, though I have no idea how he knew his name.

Mr Butcher grumbles something to himself in a language I've never heard before. He is weird and springs up out of nowhere at random moments. But *immortal*? That's *impossible*. I can explain who I am to anyone, with one wave of my hand. All Mr Butcher has is his word, and not a very trusting one at that.

'So, you're saying you can't die?' I say, sensing the imminent heat rising from my feet, already anticipating my next move.

'That's right,' he says soberly.

I don't waste time considering his answer. With a flash of heat and light and without giving my intentions away, a flame appears in my hand, flickering with the breeze coming from the open kitchen window. I blow heavily on it, transforming the room into the perfect platform for my fiery comet to fly across. A vibrant orange haze swirls around Mr Butcher, engulfing him in a spiral of fire.

He stands with a slightly amused expression on his face, my flame spear having no effect on him. He pretends to dust off his clothes as the last spark fizzles from his thick, woollen jumper.

I close my hand and extinguish the flame.

'Believe me now? Do you really think you're the only one in this world with the power to shock? With all that you now know, am I so impossible to believe in?'

My brain is empty. No words exist. I want to ask questions, but I don't know where to start. I'm at a total loss, but River is worse. Then the reality of what I have done finally sinks in. What if he was *mortal?*

'Oh my God, I could've killed you,' I mumble into my hands. I slump back into the chair, staring up at Mr Butcher.

He brushes off my concern. 'I think an explanation is in order,' he says, his voice calm and composed. He paces back and forth a few times before stopping in front of the kitchen doorway. His hands remain behind his back. 'I finally came to terms with my immortality as I walked inside the belly of that volcano, you know, the one that I supposedly jumped into.' His eyes take on an unnatural haze, like frosted glass. He doesn't seem to be talking to anyone in particular, and I desperately want to ask him what it was like. Was it as hot as hell or hotter? 'But for the record,' he says, 'I *didn't* jump. I was pushed.' The glazed look is gone, replaced by fire and determination. I want to circle back to that one.

He begins to pace again. 'I came to believe, over time, as I outlived my peers and family that something was different about me. The first time I tested my immortality, I was on a ship near Italy. I decided to throw myself overboard. The water, cold at first, streamed into my lungs, and for a moment I believed everything I lived by was a lie. That was until my body began to absorb the water like air. I became one with the sea. The waves cradled me like a lost child and the water was as warm and as comforting as my own bed. Later, I tried to throw myself from a carriage, aiming to break my neck, yet the ground was softer than any mattress I'd slept on, cushioning my fall. I next tried to hang myself but when the air lifted me higher, causing the rope to slacken, caressing my neck like a silk scarf might, I knew that death would never visit me.'

I gasp at his words.

'I now know I was sent here,' continues Mr Butcher, 'to give people knowledge about how it all began and to teach them the principles of the four elements - earth, air, fire and water, and how such powerful forces could control the earth. And by taking any one of them away, the earth would turn to dust and civilisation would cease to exist.'

Finally, he sits down. River also takes a chair.

'My human body hid the secrets of who I was until I was finally tested, the same way it was hidden from you, and the same way the secrets of creation are hidden from every human. It was only then, when I'd learnt the truth of who I was and what my role in evolution was, that my memory came back.'

'Sent from where?' I ask.

'And by who?' adds River.

Mr Butcher answers both questions with one answer. 'The Creator,' he says with a wry smile. 'You see Ember, Ra-Mon and I were created as brothers.'

'Were?' I frown.

Mr Butcher's gaze disappears through the wall to a place that has its own rules. 'Even the purest of us can have a difference of opinion, especially after spending a millennium together. He was always more assertive than I, always searching for ways to challenge himself and bring about change, whether that was in the best interest for this world … or not.' His lips twitch into a smile. 'As you know, when the earth was created, fire consumed the planet. But fire wasn't just formed, Ember … it was produced by a FlameMaker – the first FlameMaker - an immortal being who reigned over the earth, devastating the planet with her power. She was made by the Creator as a …'

'An experiment …' I blurt out.

'Well, I wouldn't put it *quite* like that, but you're on the right track. We are all beings of energy - you, me, the trees outside, even a rock buried deep in the ground. Everything gives out a vibration, and it is this that led the Creator to bring forth the FlameMaker - to witness the cause and effect of energy.'

'What about the others?' I ask.

Mr Butcher lets out a deep sigh. 'The other Elementars were created upon request.'

'By who?' asks River, leaning forward, his elbows on his knees.

'Ra-Mon, being as curious as he was, asked the Creator to craft a companion for the FlameMaker – someone equally as powerful but as different as could be. He assigned Ra-Mon and I as overseers of this world, and the WaterLover Immortal was created. For a time, the two lived in harmony.

River reaches up and wipes his hand across his forehead.

'Are you okay?' I ask. The colour in his cheeks is nearly all but gone, his skin, white like eggshells.

He nods unconvincingly, before mumbling something to do with Adam and Eve.

'Close, Mr Fulton,' says Mr Butcher smiling. 'It's amazing how the two stories have become so separate, when they were born from the same fact. As time passed, the WaterLover became stronger than the FlameMaker. His emotional needs were unfulfilled to the point his power overcame him, and an abundance of water surged onto the planet. The FlameMaker disappeared and we were left with this out-of-control emotional being.' River shifts in his seat causing Mr Butcher to pause for a few seconds. 'Something had to be done before the WaterLover lost all control. He had already covered the entire planet in water and Ra-Mon looked to the Creator to fashion a companion for him, but not a woman this time. A brother, like the brother he had in me.'

Mr Butcher's eyes grow cloudy, all lightness vanishing. We sit in silence, waiting.

'Go on,' I urge.

'The AirWhisperer was the next Immortal, and he and the WaterLover were indeed the brothers that Ra-Mon had hoped they'd be. They remained loyal to each other, but the law of evolution told us that one day, one would be stronger than the other. The AirWhisperer's powers grew, and the more oxygen he emitted, the stronger he became. Every vacant space was filled with pure, breathable oxygen, even to the point of infiltrating water. The WaterLover's powers fell and he, too, disappeared without a trace.'

River starts pacing to and fro. I raise my eyebrows. 'And?'

'Ra-Mon was becoming erratic and impatient, demanding to know where he went wrong, but, like the Creator told him, there is no right or wrong, no good or evil. There is only truth. Ra-Mon didn't believe it and took it upon himself to generate a final immortal, one who would tie the three of them together and bring unity and harmony to this world. He did so without the permission of the Creator and so the EarthHealer was made. But she also hungered for the chance to be supreme, using great amounts of oxygen from the AirWhisperer to create life and sustain her many living organisms, which as you can guess, vanquished the AirWhisperer forever. The EarthHealer then used the water and earth to accommodate her creations and fire to regenerate her beloved children when death found them.'

'Mother Nature,' I utter.

'Amazing isn't it, when you hear the story in its entirety? Parts of the truth have survived for thousands of years, parts have fallen into legend and others are now looked upon as a strange tale in a black bound book.'

'Yes,' we both whisper at the same time.

Mr Butcher's face clouds over. 'Of course, it wasn't the Immortal's fault, that they desired power. It was how they were made, without thought for anyone but themselves. We simply watched on from above.'

'Like angels,' I say, suppressing a laugh.

'We've been known by worse.'

'I bet you have,' mutters River.

'But after the EarthHealer was created, the Creator became angry and banished Ra-Mon and I from his side, not wanting anything more to do with Earth. It was forbidden to create another to combat the EarthHealer's powers and we were cast out.'

I look into my hands. It all sounds so incredible, so utterly unbelievable, yet Mr Butcher's story gels inside me in a way that can't be anything else but truth. The same way I know I am different.

'So, to end the story, The Creator stripped all of mine and Ra-Mon's powers, save one. If the other immortals were ever discovered, the Creator gave Ra-Mon and I the ability to either Generate, Operate or Destroy their abilities, … all in his name, hence the abbreviation – GOD.'

'NO WAY!' My mouth falls open and stays that way. 'Are you here to destroy me?'

My Butcher smirks. 'If I was, we wouldn't be having this conversation. I like to see myself as the *good* twin. You are an Elementar, Ember, and it is by you coming into your power that has drawn Ra-Mon to you. Your presence lured me closer as it will attract the others too. We need to be ready when they come.'

'When who will come?' asks River.

'The other Elementars – WaterLover, AirWhisperer and EarthHealer. It is your job to unite them and be ready.'

I swallow. 'For what?'

'And here is the bombshell. Prepare yourselves. Ra-Mon plans to overthrow you all, to control you and the Elementars, and use the earth as his own personal experiment.'

'*What*?' Hysteria breaks through my voice.

'That is the reason I had to reveal myself to you. I thought at first I was mistaken, and that you were one of the many fire users that have graced this planet, but when Ra-Mon recognised you at the school gate and I read his mind, I knew you were the true FlameMaker. I had to bring the two of you together so I could be sure.'

'So, where does that leave us?'

'He will come for you, Ember, when he deems you ready. He knows that duelling you now would be a hollow victory.'

'Oh, thanks for the vote of confidence,' I say, dryly.

'He wants a worthy opponent - a glorious conquest. He is a child with a magnifying glass and if an immortal could have an ego, his would be beyond anything you could comprehend. His aim isn't to conquer and rule … it is to do battle and deserve his title.'

I chance a look at River, who is still pacing. 'We do have one thing in our favour.'

'What's that?' I ask.

'Ra-Mon will only challenge you when you are at your strongest.'

'How come?'

'The stronger you are and the harder you fight, the more he can milk your strength for himself, leaving you weak and easy to vanquish you. Being on this plain, drains our immortal energy and he will exert all of his power to win, otherwise it will leave him vulnerable and open to defeat.'

'So, I'm screwed either way? Great!'

Mr Butcher says nothing.

'And if he succeeds?'

'We'll cross that bridge when we come to it.'

'But if he succeeds,' I protest. 'Fire will disappear from the earth?'

Mr Butcher's head yo-yos from side to side. 'Yes and no. Fire can still ravage through the earth but by his command only, and that can only happen when he has control over all four elements. He'll have to get through all four of you.'

I let out an exasperated sigh. 'That makes me feel loads better.'

'This is good news,' he says, conjuring a smile. 'It means we have time to train and find the others.'

'Who are they and how are we going to do that?'

Mr Butcher's face falls, his eyes interrogating, trying to peel back each individual layer of the space between us. 'They will present themselves to you at the appropriate time.' His feet shift, the same time his bold stare does. 'Before I was banished, I was told by the Creator of a prophecy of the twenty-first age. One would descend from the north, one from the south, one from the east and one from the west. Human children, with the ability to channel the elements, would step forth and save the world before time ran out.' Mr Butcher grimaces. 'If we can manage to keep Ra-Mon off your back while you and I have a little one-on-one training, and search for the others, I'm sure it would up the stakes of the game. I'm sorry I know it's not much to go on …'

'It's nothing to go on,' I snap as the mountainous task surrounds me from every angle.

Mr Butcher's face softens. 'It's not an easy life to live, you know, being an immortal. I have my own problems too.'

'But you don't have to go up against Ra-Mon, do you?'

'Believe me, I've been there and lived to tell the tale. Let's not focus on what has happened. You have to prepare. You have to discover what else you can do.'

'Why doesn't the Creator take Ra-Mon down himself?' asks River, stopping in mid-step. 'It would eliminate all of this.'

'Hmm, that would be the perfect solution, wouldn't it? But there's no way that can happen.'

'Why not?'

'Because when he'd seen what he'd created in the FlameMaker, he felt too burdened with the responsibility of it and relinquished all of his power to Ra-Mon and I, so that we could watch over the fate of the earth. He is but an observer now, listening to prayers, giving hope to those who still ask for it.'

'Then why don't you whoop Ra-Mon's arse, if you've got all this power?' River fires back.

'Believe me, I wish I could, but the Creator determined that our powers were not to be used against each other. It neutralises whenever we fight. We've tried it ... several times. Only the combined effort of the Elementars can defeat Ra-Mon.'

My head aches and tiny pink spots appear on the back of my hand as I continue to pinch myself. 'I can't believe this is happening, I just can't believe it,' I mumble into my lap.

'We need to see what you can do, Ember. We need to have an idea of where to start your training.'

River sits back down in his chair and grins. 'I'd like to see what you've got, too.'

I throw him a wicked stare and River chuckles. 'Aren't two near death experiences enough for you?' I say, trying to keep the smile from my lips. step, like I've been practising, and then make it leap from one hand, high into the air and swirl for a second before returning into the other.

'That's such a cool party trick,' River says impressed. 'I knew there was a reason I wanted to be your new best friend.'

Mr Butcher nods his head. 'You show remarkable control for a novice. Being a FlameMaker is more than simply manipulating fire and teaching it to do a few tricks, Ember. You have to learn to channel that energy, let it become you, let it live in you. Playing with it like a cat with a mouse is only the beginning. You will need to walk through it and let it consume you. Only then, will you be ready to face Ra-Mon.'

'And you'll teach me that?' I say with hope in my voice.

'Yes, Ember. I will teach you everything about becoming a FlameMaker.'

It's dark and cold when we leave Mr Butcher's place. Snow is falling in big heavy flakes, erasing all trace that we'd walked up my street only two hours ago. The fear I once felt about walking past number forty-seven seems insignificant to what is now about to happen. There are darker, more dangerous things in this world than The Creeper.

'Do you think I'm ready for this?' I ask, cuddling up to River. I can see the worry dancing between the shadows of his face.

'You'd better be, because the poor sod that comes next will struggle to keep up if you haven't got all your ducks in a row.' He is referring to the next Elementar who will present themselves. 'But enough of that for now. Butch says you've got three days before you start your lessons. So, I order you to take a nice long swim with me tonight, eat Wally's amazing vegetable korma and watch as many funny movies as you can before falling into a heap.' He kisses my hair.

The nervous tremor in my stomach, my constant companion these days, and friendly reminder, says funny movies and swimming isn't about to make this go away any time soon.

# TWENTY-NINE

CHRISTMAS Day.

Never in a million years did I ever expect to be spending my day like this. I woke to the sound of jingling bells, River standing beside my bed, still in his boxer shorts and singlet, and wearing a red Santa hat. We opened presents in front of the fire, me feeling totally guilty for the one gift I gave him compared to the three that had my name on them. I can still feel the heat in my face as I unwrapped the beautiful pendant in the shape of a flame and matching earrings. The third gift he wants me to wait until later to open. Wally then made the most amazing Christmas dinner and joined us at the table, cracking the worst jokes in history. It was nice to get to know him on a social level and in many ways, he reminded me a lot of my dad.

And now, by the warmth of the fire, our bellies full of plum pudding, we curl up together to watch a movie. Wally slips in, and out of the room, as stealthily as he does, with a cup of hot chocolate, three pink marshmallows in each. It's the exact same treat I used to share with my parents. I figure a dark shadow must've fallen over my face as I think about them because in true River style, he picks up on my change of mood almost immediately, his emotional antenna on red alert. 'It's hard, isn't it?'

I try to find all the ways to mend my broken smile. 'I miss them,' I whisper, my throat aching for them.

River leans in and kisses my temple. 'I know you do, love, and I can never replace them, but I can try to make you smile. Why don't you open your last present,' he says, reaching over me to retrieve it from the table.

He passes me a black box. I untie the red ribbon and hesitate for a moment, praying it isn't more jewellery. I absolutely adore the gifts he bought, but he's already spent so much on me. I could never repay him.

I lift the lid. On a bed of white satin, sits a miniature wooden rocking horse.

My throat wants to close over and any breath in, isn't finding a way out. My eyes ache, tears at the ready.

'Em?' There's a worried edge to his voice. 'I remember you saying your mum bought you one and I thought ...'

'I love it, River. I really do.' Tears stream down my face. He wipes them away, bringing my eyes back to him.

'Are they good tears or ...'

'Both.' I start to sob uncontrollably. He holds me for as long as my pain goes on for, and then tucks me under his arm, safe, loved, in the glow of the firelight. It takes a good hour before I feel more myself again, however, every time the picture of my parents' faces flickers beneath my closed lids, the desire to go back and rescue my crystal rocking horse jars in my head. It's the only thing left there for me now, except for Aaron, and the only keepsake that means anything and everything to me.

'I do know how you feel, believe it or not. I didn't get on with my parents half as well as you did yours, but it still hurts to be alone,' mutters River as he brushes my hair back from my face. 'I feel the same way, but nothing will bring them back. I try to remember the good times, like how my dad used to take me fishing when I was five and would sneak a package of jelly from the cupboard, so we had something to eat on the walk down to the river.' I force a smile out. The urge to ask River more about how his parents died, more about his relationship with his parents burns on my lips, although from the tortured look on his face, he isn't up for that type of conversation any more than I am.

I lay my head against his chest. 'I have something back at the Burberrys' I need to get ...'

His breath stops. His torso tenses.

'You're not going back there.' His voice thunders in my ear making me sit up. His face is somewhere between shock and horror. 'Over my dead body, Em. What are you thinking?'

'My crystal rocking horse is the only thing I have left to remind me I once had parents,' I protest feebly.

River presses pause on the movie and throws the remote on to the coffee table as he gets up. 'You have memories. Real memories up here,' he says jabbing himself in the temples. 'Aren't they good enough?'

Clouded memories chase across my vision. 'No, they're not enough. Maybe they are for you, but it doesn't work like that for me. It was the last thing my mother gave me. It's beyond special, it's my most precious belonging.' I swallow, keeping my teeth clenched - anything to keep back another wash of tears. 'Besides I don't want *him* to have it.'

River rubs his chin. 'I don't want you going within ten feet of that house without me. You may not remember the state you were in the last time you were there, but I do. It wasn't pretty, and if you think I'm going to stand here and let you go waltzing through that door again, you're fucking nuts.'

It's the first time he's sworn at me and my shoulders wilt. I crumble back into the sofa.

I stare pointedly at the necklace around his neck. 'You of all people should know.'

He catches me looking at it and rubs the disc between his thumb and forefinger. 'That's a cheap shot, Em.'

I feel instant guilt. A moment of silence.

'Promise me you won't go back there.' River's face is as fearful as I've seen it. I open my mouth to say I promise but all that comes out is a meek 'okay.' Technically, I never actually promised anything.

River restarts the movie and even though my eyes are fixated on the TV, my mind is busy formulating a plan to get into the Burberrys' without The Creeper or River finding out.

My opportunity arrives the very next day.

River has barely taken his eyes off me in last twenty-four hours, and for reasons I can't come up with, his time away from the pool reflects in his sallow skin and more frequent mood swings.

'Are you sure you don't want to swim?' he asks, almost begging. 'It'd really pick you up.' It's the fifth time he's asked me in an hour and dead obvious how desperate he is to keep me in his sights. It's now or never and I know it's the only time I will be able to slip away.

'No, it's okay. You go. I've got … tummy pains,' I lie. River's face, including his ears, flush a deep shade of beetroot. 'I'm going to finish watching this,' I say, gesturing to the TV. Laying it on extra thick, I rub my stomach in a clockwise direction. River winces and begrudgingly leaves the room.

After a few minutes, I creep down the hallway and loiter outside the swimming pool door. The second I hear his body splash into the water, I fly upstairs and grab my coat and shoes. I check every corner, for Wally and tiptoe down the stairs, pulling the door softly behind me. I am up the road and out of sight within minutes, leaving a note on the hallway table saying sorry but the rocking horse means more to me than life itself.

The black, icy slush takes no time at all to soak through my shoes, but my mind is pre-occupied, hoping that Rose and Celeste are at the Boxing Day sales, as usual, whilst The Creeper and Aaron have their "father and son" time, sledging down the hills just outside of town.

The usual butterflies, which have mutated into fully grown eagles, take flight inside my stomach as I draw closer. I haven't considered if what I'm doing is courageous or irresponsible. All I know is I don't want anything I love so much to remain in that house a moment longer.

As I contemplate asking Mr Butcher for help, the front door opens, and Aaron and The Creeper appear. I throw myself into the bushes of number nineteen and watch from between spindly branches as they strap themselves into his ancient green Rover. Confidence blossoms in my chest and I let out a breath as they pass me, unseen.

Score!

I open the front door and creep into the hallway, listening so intently my ears ring. My heart thumps madly and erratically. All clear — Rose Burberry and Celeste have gone, too.

I take the stairs two at a time and slip into my old bedroom, noticing the spot where the bolt should have been on the door. There isn't even a filled-in screw hole. Rachel was right – it's a new door.

My room looks the same as the day I'd left, except the boards have been taken down from the window and the glass has been repaired. It still smells of The Creeper and of me. Fear passes over my body at the mere memory of my last moments here and then is gone. A fear I will never experience again.

Now that I'm here, it isn't just the rocking horse I want. My things are all around me and certain items beg me to take them too. I pull down the burgundy fabric suitcase from the top of my wardrobe, the same suitcase my old life had been packed into and throw back the lid. There isn't much of this life I want to be reminded of and after placing a few favourite items of clothing, a pair of nearly new shoes, all my school paraphernalia and the keepsakes off my chest of drawers, I turn to my beloved rocking horse.

It is missing.

There are only two people in the world who would think to take it and they share the same surname.

I race into Celeste's room. It would be just like her to take it after the incident at school. Spite could double as her middle name and I'm convinced it courses through her veins because blood belongs to those who have a heart. I wrench open each drawer in turn, rummaging through clothes and yet more clothes, noticing my own long-lost garments amongst the bundled together t-shirts and jumpers. Each precious second is luring me into dangerous territory. But I can't leave without it. It's what brought me here. I don't care about the clothes. I want my rocking horse and I'm not going to leave without it.

The front door slams.

The Creeper's voice and Aaron's laughter carry up the stairs. I force back the urge to vomit.

My hands freeze to the handles of Celeste's wardrobe.

I tiptoe across Celeste's thick cream carpet to the door and open it slowly. I can hear The Creeper's voice coming from the kitchen. My failsafe plan to get in and out undetected has been foiled.

'Go and find it and then we can get out of here,' I hear The Creeper say to Aaron. He doesn't sound grumpy, but that will soon change if he finds me here. Seconds later, Aaron's fluid footsteps up the stairs have me recoiling back inside the room.

I opt for plan B.

If they are on their way back out again, I could hide and wait for them to leave. It's a much easier option than confronting The Creeper and exposing who I really am because that's what it will take for me to get out of here alive.

I push the masses of clothes aside in Celeste's wardrobe and sit down among the endless pairs of shoes … waiting for the sound of the front door.

'I've got it, Dad,' Aaron calls out. 'It was under my bed all along and I found my old toothbrush under there too.' His little voice brings a smile to my lips. I hear him muttering to himself as he races back down the stairs. A few minutes later the front door clicks shut.

I sigh heavily and fall against the fake wood backing of the wardrobe.

That was close.

I kick open the door and crawl out. I will take one quick look around and then leave. Staying any longer is tempting a fate I have no desire to confront.

With renewed inspiration from Aaron, I lift the hot pink valance that runs around Celeste's bed and peer underneath. Apart from two of my t-shirts that have been missing for six months, there is nothing.

'Looking for this?' sneers a voice.

My head hits the base of the bed with a dull thud and I close my eyes wishing I didn't have to move. Slowly, I back out and look up at the only person who has ever truly made my skin crawl. He is standing in front of me in an old black tracksuit, too small at the waist, his glutinous stomach straining the two sides of the zip to bursting point. His face is light but not surprised to see me. I wonder what gave me away.

'Your perfume.' The Creeper smiles smugly as though he's read my thoughts. 'I would know it anywhere.' In his hand sits my crystal rocking horse. 'Somehow I knew you'd come back for it. You're so predictable, Ems.'

My blood begins to boil as I watch his fat, girlie-soft fingers caress the body only I had ever touched. I stumble to my feet, my body on the brink of eruption. Beneath my skin, the fear in my blood transmutes into anger. I feel it

310

stream through my veins, spurring me on, giving me confidence.

Staring him down, I hold out my hand, aware of the slight tremble that runs to my fingertips. 'I'd like that back,' I say firmly.

His face changes and, for the first time in my life, I see a flicker of fear pass over his eyes. It makes me smile on the inside and I wonder if he can see the molten lava dancing around my pupils.

The Creeper manages to compose himself and a cruel smile kicks up the corners of his mouth. 'You have to come and get it,' he purrs. He raises the horse to his mouth and kisses its delicate body, defiling the only innocent thing left in my life. I've never wanted to kill someone as much as I do right here, right now ... and with my own hands, twisting the life out of him, until his neck snaps or his breath ceases. 'You really haven't put two and two together yet, have you?'

I frown.

'I had my eye on you long before you came to me.'

Air rushes out of my body in a big hurry, leaving me lightheaded and nauseated. Ice instantly replaces my blood. 'What?'

'You were so naïve, you didn't even know I was watching you.' The brakes to my life screech to a horrifying stop. Dark lights want to take over me and put me to sleep forever. The only word in my brain is no, no, no, no, no, no, no, no, no, no. 'The day your parents were killed was the day you were meant to be mine.' The slow realisation that I hadn't been randomly placed in foster care, swiftly surfaces. He had planned this. 'And blacklisting your little friend's name was easy.'

I feel all control slipping. I bite my lip hard, hoping the pain will revive me and remind me who I am. 'I'm not playing anymore of your games,' I spit out furiously. 'You can't control me anymore. I am *not* your plaything.'

311

His eyes, as always, undress me layer by layer. 'Oh, but you are.' He licks the rump of the horse. 'You want this? Then I want something in return.'

I bite down harder on my lip, this time tasting blood. *No way, no way, no way.*

'I want you to give yourself to me, wholeheartedly, and I will never bother you again.' It's another of his games, another one of his sick, deceptive ploys to get to me. I will never bargain with him, especially not with my body. I'm ten days pure for crying out loud. There is no way I'm going to break that, not even for my most cherished possession.

I let out a scornful laugh. 'You think I would willingly give myself to you … an old … unattractive … overweight creep who can't satisfy his own wife, so preys on an innocent young girl. You're pathetic.' His lips tighten, losing all colour. I have angered him, and yet I'm not as scared as I used to be.

I look towards the door and The Creeper senses my anticipation. 'You still have to get past me.' Fire tingles in my fingers, ready and waiting for my command. 'And there's only one way out, Ems, unless you wanna go through the window.'

I know I can pass him in a flash, take the horse and be on my way but I can't help wondering where Aaron is. I don't want to scare him or knock him flying on my way out.

I take a bold step towards him. 'Where's Aaron?'

'Aah, yes, Aaron. Your little Achilles heel. I'd almost forgotten about him sitting in the car. Thank you for reminding me.' His eyes blacken, sanity fades and the look of death takes over.

'Don't you dare,' I hiss, my own voice louder and casting an even fiercer shadow over his.

'And still, You. Do. Not. Learn. Never … *never*,' he yells. Spit froths at the side of his mouth, 'ever threaten me, my girl, or you'll find yourself worse than dead. I'll lock you up permanently and there will be no more Mr Nice-guy.'

As serious as his threat is, maybe three months ago it would have had me in tears or praying to the universe for help. Now, his words are no harsher than something Eliza might say. In fact, it's funny. I hold back my laugh, but my wide smile is much harder to hide.

His eyes bulge.

He takes a confident step towards me, his fist clenched, and his arm pulled back, ready for the biggest haymaker in history.

'Dad? Are you ready? How much longer are you going to be?' Aaron's footsteps thump up the stairs. 'I can help you look for it if you like?' I want to call out to him and tell him to wait downstairs but the door's already opening and his sweet, overjoyed face pokes around and sees me. He runs up to me and throws his arms around my waist.

'Em-ba, where have you been? Are you coming home? Dad said you were visiting friends. Are you staying?' His words trip over each other in his excitement. I dust the top of his head with my palm.

'No, honey. I'm not coming home. I'm sorry, but I can't live here anymore.' I glare at The Creeper for the sadness I have caused Aaron and the heartache I'm inflicting on him.

'Aaron … get in the car,' orders The Creeper. 'I'll be down in a minute.' Aaron holds on to me, not wanting to let go.

'I'll go with you. It's okay. I'm here,' I soothe, feeling the wardrobe doors sliding across my back as I keep my distance from The Creeper. I half drag Aaron into the hallway.

'You're not going anywhere, Missy,' bellows The Creeper. 'We still have things to sort out.'

As far as I'm concerned, we are done. 'You can keep the rocking horse as a gift, or as a reminder of how twisted you really are. I wouldn't want it back after your filthy hands have been all over it.'

Aaron looks up at me with frightened eyes. 'What's going on, Em-ba?'

'Nothing, honey. Everything's all right.'

'Everything is not all right,' growls The Creeper.

In the second it takes for me to react, two things happen in quick succession. The Creeper throws the rocking horse at me, hitting me in the forehead. I gasp as my skin splits open and a rush of blood streaks down my face. I ease my grip on Aaron's shoulders as my hand flies up to my face giving The Creeper time to snatch Aaron out of my grasp by the collar of his shirt. He holds him precariously close to the top of the stairs.

Aaron screams out. 'Dad, what are you …?'

'Shut it,' snarls The Creeper. He tightens his stranglehold on Aaron who frantically reaches up to try to loosen them, his hands clawing at The Creeper's hands. He is choking.

'Get your fat, grubby hands off him,' I say between clenched teeth. 'Now!'

In that moment, heat, no … fire, no … flames, all three together, rip through my body, impatient and demanding to be unleashed.

'What can you possibly do to make me?' demands The Creeper. I know of one way, my way, but Aaron is dangerously close. I will have to wait until I get a clear shot.

'I could turn you into ash,' I spit. 'You remember the lips … that was me. I did that to you, and I would rather cut off my own lips than taste your disgusting breath in my mouth again.'

Death has disappeared from his eyes. I don't recognise this new monster. He is more than cunning, more savage than I'm used to. The last remnants of his sanity slip away, leaving his expression parched and without remorse.

314

The Creeper lets go of Aaron's neck and gives him a solid push. I watch helplessly as Aaron tumbles down the stairs, wailing as he falls. His small body stops in a crumpled heap at the bottom. He doesn't move. His arm and back are shaped at an odd angle and water fills my eyes as the rage inside me boils to volcanic proportions.

'You're a disgusting waste of space that should never have been born. I've waited a long time for this, but now I can make sure you never lay a hand on anyone again ... EVER!'

Like a cornered animal, I cower, desperate to blend into my environment, yet ready, so ready. He advances, experience and size on his side. I shiver and open my hand. 'Flame and fire, I need you.'

A small flame willingly leaps into my hand and bobs about waiting for directions. The Creeper's pupils dilate and the area around his eyes tightens. The horror I see gives me more pleasure than I ever thought possible.

He *fears* me.

He fears *me*.

His mouth drops open and his hands come up to protect himself. My hands, hotter than soldering irons, tingle with warmth.

The Creeper doesn't utter a single word when my hands make contact with his. His scream echoes down the hallway and the smell of burning flesh and searing muscle suffocates the small landing.

I release my grip and he drops to his knees. His hands are black where they should be peach. Bleached white bones protrude through what is left of his ashy skin. The pudgy moistness is gone, melted off the bones like an overcooked lamb roast. His hands will never be able to touch anyone again, never be able to feel or give him pleasure.

I dig my index finger underneath his chin to make him look up at me, chiselling a hole into the fleshy folds beneath.

315

'Stick out your tongue.'

His jaw trembles.

His soft whimpers for help, for me to stop, the pleas for mercy, mean nothing to me.

'NOW,' I demand.

He opens his mouth slightly.

'Wider,' I snarl.

His lip quivers and I run my thumb first over his top lip and then over the bottom, searing the flesh as I go. The flesh melts away, removing the shape and definition of his lips, exposing his gums. His cries go unheard.

I have no intention of disfiguring his tongue or harming it in any way. I want him to be able to talk about what he's done to me if and when that time comes. No. I want to instil fear into him. The same fear he has inflicted on me. Fear that he will remember for the rest of his life.

'And one more thing. I want access to my money. I want four hundred pounds from my parents' estate deposited into my bank account every month and if you tell anyone what happened here today, it won't be the only appendage you'll lose.' I kick him hard in the balls. 'Get. My. Drift.'

I hold out my hand and a thunderbolt of fire the size of a tractor tyre spirals furiously in my palm. 'All you need to say is you tripped on the mat and fell forward into the fire. Got it?'

The Creeper nods fearfully. It's obvious he's in shock, but I don't give a shit about what he's thinking or feeling. He deserves everything he gets and so much more. I snatch up the rocking horse, that's broken in three places, drop it in my pocket and fly down the stairs to Aaron.

'Oh God, Aaron. I'm so sorry. It's all my fault.'

He is breathing … but only just.

# THIRTY

*THE* morning of Aaron's funeral is a day I'll never forget.

I feel responsible for his death even though my hands weren't directly the ones to cause it. I have tortured myself relentlessly night after night until I've made myself physically sick. If I hadn't been there, none of this would've happened. If it hadn't been for that damn rocking horse that no longer has the flavour of my parents attached to it, he would still be alive.

River was right.

The memories of my parents *are* locked safely away inside me. Throughout the five days I sat by Aaron's hospital bed, praying for him to wake from the coma he'd fallen into, I wrestled with my conscience. Rose Burberry hadn't shed a single tear at the hospital, and all that Celeste could do was glare at me as though Aaron was her guiding light and reason for living. The Creeper's injuries were seen to and paled in comparison to Aaron's death. He received no attention from anyone and sat as far away from me as he possibly could, twitching and tapping, bandages around his hands and some kind of adhesive over his lips and chin.

No amount of reassurance from River makes me feel any better and of course, he was furious that I went. He'd patched up my head, which luckily needed less of Wally's paramedic skills, although hasn't spoken more than a few words to me in the days that followed. I'm sure, but for Aaron's tragedy, he'd still be mad at me.

I've cried so much over the last week, whatever fire I have inside me I am sure has now been doused. No more sweet chirps of dinosaurs. No more walks to school. No more *anything,* for the little brother I never had. His death brings forth memories of when my parents died, although their coffins were empty as I teetered over them. Aaron is inside that tiny box, all alone, cold and dead. He will never smile again.

Poor Aaron.

Tears blur my vision as I stand by the graveside, barely able to make out the tiny white coffin sinking into the dark, cold earth. All I can think of is, I wish to God I had taken that bloody swim.

I ache all over and my body wants to give up and join him because my wants have resulted in his end and I want to scream … really scream out to the world that I didn't mean for this to happen and that I'm sorry. I'm sorry. I'm so so sorry.

I feel the weight of River's arm around my back and almost take up the support that he offers until I see The Creeper staring at me, his hands still heavily bandaged. I straighten my back immediately as the vicar's heartfelt words wash over me. My gaze flicks across to Rose Burberry, who is now sniffling into a hanky, Celeste beside her, gripping her arm. I don't doubt that Celeste loved her brother but this lesson on family conduct and sibling love is something I am sure will plague her forever.

'It's over,' River says as people begin stepping back from the graveside. I start to walk away when I hear Rose Burberry's voice.

'Ember, do you have a minute?'

I stop and turn, surprised that she has anything to say to me. I offer a commiserating smile.

'I have something for you,' she says and opens her bag. My brow furrows as I take the small dusky pink note from her trembling hands. Rose Burberry leaves, hunched over in her grief, clutching hold of Celeste's arm.

I unfold the paper and read:

> *Dear Ember,*
>
> *I want you to know, I'm leaving my husband. No words can express how sorry I am for what he's done to you. It may seem that I sat back with blindness and ignored the abomination that was going on under my own roof, but I had my reasons, and as sad as my life is, and as cowardly as I am, it was the only way I could keep him away from my own daughter. She's not perfect, Ember, but she's mine and she's all I've got. I hope one day, Celeste will truly understand the sacrifice you made for her. It is a debt, I know, I can never repay. I am not proud of what I have done but one day, you will understand, a mother will do anything to protect her child, ~~even if it means hurting someone else's~~. I will have to live with this for the rest of my days and there won't be a single day that passes that I won't think of you with grace and gratitude.*
>
> *Rose Burberry.*
>
> *PS: I'm sorry Ember, but I think Aaron would have wanted me to write this letter.*

319

'Wow,' I mumble under my breath, tears streaming, hands shaking. River is reading over my shoulder.

My knees wobble and I feel myself falling.

I collapse on the ground, wishing the earth would split open and swallow me instead of Aaron. River's arms, comforting and warm, hardly touch my heart as tear after tear falls onto the frozen ground. His kisses are numb against my cheek, trying to wipe the sorrow away with his lips and yet a freedom, a piece of my soul, has finally knitted its way back together. Rose's letter by no means excuses her husband's behaviour, but her apology and acknowledgment are enough to allow a healing process to begin.

The next few days, are either spent in bed huddled under the duvet or wandering the lonely hallways of River's house. Minutes drift into hours, hours into days and still the pain will not ease. Knowing I will never see Aaron's cheeky little smile or hear his incessant ramblings brings a fresh flood of hot, stinging water to my eyes.

'Miss Ember, a gentleman is at the door for you.' Wally's voice startles me out of the darkness.

'Sorry. What? Who? Where's River?' Blood leaves my face in a hurry as a gentle hand touches my arm.

'It's okay, Miss. It's not …' Wally clears his throat. 'It's a taller gentleman with greying hair and Master River is still in the pool, Miss.'

I push myself out of the armchair and follow Wally to the door. As I suspected, Mr Butcher is standing in the foyer. He doesn't look as gigantic in this spacious room where the ceilings are far enough away to resemble low clouds.

'Miss Riley, I'm so sorry for your loss.'

My teeth grate across each other as I pull the reins up inside me to stop that terrible tremor again. 'Thanks,' I mutter.

'Look, I know this is upsetting for you, but too much time has been wasted.' Wally elusively extricates himself from the room.

'Come through,' I say, gesturing to a door leading into the formal lounge. Mr Butcher sweeps past me, leaving a blast of cool air behind him. I join him in front of the fireplace which is already alive with colour.

'You need to train, Miss Riley. You have no idea how important it is if you're not ready when Ra-Mon returns.'

'Enlighten me.'

Mr Butcher's face creases one minute and then softens the next, repeating this cycle as though the very words are too painful to say.

'When I said you and the other Elementars are here for a purpose, and that you need to stop Ra-Mon from gaining control over the earth — well ... there's a little more to it than that.'

I thought as much. 'How much more?'

'You need to prevent the release of the first Elementar.'

'I feel my forehead crease. 'I don't understand.'

Mr Butcher grimaces. 'Nuria, the first Elementar lives inside you, which is why you can call on her power. Her name means God's fire and she is the original FlameMaker responsible for torching the earth fifty million years ago. The first three Elementars have been hidden for thousands of years and when I began to teach in the ways of the elements, it all became clear. These Elementars have jumped from body to body since the beginning of time. Once Ra-Mon overthrows you, Nuria will be vulnerable.'

A breath filters into my lungs, down deep and deeper still to where I often envisage a part of me is hiding. I hold on to that thought, searching, listening for any sign of the immortal residing somewhere within. I blow out my breath and hope for a glimmer of recognition, some forgotten secret, but I feel nothing.

'If Ra-Mon defeats you, he will draw Nuria from your body like blood from a syringe. You will syphon her power

321

to defeat him, but ultimately, it will make her weak and at the mercy of Ra-Mon. You have to do whatever it takes, to hold him off.'

'So, either way I'm screwed. If I don't fight back, he will kill me, and then Nuria will find someone else to inhabit,' I look to him as he nods, 'and if I do fight back, he will take Nuria anyway and win.'

'There is a much bigger plan at play here, Miss Riley. Trust me.'

I find myself quoting my father. 'Trust has to be earnt.'

My Butcher nods and scratches his beard. 'Very true. But for now, it all rests with you.'

'You said, the first three have been hidden. What about the fourth Elementar – the EarthHealer?'

'That's what I like about you, Miss Riley - your ability to see and hear what others overlook. The Earth Immortal still holds the power. Ra-Mon wouldn't dream of going up against her without the power of the three other Elementars behind him. She is stronger than he could've ever imagined. But she only appears when the balance alters - ashamed to show her face, too ashamed to ask for help. Ember, people are populating this world at a rapid rate and she knows eventually, it will cause the earth's demise. Soon there will be too many people to cater for and what do you suppose will happen then?'

'We'll turn on each other?'

Mr Butcher smothers a laugh. 'We're not that far from it now. But yes, we'll end up like animals.'

Colour drains from his face, and any hope he had before, seems lost. 'And then, when this world is at its lowest, Ra-Mon will return.' Mr Butcher places his hand on top of mine. In my mind, I see images of everything he says. 'Outbreaks of wildfires will ravish the countryside. Water will come in the form of tsunamis, floods or droughts, and Air will be polluted beyond repair, destroying the ozone. The balance will be upturned and these three Elementars will be left to destroy themselves. Then he plans to start a new race. One of his own making.'

'And he can do that?'

Mr Butcher shrugs his colossal shoulders. 'I don't know. He is drawing power from so many sources, places even I can't see.' His face darkens. 'Perhaps even the Underworld.'

'Hell?'

'Amongst others.'

I shift uncomfortably in my seat. 'This is way worse than I thought.'

'That is why, only with the four of you together, can you hope to bring balance. It's not all left to you, Miss Riley. You are merely the beginning.' My head is nodding although I'm unsure if it's what I want it to do. 'So, back to the training. You need to practice somewhere nobody will see you.'

'Where?' I ask. Where would be safe from a walking volcano with erratic explosive tendencies?

'I know of just the place. I will be back first thing in the morning.'

'What about today? What about the urgency?'

'You need to use this day to get rid of whatever is holding you back. Leave it here because, come tomorrow, I want you focused and ready for battle.'

'Battle?' says River, making an entrance. His hair, shiny and wet, competes with the brightness in his eyes. He stares at me. 'Em?'

'You fill him in. And Ember, you'll need to bring a hat and sunscreen with you.'

Mr Butcher nods at River before seeing himself out.

After dinner and an extensive conversation with River, trying to answer all the questions I'd forgotten to ask Mr Butcher, I retire to my room. My eyes find a sense of peace as I gaze at the heavy snow gathering outside on the window ledge. I wonder if sleep will ever find me among the chaos and chatter. I close my eyes and for the first time pray for silence. For calm and peacefulness.

I know I've been under sleep's spell because I wake with a start. It isn't quite midnight, yet something woke me. A soft swishing sound that could have been the wind brushing its fingers against the window, except it sounds much closer.

I push my hair out of my eyes and sit up, peering through the darkness. There it is again. I almost mistake it for the trickle of blood sighing through my veins or the echo of my breath as it whistles in and out of my body - a familiar sound persisting within my veil of consciousness, hidden somewhere in my soul.

'Ember,' whispers a voice. The hair on my neck prickles and yet I feel no fear. I know the voice. I heard it just over a year ago - a soft, sensual voice that swaddles me in cuddle-rugs and loving arms. A voice that lifted me out of pain, out of danger - the same female voice I heard in the car the day my parents died, except this time, I'm hearing it through my ears and not from within my body.

'Yes?' I respond. Silence prevails as the wind presses harder and harder against my window. I close my eyes, pleading for her to say something else.

'I am Nuria.' The words bubble out of my chest as though I'd spoken them myself. 'You must find a way to defeat Ra-Mon. I cannot be his hostage.'

'How?'

'I was reckless, as were we all. You have to find the others. You are the key, Ember. The one to unlock the power.'

'What power?'

'Who are you talking to?' asks River, peeking around the door.

The beat of my heart returns to normal, the tremor in my breath steadies. I listen for her voice. 'No one.'

River comes in and sits down, his brow bearing its usual concern. 'Are you sure? You don't have to be embarrassed if you've had another bad dream. I can stay until you fall asleep.' His fingers graze mine, sending ripples of warmth up my arm and into my cheeks.

I want him to stay.

I want him to crawl under the covers and explore my body. Explore me in a way that he's so reluctant to do. Ask me, ask me, please. Ask me if you can spend the night curled next to me, and not sitting on the top of the sheets keeping watch all night like you do, and I will tell you yes, yes you can. Ask me to touch you. Tell me you want me. Tell me you need me.

He brushes his thumb over the apple of my cheek, and I lean my head into him, begging for him to pick up my emotions. Ask me now, I plead silently, before time slips away.

'Em …' His voice, strangled and tight, cuts off.

'Stay with me, River. Stay with me for the rest of the night. Lie next to me and be the first person to see what love and passion looks like from my eyes. See me as pure.' *Please, see me as pure.* A tear splashes off my cheek. Another follows the exact same path. The tear runs to my chin and lands in River's hand. He stares at it dissolving into his palm, his jaw flexing beneath lightly stubbled skin. He swallows, hard.

'Em, if only you knew how complicated it is for me …'

'Please … I'm alone. I'm so alone. I want to feel something other than pain - something more than the ache in my heart that has been ripped and torn to shreds. I want to know what it feels like to be touched, really touched, with hands that are gentle and tender and with hands that I trust. Your hands.'

'I don't want to hurt you,' says River. The sliver of light from the open doorway is enough for me to see his eyes - like smoke over water. They tell me their truth and yet I see torment in them I can't explain. It looks old, like a memory. 'I don't know how to be close to you.'

'This is all I want. You won't hurt me. I trust you.'

River's breathing pattern abruptly changes as though a chain has broken inside him, releasing demons that hold him hostage.

Slowly, his hand creeps down my neck, teasing my skin as his fingers trail behind like feathery fronds. The strap of my camisole slips down my arm as he cups my shoulder. He looks longingly at it but doesn't replace it, instead his fingers, light and delicate, dust across my collarbone, the protruding bones tickled beyond belief. I want to laugh and cry at such a feeling. I want to open my eyes and see the same desire on his face that I feel on my own. My head falls backwards, giddy, offering more area for him to discover.

I hear his breath. Almost strangled. Almost a gasp.

His hand glides across to the other shoulder, this time, his fingers entwining in the other strap for a few moments before letting it fall. The front of my camisole slips down a little further. My heart spikes.

'You're so beautiful,' I hear him mutter before his lips finds the hollow spot at the base of my throat. A soft moan trembles from my lips. Oh, please God, don't ever let this feeling go away. Instinctively, I wrap my arms around his neck. My hands catch in his hair, releasing the sweet smell of raindrops on a sunny day. My heart begins to race.

Recklessly, he pulls me into his lap. His lips trace the contour of my jaw, following the line of my throat as his fingers tickle over my shoulder to my back, stroking my body in a way that is too new, too unbelievably innocent and glorious but which scorches me with a desire that I was sure would never surface in me. His hands find their way under my top, searching, hungry as though they will never have their fill, cupping each breast over and over again, before dancing up my back in desperate caresses that want to touch every part of me at once. His breath is hot in my ear and the touch of his tongue against my neck sends fiery rockets of pleasure in every direction. My body has awoken, and I finally know what it feels like to feel love. It is so different from the kiss we shared outside the tavern.

Tentatively, I run my hands down the sides of his neck and his body responds with a light shiver. His shoulders and arms, strong and so goddamn sexy, melt beneath my fingertips as I draw irregular patterns into his bronzy skin. Every muscle answers when I slide my palms over them, each one flexing and contracting, begging me not to stop. I find the hem of his t-shirt, pausing for a second to revel in the mystery of what lies beneath and what I have dreamt of touching since I first met him. I deftly lift it over his head. My own hands, eager to explore again, ache at the prospect of not touching him. The pads of my fingertips start at his neck, pass over his shoulders and travel down his back, feeling every perfectly constructed muscle, every turn and curve.

His bare chest presses against me, warm and firm and so faultless in every way. My lips find his throat, his Adams apple, under his chin and up to his ear. He moans in a way that makes me want to do it more. My hands trace all the way down, past his waist and on to his hips until the ribbon of silken skin runs out. I dare to go lower, brushing the tips of my fingers over the waistband of his shorts as his kisses find my eyes, my lips, my throat and all the way across to the arc of my shoulder. I want to know what he feels like everywhere and every part of him eggs me on that much further. I let my hands slip beneath his shorts. The rise and fall of his chest against mine stops suddenly.

'Em ...' is all he says. I remove my hands and pull him down on to the bed. His body, pressing down on mine, is no firmer than his softest kiss. He is hard against my leg, stirring wild feelings inside me. I grip him tighter, curling my legs around him, not wanting a single part of me to go without. His eyes burn with desire and I wish I could tell him how they smoulder like molten lava, but my heaving breath will not let the words out.

He kisses me harder, wanting me more with each touch, each breath, each kiss and I can feel myself coming apart and coming together and want him more than I've ever wanted anything in my life. He pauses and looks at me, smiles, kisses the end of my nose, deliberating, waiting … for what. He wants more. He wants me more than he's saying. I see it in the way his eyes hide no lies for me.

Leaning away, far enough for me to still feel his breath on my face, I know my time has run out. The torment in his eyes is back, a hurdle he seems to be struggling with. His jaw flexes so many times I begin to look over every inch of him to see where the anguish is coming from. 'We shouldn't be doing this,' he says in gasps that say otherwise.

I bite back the tears. 'We aren't doing anything wrong.' Three words sit at the back of my throat. Three tiny, innocent words I've been longing to say forever - three words that cannot be taken out of context or be misunderstood.

I lean in and kiss his neck and the words come out in a whisper. 'I want you.'

River closes his eyes, squeezing them shut as if some terrible pain is growing inside him. 'Em, you wouldn't say that if you knew …'

My heart tumbles into my toes. 'Knew what?'

His hands tenderly brush the hair from my forehead before he kisses each eye in turn. 'I can't explain … I don't know how to tell you …'

My eyes widen, desperate to see what's going on inside him. 'Look at me, River.'

Two, four, five seconds pass. His eyes slowly open – once drunk with passion, now hardened and distant. I wish I had the courage to tell him how he had become my saviour, my hammock, my boat in rough seas and the lighthouse that guides me away from danger. I want to ask if he loves me, adores me, worships the ground I walk on, like I do with him, but for some reason the words lay silent against my tongue. They sit caged inside me, locked in a room with no door, no keyhole and behind a wall that's too high to climb over. I count the beats of my heart – ten, eleven, twelve, thirteen, but still ...What if he doesn't feel the same way? What if he rejects my love, then what? How will I cope? Where will I go?

Too many questions with uncertain answers form a ball of splintering glass at the back of my throat. I close my eyes and swallow. It scratches relentlessly, refusing to let tears fall. A breath manages to find its way into my lungs, and I blow out a random sentence. 'River, do you like spending time with me?'

'How can you even say that?' River rolls off me and gazes up at the ceiling for the longest time.

'You never tell me ... you never say how you *feel* ...' I hesitate as my teeth graze over my lips, my heart thumping so loudly, so damn fast I'm not sure he even hears me whisper ... 'about me.'

River turns to look at me, his lips soft, his cheeks flushed pink and with brilliant soulful eyes that I would willingly hold my breath and suffocate in.

'You speak of trust and love, after all you've been through, but I'm not capable of either.'

I prop myself up on to an elbow and stare at him until my eyes sting and my vision distorts. 'How can you say that when you are so good at both?'

His eyes close, shutting me out again. 'It's an illusion. A careful, simple yet effective illusion.'

'Tell me about it. Let me in. Let me help. I want to be the one you run to when you need someone.'

River's hand, so warm and so deliciously tender, cups my cheek, his thumb parting my lips. His lips find mine for all of one glorious second. 'One day,' he says sadly. 'One day soon.'

# THIRTY-ONE

*I* wake the next morning, the space beside me wide and cold and uncrumpled as though what happened between us last night was nothing more than a dream someone else had. I wish I had the time to dissect everything he said or didn't say but as I glance at the clock, I realise I only have an hour before Mr Butcher arrives. Today is about me, NOT us and I need to get my fiery shit together. A swim should sort that out.

I change into my swimsuit and pad down the hallway to the pool. Normally I go straight to breakfast, so River won't be expecting this. The thought of trying to avoid his elusive eyes and feigned smile is too much for me to stomach.

Thankfully, the pool is empty.

I dive in at the deep end and swim lap after lap, trying to drown last night's conversation out of my body. One thing is clear when I finish up twenty minutes later - I need to be more independent. If River's issues, whatever they may be, could jeopardise me being part of his life, then I need to stop looking to him for support. I need to take charge of the decisions in my life instead of handing them over. And my first decision is to go with Mr Butcher – by myself.

I towel off and head towards the dining room. The door is ajar when I get there and the voices coming from inside aren't exactly quiet.

'But she suspects something,' River says. 'How can I keep lying to her?' My hand flies to my mouth.

'Stick to the plan, River. It's the only way. Ember will understand,' Wally replies sternly.

I bite into my knuckles until the pain becomes unbearable. Fire erupts, and I use its energy and power, the only way I know how – to channel anger. I am done with the secrets, the games, the 'keeping me in the dark' scenarios. I want to know now. I deserve to know.

Using more strength than I thought I had, I push against the double doors to the dining room with such force they swing back, hitting the mantelpiece. It shudders and rings out in a tone of jingled crockery. 'What will I understand?'

Wally and River stand rigid, mouths agape.

'Well?'

Wally recovers a lot quicker than River. 'That Master River won't be able to join you today. He has … urr … errands to run.' Each of us knows, as my eyes land first on River and then on Wally and back to River again, that this isn't the truth.

'Right,' I say with more sarcasm than a stand-up comedian. I waltz out before they can come up with anything more ridiculous and retreat to my room. I close the door, not meaning to slam it. I don't want to speak to anyone.

As it happens, nobody wants to speak to me either and half an hour later, a soft knock at my door followed by a 'Miss, your visitor is here' has me scrambling off my bed to find my shoes.

'You all set?' says Mr Butcher, dressed in a pair of shorts and a Hawaiian shirt. All that is missing is a straw hat and a long-stemmed cocktail in his hand. The snowdrifts against the windows conflict with my thoughts.

'I am, but you look like you're going to the Bahamas. Am I overdressed?' I glance down at my jeans and jumper.

Mr Butcher chuckles. 'Now, I'm not going to lie to you. This next part feels a little weird. Best thing is to hold your breath and close your eyes. It helps with the dizziness.'

'*Dizziness*?'

Mr Butcher's latches on to me like a leech out of water. The ground disappears from under me in a vortex of shadows as the jaws of darkness spiral around me, pulling my body in ways gravity has never been taught. It's a fleeting moment, two blinks, nothing more. Before I can think about what has happened, a sharp jolt spears my feet back to the earth. Except it isn't earth … it's sand – thick, orangey, marmalade sand.

The breath I was supposed to be holding now flows freely from my body. With eyes wide open, I take in the view before me, which is nothing less than mind-blowing. Trying to get my brain to understand what my eyes are seeing is close to impossible.

Banks of coppery red sand rise and fall all around me in dunes that seem not of this world. 'Where are we?' I manage to ask. My vision slopes sideways as a bout of giddiness hits me.

'Easy there,' says Mr Butcher, steadying me. 'Put your hands on your knees and breathe.'

I follow his orders to the letter. 'But where are we?' I ask again as the sand shifts beneath my feet. Hot winds steal the moisture from my lips. I lick at them once and then wished I hadn't.

'Miss Riley, welcome to the Arabian Desert.'

'Arabian …wh..?' My stomach lurches. Then I vomit.

'You're ok. Not many enjoy their first wormhole without being re-introduced to their last meal.'

I wipe my mouth. 'Thanks, but I haven't eaten yet.'

'Better for you. But, it's a spin-out, isn't it?' Mr Butcher seems to be enjoying himself.

'Ye …' I try to say.

'Perks of being immortal,' he says offhandedly. 'Can go wherever I want, whenever I want.'

I suck down a few more breaths, my body finally coming back online. 'And you didn't think that it was worth mentioning before zapping me halfway across the planet to Saudi Arabia?'

'Seeing is believing. Besides, there is nothing you can burn out here,' says Mr Butcher with a smirk. 'And no one to see you either, which is a bonus.'

I straighten up slowly, my head now clearer. 'Is this where you want to teach me?'

'Miss Riley, I don't have anything to teach you. You have all that information stored inside you or *Nuria* does. All I have to do is help you to channel it. Look at me as …' He shrugs his huge shoulders, '… as target practice.'

'Hmph.' He is funny, in a weird, masochistic way.

'Right.' I yank my jumper over my head, already feeling my armpits beginning to work over-time in this heat. I'm grateful for putting on a tank top.

Mr Butcher folds his arms over his chest. 'So, show me what you've got. Don't hold back. Remember … you can't kill me.'

I turn my focus inwards. It doesn't take long to conjure up the standard ball of fire. I dig deeper, allowing it to spin faster than I've ever dared. When it reaches the size of a gigantic pumpkin, I can't help smirk. My concentration dips as Mr Butcher drops his head and shakes it from side to side. The fireball vanishes.

'What?' I growl.

'It's not good enough. I've seen this circus act ten times before. Show me something worthy of a true FlameMaker.'

My shoulder blades dive down my back. 'I don't have anything else. I've only just managed to control that.' I step out of my shoes and sink my feet into the hot sand.

'Ra-Mon will eat soup out of your skull at this rate and still have room for a main course,' continues Mr Butcher. 'Search inside, Ember. You need to find where the power comes from.' There is that word again.

'I can't,' I yell back. 'I don't have anymore.'

Since Aaron has gone and things between River and I are falling apart, my heart isn't in it. I am lucky enough to hold a flame for more than a few minutes before it fizzles out. I can't find whatever Mr Butcher is looking for. I don't want to be a frigging FlameMaker.

'Can't we go,' I ask, dropping to my knees. Tiny grains of sand run through my fingers.

'No. You will die and so will River …'

'*River*?'

Mr Butcher's irritation turns to remorse. 'River is the next Elementar. He is the WaterLover.'

'Does he know?' My voice is no louder than the sweet chirps of a sparrow.

'Promise me one thing. You will not tell him you know. It will make everything more difficult.'

'How? He has to know.'

'Because if River tries to intervene, he could get killed in the crossfire trying to protect you, which would cause Nereus to find another host. It has taken hundreds of years to find you. Let's not tempt fate.'

'But …'

'Ember, you have to do this. Worry about what you need to do and leave River's concerns to him. Nuria never had to rely on anyone or inform someone of who she was, and you must follow her lead. You need to trust her and look to the core of your being and find that part of you that keeps charging ahead as though your life and the lives of everyone around you are all that matter.'

'Ember.' A woman's voice, dark and haunting, sings its way out of the depths of my soul. Nuria?

*Nuria, where are you? Help me. What do I need to do?*

I have become a human pincushion, tiny prickles under my skin radiates out through my arms, legs and face.

I close my eyes.

In my mind, I see a vision of a woman, chained to a stone wall that runs with water. It is as clear as the sun setting behind the sand dunes. Her hair is the colour of blazing amber, streaked with tones of honey, rust, ochre and auburn. She is, without a lie, the most beautiful woman I've seen.

'Is this you?' I ask Nuria silently.

'Yes,' she whispers 'If Ra-Mon wins, I will be bound to the Waterwall forever.

'How do I ...'

'Become the fire, Ember,' she says. 'Live in it and breathe in it. Let it consume you. Let it find a place within you to reside and grow.'

The buzzing and tingling in my body stops.

'Miss Riley? Are you okay?'

I know what I have to do. 'I'm fine,' I say. 'Stand back, unless you want to be barbecued.'

I can't say, initially, where the power came from, or how I did it. Maybe it was because River was now in danger too, and if Ra-Mon defeated me, and syphoned Nuria from my body, damning her to an eternity of pain, River would be next, which would then, start a cataclysmic ball of events rolling that the other Elementars wouldn't even see coming.

A volcanic surge, unparalleled by anything I have conjured before, trembles beneath my feet. I look down to see if the earth is cracking open. I frown at my feet that are still hidden beneath the sand. Fire, flame and explosions course up my legs, slow at first, chugging steadily but gathering momentum. My waist is next to feel the full force of it, my organs ignite, fury ravaging my body with heat, filling me with an energy not of this world. I feel my body being taken over as my chest violently lurches forward, back arching, as though I'm about to vomit. My head is thrown backwards as a tidal wave of flame rises and cascades over me. The sky is bathed in red. I look down at my hand, now engulfed in blistering fire. My whole body is. I have become a human torch.

Yes, it's hot, but no hotter than a welcoming shower. And the power un-surpasses everything. I'm not thinking about me or River, or even Ra-Mon. All I see are ways to burn, to scorch and scald. Reason and sense vanish. I am fire. No thoughts, no feelings, no regrets or sorrow. Just power. I am invincible. I can take on the world with a single wave of my hand - one kiss blown through the wind could torch an entire city. The rush of what I'm ultimately capable of throbs in my body like the slow rhythmic pulses of a ticking bomb. All I need are a few more seconds, just a few more, to feel that last crescendo.

'Bravo,' says Mr Butcher, clapping.

As though I've been dipped in an ocean of icy cold water, the fire is gone. My mind is my own again, along with my thoughts, my dreams, my nightmares and the memory of what I can become. I want to scream out "why"? Why do I have to come back to this shitty world– back to these dark memories that for a brief few seconds never existed.

'Impressive, very impressive. Now that's the kind of power you'll need to exert if you want to battle Ra-Mon.'

The last of the energy slithers from my body. Every last morsel has been used up, robbing me of the strength to stand. I fall to the ground, backwards or forwards, I'm not sure which way. The only thing I remember is, it doesn't hurt.

I wake to find myself lying on the soft cream sofa in River's lounge room. My head, although still on my shoulders, could belong to the old man staring intently at me. Fogginess, with a thumping kick to it, sits in its place.

'Feeling any better?' A hand extends towards me. 'Drink this.'

'Um …' I push up into a semi-sitting position and groan as my head splinters.

'Probably dug a *little* too deep for a first time,' says Mr Butcher with a sympathetic smile. 'At least we know what you've got now.'

But how much does he know? Does he know how it consumed my soul, begging me to do its bidding? Does he know how much I wanted it to? Does he know that I felt Nuria rising, ready to burst forth into a world that has already vanquished her once? Does he know that the next time it happens, I might not have the control, or the desire, to pull myself back, or Nuria come to that, from the precipice that has every intention of devouring me in its power-driven fire-pit?

'Yeah,' I answer vaguely. I pass the glass back and sit up. The water dowses whatever heat is left in me. 'Where's River?'

'No one was here when we got back,' says Mr Butcher with a grimace and a heave of his colossal shoulders.

Mr Butcher has an odd expression on his face. 'I have a confession to make, Miss Riley.'

'Oh.'

'When I told you, I know everything that has been going on, it was my way of telling you I know of your family environment.'

What is left of the anger inside, bubbles to the surface. 'If you knew, why did you do nothing?'

His face contorts in sympathy, creasing his already lined face. 'I cannot intervene in the lives of humans. It is forbidden. However, I was able to manipulate certain devices, namely smoke detectors and alarms at critical times to help you.'

I almost laugh. 'That was *you*?' Those prayers I sent out, actually were being answered.

Now that we seem to be "friends", I want to question him about something. 'What's the deal between you and Mr Fisher?'

Mr Butcher booms out a hearty laugh. 'Robin Fisher and I were at the same school.'

I frown. 'And?'

'He was one of *my* students.'

'Oh.' I allow this information to marinate for a few seconds. 'And you haven't aged, right?'

'Precisely. I keep telling him it was thirty years ago and that I'm not the teacher he thinks I am, but he's convinced I'm a vampire or something.' He laughs again and this time I laugh with him.

The front door slams shut and River appears at the doorway. He looks more stressed than before. 'Hey. You're back.' He doesn't wait for my response. 'If you need me, I'll be in the pool.' Wally skulks past, giving me a courteous nod.

I let out a sigh.

'I can see you have your hands full here, and I need to get home … and do some *washing*,' says Mr Butcher. I look at him in surprise. 'Yeah, I know what you're thinking. All those powers and I still have to take my clothes to the laundrette.' I holster a smile. The more Mr Butcher speaks, the more I like him.

He lets himself out and I stumble up to my room in desperate need of sleep. I can't face River, no matter how much I want to clear the air. I can't look at him, knowing he is the next Elementar and that I'm forbidden to tell him. It makes total sense to me now – his love of the water and how much time he spends in it. But the secrecy, the constant redirections and that air of mystery that hang over him are more obscure to me than ever.

# THIRTY-TWO

*THE* day I've been dreading is finally here - the excursion to the North-Western Fire Brigade. I'd be a fool to believe the looming tension that's been building the last forty-eight hours, luring me in like some unsuspecting mackerel, is just my imagination, except it isn't. It's my very own internal warning system, now matured, and enhanced, and gifted from my mum, for what lies ahead.

I gaze over at the alarm clock, wiping the sleep from my eyes. The thought of breakfast has me burying my face back into my pillow hoping to find the answer there to how I'm going to survive the next twelve months of this living day to day stuff and looking over my shoulder bullshit at every little noise and squeak. Two weeks of trying to blend back into my school environment has been tough and more alien to me than the *being* trapped inside me.

The alarm goes off and I reach out and flick it off. River pops his head around the door and offers a comforting smile. A heightened sense of panic manages to find solace amongst my bones.

Sitting on the packed mini-bus, River's hand tightly wrapped around mine isn't helping much. The talk I wanted to happen, didn't, as such, although he did tell me he would come clean with everything when the time was right. I have no idea when that time is. I can only hope it's soon.

I catch him staring at me, and as always, his eyes tell me not to worry, but I can't help it. The feeling that this day isn't going to end well resonates so well with me, it's almost *normal*. I laugh on the inside. Who would've thought this kind of sanity would become my new kind of normal?

I watch as his fingers brush over mine for the tenth time, delicately fondling each digit in turn as though they're made from glass. It's hypnotic, in a strange way, and the constant repetitive action dulls my senses and takes the edge off the anxiety. He is my own bottle of lavender.

Cherie is up and out of her seat the second the bus stops, her ponytail swinging in every direction. Naomi Bell, Cherie's sidekick for the day, is close behind her. 'I can't wait to see our instructors. I love guys in uniforms,' says Cherie, making no attempt to curb her volume.

'Me too,' parrots Naomi, applying a thick wad of lip gloss.

The stony car park seems to be a good place to gather everyone into a semi-circle, and as Mr Butcher completes his final head count, his gaze falls to me. I know he wants to ask me how I'm feeling, instead he throws his hands into the air.

'Listen up,' he bellows, 'today, is going to be rather full-on, so you'll need to stay alert, watch your back and the person either side of you, and concentrate at all times.' Regardless of how many people are standing here, I know his words are meant for me. River squeezes my hand, as if he understands. As if I need any more reminding. Something tells me it isn't *if* Ra-Mon shows himself, it's

340

*when*. I tune out the remainder of Mr Butcher's speech about being prepared, focus and doing the best I can.

Cherie and Naomi twitch and fidget, elbowing each other childishly as two men wearing matching navy-blue overalls, draw closer. The men stop, fold their arms across their chests and wait patiently for Mr Butcher to finish.

'This is leading firefighter, Tyler Casey, and sub-officer, Christian Romano.' The two men nod and say hello and yet all I hear is Cherie calling dibs on the dark-haired one. 'They will be taking you through your program today and I urge you all again. Pay attention, ask questions if you're not sure, and be prepared.' I'm getting sick of his pep talks.

Sub-officer Romano steps forward. 'Welcome to the North-Western Cadet Program. Like your teacher said, this is going to be a full-on day. To make it easier, we are going to split you into two groups, one with me and the other with leading firefighter Casey.'

Cherie and Naomi shuffle closer to Leading firefighter Casey as he smiles and nods at everyone. The braces on his teeth sparkle like he's swallowed a mouthful of glitter. 'We will take you through the theory of fire-fighting, safety and general housekeeping this morning. We'll then break for half an hour. Then group one will go off with leading firefighter Casey and extinguish some small fires that have been specifically set up for training purposes, and then on to the fire-pad for a group training session, while group two will battle the notorious smoke house.' He pauses giving everyone a brief smile. 'After that, we'll break for lunch, and then in the afternoon we'll swap over and whoever is interested, will get the chance to climb some ladders and maybe break down a few doors.'

Cheers go up from some of the boys. 'Like your teacher said, it is dangerous, and if anyone is caught acting in a manner deemed unsafe, then that person will be escorted back to the training room immediately, where they will spend the rest of the day completing theory sheets. Is that clear?'

A mumbled response echoes around the group.

'There is no room for error when dealing with fire.' He looks right at me when he speaks as though he and Mr Butcher are somehow in cahoots with each other. 'Right then, let's divide into groups.'

Sub-officer Romano cuts his arm through the centre of our huddled group, dividing us into two equal parties. In total disbelief, I discover that Cherie and Naomi, flocking obsessively close to leading firefighter Casey, are in my group ... again.

The training room is set up as a standard classroom and piled up in the furthest corner are a mountain of green overalls. We work steadily through the handouts and by the time I turn to the last page, the queasiness I'd try to ignore, finally gets the better of me. I need to use the bathroom.

Mr Butcher, who is talking quietly to leading firefighter Casey, casually looks over as my hand creeps up above my head.

Sub-officer Romano points at me. 'Yes, you have a question?'

My face twists with embarrassment. 'It's not really a question,' I half mumble. 'I need to use the bathroom.' Cherie and Naomi turn around and roll their eyes at me. My stomach kicks out and I cup my hand to my mouth.

'Out the door, second door on your left.'

River's eyes beg me to tell him what's going on but all I can do is shake my head. Mr Butcher seems overly keen to know, too, trying to read my thoughts with his heavy frown.

I slip out of the room and head along the pale blue hallway, dotted with posters of fire and flames, which instantly quicken my step. I lean into the bathroom door and rush over to the first sink. The breakfast bar that River had given me on the bus makes a swift exit.

I rinse my mouth out and splash water over my face. I look around. Shit. No hand towels. Water glistens off my skin. I pat my cheeks against the sleeve of my shirt.

Out of habit, I lift my head, not particularly wanting to see my reflection in the mirror, it's something you do when you're searching for answers. It's then I see Ra-Mon looking down at me from above the toilet cubicles. His long silvery hair hangs over both shoulders as his cold, soulless eyes, no neon blue lights this time, just dark hollow sockets, drill through me.

Instinctively, my hands flare with heat.

'Not yet, FlameMaker. When I say.'

I swing around to look at him, only to find he isn't even there.

By the time I arrive back in the training room, everybody is stepping into pairs of overalls. Mine have been draped over my desk.

'You okay?' asks River.

I nod, but I'm not. I begin to pull the overalls on over my clothes, trying to avoid everyone's questioning eyes.

'Don't you have any smaller ones?' chirps Naomi. 'Mine's too big.' They are all big, though River looks close to perfection in his. His body fills it out nicely. He throws me a wicked grin and shrugs as though he knows it himself. I hide my smile underneath another wave of anxiety.

'Mine too,' complains Cherie, pulling the material away from her chest.

'No one's going to see ....'

'*You* can,' says Cherie before sub-officer Romano can finish.

He takes a deep breath. 'Anyway, you'll be glad of them in case of an emergency. They're fire-retardant.'

Naomi and Cherie groan in unison. 'He's fire-*retardant*,' whispers Naomi.

'I want you all to get into your groups from this morning. My group will be visiting the smokehouse first,

343

whilst leading firefighter Casey's group will tackle the fire pad and fire drums. We'll swap around after that. Everybody ready?' Peter Capelli is the only one to respond with a fist pump and an energetic 'yes'.

'What a dick,' mutters Cherie. For the first time in my life, I can't believe I'm agreeing with her.

Firefighter Casey leads us outside to a large concrete playground, minus the netball and basketball lines, and rallies us around him. Six old oil drums are a short distance away, overflowing with bright blue bricks that have already been set alight. I glance over to a raised square platform, half the size of a netball court.

'Must be the fire pad,' says River, reading my thoughts. I fake a smile but lean that much further into him. That whole 'standing on my own two feet thing' and the 'I need to stop looking to River for support' speech, died an early death this morning and, being at the edge of the group, I'm glad no one can see his arm around me, rubbing warm, soothing circles into my back.

I swallow as my gaze pans back to the oil drums. Surely, Ra-Mon wouldn't do it here … not in front of everyone. Maybe he wants an audience, like Mr Butcher implied. Maybe that's Ra-Mon's aim, to humiliate me in front of my own kind. I search deep inside, begging for Nuria to hear me.

*'Don't let him kill me,'* I whisper to her, *'and don't let him near River, either.'*

'First off, leading firefighter Casey is a bit too much of a mouthful when it comes to a) emergency situations and b) constantly calling out my name to ask questions. For this exercise, you can refer to me as Tyler or Ty,' says leading firefighter Casey.

Cherie and Naomi giggle and poke at each other. 'Tyler, do you have a girlfriend?' asks Cherie, flicking her hair out.

'No, and you'd better tie that mane back. You don't want it going up like a haystack if a stray *ember* floats your way.'

Call it hysteria setting in, I don't know, but a laugh shoots out of my mouth. All eyes fall on me, but it's the snarl that grows on Cherie's face that makes my smile the widest. 'He isn't talking about you, *Ember* Riley, in case you're wondering. It's just a random word. Not all words to do with *embers* are about you.' She steps closer to me. 'Besides, he doesn't even know your name.' I want to laugh again, but I hold it back.

'Right. Listen here,' interrupts Tyler, frowning. 'I want you to get yourselves into pairs, decide who goes first and then I'll allocate you each a drum.'

Like an affectionate cat, Cherie brushes herself along River's arm. 'You can be my partner, if you want? I don't scratch much … unless of course you're in to that kind of thing.'

I edge my way around River until I'm standing in front of him and am about to let something along the lines of 'keep your filthy fake nails off him', but River restrains me. Instead, he circles one arm across my ribs, just beneath my breasts, the other around my neck and pulls me against him. His body is warm and soothing, the way it always is, and my heart soars, taking my breath with it. I wish we were sharing this moment alone.

He breathes into my ear. 'I've got this.' He then kisses my neck, longingly, lovingly, in front of not only Cherie, and Naomi, who are now gawping at us like we've sprouted horns, but the rest of the class too. It's over and done with in less than a second leaving my knees trembling, and my body aching in a way too sensual to be real.

'I'm with Ember, Cherie … on and off the playground.' River's cheap shot hits her where it hurts the most … her ego. I see the fury simmering beneath her thick layer of orange foundation.

'What a waste,' she hisses spitefully and retreats back to Naomi, who is still standing with her mouth agape. They link arms and barge their way through the group, closer to Tyler.

'Now, you guys, all wait here. I'm going to demonstrate the correct method for extinguishing a fire. The same way you learnt in your workbooks this morning.'

Tyler picks up the fire extinguisher, a few feet from the drum, and douses the fire in less than five seconds. It looks easy enough, but I still think *my* method is better.

'Inform me when the first of you extinguishes the fire and I will come around and relight it for the next person.'

There is no getting out of this.

This is happening.

I'm not scared about putting out a fire. I'm scared about what will happen when I confront it. Will Ra-Mon appear?

'Chill, Em, you're making me feel nervous,' utters River, rubbing his stomach. 'I'll go first, if you want me to?'

'Thanks.'

River steps up to the drum.

Ten seconds later, he hands me the extinguisher, looking incredibly pleased with himself. Most of the other pairs have successfully put out their fires and Tyler is simultaneously relighting the drums.

'You're good to go,' says Tyler, walking back towards us with a mini flamethrower in his hand.

I front the drum, the extinguisher shaking in my hands. Please don't come out, please don't come out, I chant. I squeeze the trigger and close my eyes.

'Em, it's out,' says River softly in my ear. His hand covers mine and I slowly prise my fingers away from the handle. Fearfully, I look up, all around and behind me, expecting to see Ra-Mon's ghostly figure floating close by. There is nothing. I swallow down the emotional cocktail of relief and fear adding an umbrella of apprehension just for good measure.

River kisses the side of my head. 'I'll be here, right next to you, every step of the way.'

'Well done, everyone. I'm sizeably impressed,' says Tyler. His dark brown eyes wrinkle in the corners as he smiles. 'So, let's see what you can do with something a little more intense.'

River is right. The square platform we looked at before, is the fire pad.

'This is what we call the fire pad,' says Tyler, standing in front of it and gesturing his arm behind him. 'It's a combustible material that when lit, will slowly spread out until it covers the entire pad. We use it to teach new trainees the importance of where to extinguish the fire. I'll demonstrate.' He looks up. 'I'll need a couple of volunteers.'

Cherie and Naomi elbow their way to the front. 'We'll help you, Tyler,' coos Naomi.

'Yeah, with *anything*,' adds Cherie. I roll my eyes at her blatant attempt to bewitch him.

'Great,' says Tyler, although it doesn't sound great from the way he says it. 'And a strong, burly lad. You,' he says, pointing to River.

River unlaces his fingers from mine and steps into an arena of swishing hair and fluttering eyelashes.

Tyler picks up a long hose, snaking its way across the pad. Helped by River, he drags it around the edge to where Cherie and Naomi are standing. 'This is called an attack hose and it can reach up to 100ft in length. The pressure behind it is around 290 psi and can discharge up to 140 gallons of water a minute – that's twelve times that of your average garden hose.'

A ripple of comments hum around the group. 'Okay, girls. Which one of you is the strongest?'

'I am,' says Cherie sticking out her chest.

'You see that wheel close to the pumphouse.' Tyler points to a thin, red wheel attached to the station wall. 'Trot on over there, and when I give you the thumbs up, turn it clockwise.' That's the second time Tyler has referred to Cherie as a horse, and by the look on her face, she picks up on it too. Her ponytail swings wildly as she storms across the fire pad.

'The idea is you have to make sure you apply the water directly to the seat of the fire.' Tyler pauses and readjusts the hose in his arms. River has already dropped his end and is standing beside me again. 'The seat is the base of the fire, where all the combustible materials are, and where you should be aiming. It's what adds fuel to keep the fire ignited. I'll show you.'

Tyler turns to look at Cherie, who is standing with her hip jutting out and her arms folded. 'Now this young lady will stand behind me and keep a watch to make sure my hose doesn't get a kink in it.' Naomi stands directly behind Tyler, too close in my opinion, looking everywhere but at the actual hose. 'Everyone else take ten steps back, please. This can get a little hot.'

'What about me?' whines Naomi.

'Don't you want to top up your tan lines?' Tyler asks. A titter of laughter echoes around the group. Naomi looks furious. 'Don't worry, you won't feel it as much behind me.'

Hot, I think, bring on some heat. The temperature outside is close to freezing, despite the extra article of clothing we are all wearing, and with few buildings surrounding us, winter's breath has us right where it wants us.

Tyler sidesteps over to a foot pedal I hadn't noticed before, opening the grate of a furnace. Flames spring to life in the middle of the pad, spreading its angry web of orange everywhere. Tyler gives Cherie his thumbs up and Cherie begins turning the wheel.

'Keep going,' yells Tyler. Water spills out of the nozzle, slowly at first and then thick and fierce. 'You okay?' he shouts back to Cherie, who still looks petrified. She doesn't answer.

Tyler shows us how to attack the fire in the most effective way, and within a few minutes six out of the eight square mats have been extinguished, leaving only one remaining. He presses the pedal on the floor to close off the oxygen.

'Who wants to have a go at the pointy end?' All the girls step backwards, except for me. The natural instinct to be afraid of fire isn't there.

'A volunteer,' cries Tyler. 'Step up, step up. Don't be frightened. I'll be right next to you.' I see the scowl on River's face as I move out of his circle of protection.

Tyler hands me the hose, the shutoff valve, closed. It's heavier than I thought it would be and my arms buckle at first when I hold it. River is there in a flash, taking the weight of the hose behind me. I feel his warm breath against my neck and his presence steadies my trembling hands. If Ra-Mon is coming for me, now is his chance.

Tyler hits the switch on the ground, waking the sleeping fire giant once more. Three pads light up in a flash and the intensity of the heat grows, causing flames to swirl ten feet into the air. I aim the hose at the base of the fire, the way Tyler had instructed.

'Great. You're doing great. Keep it low … that's it,' says Tyler. His encouragement, and River right behind me, pushes my confidence. I'm already down to two pads when out of nowhere a mountain of fire, more brutal than any active volcano, flares up as though the earth has cracked open and the flames of hell have leapt from its fiery hole.

'What in God's name,' shouts Tyler, grabbing for the hose. 'Give it here.' He yanks the hose out of my hand, pushing me back with his body. The water isn't making any impact on the blaze, the whole area now a huge sauna.

'Must be a fault in the main gas vent,' he yells at nobody in particular. 'Stand back everyone.' But I know it isn't any vent.

Ra-Mon is here.

I feel his presence.

It has begun.

The fire engulfs four pads, then eight. It's totally out of control. 'I've never seen anything like this in my life,' shouts Tyler.

'Do you want me to go and get somebody?' I ask as wave after wave of heat rolls towards us.

'S'OK, part and parcel of being a fire fighter,' yells Tyler, over his shoulder. He aims the hose lower and with a little more determination this time.

'It's Ra-Mon,' I whisper to River. 'I saw him in the bathroom before. He's come for me.'

Startled, River spins around, his eyes searching every roof ledge, every shady corner, every doorway. 'I won't let him hurt you.' I think back to what Mr Butcher taught me and what Nuria had said - become one with the fire.

I slip out of River's embrace. 'I think I know what I have to do.'

'Em, no,' groans River, the pain evident in his voice.

The wall of steam around us is all the cover I need. Walking into a fire with a group of teenagers watching, isn't exactly the wisest move. *Gossip*? I'd have to move to a new country to escape that, let alone a new town. Plus, that mental institution that has my name all over it, is looking more probable every second. The vision of being used as a government experimental weapon glazes across my vision.

The cover is good, and the steam is so heavy it could pass for thick fog. It takes a couple of seconds to locate the navy blue of Tyler's overalls and I weave around him and stand at the edge of the fire pad. The heat greets me in a way I can't possibly explain, except to say that we feel like old friends who haven't met in a long time. Without fear or thought, the soft carpet-like pad finds my feet, nurturing each step I take as I stroll headlong into the furnace to meet Ra-Mon.

The dulcet tones of Nuria's voice wafts through my body like the first sweet breath of spring. 'Ember, go into the middle and sit down. Allow the energy of the fire to become your strength.'

I walk into the middle, leaving the oranges and reds behind, passing the yellow until I stand at the core of the fire. To me, it's how I imagine heaven – whiteness everywhere and the feeling of complete peace. I feel like I finally belong.

I sit down, cross my legs in front of me and rest my hands in my lap as the fire rages around me. I can just make out Tyler's voice as he continues to battle something in which he has no skill in overcoming.

This is down to me.

I close my eyes and will the fire into my body, asking its permission to fill my throat and lungs, my organs and bones, urging it to consume me as though I am the fuel and my body is the wood that starts it.

I sense Ra-Mon is near before I open my eyes. 'FlameMaker, you have impressed me with your skill.' He is dressed in a cloak of blood-red. The hood is up, although his face is lost in shadow. He's come dressed for war.

Flames leap down my throat when I open my mouth to speak. 'What exactly do you want from me?' My lips draw a thin line across my face.

His hood retracts of its own accord. 'You know what I want,' says Ra-Mon, appearing slightly amused. Sunken pits where his eyes should be, now glow red instead of blue. 'You have something I want.'

More heat finds its way into my body, sending a surge of confidence through me. 'You mean, Nuria?' I ask.

Ra-Mon advances towards me as though his feet are gliding over ice. 'He told you. I *am* surprised. My brother, coming to everyone's rescue. How sweet.' The tone of his voice is soft enough to soothe a child, yet the snarl on his face will keep me up in many nights to come, if I survive this. His gnarly white fingers, each one long and twisted, tap together in front of him.

'What about me?'

'I don't care for you, as hard as that may be for you to hear. If you live or die, that is of no consequence to me.'

My heart starts to race. Ra-Mon throws back his head and laughs. 'All I want is Nuria. And I will take her when you are ready. She will become my ...what do you call it,' he says, pausing. He smiles. 'My pet. I will use her whenever I need her, and she will answer to me alone.'

The bottom falls out of my stomach. He sounds just like The Creeper and my first impulse is protection. 'You will not take her.'

He laughs again. 'I *will* take her, by force if necessary, which will be painful for both of you, or you can give her up now, resulting in no pain, and we can both go on our merry ways.' I glimpse the smile that crosses his face before he bows low to me.

I'm used to pain. We've shared time together in so many ways. Pain isn't something I'm frightened of. I know its rhythm. I understand how it spreads like a disease. But losing another part of me ... that instils real terror. I will not give her up, and I will fight, harder than I've ever done before, to keep someone else from taking her from me ... whatever it takes.

I slowly get to my feet. The breath of fire living inside me, lies ready at my command, ready to do my bidding. Scorching power surges up my spine and waits at my throat. 'I'm not giving her up.' Flames leap out of my mouth as I speak.

Ra-Mon shakes his head and tuts. 'Wrong answer, I'm afraid.'

I don't wait for him to say anymore, not when I'm packing heavy artillery.

One breath, one small breath in and then out. Flame, spurred by desire, rips out of my mouth in one rapid thick stream, hitting Ra-Mon square in the chest. His look of surprise brings a smile to my face. I toy with it for a second, wondering what his next move will be. Whatever it is, I'm ready.

Drastically underestimating my opponent and a dose of over-confidence is my downfall.

I know that now.

A sharp and powerful blast, too quick for me to even see, streams out of Ra-Mon's eyes and thumps into me, knocking me clean out of my shoes. My vision doubles as I look up, wavering long enough for me to see Ra-Mon's face hovering over me with a smile, before I'm sucked into a tunnel of black.

# THIRTY-THREE

*A* hundred bees buzzing around a newly opened rose, reassures me I'm not dead. Their humming tones, some higher than others, criss-cross over me as though I'm caught directly in their flight path. A smile tries to pull at the edges of my lips.

I'm *not* dead.

I'm not *dead*.

The buzzing gets progressively louder until it isn't buzzing at all.

It's voices.

Lots of voices.

It isn't that I can't open my eyes. I don't want to. I don't want to open them to find twenty faces peering down at me, wondering whether I'm dead. One voice stands out among the rest. I hone into that sound, wishing it is only him and me. The pain in his voice as he repeats my name over and over, begging me to wake up, is the most sorrowful words that have ever come out of his mouth.

'Please, Em. Wake up.'

The touch of his hand … that familiar feeling that transforms my used-up body into a desirable, excitable entity, washes through me the same way his eyes tell me he will never let me go without a fight.

I love him.

I want to tell him I love him and that I will love no other as long as I live. That I will lay down my life and sacrifice myself if I have to, to keep him safe. His grip tightens around my hand as if squeezing his life force into me. I have to put him out of his misery. I have to let him know I'm alive.

My eyes barely flutter open before I feel his lips on mine. 'It's over,' I whisper as he lifts me into his arms, my cheek finding the soft crook of his shoulder.

'Stand back, stand back. Give her some room.' I hear the distinct deep tones of Mr Butcher in my head. 'Mr Fulton, bring her inside.'

With my head resting against River's chest, I listen to the familiar sound of his heartbeat, slowing, no longer stressed, no longer beating faster than it's natural capacity. Beating … strong … dependable … lovable.

'You're all right,' reassures River, brushing my hair from my eyes with his lips. 'I'll never let anything happen to you.' *He keeps saying that, and yet it still does.*

The fluorescent lights sting my eyes as we enter a building.

'Put her in here,' I hear a voice say. It sounds like Tyler.

I feel myself being lowered down until the solid base of a chair touches my thighs and back. My overalls have been removed, though I have no idea when, or by who, and the sleeve of my jumper is pushed up to my elbow. A hand, much bigger and rougher than River's makes contact with my arm.

'Miss Riley?' Slowly the world comes back to me.

'Mr Butcher?' Two worried faces, and one confused face stare back at me.

'How did you manage to find your way into the middle of the fire pad?' asks Tyler, looking around at everyone first before stopping at me. 'And not get burnt.'

'I don't know,' I mumble into my lap. 'I can't remember anything.'

'Are you hurt?'

Checking in with my body, I simultaneously scan each limb for injuries. There is nothing, apart from a slight ache on the back of my head. I reach up and touch it.

'Easy, now,' says Mr Butcher. 'Maybe an icepack might be in order, Tyler?'

'Oh yeah, right. Ice.' He promptly gets up and leaves.

Mr Butcher turns to me. 'Was it Ra-Mon?'

Biting my lip, I lower my eyes and nod.

'Did he get what he was after?'

'You mean, Nuria?' I ask, meeting his gaze.

A flicker of concern plays across his vision. He nods.

'Who's Nuria?' asks River.

'Yes. He told me he wasn't after me.' I glance over at River. 'He wants the Elementars, just like you said.'

'Did he say why?'

'Who's Nuria? River repeats louder this time.

'Yeah, of course he did,' I say, rolling my eyes, 'we had a nice cup of tea and chatted for hours.' Like two sleeping caterpillars, his bushy eyebrows slowly crawl upwards. I've overstepped the mark. 'I'm sorry. No, he didn't tell me anything. As usual, I'm the last one to find out anything.'

'You're not the only one,' says River.

'And Nuria?'

River groans, rolling his eyes.

I close my eyes, letting go of my senses. My breath slows to almost no breath at all. *Nuria, are you still there?* Please don't say I've failed. Please don't say that it was all for nothing. That Ra-Mon has won. Please, say that you are still fighting alongside me, that you won't relinquish that easily. My eyes close tighter. Every inch of my body begs to hear her sweet voice, to believe we are still part of each other, and that Ra-Mon has failed. *I'm here, Ember, but I don't know how much longer I can hold on. Ra-Mon is milking my strength.*

My eyes float open. 'She's still here,' I say with a smile.

River drops my hand and heads for the door. 'If you don't want me here, you should tell me now.'

'Wait, River ...'

'Let him go,' says Mr Butcher. River turns back to look at me and closes the door behind him. That whole feeling of my heart falling through my stomach is back. 'He will have his time. Now, Ember, focus. Did he say anything else?'

I shake my head. I tell Mr Butcher about the blast in the chest I'd delivered to him. 'The last thing I said to him was that I wasn't going to give Nuria up, and he'd said, "wrong answer".'

A dark cloud passes over Mr Butcher's eyes and his brow heavies. 'This isn't the end of it. He'll be back and there won't be any time for conversation next round. He means business and don't think for one minute that that cheap fireball shot hurt him. He probably wasn't even winded. He is preparing, Ember, changing his strategy.'

A lonely flame lights up inside me, igniting the fire for the most important moment in my life. 'Well, I'm not exactly licking my paws here either. I'm ready for him.'

'I admire your confidence, but he won't give up ... not without a real showdown.'

I've heard enough. I need to see River and explain what is happening. 'Are we done here?' Mr Butcher, who had been kneeling at the foot of my chair, shuffles away and stands.

I rise, too, and go for the door as Tyler comes back in. I raise my hand to the back of my head and rub it vigorously. 'Thanks, but I don't think I need that now. It's fine.' I slip past Tyler and half walk half run down the corridor to find River.

I eventually find him, and everyone else, in a similar training room, eating lunch. His eyes skim over me with mild curiosity and that's all.

No heart pounding desire.

No hypnotic trance.

Nothing.

My breath catches in my throat. *Please* don't let me lose him this way.

Leaning up against a bookcase, away from everyone else, he stares, unblinking at the wall. I sit down, waiting for him to look up. When he doesn't, I reach for his hand. I'm half expecting him to withdraw it from me, but his fingers fold around mine, holding them tight.

'River ...'

'Don't. It's okay.'

'But, I want to tell you what happened.' I need to tell him.

'I was being selfish. You need time ...'

'I don't need time. Stop telling me I need time. I know what I need, and what I don't, and I need ... you.' The lines on River's brow grow denser and his eyes portray utter defeat. I don't understand what it means but I take the moment to pause and steady my breath. 'I need you ... to listen.'

'Ember, I need to tell you something too.' I finally have a chance to peek into the mysterious world of River Fulton. The word 'what?' waits patiently on my lips, but I know it's not the right time. This time belongs to me.

'Nuria is the first Elementar, the first FlameMaker, the one responsible for covering the earth in fire millions of years ago. She disappeared after she was vanquished by the WaterLover Elementar and has remained hidden until recently.'

As though a ray of sun has found its way into the room, River's face brightens. 'Go on.'

I look up, to make sure no one is listening, and lean in a little closer. 'She's inside me.'

River draws back from me, looking at all the different parts of my body trying to see where she might be.

'I've heard her speak to me.' How ironic, I think as I recall one of our first conversations, when I'd told him I was hearing voices. How the truth turns itself around on you.

River seems to be struggling to construct a simple sentence. 'Is that why Ra-Mon is after you – to get to Nuria?'

'Yes.' Regardless of how many pairs of eyes, including that of Mr Butcher and Tyler, who entered a little while ago, River pulls me into his lap and wraps his arms around me.

'We'll get through this. Just stay close to me.'

I soften in his arms, breathing in everything that is good and calm about him. His lips brush over my forehead.

'Ugh! That's disgusting,' says Cherie, staring at us. Others look our way and reluctantly, I draw away from him.

'If everyone's ready …' Tyler gestures to me and I nod my reply. 'Then we'll get on with this afternoon's activity. My group, when you're packed up, go and line up outside the building, and sub-officer Romano's group can wait here until he comes and gets you.'

In a matter of minutes, we are back out in the cold. This time, I button my overalls right to the neck, wincing as the northern wind tries to steal another morsel of warmth from my body.

We follow behind Tyler, passing two large grey rendered buildings, which he mentions contain a gym, swimming pool and accommodation for recruits. Another five hundred yards across a sports oval on to a winding path, partially covered with trees either side, brings us upon a large brick house with black windows.

'What *actually* is a smokehouse?' asks Naomi.

'Good question. It's a specifically designed house, filled with smoke that prepares and teaches new firefighters what a real-life house fire feels like.'

'So, there's no fire inside at all?'

'None whatsoever. Only smoke. It is what we call a primary search, although you guys won't be searching for anything. We'll do what's called a walk-through.' Naomi looks relieved. 'And, because smoke is as dangerous as the fire itself, you will all need to wear breathing apparatus.'

'Do we have to?' asks Cherie. 'It'll smudge my makeup.'

'No, you don't have to, if can hold your breath for four minutes and keep your eyes closed the whole way.' Tyler smirks. 'It's not for everyone, so if you choose not to go through, that's fine. You can wait here with me and watch the others come out.' Embarrassed, Cherie sticks out her lip. 'I'll go.'

The breathing apparatus is similar to scuba gear, except the bottles are no larger than a standard drink bottle and hook onto our belts. The mask also goes over the entire face, including the mouth.

'Only five can go through at a time,' says Tyler, checking everyone's equipment.

River and I stand in line, waiting for the first five to go.

'Once the door opens, you will need to follow the painted yellow arrows on the floor, which will take you in and out of each room, until you come to a door with the word EXIT written on it in bright green. Hit the buzzer on the door and I will open up and let you out. Do not take your masks off at any time. I don't want to be performing CPR on anyone today.'

I gaze into the eyes of those about to leave, especially Peter Capelli, who looks about ready to vomit. 'If anyone gets scared or feels panicked and wants to come out right away, hit the red button on your belt. It acts as an alarm. It will be activated on my terminal here,' says Tyler, pointing at his belt, 'and I will come in and get you. It's also a great idea, to hold on to the person's overalls in front of you.'

Cherie, dragging Naomi with her, shuffles up a few people so that she's in front of River. She turns and winks at him. It takes every ounce of restraint not to thump her in the face.

'Ready? Let's see, a thumbs-up,' says Tyler. Everybody sticks their thumbs in the air and Tyler wrenches open the steel door. It sounds like the hatch of a submarine opening.

The first five people file in and we wait as Tyler disappears around the side of the house for a few seconds before stepping out wide, keeping us in his sights. In no time at all, the others are out, declaring how cool it was.

'Second team, prepare,' calls Tyler. It's our turn and my legs have transformed into two steel girders, too heavy to lift. My fiery warning system is on full alert.

'In you go,' says Tyler, opening the door wide.

I grapple for the back of River's overalls, fully aware he is holding on to Cherie, by the way she keeps telling him how warm his hands are, when she can't possibly feel it through this thick material. Resembling a line of shackled convicts, we shuffle in.

In the same way, my mother knew about her migraines coming, and the same way I know when The Creeper is about to visit, the moment the door slams shut, I know that Ra-Mon is waiting for me. I realise now it isn't a curse. Fear had turned on that aura to help me, to train me for this one moment.

Thick smoke fills the narrow hallway at an alarming rate. River turns and nods at me, his eyes partially hidden. His head tilts in the direction of my hand that is gripping his overalls, his attempt to speak distorted behind his mask. Communication is out, unless he removes it, but I know what he's gesturing to.

I loosen my hold, so I can grab a fuller handful, when River is wrenched from my grasp. Suddenly he is gone and

I'm alone, smoke too dense to even see the markings on the floor. As though the roof has been ripped off by a giant claw, the face-creasing, eye-closing crack of thunder that shakes the building, tells me things about to get real.

Barely seeing the tips of my shoes, I edge up the passageway leading into the first room. The smoke is thinner in here and I can make out the arrows on the floor. The room, however, is empty.

Icy fingers and a familiar icier breath against my neck stops me in mid-step. I spin around. Ra-Mon is hovering over me.

'FlameMaker, so good of you to join me.'

'Like I had a choice,' I mumble into the mask, knowing he can't hear me.

He steeples his fingers in front of him as though he's about to give a sermon. 'It is time,' he says. I squint at him through the mask, knowing I can't remove it to speak.

I shake my head no.

'You do not choose when the time is right, fledgling.'

This is when I realise this isn't about a fair fight. It isn't about me gaining my strength or learning how to manipulate fire or how to duel a fair fight. It's about luring me into a false sense of security. He wants control. He wants to call the shots. It's just another game in my life, a calculating and well-planned game.

Ra-Mon swoops down in front of me, pressing his face to my mask. 'You need some persuasion then?' His mouth cracks open and a haunting laugh turns my blood to ice.

He vanishes.

Then terror fills my ears as wild, panicked screams come from the room next door. Screaming means someone has their mask off. I turn and run as best I can, half blind and in oversized overalls. My shoulder slams into the edge of the doorway as I misjudge the opening, knocking me backwards several steps.

The screaming continues. A sound I remember so well from the shower incident.

The alarm button on my belt flashes. Tyler is aware something is wrong. I press it twice, praying for a rescue.

The next room I find myself in is larger than the one before, and I rub the front of the mask desperate for a clearer visual. Smoke starts to dissolve before my eyes, and I see a body slumped against the wall.

It is Naomi.

The fear in her eyes tells me she's had her first encounter with Ra-Mon.

'Where is he?' I ask, my voice inaudible.

She looks up, the life drained from her face.

I shake her shoulder.

Naomi stares up at me, her eyes icy blue, shock seeping out of every pore. I have to leave her. There are still three others left in here, one being River. Yellow arrows direct me to the next room where Nigel Farrington is standing with his body flat against a wall. He too has those icy blue eyes and the same catatonic look.

I push on and into the next room, wondering how many more rooms are left. The smoke house hadn't looked that big from outside. This room is empty apart from a painted fireplace on one wall. I've had enough of this sneaking around. I slip my mask upwards.

'River!' I yell.

'We're in here, Ember,' he says in a calm, controlled voice. I follow the direction of his voice and find Cherie clinging to him, her eyes the same shade of blue as Nigel and Naomi's. River has the same beautiful blue eyes as he always has, piercing through the smoke, acting like runway lights, drawing me in.

'Where is he?' I ask, removing the mask. For some reason, the smoke doesn't affect me. It tastes dusty, and charcoaled, and tickles at the back of my throat a little, but it's breathable. I notice the door River is leaning on, is the exit.

River clocks my eyes and lifts his mask. 'It's bolted. I've pressed the buzzer but it's not working.'

'Of course, it's not working, dear boy. I have disengaged the alarm system,' says Ra-Mon.

The ghostly figure, appearing more solid and more human every passing second, drifts towards us until he is right in front of me.

'I, Ra-Mon, am here to challenge you, Child of the FlameMaker, and rid you of the cowering entity that refuses to face me.'

I stand tall and puff out my chest. 'I obviously didn't make myself clear before, but you can't have her. She is part of me, and I am part of her. If you want her, you'll need to go through me first.'

'No,' yells River, removing his mask to speak. He takes in a deep breath, seeing me breathing with ease, and coughs before replacing it.

'Just what I was hoping you'd say, girl.'

'Let me prepare.'

Ra-Mon nods.

First, I take off my belt and throw my mask on to the floor. I call to Nuria, silently invoking her. I need you.

*I am here, Ember. I will help you all I can, but I am weak.*

I close my eyes, envisaging a volcano, a fiery, tempestuous volcano that spreads out far and wide. I see the earth burning under my closed lids. As though the gates of hell have been opened, fire and brimstone, flame and heat, bubbling, boiling, lava floods the grasslands and streets, engulfing houses and shops and office blocks. There is nothing but reds and oranges and searing white hotness, too hot for colour to hold on to. I feel it building in my body, fuelling me with energy, living inside me like before, willing it to take over, giving into the power that wants its' fill.

I open my eyes and see Ra-Mon between the flames that dance in my vision.

'Whoa,' mutters River. I turn and smile at him and his eyes widen even further. I can only imagine what I must look like.

I return my gaze back to Ra-Mon. 'Now it begins.'

A surprised look wavers on his face for a split second before being replaced with coldness. The hollows where his eyes should be, glow pale blue, and the tips of his fingers are charged with an electrical current that snaps and crackles when he flexes them.

I don't feel fear, only power, and my body convulses with it as a fireball forms between my hands. It's the most exhilarating feeling I've known. More personal than a kiss and more powerful than a kind word.

A burst of light flies towards me but I'm ready for it. The orange ball, swirling and spitting out sparks, opens like a vortex and swallows Ra-Mon's feeble effort in one gulp. I smirk back at him. I shoot out a flamethrower type spear that soars across the space between us. He bats it away like an annoying wasp. I dig deeper and fire out another flame spear, more powerful and with more speed. Ra-Mon steps back to deflect it and his eyebrow twitches upwards in what looks like disbelief. It sails over his shoulder and slices a hole in the wall behind him. A fire breaks out.

'Upped the stakes there, little one?' says Ra-Mon with a curious smile.

'River, get behind me,' I say.

The grin on Ra-Mon's face changes. His eyes pierce through the smoke to where River is standing. Laughter like I've never heard before, the kind that fills every inch of your body with bone-chilling terror, stalling your thoughts, slowing your blood, turning you to stone and jelly at the same time, taking you down a dark, desolate road, where invisible footsteps and monsters dwell, spews from Ra-Mon's mouth.

'This keeps getting better and better. How fortunate I am today, that I can take care of two little fledglings at once.'

'Don't you dare threaten him,' I growl. I'm not sure if River can hear Ra-Mon above the noisy gurgling of the breathing apparatus.

Ra-Mon looks a little bemused. 'He *doesn't* know? He doesn't *know*. Oh, how delicious.'

I pull River closer, Cherie dragging behind, still clinging to his arm.

'Don't keep him all to yourself, child. Weren't you taught to share?' A bolt of blue light shoots out of Ra-Mon's hands, flies past my head, and slams into the wall less than an inch away from Cherie's shoulder. She doesn't even flinch.

'What have you done to my friend?' The word friend sticks in my throat as I say it.

'She has been disengaged, just like this pathetic alarm system. There's no way out for you, or any of your friends.' Darkness falls over his face, transforming whatever human-features he had into something more beast-like. 'Are we stopping for more conversation, girl, because I need be on my way?' His voice has changed too, a deep, gravelly bark that resembles a drool-swinging, blood-seeking creature from hell.

'I need answers,' I say boldly. The fireball, which is still in my grasp, spreads up my arms and into my chest. I'm positively alight.

'Enough!' he snaps. 'I need Nuria and if you don't hand her over now ….'

I don't let him finish. I discharge the fireball, throwing my arms forward so fast, a gentle pop sounds from my shoulders.

Ra-Mon is in his element. He catches the fireball and toys with it, slowing it down and then speeding it up as though it obeys his will and not mine. I'm stupid to think

366

I can go up against an immortal. I drop to the ground – totally exhausted.

'*Get up,*' Nuria whispers inside me. '*Get up, and fight for me, Ember.*'

'I can't,' I whimper.

'*Now. I don't have much time left.*'

I stumble to my feet and hold up my hands in a feeble gesture.

'You are weak, and not worthy of me,' says Ra-Mon. 'If you will not fight, maybe he will.' Ra-Mon looks straight at River. My heart turns over in my chest.

River gets up and shrugs Cherie off his wrist as I watch him and Ra-Mon face off.

'So, you're the child of the WaterLover,' says Ra-Mon. 'I didn't think I would be seeing you so soon, but nevertheless, I'm delighted you could come to our little soiree.'

'Don't you touch him,' I scream through my teeth.

'A fighting spirit, FlameMaker. That's what I like to see.' But isn't Ra-Mon's plan to challenge River, even when another spear of blue electricity buzzes past my face, heading straight for him.

'You idiot. I'm here,' I yell again. 'Are you blind?' The fact that he doesn't have any eyes, so to speak, is irrelevant.

'Rising steadily off the ground, Ra-Mon stretches out his hands and emits a charge, twenty times more powerful than the previous one, hitting me between the ribs and hurtling me from one side of the room to the other. I cry out as I smash into the brick wall. Hot, splintering pain races across my shoulders and neck. I try to ignore the sound of something snapping and the warm trickle of blood sliding around the back of my ear.

'No,' I choke out as River sprints straight for Ra-Mon. Ra-Mon laughs.

River doesn't get within two feet of him before he is slammed into the opposite wall with a flick of his wrist. I wince as he lands in a heap.

Gingerly, I try to push myself up, but my shoulder gives way. I scream out again, agony slicing through me. My eyes find the floor, mesmerised by the red lake pooling around my left thigh. A ten-inch piece of steel protrudes unnaturally from my thigh. It doesn't look real ... like it's happening to someone else. Two attempts to remove it has me almost passing out. Blood spreads quicker than wine, soaking my jeans with red.

I glance up to see Ra-Mon extracting a larger piece of steel from within the roof cavity. It lights up in a blaze of electric blue as he powers it up and fires it at my chest. I move, but not quick enough. My vision distorts, my hands automatically fly to my stomach. The piece of steel jutting out of my thigh is nothing compared to witnessing a spear the size of a javelin extending from your abdomen.

The room becomes darker.

There is no pain now, only darkness.

'Not yet, girl,' I hear, whispered into the night. 'You die when I say you die.'

My body feels light, ready for death, ready to meet my parents. In the blackness, something red and fiery comes closer. Blurry at first, and yet with each passing second, I can make out the shape of a woman. It is Nuria standing before me, her auburn hair curling over her shoulders, her hands turned upwards.

*Ember, I relinquish all of my power to you.*

You cannot, I say. Ra-Mon will take you captive.

*For now. But you will live to fight another day. Promise me, you will not give up the fight. Promise me you will set me free.*

I promise.

The beautiful woman, who has been the angel on my shoulder, dissolves before my eyes.

My eyes open, a renewed sense of power. Gritting my teeth, I grip the spear and reef it out of my flesh. It leaves behind a biting, burning sensation. Blood spills out of the wound.

I struggle to my feet, using the wall to push myself up, my left arm useless and hanging much lower than my right. I raise my good arm, the blazing spear of fire ready for action. Before I can throw it, a twist of light, gnarly like Ra-Mon's fingers, dives into my stomach where the spear had been embedded. I fall backwards, looking over at River as he lays nearby, his eyes closed. My body jerks and shudders as Ra-Mon probes inside me, in search of Nuria. A vicious claw, ripping, layer by layer, tearing me apart. All I can do is watch River, his lids closed, and pray that he isn't dead, all the while wishing his blue eyes were there to save me.

The digging continues, unravelling the only thread that's holding me together. My body lurches forward. I'm being drawn closer to Ra-Mon by my belly button as though he's attached an invisible cord to me. I can't bring myself to look down and see if my stomach is still intact because it feels spread open, my organs scooped out and lying beside me. The slicing and rummaging inside persists as I involuntarily inch across the floor until I'm lying beneath Ra-Mon's feet.

'In the end ... they all bow down,' I hear him say. One final tug sees me come undone. I scream out – my soul stolen, my core beaten to a pulp, and I know, before I have the chance to ask her, Nuria is gone. Her faint cry, as she left my body, scratches a scar much greater than any abuse ever could.

A shadow passes over me and at first, I think death has finally found me. Two bare feet, misshapen and icy white, shield my view of River. A solitary foot slaps against my cheek. Smoke that had once smothered me as we entered, is now clearing.

'Tell him,' says Ra-Mon, pointing at River, 'that I'll be back for Nereus.'

'What?' I mumble, my throat, swollen and tight.

'Nereus. He's next on my list. So … my advice to you, FlameMaker, now that you have nothing else I need, would be to wise up your boyfriend and let him in on our little secret.' His playful voice is back and his face, although inhuman, is now bearable to look at.

The sound of doors opening, and the rush of voices that follow, is Ra-Mon's cue to leave. His spooky blue vapour mingles in with the smoke as the blackness welcomes me home.

# THIRTY-FOUR

'*STOP* fussing,' I groan for the tenth time. 'I'm okay.'

Any idiot can see I'm not. And River isn't buying it for one second.

'Can you feel this?' asks Mr Butcher, squeezing the tips of my fingers.

'Yes, I can feel that.'

'You know, it was touch and go there for a while, Miss Riley. I didn't think I'd be able to bring you back.' I have no memory of leaving the smokehouse, or of Mr Butcher's magical healing powers. I woke to find him leaning over me, his hands resting against my stomach.

'Yeah, I suppose I'm lucky, I guess. Now, will you both bugger off and leave me alone for a moment.' It does feel good though, to be back in my own bed at River's house, but right now, I need some time to myself.

Mr Butcher takes a step back and River, who is sitting on the edge of my bed, reluctantly gets up. He wavers, wondering if I'm about to change my mind.

'I apologise, I can't do anything about scars,' he says, gesturing to my stomach. 'But your shoulder popped back in nicely.'

Visions of the almighty spear protruding from my stomach and leg seems to have faded considerably and I can't help wondering if Mr Butcher altered my memory like he did with the firefighters. Only after intense questioning did he finally admit the reason the blessed incident had been put to bed was because of his special memory enhancement, as he called it. Lucky too that it worked for Cherie, Naomi and Nigel. As far as they know, I am no weirder than I was yesterday.

I gingerly rub a hand over my stomach and then my thigh, the pain nothing worse than a hard day at the gym.

'Bones are a bit easy to knit back together, if I say so myself. Click clack and back to normal. I think you'll find your three ribs and collarbone have mended exceptionally well too.'

'Great. Now that nobody is coming to get me anymore. Please. I just want to rest.'

'Very well,' says Mr Butcher sighing. 'You heard the lady. She's had enough.'

River still seems to be stalling. 'I'll be downstairs if you need me.'

'I know,' I say softly. 'Thanks.'

After a long, slow glance over his shoulder, River closes the door behind him, leaving me alone.

I want them gone because I'm not sure how much longer I can hold it together. My eyes ache with fullness. Tears are waiting.

Nuria is gone. I failed her.

All this time, she has been by my side. That unknown entity pushing me on, giving me courage and always there in my darkest hour.

Heat fires up in my chest, but it isn't real fire, not like before. I tiptoe out of bed, body aching, bones as brittle as matchsticks and cross to the bathroom. Although doubtful,

I need to know whether I can still conjure fire. I have to try.

Sitting on the edge of the bath, I open my palm and focus my energy. A small flame, barely alive, flickers for a second before dying a quick, painless death. I try again and again, each time heat builds, but it is never enough to sustain a flame for longer than a few seconds. Nuria is gone and so, I decide, is my power. My ability to be someone new, someone who isn't frightened to stand up for herself, someone worthy enough to stand beside, is gone.

My thoughts return to Nuria and to the look in Mr Butcher's eyes when I'd told him I'd failed. He smiled, of course, telling me it wasn't my fault but, like I said to him, if it wasn't my fault, then whose fault was it? I haven't managed to tell him about Nereus though, as River hasn't left my side for a single minute.

I sneak back into bed and pull the covers over me, taking a minute to rub small circles into my abdomen. Nuria … where is she now? How am I going to make it without her silent encouragement? Sobs rack my throat and the painful sting of loss rips its way out of my mouth until my breath runs out. My body judders, sweeping every ounce of happiness out with it. I want to curl up and die. I want to wake to find my mum and dad standing over me, telling me it is all a bad dream and that if I go back to sleep, everything will be all right in the morning. But it won't be all right - the ache in my stomach and the absence of my soul sister assure me it's real and there's more to come.

I draw the duvet up higher and turn my head into the pillow. My eyes finally find peace in the darkness as I close them, a throbbing at my temples and the emptiness inside, lull me into unconsciousness.

My life is normal now – everything I ever wanted it to be. And I couldn't be sadder.

I feel like I've slept for hours, but on closer inspection of the clock, I see it's only 1am. River is sitting at the end of my bed, looking into his hands. I reach for the bedside light.

'Leave it off,' he says, his voice cold, hard, distant.

'What's wrong?' I ask, wiping my eyes awake.

'How long have you known?' he asks me.

I can't quite see his eyes in the fading light but something tells me they aren't the warm and caring lagoons I want to see. 'Known? About *what*?'

'Don't play games with me, Em. I asked you a serious question. I asked you, how long have you known about me?'

I pinch the skin on the back of my hand.

It hurts.

I'm not dreaming.

'I don't know what you're …' River turns his head from me. He looks hurt, as though I've insulted him.

'How long have you known about Nereus?'

Now he has my full attention. I sit up higher and switch on the light. Dark, moody circles replace his blue, blue eyes.

'You know?' My voice raises an octave or two.

'I know of him.' The confidence in his voice makes me gasp. 'And you called out his name in your sleep.' Heat filters into my cheeks. What else have I said?

'So, you know who you are then?'

'Yes. I've known for a while, although I had no idea of Mr Butcher's involvement until he told us.'

'Yeah, it's not every day your science teacher tells you he's immortal.' My attempt at humour goes astray and I circle back to his last comment. 'Why didn't you tell me who you were when I found out who I was?'

River's face tightens, his lips twisting in anguish. 'I swore an oath.'

*Another promise.*

'To who and on what?'

'You remember saying you had secrets, well, this is one

374

of mine. For now, please don't press me for more info because I can't and won't give you any. One day, I will, but for now I have to think of the safety of the other two.'

The other two? 'The air and earth Elementars?'

River refuses to answer. 'Tell me what he said to you about Nereus?'

'Nothing much, only that he was the next one on his list. Ra-Mon is coming for you.'

'I know. Butch already gave me the heads up while you were sleeping.'

'And?'

'And he reckons we'll have some time up our sleeves. Ra-Mon will be busy with Nuria. He has to perform some kind of a ritual to prevent her from returning to earth.'

Guilt smothers me. I swallow hard. 'What kind of ritual?'

River shrugs. 'He didn't say. Some kind of binding ritual. I suppose that's one of those, 'need to know' issues.' His eyes wander off to the corner of the room and stay there.

'But that's not all ...' I wait until he looks at me. 'Is it?'

He shakes his head solemnly.

I suddenly feel like I'm intruding. 'You don't want me here anymore, do you?'

He runs his hand through his hair. 'It's not that.'

'Then what is it?' That raspy feeling returns to my throat and my body is ready to cry all over again.

The vibrancy in River's eyes wane. 'I'm not good for you.'

'How can you say that? You're everything.' I want to add, "to me", but from the pained look on River's face I might as well have told him he had six weeks to live. 'I thought we got on well,' I say, a little softer this time.

'We do,' he fires back so quickly I jump.

'Then I don't see what the problem is.'

'You wouldn't say that if you really knew me. You wouldn't be lying in my bed, pouring your heart out to me,

375

trying to convince me I have one ounce of goodness in me.'

I grind my teeth, knowing my next words will either have me wrapped in his arms or homeless. I have no choice. I have to know where I stand and what he thinks of me. Rolling my bottom lip between my thumb and forefinger, I take one more second to make up my mind.

'I know there is goodness in you because I couldn't love someone as bad as you say you are.' My chest trembles as I inhale.

'Love ... No Ember, no. You can't love me, I forbid it.'

'You can't tell me how to feel. I choose to love you.'

'There are a lot of things about me, Em, things you don't know, and after everything you've been through, I don't want to add to that pain. I'm not who you think I am. I have a past.'

My throat tightens. 'Don't we all,' I blurt out.

'Yours has been inflicted upon you. Mine is different.'

My head begins to ache. 'What do you mean?'

River disregards my question. 'I've caused you to fall in love with me, forced you against your will, and it's the one thing I promised myself I would never let happen.'

I'm even more lost now. 'Please, River, I don't understand.' My voice crackles.

'I don't deserve you. I don't deserve to be happy, not after what I've done.'

'Done?' Done what? He is talking in riddles.

River's jaw clenches, the same way and with the same ferocity as his eyes do. His whole body is begging me not to ask anymore but I can't help it. I have to know.

'You don't love me,' he says, sadness saturating every word, 'because who I am is a lie. It is a part of me I cannot control, a part that lures in the innocent without them knowing. It's a curse – an emotional curse.' His eyes fall heavily to the floor like he isn't worthy to look at me. 'It affects everyone, including me.'

'But I am in love with you,' I stress.

'No, you're not. It's an illusion, Em. Why can't you see that?' River stands, his distant eyes telling me he wishes he hadn't said that. His voice softens. 'You don't know how it works. How it crawls under your skin and undermines every layer of goodness, replacing it with lies and feelings you think are real. I've lived with this my whole life, Em; you've had it for a few months.'

'What exactly *do* you feel?' I pause. 'I mean, how do you feel about me?'

River hesitates for a moment; his jaw wired shut for so long, I think he'll never utter another word. He turns to face me, his eyes pooling like a moonlit lake. 'I'm in love with you, Em. I have been even before we met.'

I frown at his response. 'So, what's the problem?'

'*I* don't know if it's real. I don't know if what you're feeling isn't the same as all the other times.'

My frown becomes more rigid. 'Other times?'

River takes two tentative steps away, just within arm's reach and sits back down. He drops his head into his hands.

'I promised myself I wouldn't get involved, that I wouldn't open myself up to have another line of victims begging at my feet but I'm right back to where I started.' He is talking to himself. 'And on top of everything else, I've caught you up in this web too. The very last person in the world I swore to shield from this repulsive obsession.' My eyes widen as I watch a tear fall from his cheek. My heart is breaking wide open. 'It's all been for nothing,' he murmurs.

Very slowly and with no agenda in mind, I draw his hands from his face and hold them in mine. I half expect him to pull them away. Instead, he squeezes them tight and raises them to his lips, kissing them so tenderly that it physically hurts my heart.

'Please …'

In the swiftest of movements, River lunges towards me, scoops me into his arms and kisses me like it's the last kiss we will ever share. My hands tangle in his hair, tears

377

staining my cheeks as I hear his body whisper goodbye to me.

Our lips part, and he stares at me with that wondrously in-depth gaze that has the power to still my breath and my heart and my mind, all at the same time.

Time ceases to exist.

I don't need breath, or to feel my heart pumping, or to think of what to say.

I need him and this moment to last forever.

'I want to look at you one more time because after you hear what I'm about to say, I know you'll never see me the same way again.' Another tear runs down his cheek. Outside, the heavens open, and rain pours so furiously I feel instantly afraid.

'I want to understand.'

I plead with my soul for him to open up and tell me.

He nods, runs his hands through his hair, anguish settling on his face.

With my hands back in his, he takes a deep breath. 'Em, I'm a liar and a thief, and I prey on girls like you only to satisfy my desires.'

# ACKNOWLEDGEMENTS

The Elementar Series has (so far) been six years in the making and many people in my life have contributed to this book finally coming to life. First, I want to thank my husband, Steve, who gave me all the time I needed to connect with my imaginary friends and who stood by reverently and watched me grow as an author. I could never had done this without you.

I also want to thank my daughter, Lily, who believed in the story and characters right from the very beginning and was never afraid to give me her utmost honest opinion in everything. Never change x

Next, to my three sons, Samuel, Joseph and Jesse for being so patient with me and for giving me the time to write this book when I should've been helping you with homework.

I also want to acknowledgement my best friend, Flicky. Through thick and thin, she has supported and encouraged me to follow my dreams and be myself and has held my hand in a journey full of laughter and tears. Thank you.

Thank you to Natasha Snow Designs for my beautiful cover.

And finally, to you, the reader, for giving this story a chance.

379

About the Author

Lorraine Eljuga was born in Suffolk, England and emigrated to Australia when she was twenty. The Snowy Mountains, in New South Wales, is now where she calls home. Lorraine is a Nutritionist & an Aromatherapist and was also a Writer in the Royal Australian Navy for four years.

FlameMaker, Book 1 of the Elementar series, is her first novel.

You can visit her at https://www.lorraineeljuga.com

*Watch out for book 2 ~ WaterLover*